D1527128

THE BILLIONAIRE'S BRIDE

L. STEELE

Delafield Public Library
Delafield, WI 53018
262-646-6230
www.delafieldlibrary.org

1

CLAIM YOUR FREE CONTEMPORARY ROMANCE

CLAIM YOUR FREE PARANORMAL ROMANCE

FOLLOW ME ON TIKTOK

JOIN MY SECRET FACEBOOK READER GROUP

Edward

The darkness pulls at me. I am falling, twisting, writhing. The sound of harsh breathing, groans reach me. I turn toward it, reach out my hand. It's Baron; it has to be. "Don't hurt him." I cough. "Please don't. I'll do as you say. I'll let you do anything to me; just don't touch him."

"Is that so?" My captor's footsteps approach, and I flinch. I want to turn my face away. Want to squeeze my eyes shut and pretend whatever he is going to do is not happening to me. I am not here, not in this room with no windows.

How long have I been here? Days...weeks maybe? I've lost count of time, my entire existence narrowed to what I can feel, touch, sense...since I'd been blindfolded after I'd been taken.

My kidnappers had shoved me in a room. I had resisted and they had hit me on the head. When I'd come to, I'd heard the shuffle of other bodies, heard the breathing of the others, enough to realize that I wasn't alone. They had kept us bound, gagged, blindfolded in the same room. Then Baron had managed to reach me and free my restraints. We'd attempted to free the other boys, but didn't get far before the kidnappers had returned. One look and they could read our intentions. They'd dragged me and Baron out, separating us from the rest. They'd locked us up together, blindfolded but not gagged.

I'm scared, so scared. So is Baron, though he tries not to show it. We've made a pact, that if we get out of here alive... We'll never allow anyone else to control us ever again.

Every time the kidnappers come back, they beat us. They'll leave, but never for long. They keep coming back for more. They feed us just enough to keep us alive. My entire world has narrowed to the next thud of boots on my back, my shoulders, on my chest. Beaten and left nearly unconscious.

The next time one of them returns, he tears off our blindfolds. Asshole is wearing a mask so we can't make out his features. I have the impression of a tall man, broad shouldered and with gray eyes. He tells me what I have to do. I refuse and he beats me again, this time until I black out. When I awaken, my kidnapper is ready. He tells me if I don't give him what he wants...he'll beat Baron.

I hesitate and he plows his fist into Baron's head, into his side. I hear the sound of ribs cracking and feel the anger thrum at my temples. "Don't," I beg him. "Don't do it."

"Are you ready to give me what I want?"

I hesitate again. This time he rams his fist into Baron's stomach. I hear Baron gasp in pain and somehow, that is so much worse than being beaten up myself. Somehow, hearing him hurting is much more horrible than anything this man could do to me.

"I'll do it," I force myself to form the words. "I'll do whatever you want."

He grabs my collar and tugs me up to my feet. My knees knock together, my shoulder throbs, my stomach knots, and I hate the weakness that boils up my throat. I swallow it down, will myself to stand straight. To push my chin up, thrust my chest out. *I am not afraid, I am not.* He turns me around, shoves me against the door, reaches for my pants and tugs them down.

It hurts, it hurts. I glance sideways take in the signet ring he wears on his pinky finger; the design on its surface is a bow and arrow. I glance up meet Baron's frozen eyes. His gaze widens, but he holds my gaze as the bastard buggers me.

"I won't make it."

"You don't have a choice." Baron bares his teeth. "The only way is forward."

Then pain slices through my head.

"No." My eyelids snap open. "No." My voice echoes in my ears. I take in the white ceiling, the walls, the smell of antiseptic and that sense of suspended reality that clings to a place which can never be a voluntary destination for anyone. Clearly, I am in a hospital. I try to rise up, but my body protests. My chest hurts. Pain slices through my side and I groan.

"Edward." A face appears in my line of sight. "You're awake?"

I stare up into her green eyes, emerald light, welling with emotions. A tear slides down her cheek. I reach for her and my shoulder protests. I grimace.

"You were shot." She glances down at my chest.

I follow her gaze and spot my left arm in a sling. I am wearing a hospital gown that gapes in the front to reveal a bandage around my chest.

"I'm alive," I mutter. That has to count for something, right?

"You were very lucky. The bullet grazed your side; a few inches more and—" Her bottom lip quivers and tears fill her eyes.

"Hey," I grip her arm and tug. She sits down on the side of the bed. "I didn't make it this far to die."

"Where did you go, Edward?" She swallows. "Why did you leave me?"

I blow out a breath. "I had to, Eve. I just had to find a way to get my head screwed on right. I needed time to sort through all of my feelings."

"And did you?" She tugs on her hand and I release it. "Did you manage to clear your head?"

"No." I twist my lips, "No, I couldn't stop thinking of you. Every moment I spent away from you was a mistake."

"Oh." She wrings her fingers together. "I... I don't know what to say."

"There's nothing to say; I am back now and—"

She rises to her feet, puts distance between us. "You left me, Ed. You shagged me, then walked out on me with no explanation."

"I was confused, Eve." I struggle to sit up. My side twangs, pain slices up my spine and I push it away. "I had just given up the one thing that had grounded my life until then. I walked away from my faith. I was ready to leave everything behind... I wanted to get away from it all. Instead, I found myself on your doorstep.

"You broke your vows." She adds quietly, "You shagged me."

"I needed you, Eve."

"And I needed..." she raises a shoulder, "a man who would stay with me after taking my virginity."

I swallow. "I was your first; I'll never forget that."

"I...tried to forget you. I didn't want anything to do with you, not after how you treated me."

My heart begins to race. The pulse pounds at my temples. "And now?" I clear my throat. "How do you feel about me now?"

She trains her gaze on me. "I don't know." She glances away, beginning to straighten my bedclothes, "When that bullet hit you and you collapsed and I thought I'd lost you..." Her chin wobbles, "I knew then, that I still had feelings for you."

My shoulders relax, some of the tension draining out of me.

"As do I, for you."

"But it's not enough." She squares her shoulders. "I can't forget how you abandoned me. You didn't even have the decency to tell it to my face. You simply walked out."

"I'd told you I would have to leave."

"You didn't even wait until I woke up."

"You'd have stopped me," I point out. "I had too much shit to sort out. I knew if I stayed, I'd be too taken up by you. As soon as I slept with you, I knew it was a mistake."

She stiffens, and I firm my lips. "I didn't mean it that way."

"Sure, you did." She scowls. "You regret sleeping with me."

"No." I sit up. Every part of me protests, and I wince.

Ava protests, "What are you doing?"

"I am fine." I push my legs over the side of the bed and stand up. My knees protest, my thighs spasm. Sweat breaks out on my forehead and I feel lightheaded, but at least I am upright. "See?" I say through clenched teeth. "I'm standing, aren't I?"

"Edward," she admonishes me, "get back into bed."

"Why don't you make me?" I take a step toward her and my entire body protests. I grit my teeth, forcing myself to stay upright. "Come on, Eve, tuck me in."

She scowls. "I only stayed to make sure you were okay."

"I'm not okay."

"You're standing, aren't you?" She blows out a breath. "I... I need to get going, anyway."

"Not yet." I straighten my spine, "I need you, Eve."

She shudders, closes her eyes. "I... I am not sure what I need."

"You still want me," I insist.

She takes a deep breath, pushes her shoulders back. "I survived without you all these days."

"Is that enough for you? Surviving?"

"I did a good job of it, thanks to Baron."

"Baron?" I draw in a breath, trying to figure out how she knows about him. I asked him not to contact her. "Did he look after you while I was gone?"

She tips up her chin. "I don't need a man to take care of me."

"Too bad," I set my jaw, "I did what I thought was best in the circumstances."

"Best for you or for me?"

"Best for all three of us."

She laughs, "You have no idea what you are talking about."

"Don't I?" My legs tremble; the dull thud of pain in my side ratchets up. Damn it, I can't afford to be weak. Not when I have to get back on my feet as soon as possible. It's the only way I can show her that I am worth forgiving. Sweat beads my forehead. *Stay on your feet, don't you dare collapse on the bed.*

"I knew I couldn't leave you unprotected, and I didn't trust anyone else to take care of you."

"Except Baron?"

"Except Baron."

"He got there in time that day. If it weren't for him reaching me, I… I'd have —" Her chin trembles. Tears gleam in her eyes.

A hot sensation stabs at my chest. I close the distance between us, wrap my free arm around her " Don't cry, Eve." I tuck her head under my chin. The scent of jasmine laced with that lush womanly scent of hers, fills my lungs. I am instantly hard. *Shit.* I am trying to comfort her, yet being this close to her is sheer torture.

"Why did you do it, Ed? Why did you send him to me?"

I stiffen. "Did he hurt you, Eve? Did he do something to upset you?"

She rubs her cheek against the rough hospital gown. "The only person who's hurt me here is you."

I squeeze my eyes shut. "Don't say that, Ava."

"It's true, though." She pushes against me, but I hold her close for just a second more before releasing her. She steps away, putting distance between us, and my gut twists.

"Eve," I frown at her, "what's wrong?"

"Nothing." She twists her mouth. "Everything."

"What do you mean?"

"Just that," she folds her arms around her waist, "I am not the same woman you left behind."

"It's only been two weeks."

"A lifetime."

I purse my lips. Who'd know that better than me? My life had changed in an instant when those bastards had abducted me. Seven lives...changed in the blink of an eye. We'd never been the same again. So yeah, I know what she's talking about, but still... It hasn't been that long. I drag my fingers through my hair, wince when every nerve in my body seems to protest. Shit, I must be more beat up than I'd realized. "So...what are you saying?"

"That, it's best if we spend some time apart."

"No fucking way that's happening." I take a step toward her and she skitters back. That stops me. "You afraid of me?"

"No." She shakes her head. "Of course, not."

I scowl, "Then why—"

The door opens then, and Baron walks in. He glances between us. His gaze takes in my features, sweeps over my bandaged arm, before coming to rest on Ava.

His brow furrows. "Are you okay?" He walks toward her, and she holds up her hand.

"I… I'm fine, just need some space."

"Not happening," he snaps. "You were attacked, and from what that man said before I took him down—"

"You mean before I took him down?" I interject.

He turns to survey me, "You look like shit."

"No thanks to you," I growl.

"I shot you by mistake. You know that, right?"

"Is that right?" I take in his jeans and shirt, the ruddy glow of his features. Bastard looks in the peak of health, while I feel like I could keel over at any moment.

"You know it is." He frowns. "I was aiming for the guy who broke into the studio."

"Only I got him first."

"About that," Baron scowls, "how did you have a gun on you?"

I arch an eyebrow, "Because, I am one of the Seven?"

"But..."Ava swallows, "you were a priest."

"Precisely." I dig my heels into the floor to stay steady, "Because I was a priest, I know people from all walks of life, enough to be able to procure a gun. Besides, no way was I returning unarmed. Not when I knew I'd need to keep you safe, Ava." I glance between them. "Turns out, I was right to do so. If I hadn't arrived in time, I'd never have shot that asshole."

"He's alive, by the way," Baron offers.

"Too bad." I glower. My legs begin to tremble. I sway. Both Baron and Ava step toward me. Their shoulders brush and she stiffens. So does he. They spring apart as if an electric current shocked them. More likely, an electric connection did pass between them. I sit down on the bed, look between them, before turning to him.

"Did you fuck her?"

2

Ava

Shit, shit, shit, I knew it was a mistake being in the same room as Baron and Edward. But how could I stay away? Edward had been hurt. He'd been in and out of consciousness for the last two days. I'd stayed by his side, only to make sure that he was okay. That's it. It has nothing to do with the relief that had swept through me when I'd seen him framed in the doorway of the studio. Right before he'd been shot—by mistake—by Baron.

Now, Edward glares at Baron, a suspicious look in his eyes. Of course, he'd spotted the body language between me and Baron. Too bad. Not that there's anything between me and Baron anymore, not after he'd left me too. But he'd rescued me again, when he'd walked into the studio. If it hadn't been for him arriving when he did... I swallow. Still, I hadn't been prepared for Edward to figure out what had transpired between me and Baron so quickly. And no, I will not feel guilty about that. After all, it's Edward who left me in the first place, didn't he?

Now he fists the fingers of his free arm at his side. "Did you?" he growls. "Did you shag her?"

Baron raises his shoulders and drops them. He opens his mouth, shuts it, shuffles his feet. Shit, if that isn't a dead giveaway for guilt, I don't know what is.

And damn, if we have done anything wrong. Yeah, you only slept with his friend while he was away.

But it's not like I had been in any kind of committed relationship with the Father... I mean, Edward. It is going to take some time getting used to not seeing him as a priest anymore. And the man in front of me with his bloodshot eyes, hair standing up every which way, anger bouncing off of him...is as far away from the calm, collected, Father as I can imagine. It's as if he left as one person, and returned as someone else. The change had already been underway the last time he'd seen me—when he'd fucked me, made love to me in a passionate blaze that had burned into my skin and imprinted itself in my cells. I swallow, glancing away.

"It's... just..." Baron starts to speak then purses his lips.

"Oh, for fuck's sake," I burst out. "Yes, he shagged me. I shagged him. Does that answer your question?"

Both men turn to glare at me. Edward with those golden eyes that seem to be ablaze in a way I've never seen them before. And Baron with those twin beams of laser blue that seem to cut me to the bone.

"What?" I demand. "What did you think would happen, Ed? You abandoned me—"

"—Left you while I took some time to figure things out," Edward snarls.

"Then called your best friend to come back to the life he'd left behind—"

"—to watch over you." He squares his shoulders.

"Knowing full-well that I was in a vulnerable position." I purse my lips.

"—I wanted to make sure you weren't alone."

"And that Baron, here, was trying to cope with life after everything that he'd been through," I insist.

"—I was giving him the chance to mend fences with the rest of the Seven."

"You pushed us together, knowing there was a good chance that we'd develop feelings for each other," Baron interjects.

"I trusted you," Edward roars, and I jump. Whoa, hello! What the hell happened to the Father who was always tightly in control? Who wore his serenity like it was the most important part of his personality?

To be fair, I'd always sensed that burning intensity just below the surface, only I'd never seen him lose his cool before. Not like this, and sensing how full-on Edward is now, compared to how he never showed his emotions earlier? It's something else altogether.

Silence descends in the space, broken only by the muted sound of footsteps outside the door.

"You were supposed to watch her... From a distance," Edward growls. "You weren't supposed to make contact."

"What can I say?" Baron drawls. "I screwed up. Oops."

"Why you—" Edward's jaw tics. A vein pops in his temple. Anger pours off of him as he glares at Baron, who meets his gaze with a stoic countenance.

OMG, this can't be happening. I cannot believe this is actually unfolding in front of me. I mean, I can't possibly be witnessing this kind of a showdown, and with two men...at the same time, right? Both of whom I fucked; no excuses. And who were—are? —close friends...had clearly been through a lot together.

Now, because of me, they are eyeing each other like they hate each other... Maybe they already did, to some extent, if I've correctly read between the lines of how they had spoken about one another. Still, I can't live with myself if I destroyed whatever little bit of trust remained between the two. Going by how the two of them are engaged in a game of who-blinks-first... Well, I'm afraid things are going to get a whole lot worse.

I drag in a breath, then step between them. "Stop it, you guys."

"Get out of the way, Ava," Baron snaps.

"Don't talk to her like that," Edward snarls back.

I throw up my hands, "No seriously, you guys, this is not the time or the place to engage in a game of who has the biggest dick."

Both sets of gazes train on me. I glance sideways at Edward's glowering face, then at Baron's stony one. Shit, I had to go and say that, right? Of all the things.

Baron opens his mouth and I hold up a finger, "Don't even think about it."

"You don't know what I was going to say."

"Oh, please." I toss my hair over my shoulder. "The way the two of you pounced on that comment—which is a figure of speech, by the way, I'll have you know—you think I don't know what's going through your minds right now?"

"Actually, I don't," Edward drawls.

"Neither do I," Baron widens his stance, "but I'd sure like to know."

I stare between them, "Seriously, now the two of you are going to unite against me?"

"Of course, not, " Edward bites out.

"No way," Baron retorts at the same time.

The two glare at each other again. The tension in the room ratchets up. Now we are back to square one. Lovely.

"Enough. Really, you two, cut it out." I fold my arms across my chest.

Edward scowls.

Baron's jaw hardens.

The animosity in the room seems to hit a fever pitch. The hair on the back of my nape stands on end.

"Step aside, Ava," Baron's voice lowers to a hush.

"No, no, no." I wring my fingers. "Don't do this."

"Do it," Edward says in a hard tone. Then he turns his gaze on me, and his features soften, "Please. Baron and I we need to sort this out."

"But… You're hurt," I burst out.

Edward rises to his feet. He pulls his arm out of his sling. Sweat beads his brow, but his features don't change. "You mean this?" He smirks. "It's fine, just a scratch."

I blink down at his arm, then at his face. "You are crazy," I mutter.

"I have been since I met you," he agrees.

Baron growls deep in his throat and the hackles on my arms rise.

"Now, Ava," he snaps, and I skitter back.

I feel the breeze a second before he throws up his fist.

3

Baron

What the hell am I doing? Edward's hurt, for fuck's sake. And yet, he'd challenged me. Knowing full-well I wouldn't be able to resist it. I throw a punch, aiming for the unhurt part of his face. He rises to his feet, ducks at the same time. I stumble forward. Edward wraps his good arm about my neck, tugging. Motherfucker's hurt but his grip is powerful. Apparently, the ex-Father has been keeping in shape.

"Stop! Stop it, you two!" Ava yells, just as Edward yanks his arm tightly against my neck, cutting off my air supply. I try to take in a breath and my lungs burn.

"I am going to get help." From the corner of my vision, I sense Ava run for the door.

I cough, grip Edward's forearm, tugging. He grunts, then with a sharp twist, digs his elbow into my windpipe. Darkness flickers at the edge of my conscious mind. Fuck this. Hurt or not, I am going to have to bring him down. I bring my elbow up, shove back.

Connecting with his chest.

A growl rips from him. His grip loosens. I break free, turning on him, to find him reeling back. Blood stains his hospital gown. His breathing is harsh, his face pale.

"Shit, shit, shit."

He sways on his feet, and I grab his shoulders, turn and ease him onto the bed.

"Why do you have to be such a stubborn motherfucker?

"Why do you have to...be?" He glowers up at me, pulls away, then huffs again. Sweat beads his forehead, as he collapses back.

"I am sorry, Ed. Truly, I didn't mean to shoot you."

"Yeah," he says through clenched teeth. "I know, even though a part of me wishes that you had done it on purpose, just so I could find a reason to hate you."

"Like you don't have enough basis to do so now?"

"You and Ava." He curls his fingers into fists, "How could you, Baron?"

"It wasn't something in my control," I snap.

"I sent you to her because you were the only one who could keep her safe."

"You sent me, knowing you were putting me in temptation's way." I drag my fingers through my hair. "Admit it, Edward. You knew we'd be attracted to each other. You were testing her... Testing me."

"You think that's what this is?" he snarls. "Some trial by fire bullshit?"

"Isn't it?" I glare back at him.

He clenches his fingers into fists. "Is this some bullshit explanation that you've come up with to assuage your conscience?"

"It's the truth, something you are not able to admit to yourself."

"Your conscience is playing tricks on you."

"Your sub-conscious is double-crossing you."

"Like, you did?" He bares his teeth.

Anger suffuses my blood. "Why you—"

"What have we here?" A new voice sounds behind us. I turn to find Weston walking in. He's wearing scrubs, a white coat over top.

"Ava told me you two were fighting but I wouldn't have believed it if I hadn't seen it with my own eyes."

"Aren't you a cardiologist or some such shit?" I mutter.

"Yeah," Edward doesn't take his gaze off me, "shouldn't you be sending someone more common in to check in on me?"

"I would have, except apparently, I care enough about the two of you to make sure that you don't kill yourselves. A feeling which neither of you seem to share, it seems." Weston walks around the bed, taking in Edward's pallor, then glares at me. "Out."

"But..."

"Get out, Baron," he says in a calm voice, "now."

Something in his tone cuts through the chaos in my head. I pivot, walking out of the door, up the corridor to the windows at the far end. Reaching it, I ball my fists at my side, then bang my forehead against the pane. "Fuck," I growl. "F-u-c-k."

I scent jasmine, and below that, the whiff of ripe raspberries. A second later there's a touch on my shoulder. I stiffen, but don't turn around.

"Baron?" Her soft voice wraps around my heart. Her scent intensifies as she comes around to stand abreast with me.

We stare outside the window at the large semi-circular driveway that leads to the road. A car stops, drops off a man and a woman, before driving off. To my right, a patient in a wheelchair with an IV attached to his arm sucks on a cigarette as if his life depends on it. What foolish creatures we humans are. We cling to life with every last breath we have, even as we inhale poisons that hasten us to the end.

Am I poison to her? Why did I taint her life? I should have stayed away. Instead, I had complicated things for her, for me, and for that asshole, Edward. Somewhere along the way, I had become addicted to her. I can't live without her. I'm not going to give her up that easily, not without a fight.

"You okay?" She glances at me from the corner of her eye. "I'm worried about you."

"Don't be." I draw myself up to my full height. "I'll be fine."

"You sure?"

I glance at her in time to see her chew on her lower lip. My blood instantly drains to my groin. Shit, my friend—okay, ex-friend—is lying there hurt. After I'd shot him. And here I am, lusting after his girlfriend. Well, technically she's mine now, and I'm not letting her go.

I close the distance between us, fit my knuckles under her chin and tip up her head. "Yeah," I murmur, "I've never been more sure in my entire life."

Her breathing grows shallow. Her pupils dilate. "Baron," she whispers.

"Hmm?" I rub my thumb across her lower lip. So fucking soft, she is such a bloody temptation, I can't keep my hands off of her. I lower my head to hers and she parts her lips. I share her breath, and that sweet scent of her arousal goes straight to my head. I brush my mouth over hers once, twice. She shudders. She digs her fingers into the front of my shirt. I slide my hand down her back, to the curve of her hip. That dip of where her waist meets her butt... Fuck me, but I could lose myself in that sweet roundness. Come to think of it, I have.

I deepen the kiss and she parts her lips. I lick into her mouth and a moan bleeds from her. I gaze into her eyes as I slide my tongue across hers. She shudders, pushes herself closer, but I clasp my other palm around the nape of her neck, hold her immobile as I devour her mouth. She wriggles her hips, tightening her grasp on me. I palm her butt and she gasps. Her head falls back and her eyelids flutter as she submits to me... My cock thickens, and fuck me, if I don't have her right now, I am going to—

Footsteps approach and the sound of someone clearing their throat reaches me. Her eyes snap open and she tries to pull away, but I don't let her. I continue to devour her mouth, watch as her eyes glaze over with lust again. Good, no-one, no-one can stop me from wanting her. Except him... He can. I tear my mouth from hers, release her so quickly that she stumbles. I grip her shoulder, make sure she finds her balance before turning to face the intruder.

"Yes, Doc?" I tilt my face toward a wary Weston. His gaze narrows on me.

"I patched him up. You can see him, now."

"Oh, thank God." Ava brushes past him and walks to the room. I watch as she disappears inside. Fuck, I can't stop her from seeing him. But I can do my best to ensure that she doesn't think of anyone but me. Doesn't want to be with anyone but me. Can't stop loving me. Only me.

I grip my fingers at my sides with such force that pain tears up my arm.

"Easy, ol' chap," Weston drawls, "you don't want to burst an artery."

"That would be the least of my worries." I stare at the hospital room door through which she'd disappeared. What's she doing inside there? Is she touching him? Kissing him? Does he have his hands on her? Are they plotting how to be together? A growl rips up my throat. I take a step forward and Weston grabs my arm. "Don't be stupid, Masters."

"What-bloody-ever." I try to shake off his arm but his grip tightens. "Rein in your impulses," he cautions. "Don't do anything that will spoil your chances with her."

I pause, "Why are you so concerned about that?" I shoot him a sideways glance. "Thought you were on Edward's side."

"I am on the side of whatever—whoever Ava chooses." He tilts his head, "After all, it is her choice."

I press my lips together.

"It is, isn't it?" he says in a warning tone.

"Of course." I tug on my arm and he releases me this time. "And no one is going to stop me from influencing that." I turn to leave, then look back at him and ask, "The man Edward tried to kill... "

"He's still unconscious."

I stare at him over my shoulder. "And the man who broke into Ava's studio... he's not conscious yet either?"

He shakes his head. "The bullet punctured one of his lungs but he'll survive."

"Too bad he's not dead."

Weston arches an eyebrow. "Look at it this way, between the two of them, we should have, hopefully, enough information to help us track down the kidnappers."

"Bloody incident," I spit out. "When I finally get my hands on those behind the kidnapping, I am going to wring their necks with my bare hands."

"Get in line," Weston says mildly. "So, what are you going to do now?" He looks me up and down.

"What do you mean?" I drawl.

He glances from me to the closed hospital door, then back, "You know what I mean."

"That's easy," I bare my teeth, "I am going to fight for what's mine."

4

Ava

"Are you comfortable?" I plump up the pillow behind Edward's neck.

Following his altercation with Baron, Weston had patched him up again, then given him more pain killers. By the time I'd emerged from Edward's room, Baron had left. I'd been disappointed, but also realized it was for the best. Standing up to one of them takes everything in me. Going toe-to-toe with two of them? That is nearly impossible. Not something I can do. So, when I hadn't seen or heard from Baron since, I'd taken it as a sign that I should focus on helping Edward recover. Not that it is something I have to do... But I feel compelled to do so... Maybe a part of Baron feels responsible for Edward getting hurt. After all, he had walked into my studio and saved me. I do owe him...somewhat.

Edward had still been asleep when I'd gone home last night, and when I'd returned today, he had seemed much better. So, I'd headed off to the studio, managed to get in the post-lunch dance class, then returned to check in on him. My plan was to head off for my late evening class, if everything went well. I'd cancelled my dance classes the last two days, but if I could get the ones in today, it would definitely help to keep some money coming in.

This time, he is awake.

I tilt my head in his direction. "There's one thing I want to ask."

"Anything." He smirks.

I frown, "It's a serious question."

He wipes the smile off of his face. "Is this serious enough an expression for you?"

"Hmm." I huff. "When did you learn to shoot?"

"I didn't?" He raises a shoulder. "I saw the gun lying next to the man on the floor. I picked it up and when I saw him aiming the gun at the both of you, I followed my instinct and shot at the guy. I got lucky."

"Wasn't that difficult for you?" I swallow. "After all, you were… are a priest."

"Not anymore," he mutters. "Certainly not, after I've broken my vows in every form imaginable."

"Don't you have to tell the Church or something, that you are leaving them?" I frown.

"It's the first thing I did in the morning, before I left the city. I met the Bishop and spoke to him."

"And they agreed to let you go?"

"Canonical law states that once you are ordained as a priest, the sacrament can never be erased." His lips twist. "But before I left, I asked to be laicized."

"What does that mean?"

"I can no longer function outwardly as a priest."

"Oh, Edward." I twist my fingers together. "Why did you do that? It was so important to you, being in service of the Church and your flock."

"It was," he agrees, "until I found something more important."

He peruses my features and my cheeks heat.

"I can't accept it," I whisper. "It's too much of a responsibility."

"It was inevitable." His sighs. "I thought I could use the strictures of the priesthood to find some semblance of normalcy. Turns out, I was wrong. I thought I had overcome the aftermath of the incident, but… I had only been biding my time."

"I am not sure I understand what you mean."

He peers up into my face, "You will…in time."

"Why don't you tell me now?"

He raises his hand and cups my cheek. "So impatient," he murmurs, "so feisty." He runs his hand down my cheek, and twists a strand of my hair around his fingers. "So soft." He leans forward and sniffs, "I missed this." He peers into my face. "I missed you, Ava. Your touch, your scent, your little moans when you come apart in my arms, the way you kiss, how you get that little line between your eyebrows when you concentrate on something."

"Ed—"

"Let me say what's on my mind, Eve." He places a finger on my lips. "The weeks I was away, I swore if…*when* I came back, I wouldn't wait anymore. The distance I put between us showed me how important you are to me."

Heat spools off of his body, embraces me, cocoons me in a familiar bubble of contentment. This is Ed, remember, the man you fell head over heels in love with? The man who turned his back on everything he held dear, for you. "You still left," I whisper.

"Can you ever forgive me for that?" He winds the strands of hair around his palm and tugs. I lean in closer, until my mouth is poised just above his, until I am sharing his breath.

"I wish I could say that, given a choice, I wouldn't do it again," he whispers, "but it's what helped me sort through the thoughts in my head. It's what made me realize what you mean to me."

"It's what made *me* realize that maybe what we had was not completely right for me."

His brow furrows. "What do you mean?"

"Never mind." I shake my head. "That didn't come out right."

I rise to my feet and he grabs my arm. "Tell me what you're thinking, Eve."

"Please don't call me that," I whisper.

"Why?" he growls, and I glance away.

"Tell me why I can't call you by the nickname I gave you?" he demands.

I bite the inside of my cheek, refuse to meet his gaze.

"Is it because you don't like the name anymore?"

"No," I protest, "it's not that."

"Then?" He scowls. "What is it?"

"It's just that Baron... He..."

Edward's gaze intensifies. "Motherfucker," he snarls. "It's because he calls you by the same name, isn't it?"

When I don't reply, his jaw hardens. "Yet another thing he took away from me."

"I am not anyone's to take," I insist. "I am my own woman."

"And you are mine."

"I... I am not sure about that."

"Stop that." He pulls me onto his lap. "You belong to me. That's it. End of story."

"If only things were that simple."

"It is that simple." He brings his big palm up to cup my face again, in a gesture that is so Edward, so dominant, yet so sweet that I feel like bursting into tears right then.

I glance away. "It's not, Ed. Things are much more complicated,"

His shoulders tense. "Because of him."

"You can say his name, you know," I chide him. "After all, he is your friend."

"Not anymore."

"You trusted him enough to ask him to look after me."

"Big mistake," he growls. "I wish there had been another way out."

"You could have stayed," I remind him.

"I'd have only destroyed whatever it was you felt for me, if I had."

"You changed what I felt for you."

"Did I, Eve?" He rakes his gaze across my features, "Or are you simply confused because he fucked you?"

"Edward!" Only when his head snaps back, do I realize that I've slapped him.

"Shit." I pull away from him, "Shit, shit, shit." *What's happening to me?* First Baron, then Edward. I've slapped both of them. Before I'd met them, I'd never slapped a single person in my life... If you didn't count my sister, growing up. But really, I've never lost my temper and now... I can't go a day without striking one or the other.

"I'm sorry," I mutter, "it's just what you said —"

"No, I'm sorry." Edward sits up against the pillow. "That was wrong. I shouldn't have said that. It's just, coming back to being shot, then seeing the two of you together..." he shakes his head, "I am making excuses. Nothing pardons how I insulted you." He drags his fingers through his already mussed-up hair. The usually composed Father — no longer Father — the usually unflappable Edward, all riled up and wearing a hospital gown... Not to mention that he's unshaven. The beard on his chin only adds to his rumpled appeal. And then, he had apologized. Not to say that when he'd been Father Edward, he'd been impolite, but his dominant traits had been tightly leashed. Hidden under a control that had been both thrilling and scary to observe. Now, it's as if his personality is tumbling out and he isn't quite sure how to handle it.

He stares at me, then holds out his hand, "Come 'ere."

I glance at it, then back at him, "I don't think that's a good idea."

"Come here, Ava." His voice lowers to a hush, and damn him, but I can't stop myself from obeying him. I walk over to him and he, once more, pulls me down into his lap.

"I missed you, Eve."

Something warm pools in my chest. I push the thick silky hair away from his forehead. "I did too," I say honestly.

"I want you to know that I don't blame you for what happened."

"You don't?"

He shakes his head. "Baron can be a little overbearing. And you are the most beautiful woman in the world. Of course, he made a play for you."

"It wasn't exactly like that," I mutter.

"He and I, we have a lot in common. If anyone knows how he operates, it's me. I know he must have come onto you hard, and before you'd realized what was happening, he'd have moved in."

"Edward, no, it wasn't all him," I insist.

"It's okay, Eve." He rubs his thumb across my cheek. "Whatever happened, it's only a temporary setback. Nothing we can't recover from."

"Hold on a second." I push at his chest. "Whatever happened was consensual, Edward."

He frowns. "You were distraught, not in the right frame of mind. Baron took advantage of you."

"No, he didn't," I maintain.

"Of course, he did." He peers into my face. "He must have." His jaw tics. "It's why you slept with him."

"I fucked him, Ed." I hold his gaze. "I wanted to be with him, and it wasn't only because I was missing you."

His amber gaze catches fire. A vein beats at his temple. "What are you trying to say?"

"That..." I swallow. No other way out, best to come out and say it. "I was...am attracted to him." I shake my head. "No, actually, it's more than that, Ed. I have feelings for him."

5

Edward

Something hot stabs at my chest. I fist my fingers at my sides. She has feelings for him. Of course, she does. Baron had swept onto scene when I had left. I had sent him, precisely for that. Of course, to keep an eye on her, without moving in on her. I had been so sure that he'd do that. It had never crossed my mind that he'd make contact with her... Okay, it had crossed my mind, but I had been so sure that Ava was mine, that she wouldn't be attracted to anyone else.

I should have known Baron is too similar to me. Oh, physically we are different, but our approach to life, it's similar. Perhaps that's due to our formative years being poisoned by the same toxin that tainted the lives of the rest of the Seven. They had moved on, found the loves of their lives, while Baron and I? We are still struggling.

And now we are both involved with the same girl.

Shit, shit, shit. What a mess this is turning out to be.

"Edward?" Ava asks, her voice subdued. "Are you okay?"

I'll never be okay. I'll never forgive myself for leaving her when I should have stayed. I hadn't been thinking straight, and you know what? I am not going to regret what I did. What is done, is done. It's time to move on.

"I'm not," I confess, "but I will be, once I figure out what I need to do to win you back."

"Edward, please." She rises to her feet, and when she tugs on her hand, I release it. I watch her as she drags the heavy cloud of hair off her neck and over one shoulder. "This is not a competition."

"Isn't it?"

The door opens and Baron enters. He glances between us, then walks over to Ava. "You okay, Eve?"

"Don't call her that," I snap.

"Oh, and why is that?" He leans forward to slide his hand about her neck and Ava freezes. "Baron, please, don't."

He frowns, looks like he is about to protest, then nods. He lowers his hand to his side. "Why can't I call her Eve?" He frowns at me and I glower back. Anger pounds at my temples and I clench my fists at my sides.

"You know why," I growl. "I call her Eve. I referred to her as Eve on the phone when I called you."

"So?" Baron raises a shoulder.

"So, I called her that first; I get dibs on it."

"Dibs?" Ava barks out a laugh. "Did you just say 'dibs'?"

My neck heats. Yeah, I did. What can I say? She does that to me —totally wrecks my self-restraint. Makes me recede into the most primitive corner of my brain, which I'd hoped I had gained control of a long time ago.

"Yeah, did you?" Baron drawls. "How very mature of you, Chase."

"Fuck off, Masters," I snap.

"I see your time at whichever-beach-you-decided-to-spend-the-last-few-weeks did a whole lotta good for your temper." Baron smirks.

"It was a monastery, you bastard."

"Oh, is that what they are calling it nowadays?" Baron's grin widens. "Tell me, how much of the time did you spend high? How often did you have to say your prayers? Oh, wait," Baron pretends to think, "that was when you were a Father. Now that you are not, you don't have to pretend to have conversations with God, and all that other bullshit."

"I am going to shove your balls up your arsehole." I throw off the bloody sheets, swing my legs onto the floor.

Baron's chest seems to expand. He bares his teeth, throws up his fist, just as Ava steps in between us.

His knuckles brush the side of her cheek and anger explodes behind my eyes. She stumbles back. I snatch her toward me, pushing her behind my back, then plant my fist in Baron's face.

He stumbles, straightens. A drop of blood drips from his face. A stricken look twists his features. "Shit, Ava, did I hurt you?"

"Yes, you did," I snap.

"No, it's fine. Really. It was just a tap," she protests.

I turn, survey her features. "Does it hurt?"

"No." She shakes her head. "He barely brushed my cheek."

"Let me see." Baron, the asshole, tries to brush past me and I turn on him.

"You've hurt her enough."

"I'm not the one who left her and went off gallivanting to wherever it is that you went." He glowers.

"I'm not the one who turned his back on the man you swore to stand by."

"I saved your life, you asshole." Baron growls, "I did everything possible to help you through the aftermath of the incident."

"Saved your life?" Ava pushes at my shoulder, trying to glance around me, "What the hell does that mean?"

"Nothing," I snap.

"Nothing," Baron mumbles.

"Shit, this is crazy." Ava shakes back her hair. "The two of you can't be in a room without coming to blows, yet there are so many things you two agree on. And the secrets you two seem to have?" She glances between us. "Seriously, it's unnerving, it's like you have a secret code or something."

Or something. I rub the back of my neck. Baron stares at me, then turns his gaze on Ava. "It's not intentional," he mutters. "Asshole, here, gets on my nerves."

"Makes two of us," I gripe.

"Glad we agree on something."

"Oops, do we?" I scoff. "I must be more wounded than I thought."

"Too bad the bullet didn't hit home."

Silence descends, then Baron's features twist.

"Fuck," he growls, "I didn't mean that."

"I know," I say quietly. "When you get upset, you tend to speak without thinking."

"So do you."

"Yeah." I shuffle my feet. "Guess we got off to a bad start."

"It happens." Baron lowers his chin. "It's not every day that you meet a ghost from your past you haven't seen in twelve years."

"Twelve fucking years." I nod. "Wouldn't have thought I'd make it this far."

"Me neither, man," Baron says wryly. "What say we bury our differences long enough to figure out what we are going to do about us?"

"Us?" I scowl. "There's no us… There's only—"

"Edward, seriously?" Ava slips past me, stands facing the both of us. "Baron's calling a temporary truce. Why don't you take it?"

Because I don't fucking want to. Because a part of me is already mourning that I have lost you. Because I know I'll never measure up to the kind of man you need me to be. Because I am tainted but I can't let go of you.

"Edward?" Ava prompts. "Please, can you two stop fighting?" She swallows. "Just until we figure out what to do next?"

I scowl. Baron meets my gaze. "You know we need to figure this out," he mutters. "Trust me, I don't want this truce either, but it's the only way to move forward."

F-u-c-k. He's right. Doesn't mean I am going to make this easier for him. I fold my arms over my chest. "Fine," I snap, "let's talk this out then."

6

Baron

"You propose, what?" I stare at Ava. "No. No way, am I going to agree to that."

Edward folds his arms behind his neck. Asshole leans back in the hospital bed, like he's king of a fucking kingdom. And based on what Ava just said, I almost understand why he's smirking.

"No way, am I allowing him to move in with you," I growl.

"It's only until he is fully recovered," Ava pleads. "Look, the doctor told him he won't be up and running for a few more days. He'll need help, and I don't want him to be alone during this time."

I glower at Ed, who grins back at me. I ball my fists at my sides.

"Why can't he get a place of his own?"

"I will." Edward nods, "Just waiting for the paperwork on the apartment I am going to rent to come through."

"Why can't Saint put you up in one of his many hotels?"

"It still means he won't have anyone to take care of him," she replies.

"I'll hire him a nurse. Hell, I'll make sure he has round-the-clock attention," I snap.

"It's not the same as someone you know looking after you." Her forehead furrows. "You understand that, right?"

No, I don't. I set my jaw. "If you're alone with him, he'll take advantage of you."

Edward's expression sours. "I'm not the one who moved in on my friend's woman while her boyfriend's back was turned."

"Boyfriend?" I growl, "You were nothing to her; you barely knew her."

"Like you've spent all that long with her?" He sits up. "You tosser, and after everything I did for you, this is how you repay me?"

"Finally," I bare my teeth, "now you show your true colors. Keeping track of everything I owe you, eh? You did what you had to do, out of some twisted guilty conscience, you—"

A piercing whistle blows through the space. I whip my head around, and so does Edward.

Ava lowers her fingers from her lips, her cheeks flushed, her eyes blazing. "The two of you are incorrigible. Here I am, trying my best to figure out how to move things forward, and all you two can do, is fight like you are ten.

She stares between us. "You know what?" She plants her hands on both of her hips, "You guys can figure this out. I have had it with both of you." She marches to the door.

"Where are you going?" I scowl.

"Some of us need to work for a living," she snaps back, "and I am already running late for my first class."

"I'll take you." I take a step forward and she turns on me.

"Don't you dare come near me." She points a finger in my direction. "In fact, don't leave this room, until you two sort out whatever it is that has the two of you at such loggerheads."

"So, am I moving in with you?" Edward ventures.

"No," I snap.

"Why not?" He frowns. "I thought we'd just settled it?"

"No, we haven't."

"I am sooo out of here." Ava turns to the door, then looks back and adds, "When you two have a plan figured out, call me, or... You know what?" She pauses. "Don't. If I don't hear from either of you, I'll be happy." She marches out of the door.

Silence descends. I glare at Edward, who glowers back at me.

"Well, that went well," I drawl.

He seems like he is about to respond, then slouches back against the pillows. "Shit, we really pissed her off, didn't we?"

"What did you expect?" I walk over and slump into a chair. "The two of us can barely look each other in the eye when we speak, let alone try to work out what is clearly a sticky situation for all of us."

"Not my fault," he mutters.

"Edward, seriously, man." I rub the back of my neck "What the hell happened to you out there? You seem to be coming apart at the seams."

He draws in a breath, then shoves off his covers. "What did *you* expect? I've been cooped up in here for the last three days. Of course, I am going out of my head."

"Is that what it is?"

"What else can it be?" He frowns.

"When are they going to discharge you?"

"How about right now?" Weston walks in, this time dressed in jeans and button-down shirt, with his white coat on top. "Your test results are all fine. You're free to leave."

"Hallelujah." Edward swings his legs over and stands. "About fucking time."

Weston stares at him, "I can't remember the last time I heard you swear so much."

"Maybe before he joined the seminary?" I volunteer.

"So, it's definitely over, then?" Weston makes some notes on his clipboard, his voice absentminded in the way of most doctors when they are processing a few different streams of thought in their mind.

"What is?"

"Your priesthood?"

Edward stills. "Seems that way," he says, in a voice devoid of all emotion.

"How do you feel about that?"

"About what?"

Weston pins him with a stare. "Don't bullshit me, Ed," he snaps. "Being a priest was a big part of your life. How are you adjusting to life in the aftermath?"

"I..." He rolls his shoulders. "I am not sure yet, and that's the honest truth."

"Hmm." Weston looks him up and down. "You have a place to go, now that the rectory is out for you?"

"I'm trying to figure that out." He glances around, heads for the chair in the corner where his clothes have been folded. He pulls off the sling, winces, then struggles into his jeans and shirt. Then he sits in the chair to put on his shoes and looks up at us. "What?" he growls.

"You know you can stay with any of us, right?" Weston adds.

Not with me, though. I fold my arms across my chest and Weston slaps the back of my head. "What the fuck?" I sputter. "Seriously, Doc."

"Aren't you forgetting something, asshole?" Weston growls.

"What, what?" I glare at him. Weston glowers back and I blow out a breath. "Yeah, yeah, you can stay with me." I mumble, "It's a studio, but hey, I am sure we can work something out."

"Oh, fuck off, Masters," Edward mutters. "I am sure you'd be glad if I took you up on your offer, but it's not happening. I am staying with Ava."

Anger thrums at my temples and I shove it back. *Don't lose it. Don't lose it. For Ava's sake.* You need to win her over and that's not going to happen unless you get back in her good books.

Which means, having to pretend to get along with your once friend. *It's the only way she'll realize that you are serious about her.* Fuck! I don't have a choice. I am going to have to grit my teeth and get through this.

"You ready to go?" I say through clenched teeth.

"You offering me a ride?" Edward arches an eyebrow.

"For my sins." I rise to my feet, heading for the door. "Don't blame me if you can't keep up."

. . .

Forty-five minutes later, we draw up in front of Ava's home. The drive had been tense. Neither of us had spoken and I had turned on the radio—because, yeah... That's how much of a coward I am. I figured it was best to fill the silence so neither of us had to speak. Fucking hell, the last I checked I still had my balls about me, so why the hell can't I have a direct conversation with this man I've known more than half my life? Maybe some things are best left unsaid? *Like, why the fuck didn't you called in all those years you had my phone number... And when you finally did, it was only because you needed my help with something?* Typical Edward.

To the rest of the Seven, he's always been the voice of reason. The calm and collected teen who'd become a voice of conscience for them. Me? I know better.

I know that hidden under that exterior is a man who is angry with the world, with himself, with everything that happened to us when we were kidnapped. I know, because I was there. I know, because I bore the brunt of what happened during the incident, along with Edward.

I know, because neither of us have ever discussed what happened during that time. Not with each other... And definitely not, with the rest of the Seven. There are some things you take with you to the grave, for if you mention them aloud, they became real. Too real. To the point that it would consume your every waking moment. Some things... You are never prepared to face, no matter how much time passes. Some things are best forgotten, because to acknowledge them would mean you have to face the consequences of the aftermath, something which I refuse to deal with.

I park the car, shove open the door, and head up the garden path. When I unlock her front door, he stiffens. "You have a key?"

Clearly, I do. I push the door, walk through, and drop the keys on the table in the hallway. I leaf through her mail, just to irritate him, then gesture to the couch. "Make yourself at home."

He frowns at me. "Like you?"

I smirk. "Yeah, I misspoke. Make yourself comfortable," I pause for effect, "but not too comfortable." I walk to the kitchen, top off the coffee maker with water and coffee grounds, then switch it on. I turn to find Edward leaning a shoulder against the doorway.

I tilt my head, "I've been staying here."

He stiffens. "You stayed here?"

"Yep." The coffee maker begins to bubble and I move away to grab two mugs, place them on the counter.

"You moved in with her?" he growls.

I allow my lips to curve and his expression darkens. "Don't fuck with me, Masters." His jaw tics.

I snatch up the coffee pot, top off both cups, then grab both off the counter. I walk over, hand one to him, then brush past him to sit in the chair in the living room.

Edward follows me. He sinks into the couch, then glares at me. "Well?" he growls. "You sleeping in this house with her?"

"I am sleeping in this house."

A nerve pops at his temple and my grin widens.

"Chillax," I drawl. "I slept there," I point to the couch where he is sitting, "until I didn't."

He curls his fingers into fists. "You just had to rub that in, didn't you?"

"Sorry, ol' chap." I raise my shoulders. "You'd prefer I lie? Truth is, \your loss was my gain."

"So, this is how it's going to be?" he says in a hard voice. "The two of us always baiting each other, always at loggerheads, and never able to see eye to eye?"

"Guess nothing much has changed, huh?"

"Damn right." He scowls down at his cup of coffee, then stares at me, "You need to fuck off, Masters. You're not needed anymore."

"Didn't hear you say that when you called and asked me to step in."

"I changed my mind."

"I cleared up the mess you left behind at the church, by the way," I lower my chin, "and you are welcome."

"Considering how you fucked up everything else, you'll have to excuse me if I can't muster a thank-you."

"The man you thought you strangled," I tip up my chin, "he's alive, by the way."

Edward stiffens. "Too bad," he mutters, "he deserved to die."

I take in his features. "You didn't used to be this bloodthirsty."

"And you used to be my friend."

I wince, then drag my fingers through my hair. "Guess I deserve that."

"And much more." He takes a sip of his coffee, places his cup back on the table, "If you think you can come between me and Ava, you are mistaken."

"Correction." I set my jaw. "I didn't come between anyone. You left, remember?"

"And now I am back."

"I guess you're entitled to your opinion." I scowl.

He glowers back. The tension in the room escalates. Shit, this isn't how I'd wanted it to be. I'd known Edward would return, eventually... I'd hoped I'd have more time. I didn't expect for him to come back so quickly. Not before I'd consolidated my position with Ava. Before I'd won her over completely. If it means I am being greedy and duplicitous, then the fuck I care? I am not letting go of the one thing that brings me joy. I am not letting him take Ava from me, and if that means I need to play along with him for a while, even win his confidence, then so be it.

I hold his gaze, then blow out a breath, "Can we call a truce temporarily?"

His forehead furrows. "Why is that?"

"I don't know about you, but I can't fight on an empty stomach, man." I lean back in the couch, "Can we order some pizza first?"

7

"If we haven't been visited by people from the future yet, does that mean time travel will never be invented? However, these people that may have come back may have kept themselves hidden so we don't know they've come back, so the future is unchanged.... Um, does that make sense? Guess the past should stay in the past — we shouldn't change it but only learn from it. Besides there is no future yet, so how can someone come back from something that hasn't yet existed?"
-From Ava's Diary

Ava

I walk inside the house and the smell of cigarettes laced with coffee and a deeper, edgier smell I can only identify as testosterone hits me. What the—? I glance at the two men sprawled across from each other. Between them are used coffee cups. There's also an ashtray—a previously unused one which I'd shoved to the back of one of my shelves… Who'd found it? I narrow my gaze on the cigarette butts that have been stubbed out.

"Have you been smoking?" I scowl at Baron.

"Don't look at me." He jerks his chin in Edward's direction.

"You?" I turn on him, "You, Father? I mean, Edward. Really?" I scowl. "Since when did you start smoking?"

"Since I left you and realized how much I miss you?"

My cheeks heat.

Baron makes a sound deep in his throat. I ignore it. I drop my bag on the edge of the couch farthest away from Edward, then stoop to grab the ashtray. "Well, next time, take your butts outside."

"As long as you park your butt next to mine."

Before I can turn he's patted me on my arse.

"Hey," I straighten, "that was uncalled for."

"Sorry," he raises his hands, "I couldn't resist."

I glance over to find Baron curling his fingers into fists. "Keep your hands off her, you prick."

"I apologized, didn't I?" Edward drags his fingers through his hair. "It was a moment of weakness, okay."

"As long as it doesn't happen again," Baron snaps.

Edward jerks his chin. Baron, glowers, but doesn't say anything else.

"Hmm." I stare between them, "I assume you've come to some kind of understanding."

Neither speaks.

"Well, have you?" I frown. "Go on, you can tell me."

"We…may have." Baron concedes, "but first," he holds up his finger, tilts his head as if listening. "Wait for it, wait for it." The doorbell rings. "Pizza." He springs up, heads for the door.

"Pizza?" I blink

"Yeah, we have to eat sometime, don't we?"

I take in Ed's pale features, his rumpled clothes. He seems tired but not in pain. "How's the wound?" I ask.

"I'll live." He smiles lazily, and my breath catches.

Shit, this, being surrounded by all these acres of hot manliness isn't helping me at all. I turn away, "I think I am going to take a shower."

Baron returns just then with two massive pizzas.

"Everything okay with Archer?" he calls out after me.

"Of course." I glance at him over my shoulder. "He's a good man." I lower my chin. "He mentioned the two of you served together in the army?"

"We did." Baron places the pizza boxes on the coffee table. "There are only two other men I'd trust to watch over you. He's one of them."

"One of two, huh?" I say slowly. "So, there's you, obviously. And Archer..."

He nods.

"And the third man?" I tilt my head, "Who's the third person you'd trust to protect me?"

When he doesn't reply, I narrow my gaze on him. "It's Edward, right? You'd trust Edward to protect me, wouldn't you?"

Baron pauses, then resumes opening the pizza boxes.

"Well?" I prod, "You would, right?"

"Sure," he finally says, "why not?"

"Ha!" I stab a finger in his direction. "Clearly, you don't hate him as much as you say you do."

"You're right."

"I am?"

"Yep." He straightens, training that bright blue gaze on me, "It goes beyond hate. Let's just say, while I trust him with your life, I don't trust his intentions toward you."

Edward bares his teeth. "Same to you, asshole, with knobs on."

I stare between the two of them. "I get it now."

"What?" Edward scowls.

"This is why the two of you are pretending to get along?"

Baron tips up his chin at me. "We get along just fine." He coughs with his palm over his mouth, "Not!"

"Ha," I stab a finger at him, "knew it. The two of you are sitting across from each other, pretending to have a civil conversation, only so you can keep an eye on each other. So you can make sure the other one doesn't make a move on me."

Edward raises his hands, "Impressive piece of deduction there, Eve."

"It only took you what, fifteen minutes, to come to that conclusion?" Baron snickers.

I throw up my hands. "The two of you in this mood are impossible. Seriously, you guys need to chill out." I turn and head for my bedroom, when Baron calls out.

"The pizza will get cold."

"It will stay," I mumble.

"No, it won't," he retorts.

I turn, and scowl, "I need a shower."

"You can have one later." Edward nods.

I glance between them. "I am not winning this argument, am I?"

"Nope." Baron raises a shoulder, "When it comes to your well-being, I won't compromise."

Edward scowls at him, then turns to me. "Eat first, Eve." His voice softens, "You must be hungry." His gaze holds mine. "Besides, I am starving and," he lowers his voice, "I'd love to eat with you."

Heat ripples across my skin and my toes curl. He may as well as have said, *"I'd love to eat you."* My cheeks heat. Edward drags his thumb across his lips, and my belly flip-flops. Moisture pools between my legs. I take a step forward, only for Baron to plant himself in front of me.

I blink, glance up at him, "What?"

"Here, why don't you sit down?" He guides me to the chair he's just vacated. Sensations tingle out from where he touches me. I glance up, to find his lips curving in a knowing smile. I scowl.

"Not fair," I mumble. "The two of you are playing me."

He straightens, glaring down his patrician nose at me. "All's fair in love and war, baby," he drawls.

"I'm not some kind of…prey that the two of you can take turns toying with," I burst out. "I'm just a woman…" *caught between two alphaholes.* Oh, my god, how could I have gotten myself into this situation?

I stare between them. Baron folds his arms across his chest. Edward scowls from his place on the couch. The silence stretches, dense and heavy. My throat dries. I take in the pizza on the table, "May as well eat first."

No one moves for a second, then Baron nods. He walks around to sit in the chair opposite me. He reaches forward, takes a paper napkin, passes it over to Edward, who shares it with me. We each reach for a piece of pizza, then begin to eat.

"The chili flakes," I mumble, "can you pass them please?"

Both Baron and Edward reach for the packet. For a second, I am sure they are going to fight over who's going to give it to me. Then Baron retreats. Edward hands the packet over to me.

"Thanks." I rip it open, pour the flakes over my slice of pizza, bite into it. Heat suffuses my mouth. Sweat breaks out on my brow. I chew, swallow, and promptly hiccup. Yeah, that's me, always biting off more than I can chew. I never did know when things could get too spicy for me. Never did know when to stop before I burned myself, or in this case, my tongue. I hiccup again. Both Baron and Edward reach for one of the bottles of iced tea that had been delivered with the pizza. Baron snatches it up, unscrews it, and reaches across the table to hand it over to me. I thank him, tilt the bottle and wash down the pizza. The fire in my mouth subsides. I glance over to find Edward glowering at Baron—who continues to eat his pizza, his lips curled in a slight smirk.

"Oh, for hell's sake." I place down my pizza and stare between them. "This is not working."

"I don't know. From where I am, everything is peachy keen," Baron rumbles.

"Only because you won the last round," I accuse him, "and that's what this is turning out to be, right? Each of you trying to get one up on the other—"

"Sounds good to me." Baron's smirk widens.

"With me as the prize."

"Does that bother you?" Edward turns to me.

"What do you think?" I snap.

His forehead crinkles. "I think," he glances at Baron, "it's time we figure out a plan."

"You do?"

"Of course." He leans back, throws his arm across the back of a couch. "That's why we are here, aren't we?"

"Hmm." I frown at him. Why is he being so placatory? Somehow, I can't believe that he actually wants to talk about the elephant in the room, the one we have avoided talking about openly so far.

"He's right." Baron crumples up the napkin in his hand and drops it in the empty pizza box. "Let's figure this out."

They both glance at me.

"What?" I frown. "Why are you both staring at me?"

"The two of us spoke about our situation," Edward gestures between him and Baron, "before you arrived."

"You did?"

"We couldn't arrive at any decision."

I snort, "Why am I not surprised?"

"So, we agreed to disagree," Baron chimes in.

"That's a start, I suppose."

"We also agreed on one other thing." Edward's eyes gleam.

I frown, "What?" I swallow. "What did you agree on?"

"That we'd let you choose."

8

Ava

"Choose?" I swallow. "You'll let me choose?" My heartbeat ratchets up. I stare between them. They can't mean what I think they do. "Really?"

Edward smirks. "We mean, we'll let you choose how to set up a schedule to spend time with us."

"Oh." My muscles relax. What the hell? Guess I am not ready to let either of them go...yet. What does that say about me?

"A schedule?"

Baron nods. "You pick a time to meet each of us, separately."

"This way, you get to know both of us...individually," Edward adds.

"It will give you more information to base your final decision on." Baron's features close and his gaze intensifies. No doubt, he thinks the final decision will be in his favor. He wants it to be in his favor.

And if it isn't? What will he do then? How hurt will he be? And it's inevitable that someone will be, right? At some point, I'll have to choose one of them. And the other one, whoever it is, will be upset and angry, and likely, never forgive me. Likely, this would end their friendship too. One forged in such difficult circumstances that it should be able to weather anything.

But this…this is so personal, so emotional. Will the two of them be able to get through it? Would they be able to see past whoever is the inevitable winner and understand it's for the best? And if they can't? If they stop being friends, if they hate themselves…more than what they do now, will I be able to forgive myself?

"This…" I jump up to my feet, "I can't do this."

"What do you mean?" Baron snaps.

"It's because of me that the two of you are pitted against each other. I don't want to come between the two of you."

"Trust me…the disagreement between us existed prior to your coming into the picture." Edward smirks.

"That's not how it seems to me." I fold my arms around my waist. "The seven of you are supposed to be friends, right? At least, from what I've heard from the girls, you guys stick together. You have each other's backs."

They both nod.

"So, imagine how it seems to me when I see the two of you hating each other… Thanks to me."

"We don't hate each other," Baron murmurs.

I chuckle. "Sure could have fooled me."

"We just have too much stuff from the past between us." Edward leans forward. "It means our friendship will always be fraught with…tension."

"But it doesn't feel right that, ultimately, one of you is going to lose."

They both freeze.

"Or didn't you realize that?" I roll my eyes. "How did you think this was going to end? The three of us becoming one big happy family? I mean, I am going to have to choose, right?"

They stare at each other, anger evident on both of their features.

"This is what I mean," I snarl. "One of you is going to lose. And both of you hate to lose. One of you is going to end up hating the other. Your friendship will be over, thanks to me. You won't be the Seven any longer." I rake my fingers through my hair. "How do you think that's going to make me feel?"

"Slow down, Eve," Edward cautions, "you're getting ahead of yourself."

Baron glances from him to me, "He's right…on this." He rubs the back of his neck. "Let's take it one day at a time. You don't know how or where this is going to end up. We are both mature enough to realize that one of us is going to get the girl." He winces, "And of course, I want it to be me."

Edward glares at him and raises his hand. "I mean, we are both sensible enough to realize that one of us is going to emerge the victor. Besides," he kicks out his legs, "fact is, we'd rather you choose one of us than someone else."

Baron stiffens, then nods. "For once, he's talking sense," he mutters. "If… When you are ready to choose, it will, hopefully, be one of us."

"You are okay with that?" I scowl.

"Not exactly," Baron's lips twist, "but if this means I am, at least, in the running to be with you, then well… It gives me hope, and I'd rather have that…than lose you."

"Agreed." Edward strokes his chin. "As long as I know that there is a possibility that I get to be with you…it gives me a fighting chance. And fight for you, I will."

"I am not giving up easily, Eve," Baron rumbles. His features soften. "You know, I'll do anything for you… If it means I need to put up with—" he stabs his thumb in Edward's direction, "so be it."

I scowl at him, "You sure about this?"

"No, I am not." His scowl deepens.

When I stare at him, he raises his hands. "I mean, of course, I don't want to share you, but if it means, at the end of this, I have a chance of having you to myself, then," he raises his shoulders, "fair enough. It's worth a shot."

I blink between them. "You guys okay to shake on that?"

Baron's jaw hardens. "No," he snaps.

"Nope." Edward sets his lips.

I blow out a breath, "And you guys think this is going to work?"

"We'll make it work." Baron's features firm. "We have to."

"You bet; we'll make sure it does." Edward squares his shoulders. "Though I must warn you," he glances between me and Baron, "I am going to pull out all the stops." He narrows his gaze on Baron. "I haven't come this far to lose."

"Save the speech, Chase." Baron yawns, "By the time I'm done, you'll wish you had cut your losses and run."

9

Ava

"You agreed to what?" Isla stares at me.

We are in our favorite bar, at the top of the British Portrait Museum near Trafalgar Square. I've always liked it because you can look out of the window and spot Nelson's Column just a block away. I lean forward, take a sip of my wine.

"I agreed to allocate separate times for each of them."

"So, you mean, you'll be spending Monday with Baron," she counts off on her fingers, "then Tuesday with Edward, then Wednesday with Baron—"

"Uh, I don't think it's going to be that regimented."

"So, what do you mean?" Her brow furrows.

"Just that I'll be taking turns dating each of them."

"Dating?" She makes air quotes with her fingers. "Is that what you kids are calling it nowadays?"

"It really is strictly dating." My face heats, but I don't allow myself to acknowledge the blush. "This is supposed to be a fact-finding mission."

"Fact-finding?"

I nod. "Yeah, that's what they wanted and that's what I agreed to."

"And what is this fact-finding going to be about?" She presses a finger into her cheek.

"Finding out more about them, their backgrounds, their preferences; giving them a chance to get to know me better."

"And why would you do that?" She frowns.

"Why wouldn't I?" I scowl at her. "It's the simplest way of figuring out who I am most compatible with."

"Thought you already knew that?" She waggles her eyebrows. "After all, you did sleep with both of them."

"It just happened, okay?" I mutter. "If I had known it would land me in this situation—"

"You wouldn't have shagged either of them?"

I purse my lips. "No, that's not true. The way things happened—" The way I'd lost my virginity to Edward…when he'd walked in and stared at me and I had known then I wanted him, that I wasn't letting him leave without losing my virginity to him… Then, being so fiercely attracted to Baron. "I couldn't have stopped any of it," I say firmly.

"So, now you are going to try both of them out…for size?"

Heat sears my cheeks. "Not like that," I object.

"Then how?"

"There's not going to be any sex."

She chokes on her drink, places her wine glass on the counter, then snatches up a paper napkin to wipe her mouth. "No sex?"

"Absolutely not." I shake my hair back from my shoulders. "I already know both of them that way."

My flush deepens, and I square my shoulders. *What the hell? Why am I embarrassed?* Face it, I did shag them both. And I enjoyed it. And they were both hot and amazing and I felt wonderful at the end of it. Don't men sleep around all the time? Though this is not the same. When I was with Edward, I'd been convinced he was the only one.

Then Baron had crashed into my life, and after how Edward had left me… Okay, so maybe I had been emotionally fragile…but I'd known what I was doing when I'd slept with Baron.

Edward had left me, and a part of me had been sure that he'd be back, I can't refute that. Yet, I had been so strongly attracted to Baron… And he'd been there while Edward wasn't. And it hadn't felt wrong… I had followed my instincts. Which is how I had ended up in this situation, right?

Maybe my instincts aren't so reliable, after all. All the more reason to stick to the plan; approach this in a more practical manner, as Baron has suggested. Try things out and see what works… If something feels wrong, I can ditch it, try something else. All along the way, I'll be gathering feedback on what works. It's the only way forward, right? It has to be.

The alternative is to be stuck with both guys angry and snarling at each other, and gosh, how I hate that. If there is even a chance for the three of us moving on from this, to live somewhat normal lives, then I have to give this a shot. "Besides, this is about figuring out whom I am most compatible with on an emotional level… And sex only muddies the waters… So yeah, no sex."

"Hmm." She purses her lips, "Which brings me to another question, do the guys know about it?"

"About what?"

"That sex isn't part of the bargain?"

"I may have, uh, forgotten to mention it."

Her jaw drops. "Wow," she blinks, "so you are just walking into this hoping to withhold from them?"

"Don't be crude," I mutter, "but yeah, that's exactly what I am going to do. I mean, not overtly, but I am going to make sure we don't get there."

"You're going to make sure that two hot blooded alpha males spend time with you and you don't end up in bed with either of them?"

"Umm, yeah?"

She shakes her head, then turns to the bartender, "Can you top us off, please? My friend, here, is going to need it."

"What?" I snap.

She motions zipping her lips.

"Tell me," I grumble.

"Not my place."

"Oh, please." I mutter. "Seriously, Isla, you've come this far, may as well spit it out."

"Is that what you told him?"

"What?" I frown, "Oh! For your information, I swallowed."

She opens and shuts her mouth. "Whoa, woman. Seriously, you have changed."

"It's called growing up?"

"It's called, having your cake and eating it too."

"Huh?"

"You know, dating two sexy-as-hell guys... With their permission... At the same time." She stares at me. "Honestly, despite the fact that I know you are not going to be able to stick to the 'no sex' thing—"

I make a warning noise.

"Not that you are not going to try or anything, but whether you are able to stick to it is another thing altogether. Despite that—"

"Isla!"

"No, seriously. Despite all that, I am envious of you. I truly am."

I snort, "Why don't I believe you?"

"Come on, woman, you're trying to juggle two men. Me? The only action I'm getting right now is silicone."

"You mean, by imagining yourself with Liam?"

"Ugh, that man?" She makes a face. "That full-of-himself, pricktard, who needs to get a life? The last time I met him at his wedding rehearsal, he looked at me like he hates me."

"Maybe it's because he actually likes you?"

"No, no, no, not falling for that, babe. There is no enemies-to-lovers thing happening here. The man positively loathes me. He can barely bring himself to talk to me when needed. Not that I mind." She snorts, "The less interaction I have with him, the better."

"So, you'll be happy when he gets married."

Her features freeze, then she recovers and raises her glass at me, "Nice segue, but I am not falling for it."

"Not falling for what?" I ask innocently.

"You tried to change the topic and succeeded, but I am steering us back to the issue at hand."

"What's that?"

"You and your men, Ava." She leans forward, "Surely, you do prefer one of them over the other?"

I scowl at her. "If I did, don't you think I'd have decided by now?"

"Come on," she drums her fingers on her table, "isn't there anything about one of them that outweighs the other?"

Let me see. Edward was my first love... He has that unshakeable strength inside of him that had attracted me from the beginning. Then, he'd left his faith behind for me, after which... he'd left me... But he'd returned back to me. He'd changed his life, for me.

Then there's Baron. Unshakeable Baron. Who'd broken his promise to his friend because he'd seen me and hadn't been able to stay away, although he certainly did try. The lust with him is combustible; it's like striking a match to gasoline. The attraction with him is palpable. When we are in the same room, it's like my gaze is drawn to him.

Well, to both of them, to be honest. They complete different parts of me. Edward is my first love. And Baron... He'd swept me off my feet.

My head spins. Shit, what a mess.

I lower my chin, hunch my shoulders. "No," I mutter, "I can't find anything that tips the balance in favor of either of them. They are equally matched," I raise my gaze to hers, "and not only in that way."

"I didn't say anything," Isla protests.

"You didn't need to." I grab my drink, chugging down more of it. The alcohol hits my stomach and a pleasant warmth infuses my skin. I glance up to find her watching me carefully.

"What?"

"Nothing."

"Say it, Iz."

"Hmm." She circles the rim of the glass with her finger. "You're going to think I'm crazy for even suggesting it..."

"Oh please," I snort, "as if I'll ever be surprised with what comes out of your mouth?"

She chuckles, "True that, but I don't think I've ever said anything this outrageous before."

"Which is?"

"That I agree with Summer."

"You do?" I blink.

She nods, "Why don't you enjoy both of them — ?"

"But—"

"—for now," she adds. "Don't force a decision, babe. Just be with what you have, savor them, let your subconscious decide who you want."

"And if I can't decide?"

"You will." She firms her lips.

"But when?"

"You'll know when you know."

I blow out a breath, grab my glass and drain it. When, though? When will I know who is right for me? When will I find out who is my soulmate? And why did I have to fall for both of them?

"Speaking of..." She clears her throat, and I glance at her.

"Now what?" I mutter.

She jerks her chin toward the doorway of the bar.

I turn around and the breath whooshes out of me. "What are you doing here?"

10

Baron

I walk into the bar, and she watches me approach. "You shouldn't be here," she scolds.

"Says who?"

"The deal was that I'd set up a schedule to date you guys."

"Doesn't mean I can't stumble across you in a bar, does it?"

"And is that what this is?" She frowns. "Did you walk into this bar by accident?"

I hesitate, look away. "No," I mumble, "I walked in knowing you'd be here."

"Baron," she scowls, "this is not right."

"What's not right is that you are going home to him, and you'll be spending the night in the same bed as him." I belatedly notice Isla and smile at her to disguise my discomfort. "Hi, Isla. How are you doing?"

"Umm—" Isla rises to her feet, "I need to get going."

She bends, kissing Ava's cheek. "Call me if you need anything, okay?"

She nods in my direction, an acknowledgement. Meanwhile, Ava kisses her back and waves as she walks away, leaving us alone.

"She's a good friend." I slip onto the bar stool she vacated. "How did you two meet?"

"She was a good friend of my older sister's, actually. Then we met and got along really well."

"You have a sister?" I frown. "You never told me that."

"Guess I didn't have a chance."

"What does she do?"

"She's a marketing director. Has a well-paying job with a media company. She travels a lot for work, is very ambitious, and... She's my exact opposite." She laughs.

The bartender approaches me, but I shake my head at him.

"You're not drinking?" She frowns.

"I'm driving."

"Right."

I turn to her. "What makes you think that you are so different from your sister?"

She takes a sip from her drink, hunches her shoulders. "Because she's so focused, you know? She knows what she wants, and goes after it."

"And you don't?"

"I'm a med school drop-out."

"And now you run your own studio."

"Which barely breaks even—"

"Where you create art, and do what you enjoy."

"And I still struggle to get students."

"It's what you love," I insist.

"If only passion were enough to put food on the table."

"You're only getting started." I lean forward, "If you persevere… As long as you are doing what fires you up, you are bound to be successful."

She blinks. "Wow, that's some speech, Baron."

My neck heats. "It's true, though," I insist. "You're such an incredible dancer, Ava. Don't give up."

She smiles and her green eyes light up. "Thank you," she murmers, "I needed to hear that. Maybe one of these days, I'll even have the courage to sign up for the World Belly Dancing championships."

"Oh, you definitely should. Bet you'd win the first prize too."

"I'd settle for simply not falling flat on my face." She laughs.

"You could never do that. You have too much talent to do anything but excel at anything that you put your mind too."

"Wow," she blinks, "you have no idea how much it means to me, to hear you say that."

Don't lose faith in yourself." I gaze at her earnestly. "Promise me that."

She licks her lips and my eyes drop to her mouth. "Say you promise," I coax her.

"I promise," she whispers.

Her words are soft, her lips slightly parted. I move in closer, close enough to smell that jasmine and raspberry scent of hers. The blood instantly drains to my groin. My dick thickens. My thighs harden. I lower my head to hers, and she swallows. I push the hair away from her forehead and she trembles. I place my mouth in front of hers, close enough to share breath and a moan bleeds from her lips.

"Ava," I whisper, "fuck, you're beautiful."

She stares into my eyes, her pupils dilated. Her chest rises and falls and color smears her cheeks. I brush my lips across hers—once, twice—and she sways. I slide my hand behind her neck, hold her in place as I deepen the kiss. I lick across her mouth and she gasps. I slide my tongue in between her lips and she moans. I press down on her chin and she opens her mouth. I suck on her tongue, sweep my tongue across her teeth, pull her close enough for her hair to brush my face. The scent of her sinks into my skin; the taste of her goes straight to my head. I slide off my stool, push her legs apart and step between them.

A groan rips out of me and she shudders. She slides her arms under my jacket, digs her fingers into my back, and my dick lengthens. I pull her to the edge of her stool, thrust my hardness into her center. She gasps, straining against me, thrusting her breasts into my chest. Something crashes to the floor and I tear my mouth from hers, stare at her flushed features, those dilated eyes that indicate just how aroused she already is.

"Ava," I whisper and she shakes her head.

"We shouldn't."

"Why not?" I growl. "You want me, I want you."

"It's not right, to Edward."

"Don't talk about him," I snap.

She frowns up at me. "I thought we were all going to get along."

I snort, "I agreed to tolerate him."

"You agreed to give this arrangement a chance."

"Doesn't mean I can't kiss you."

"You can." She tilts her head, "Just know that I won't sleep with you."

"Wait, what?" I scowl. "What the hell do you mean?"

"I'm not sleeping with either of you, until I figure out where this is going."

"You mean until you figure out who you're going to choose?"

She scowls up at me. "I'm trying to do what's right."

"I'm right for you, Ava." I massage her neck and her chest heaves. "See how you respond to me? How you yearn for my touch, how your body reacts to my nearness?" I lower my head to hers again and her lips part. "You want me, Ava. Admit it. You need me. You can't live without me in your life. Without my telling you what to do. You want the strength of my dominance to subsume you, you want me to throw you down and rip into your pussy. You want me to bend you over this table and fuck you in the arse in front of everyone."

"Baron," she breathes, "what are you saying?"

"You want me to take you in front of this bar, so you can cry out and show them just what a good little slut you are. You love being an exhibitionist, Ava. It turns you on, thinking of all the forbidden things I can do to you. You want me to claim you, to tell the world that you belong to me."

"No," she whispers, "that's not true."

"It is."

"No, it isn't." I sense her move. The next second pain explodes behind my eyes; my groin screams in protest.

"What the fuck—?" She kneed me in the balls. Why that little— I turn around, find her running out of the bar. Shit. "Ava, hold on." I spring forward and my body protests. I grit my teeth through the pain, force myself to move forward. I race toward the door, up the sidewalk in her wake. "Ava, stop."

She turns around, scowls. "Why should I, after you pulled that underhanded stunt on me?"

I increase my pace, closing the distance between us. She yelps, faces forward, trying to run faster. I catch up to her, grab her arm and she screams, "Let go of me."

"Ava, stop." I haul her to me and she struggles in my grasp.

"Release me, you asshole.'

"No."

"Why did you kiss me like that?"

"Because you like it?"

"How dare you say those filthy things to me?"

I yank her up to her tiptoes, clamp my hand around the nape of her neck. "Because it turns you on, Eve."

"Stop calling me that!"

"Why should I?" I haul her against me and her breasts flatten against my chest. "You make me crazy, Ava. You know that?"

"Good," she huffs, "because you do the same to me."

"So, choose me."

"I," she blinks, "I can't, Baron."

I stare into her face, and my heart begins to race. "Fuck," I swear. "F-u-c-k." I release her so suddenly that she stumbles. I grasp her shoulder to make sure that she finds her balance, then step away from her. "I'll drop you home."

Half an hour later, we pull up at her house. I grasp the wheel of the car, stare straight ahead.

"Baron, I…"

"Get out of the car, Ava."

She turns to me. "You're angry with me and it's not fair. You knew Edward would return, that this entire situation would turn out to be messy."

"No shit," I growl.

"Baron, be reasonable. I—"

"Reasonable?" I turn on her, "Why should I be reasonable, when you go home every night to sleep in the same bed as him?"

"I'll be on the couch."

"What?" I frown. "Don't do that. You won't be able to sleep well there."

"I'll be fine," she assures me.

"Why can't he move to another place?"

She blows out a breath, "We've had this conversation. As soon as he's able to fend for himself, he'll move out."

"Bet he can right now. Bet he's only playing the sympathy card so he can stay with you."

"Baron," she snaps, "that's beneath even you."

I snort, "Seriously? You have no idea what Edward is capable of. Just because he was a priest, doesn't mean he still tells the truth."

She flips her hair over her shoulder. "Do I detect the green-headed monster making an appearance?"

"You think I'm jealous?" I growl.

"Aren't you?"

"If I were jealous, would I be driving you back to deliver you into his arms?" I squeeze my fingers around the wheel of the car so tightly that pain screeches up my arms.

"Yes, you would," she mutters, "because despite how much you don't agree with the situation, you'd honor your word."

"What-fucking-ever."

"Oh, I know you, Baron Masters, better than you realize. Which is why you'll never pull the stunt that you pulled today again."

I arch an eyebrow. "Don't get your hopes too high, Sugar. I'll kiss you where I want, when I want."

"No, you won't."

"The fuck, Ava?" I slam my fist into the wheel and the horn blares. "The fuck are you putting these restrictions on me? It's fucking unnatural. I want to be able to kiss you when I want, to lick your cunt when I am hungry, to slam into your pussy when I feel like it, to fuck you like you belong to me, to own you like you are mine."

Her breath hitches.

"And I know you want it too."

"Maybe," she finally concedes, "maybe I do."

"Bull-fucking-shit," I snap. "You know you do."

"Doesn't mean I am going to let myself have it."

"Why the fuck not?"

"Because I am determined to give both of you a fair chance."

"Fuck fairness."

"Oh?" She tilts her head, "How would you feel if I walked in there and asked Edward to shag me—"

"Don't you fucking dare do that," I roar.

"My point exactly."

"Fuck, fuck, fuck." I rake my fingers through my hair. "This entire arrangement is bullshit, and you know it."

"No, it isn't." She straightens her shoulders. "I need to give both of you an equal chance, and right now, this is the only way."

"What-bloody-ever."

I shove open my door, stalk around the car to her door, but she's already stepping out. She walks up the garden path and I follow her to the door. She steps onto the patio, and I follow her onto it.

She reaches for the door and I don't move. She huffs out a breath, "I am not going to ask you to come in."

"I didn't expect you to."

"Sure, you did," she mutters, "but it wouldn't be fair to Edward if I did."

"You going to tell him about how you kissed me back?" I allow my lips to twist. "You going to tell him how my filthy words turn you on, how you like it rough? How you want to be dominated and not given a choice, how you like your every hole filled at the same time, how you like to be spanked and treated like a fuck toy, how—"

She turns on me, "Shut up," she hisses. "Just shut up."

"Yeah," I widen my legs, "thought not. He can't give you what you want; only I can."

"How do you know he didn't give it to me rough?" She tilts her head, "How do you know that's not how he fucked me already?"

Blood thuds at my temples. My pulse rate ratchets up. I step into her space, then bend my knees and peer into her features, "Is that right, Eve? Is that how he gave it to you? Is that how he shagged you, Eve?"

She pales, opens her mouth, when the door to the house flies open.

"What's happening here?"

11

Edward

Baron straightens, as the two of them continue to stare at each other.

"What the hell are you doing?" I step outside, shoving at Baron. "Get out of her face, man," I growl.

He glowers from her to me, then back at her. "This isn't over, Ava." He shoves my hand away, then turns and stalks off.

Ava watches him walk down the path; her features wear a haunted expression.

"What did he say to you, Eve?" I demand. "Did he insult you, because if he did I—"

"No," she swallows, "it's nothing." She brushes past me and walks inside the house.

I watch as Baron gets into his car, then turn and stalk back inside. "It didn't seem like nothing to me," I mutter.

She places her bag on the couch and sinks down next to it. Her hair flows about her shoulders. It's obvious her shoulders are tense.

Walking over, I stand behind the couch, push her hair to the side, then dig my fingers into her shoulder. Finding a knot in her muscle, I work at it until it loosens.

"That feels good." She leans into my touch. "Don't stop, Ed."

I use my good arm and continue to massage her shoulders, alternating between the two, until the tension fades away and she's pliant.

"Mmm." She closes her eyes and leans her head back on the couch. "Thank you, that was wonderful."

"The pleasure is all mine." I smile down at her relaxed features.

She opens her eyelids, gazes up at me from under her lashes. The curve of her lips, the relaxed set of her features, the sleepy look about her eyes... All of it pulls me in. I bend down until my face is poised over hers. She traces her gaze down my face, until it rests on my lips. She swallows and I close the distance between us until my lips are poised above hers.

"Ed," she mumbles, "we can't."

"Why not?"

"Because we shouldn't."

"Why not?"

"Because I told Baron that I wasn't sleeping with him, or with you, until I arrive at a decision."

"Wait, what?" I scowl. "What did you say?"

She leans forward. "I am not having sex with either of you." She folds her arms about her waist. "Not until I've figured out what to do about all of this."

Walking around the couch to see her face, I argue, "That's bullshit, Eve."

"Yeah, that's what he said also."

"Stop talking about him when you're with me."

She throws up her hands, "Is this what is going to happen when I am with either of you and I mention the other one? Seriously, you guys need to grow up." She stands up and begins to pace. "I am trying my best here, and neither of you is helping me out."

I fold my fingers into fists at my side. "Can't say I blame him, though."

She pauses, then turns to face me. "What are you talking about?"

"You come home smelling like another man, and you think I am going to stand by silently and accept it?"

She pales, "It…it's not like that, Ed."

"Oh?" I round the couch, and walk toward her, "Then how is it, Ava, explain it to me?" I take a step forward and she skitters back.

"It's really not how it seems."

"Oh?" I allow my lips to curl. "Are you denying that you kissed him?"

Her gaze lowers.

"Thought so."

I move toward her and she stumbles back another step.

"Did he touch you, Eve?" I growl. "Did you let him press his lips to yours, thrust his tongue in between your lips, as he felt your shoulders, your breasts, the curve of your hips? Did he wind your hair around his fist and yank on it as he closed his mouth over yours?"

Her breath hitches, then her face pales. "Stop it," she snarls. "Stop it, Ed."

"Why should I?" I close the distance between us, and she slides back until her body touches the wall. She stiffens, looking around her, "Don't even think about it," I warn. "Tell me what he did to you, Eve."

"Nothing," she snaps.

"You're a liar." I lunge forward and she screams.

"Don't come closer, Ed!"

"Why?" I allow my lips to curl. "Scared I'll kiss you and then you'll forget him?"

"This is not a competition," she snarls

"So, you keep saying, and you know what? I am fucking tired of it." I plant my hand on the wall next to her head and she freezes. Her breathing quickens. She darts her gaze from left to right and that's when I push my hips into hers.

Her gaze widens; she tips up her chin and stares into my face. Her pupils dilate. I pin her to the wall and I know she can feel every last swollen inch of my hardness. Color smears her cheeks, she buries her teeth into her lower lip and blood rushes to my groin.

"See what you do to me, Eve?" I growl. "When I am in the same space as you, I can't fucking keep away from you."

"Don't, Ed," she whispers, "please don't."

"Of course, you'd put the onus on me. You want me to take the choice out of your hands. Want me to show you what you're missing, Eve?"

"Edward." She searches my face. For mercy? Fat chance of that. "I know this is not you speaking. This is your ego, your fear, that's making you say these things to me."

"Ha," I scoff, "of course, you don't want to believe the worst of me. You think, just because I was once a priest, that I'll play by the rules. You think I'll stand by and watch as he uses every opportunity to seduce you, to convince you to choose him. You think I'll let it slide when he puts his hands all over you, then drops you home, knowing it will tear me apart to see him with you?"

"Ed, stop, please." She scrunches up her forehead. "You don't know what you're saying."

"You're right."

"I am?"

I nod. "It's time to stop speaking and show you how I feel, Eve."

Her gaze widens. She shakes her head, "Don't, Ed. Don't you dare."

I lower my head, place my lips close to hers, "Tell me you don't want me to kiss you."

She swallows.

"Tell me you don't want me, Eve."

"I..." She licks her lips, "I can't."

"Ask me to kiss you."

She shakes her head.

"Do it, Eve," I growl.

She raises her gaze to mine, peers into my eyes, and in hers I see a pleading, a request, a need, confusion and lust. Arousal and uncertainty.

"Fuck." I lean my forehead against hers. "I want you, Ava. I need you. You know that, right?"

She nods.

"Then let me kiss you, let me feel your lips against mine. All the time I spent away from you, the only thing that kept me going was knowing that I was going to come back to you. Don't deny me, Eve," I hold her gaze, "please."

She draws in a breath, squeezes her eyes shut, before opening them. "Okay." She nods.

"Okay." I rub my nose against hers. "Okay." I lower my lips to hers, brush my mouth over hers once. I lean back and she makes a sound of protest. My lips kick up. I lean my face into hers, press my mouth to hers again. I lick across her lips and she parts them. I slide my tongue over hers, and a moan tumbles from her mouth. I tilt my head, suck on her tongue, and she shivers. I deepen the kiss, licking into her mouth, dragging my tongue across her teeth, as I press my hips into her.

Her entire body shudders. I pour all the longing, all the frustration, the loneliness I felt when I was away from her... The helplessness at not being able sift through my emotions, knowing how much I missed her, despite knowing I needed time to figure things out... Still having to figure things out... The lust, the complete awe that I found her... I pour all of it into the kiss.

I press my body into hers so we touch at chest, hips, and thighs, until every part of me is imprinted on hers. I draw in her breath, share my own, then lick into her mouth again, and she pushes her hips into mine. I plant a thigh between hers, pressing down into the soft, luscious center of her, and a groan bleeds from her. She wraps her arms about my shoulders and holds on as she begins to ride my leg. I deepen the kiss even more, until it seems like we are sharing the same breath, until her breasts are flattened against my chest. I tilt my hips and press into her soft core, giving her the friction she so craves. She pushes up against the column of my thigh, digs her fingers into my shoulders and rubs her core against my leg, over and over again. Her body tenses, her shoulders jerk, her entire body goes rigid. That's when I tear my mouth from hers, and stare into her eyes. "Come for me, Eve."

12

Ava

"Get yourself off on me. Come now, Eve," he commands, and I shatter. The climax rips up my spine. Sparks flare behind my eyes. My shoulders snap back as I cry out, then slump against him. The aftershocks ripple through me as I rest my forehead against his chest. He holds me there with his arm around my shoulders. I bury my nose in the strip of skin bared between the lapels of his shirt. Draw in the scent of cut grass, and below that, the faint trace of Frankincense which still clings to him.

"Do you miss it?" I whisper. "The priesthood, I mean?"

He stills, then drags his fingers down my hair. His fingertips catch on a knot at the ends and he carefully untangles it.

"Do you have a brush?"

"What?"

"A hairbrush."

I tip up my chin, "If you don't want to answer the question —"

He places his finger on my lips. "A hair brush," he repeats. "Do you have one?"

I scowl, but damn, I am so relaxed right now, I don't want to fight with him. "On my dressing table," I murmur.

He steps back, only to wind his fingers around my wrist. He tugs and I follow him to the bedroom. He leads me to the dressing table, urging me onto the stool in front of the mirror, then reaches for the brush. He starts near the tips of my hair and patiently unravels the knots. Brushing a few centimeters more every time, he gradually works his way up to finally have the full sweep from scalp to tip.

I lower my chin, close my eyes and enjoy his soothing strokes. For a few seconds, there's only the steady rustle of the teeth of the brush through my strands. The sound of my breathing, the heat of his body, the slide of the fabric of his pants against the edge of my seat.

Then, "I don't miss wearing the robes." His voice rumbles and he draws the brush down another portion of my hair. "I don't miss the discipline and the routine, something I thought I would." His voice is pensive. I try to turn my head but he clicks his tongue. "Stay still," he scolds and I turn to face forward, watching his face in the mirror.

"But you do miss some parts of it, surely?"

"I miss..." His voice lowers to a hush, "Helping people, I suppose."

Of course, he would. He may be an alphahole, but that is just a part of him... Just as much as that something inside of him, that wants to do something for the greater good. Perhaps it's that core of him I had sensed, which had been as attractive to me as the strength of his presence?

"You could still do that, you know?" I survey his reflection in the mirror. "You could still help others."

"I am not sure if that's what I want to do...now."

"What do you want to do then?"

"I want to do...you?" He raises his gaze to meet mine. The look in his eyes... OMG, it's hot and smoldering and so bloody intense. That's the thing with Edward. Nothing about him is ever half-way. It's like he always gives one-hundred percent—no one-thousand percent—of himself to everything he does. His amber eyes flare with that inner fire I recognize and I have missed. I may not have known him for very long, but the time I have is imprinted inside of me. How could someone have had such an impact on my life in so little time?

"Ed..." I whisper and his lips twist. That smirk? Jesus, it's so hot. And so mean. Why is it that I am always attracted to the bad boy? Not once, but twice over? Clearly, I have a type. And clearly, this type of thinking is not getting me anywhere.

"Ed, please don't," I plead.

"I'm not doing anything." He turns back to the task of grooming my hair. The rasp of the brush against my scalp makes goosebumps erupt on my skin.

"Ed, please." I pull away, rise to my feet, then pivot to face him. "It's not fair," I protest, "what you're doing to me."

"What am I doing to you?"

"You know exactly what." I scowl. "You're trying to seduce me."

"No, I am not."

"Yes, you are." I fold my arms round my waist. "You know, I am not going to sleep with either of you."

"But you're okay to kiss him, you're okay to rub yourself up against my thigh and come, you're okay to—"

"That's not fair," I burst out. "You begged me to kiss you."

"And you fell for it?" He raises an eyebrow and anger sparks at my nerve endings.

"You...you bastard."

"If you couldn't pass this test, I wonder what else you've been up to with him."

"You were testing me?"

"Of course," he smirks, "did you think I'd actually beg you for anything?"

I swallow. "How dare you?"

"Just trying to establish that your game of not sleeping with either one of us isn't working."

"You're right," I swallow, "it isn't. In fact, I was wrong to have thought that I could actually stick to this ridiculous notion...of trying to give each of you a fair chance. Especially when both of you seem to turn everything into a competition. When neither of you wants to play by the rules, what chance do I have?"

The blood thrums at my temples. What the hell had I been thinking? Trying to make some sense of this crazy, twisted relationship... Or whatever it is that exists between the three of us. I am the only one who seems to want to find the solution. Both of these...idiots, clearly, don't want to find a way out. I am the only one trying to play fair, when neither of them wants to respect the boundaries I have tried to create. Obviously, I am going about this all wrong. There is only one way out.

"Leave," I say in a low voice.

"What?" He frowns. "What do you mean?"

"Last I checked, this was still my house," I firm my lips, "and I want you out."

"What the hell?" He glowers. "I am not going to leave you alone."

"Ha," I snarl, "should have thought about that before your little... act, earlier."

"I am not leaving, Ava." He draws himself up to his full height. "Not until we figure out who the hell is behind the attack on you at your studio."

"I don't care," I snap. "I want you out of my space, Ed. Now."

"You're angry. I understand." He rakes his gaze across my features. "You've been through a lot."

"You have no idea."

"First Baron, then me, turning up out of the blue... And the attack—"

"Was nothing compared to how you and Baron seem to play so easily with my emotions."

"That wasn't what I intended—"

"Oh, yeah?" I take a step forward. "Didn't seem like that to me. In fact, from where I am, you and Baron seem so consumed with trying to take the other one down you don't care how it's hurting me here."

"Shit, Ava." His features twist. "That wasn't my intention...and while I can't speak for Baron, I am sure he didn't mean to cause you any pain either."

"Well, too late, buster." I take a step back from him. "I suggest you be on your way."

"I am not going to leave you here on your own."

"You don't have a say anymore."

"What do you mean?"

"It means..." I swallow, glance around the room. Am I going to do this? Guess I am going to do it. I don't have a choice. It's not working this way and I can't allow myself to be torn apart like this between the two of them. For my own sanity, maybe this is the only way out. "I need a little time away from both of you."

"No." His features darken. "You don't mean it."

"See," I stab a finger in his direction. "There you go again, telling me what I do or don't think, and honestly, I am tired of it. I just need some time alone to think about where this is all going, about what I want to do with my life, without either of the two of you meddling in my affairs or ordering me around."

"Don't you dare do this, Eve."

"Oh, fuck off." I throw up my hands, "Both of you call me by the same nickname. Do you have any idea what kind of a mind fuck that is? I mean, what are the chances? Two men, best friends... Or at least, once-upon-a-time best friends, call me by the same bloody nickname, and of course, I have fallen for both of them."

"Wait," he shakes his head, "you have fallen for both of us?"

I gape at him. "Hello? What do you think this entire," I shake my hand in the air, "situation is about."

"I thought..." He scowls. "I know you said you have feelings for him, but you have fallen for him as well?"

"Oh, my god." I slap my palm to my head, "I can't even... I mean... Seriously?" I march to the door of the bedroom, "Get out of my house."

"No."

"Edward," I slam my hands on my waist, "I want you out of my sight, right now. I mean it."

He places the hairbrush on the dressing table, then turns to me. "I'll leave—"

I release a breath.

"This bedroom. I'll spend the night on the couch."

"What the—?"

"Before I leave, I need to make sure there'll be someone watching the house at night—"

I make a rude noise.

"And that Baron..." his features harden, "has arranged for round the clock surveillance."

"Whatever."

He prowls toward me, and I watch him draw closer, closer still. He pauses in front of me, his big body blocking out the rest of the room from my line of sight. I gulp. A ripple of desire pulses down my spine. I jerk my chin toward the doorway. "Leave, please," I mutter.

"This isn't over, Eve." His jaw tics. "Not by a long shot."

I hold his gaze. I will not look away. Nope, I need to hold my own if I have any chance of getting through this in one piece. Hah! Famous last words. I am already broken inside. And confused. And at my wit's end about what to do. Time away from both... Yes, that is exactly what I need. A little time apart, without either alphahole breathing down my neck or getting jealous about the other. Yes, totally what I crave at the moment. Some peace and quiet please?

He lowers his knees, peering into my eyes. "Is this what you want, Eve?"

I nod.

He holds my gaze a second longer, then nods, straightens, and walks out of the room. I close the door behind him, lock it. Bet he heard that. Too bad. Right now, it's self-preservation. That's my focus. I head for the bathroom, take a quick shower, then change into my sleep shorts and cotton-camisole. I slide into bed, switch off the light and pull up the covers. Shit, I didn't get any pillows or a duvet for him. I roll on my side. Too bad. He'll just have to do without it. Alphahole has a thick hide; that should keep him warm. And the bathroom... There isn't another in the house, and I locked the door. Forget it. If he wants to use it, he can knock. For once, it will be him asking me for something... Instead of the other way around. I close my eyes and must have fallen asleep, for the next thing I know, it's morning.

I throw off the covers, head to the bathroom, brush my teeth.

I walk back into the bedroom, just as my phone pings with an incoming message. I pick it up, swipe the screen to read the message.

Raisa: *I've emailed you all the details of the wedding. Dad will be gutted if you don't come. Please Ava, don't be selfish.*

Am I selfish? Is that why I'd fallen so quickly for Baron, right after falling for Edward? Is that why I am holding onto both of them, because I can't let either of them go? Is that why I am so confused, because I want everything? Is that so wrong, though? To not settle for what doesn't feel right?

It's why I had dropped out of med school. And not that embarking on a creative career is any easier, but at least, it feels right somewhere inside of me. Just like... It doesn't feel right to make a decision about the two of them...yet. And going to Dad's wedding? I sit down on the bed. I had read Raisa's email, and know that the wedding is in the backyard of our family home. It's only a few days to the event now and... Shit, I don't want to break his heart. Truly, I don't.

I reach for the phone to answer her message, keep my fingers poised over the keyboard, but the words don't come. I place the phone aside. Head to the closet, drag on a sweatshirt and leggings then walk out of the bedroom.

When I reach the front room, I find it's empty.

13

Baron

I open the door to my apartment and Edward stares back at me.

"What the hell do you want?" I growl.

"We need to talk." He scowls back at me.

"Like hell, we do."

I am about to shut the door on his face, when he says, "It's about Ava."

I glower at him, "We've already spoken with her about how she's going to spend time with each of us—"

"She doesn't want to see either of us."

"What?" I frown.

"She threw me out of the house."

I can't stop the smile that curves my lips. "She did, huh?"

"She wants time apart from *both* of us." He shoves past me and I watch as he prowls over to the window in the far corner of my loft-apartment.

I shut the door, walk over to stand in the center of the room.

"What do you mean? What the fuck did you do?"

"I mean exactly what I said." He drops his backpack on the floor. "We've both been pushing her... Too much, too quickly... Of course, it was bound to happen."

"Don't go putting the blame of your desertion on me."

"It wasn't desertion." He bites out the words as he stares out of the window. What does he see? The view of London spread out before him? His past...our pasts...as intertwined as it is because of the incident and what happened to us? His future...my future? Which, for some reason, seems to be just as closely twisted together... Thanks to one auburn-haired, green-eyed beauty who has ensnared both of us.

"What do you call it, then?"

He pivots to face me. "It's called putting distance to get perspective, which I guess is what she's trying to do right now."

"Is that what you think?" I scowl.

"What I think is not important." He leans forward on the balls of his feet. "Nor is what you think of consequence."

"Is that right?" I growl.

He nods. "The only thing that matters is that we respect her wishes—"

I open my mouth to speak and he raises his hand "—for now."

I set my jaw. "I'm not sure that's wise."

"Why not?"

"If she has time alone to sort through things, what if she decides that she wants neither of us?"

"You mean, what if she decides that she doesn't want you."

"Ava belongs to me," I grit out. "She was mine from the moment I saw her."

"She saw me first."

I ball my fists at my sides, and his lips twist. "Hurts to hear the truth, doesn't it? I am her first love."

"She doesn't love you."

His smile widens. "She does."

"Has she told you that?"

"You think I'd reveal that to you?" He looks me up and down.

"You'd say anything to get a rise out of me," I growl.

"You know, I am not lying." He raises a shoulder. "Besides, she understands and appreciates the sacrifice I made for her."

"If you mean leaving the priesthood, that was a long time coming, precipitated by your inability to keep your temper in check."

The smile vanishes from his face. Good.

"And we all know you joined the Church, purely as a means of escape." I scratch my jaw.

"Escape?"

I nod. "Fact is, you couldn't deal with reality, you didn't have the balls to face what had happened, so you turned your back on the world."

His features harden. "You should talk. You shipped out and joined the army. If there's a deserter here, it's you."

"Ah, see, that's where we differ." I rock back on my heels. "At least, I was out fighting a battle. I was facing my fears while doing my best to protect innocent people, while you?" I shove my hand in the pocket of my slacks. "You were merely hiding from the inevitable."

He balls his fists at his sides, "Inevitable, huh? What's that?"

"Revealing to the world that you are a coward, Edward." I bare my teeth. "You were a coward then, as you are now."

He takes a step forward and I hold up a hand, "Think carefully before you do anything else. We both know I am in far better shape than you. It won't take me long to take you down."

"We'll see, shall we?" He throws up his fists at the same time that there's a hammering on the door.

We glare at each other.

"Were you expecting someone?"

I shake my head, glance around the space for a weapon, when a voice calls out, "Open the fucking door, wanker."

My shoulder muscles relax as Edward blows out a breath.

"Fucking Saint," he mutters.

"What the fuck does he want now?"

I pivot, head for the door, and fling it open. Saint stalks forward.

He shoves my shoulder with his as he brushes past me and heads for Edward.

"Hello, asshole." Saint tilts his head.

Edward scowls back. "What the hell are you doing here?"

"You could be happier to see us now, considering we are child-hood buddies and such?" Sinner saunters in through the door, followed by Damian, Arpad and Weston. Damian flings himself on the couch. Arpad wanders over to the bar in the far corner.

Weston walks toward Edward, "How's the wound coming along?"

"I'll survive," Edward snaps.

"Make yourselves comfortable," I call out sarcastically.

"No formalities, bro." Saint raises a hand, "You know us, we treat each other's places as our own."

"Don't I just?" I slam the door with enough force that the painting above the fireplace crashes to the floor. Good thing it came with the place, which I purchased a few years ago but never bothered to furnish. Considering I only crash here on the rare occasion I am in town. Not that any of them notice my little burst of temper. Short of dying…

"Whiskey." Arpad pulls a bottle of Macallan's from the bar. "Don't you have any fucking vodka?"

"Since when do you drink fucking vodka?" I scowl.

"Since he met Karina?" Damian chuckles.

I glare at Arpad. "You don't even like fucking vodka."

"Guess I do, now." He places the bottle of whisky on the bar counter. "You missed out on a lot, ol' chap.' He tilts his head at me, "It's good to have you back though."

"Yeah," I rub the back of my neck, "it's still no excuse to drink at," I scowl at the watch on my wrist, "ten a.m.?"

"Oh, that's where you're wrong." Arpad smirks. "This drink isn't for me."

"Who is it for, then?"

Five pairs of eyes turn on me.

"What?" I glare.

All of them shift their gazes to Edward.

"What?" He glowers at them. "This isn't a fucking tennis match."

"Sure, could have fooled us." Saint cracks his neck. "That's why we're here anyway—to referee."

"We don't need a referee," I growl.

"Oh?" Saint folds his arms across his chest, glances between us. "You two have some shit to sort out."

"That's putting it mildly." I snort

"And we're here to ensure you two don't kill each other," Damian adds from his position on the settee.

I shoot him a glare, and his smile widens. Asshole's enjoying himself.

Hell, all of them are. Tossers who have their lives all set up, wives, and kids on the way. They've managed to put their pasts behind them, managed to set to rest the ghosts from the incident. They've found their homes, have a future with their loved ones.

Me? I have none of that. Nothing, except a past as a soldier, the security company that I set up with Archer, and a future career as an investor; one which is going to take some adjustment. Not to mention a former best friend who is now my most hated enemy and a woman...who doesn't belong to me yet. And am I going to let go of her that easily? Of course, not. She is all I have left in this world. The hope of being with her is the only solace I have left to look forward to. I cannot let go of this opportunity, to find out how it would be to be with someone who satisfies that craving deep inside of me.

"We are not going to kill each other." I blow out a breath, "We were merely discussing strategy."

"Strategy, huh?" Sinclair smirks. "Is that why the two of you were yelling at each other?"

"We weren't..." I glance at Sinclair, who tilts his head.

"We could hear you all the way down to the street," Damian pipes up.

I glower at him and he chuckles.

"Okay," I rake my fingers through my hair. "Yeah, so we had a bit of a disagreement."

"Nothing the two of us can't sort out," Edward mutters. "We certainly don't need the rest of you here staging an intervention."

"Too fucking late." Saint grabs a chair, turns it around and straddles it. "You should have thought of that before you guys couldn't keep it in your pants."

"What the fuck are you talking about?" I growl at him.

"You know what he means," Weston drawls. "The two of you are involved with the same woman."

"None of your bloody business," Edward snaps.

"Much as it pains me to do so," I scratch my jaw, "I am forced to agree with Edward on this."

Saint shakes his head, "Afraid that's not how it works, ol' chap."

"What the fuck do you mean?"

"He means, since the two of you haven't been able to sort things out, we are going to have to step in."

"What the fuck?" Edward glares around at the five of them, "It's best you wankers stay out of this."

There's silence, then all of them burst out laughing.

"Fuckin' hell." Saint pretends to wipe a tear from his eye. "You guys hear what dear Edward, here, just said?"

"Yeah," Damian leans forward in the couch, "anyone want to remind him how he was part of each and every intervention on behalf of the five of us?" He turns to me, "Not you, of course, considering you missed all the fun…. Not," he mutters. "Anyway," he turns his gaze on Edward, "sorry, buddy, you're going to have to man up and take your share of advice on your love life… Which, considering the mess the two of you have gotten into... I'd say, should be welcome."

Edward glowers back.

"Or not." He raises his shoulders. "Doesn't matter, either way." He jerks his chin at Weston, who leans forward on the balls of his feet.

"Fact is," Weston looks between us, "you guys have two choices."

"We do?"

"Yep." He nods and begins counting off on his fingers. "Shut up and listen to us or... Shut up and listen to us."

"Har, har." I deadpan, then walk over to lean against the bar. "Go on, get it out of your system."

Saint drums his fingers on the back of his chair. "So," he turns to Edward, "you love her?"

"What the fuck?" I growl at the same time as Ed.

"I'm talking to Edward," Saint says in a mild voice. "Go on, Ed, I asked you a question."

"What the hell kind of a question is that?" he objects.

"Answer the question, you piece of shit," Sinner growls.

Edward shoots him a dirty look, then turns to Saint, "Of course, I do, you dickwad. Not that it's any of your business."

"Hmm." He rubs his chin, then turns in my direction, "And you?"

"Me?"

He nods. "Do you love her?"

"Fuck off, you fucktard."

"Very original." Saint chuckles. "Still doesn't answer my question."

I bunch my fingers at my sides, taking a breath, then another, "I am not going to tell you what I feel."

"Why not?" Damian frowns. "It's not anything to be ashamed of, soldier."

"We've all been through it." Arpad nods.

"Consider it another coming-of-age rite," Weston adds.

"What-bloody-ever." I rub the back of my neck, begin to pace. *Of course, I do, so why is it so difficult to admit it aloud? Why hadn't I told her so earlier when I had a chance? So, it has only been two and a-half weeks since I met her. So what? When you know, you know, right?*

Something inside me insists that she's the one for me. *So why the hell can't I say what I am feeling aloud? Argh!* I dig my fingers in my hair and tug. *Jesus H Christ, what the fuck is wrong with me?*

"Well?" Saint prompts, "Do you?"

I turn around and face them. "And if I do?"

"So, you do?"

I fold my arms across my chest. "What's it to you, assholes?"

"I understand how difficult this seems," Sinner says in a low voice. "Trust me, when I met Summer I was confused as fuck. I had no idea why whenever I saw her, I wanted to run away yet simultaneously, shove her behind me and hide her away from the world."

"Whoa." I blink, "Did you just wax almost-poetic...about a woman?"

"My wife and soon-to-be mother of my child." He half-quirks a smile, "Who'd have thought, eh?"

"Not me," I mutter. "Mr. Ruthless Billionaire Bastard with hearts in his eyes... Fuck me dead."

"Right?" Sinclair smirks. "And you know what the starting point was?"

"No," I frown, "what was it?"

"It began with accepting that I was a piece of shit who didn't deserve her."

"Hear, hear," Damian agrees.

"It began with being very honest with myself about who I am."

"A fucktard?" I offer.

"That too." His smile grows lopsided. "But also, that I was a selfish bugger in everything, and even more so when it came to her. Only, when it came to doing things for her, I discovered I could be the most selfless person."

"You're not making any sense."

"My point, exactly." He widens his stance. "What I am trying to say, you piss-tard, is that it began with me facing myself. It began with me accepting what I felt for her."

"Which was — ?"

Weston ambles over to me, "You just obtuse, or did your stint in the army addle your brains and other parts of you completely?"

"My parts are all in fine working condition," I mutter, "which is more than I can say for many of you."

"Afraid most of us here have proven our manhood, ol' chap," Weston drawls.

I open my mouth, and he shakes his head. "And I don't mean fucking or getting our women pregnant."

I tilt my head and he pauses next to me, "Every one of us had to bare our soul, lay our heart on our sleeve, and swallow some very hard lessons."

"Not to mention, coming clean and admitting our feelings for them," Damian interjects.

"You mean groveling, don't you?" Arpad mutters.

"Lots of groveling," Weston concurs.

"A whole lotta groveling." Saint winces.

"That doesn't seem like the recipe for a happy relationship." I frown.

Weston smacks me on the back of my head, and I wince, "The fuck, asshole?"

"Is that all you took away from this rather protracted and painful conversation?" He glares at me.

"If you want to tell me something, why can't you guys simply come to the point?"

"The point," Sinclair arches an eyebrow, "is you need to come clean about your feelings."

"So, you may as well start practicing now," Saint adds.

"Now?" I grumble.

Damian and Arpad nod.

Weston raises his hand and I glare at him, "Don't you fucking dare, you bastard."

"Oh, I fucking will, you douchebag, unless—"

"Unless?"

"Unless you spit it out."

"What?"

He claps me on the back of my head and I wince, "Fine, fine, I'll say, it, I love her. I fucking love her."

I stare at Edward, who frowns back at me. Like that helped with anything.

"What a fucking mess," I mutter.

He narrows his gaze.

"Now that we have that out there." Sinner turns to Edward, "What are you two gonna do about it?"

14

Edward

"Why are you asking me?" I growl. "I am not the one who got us into this mess."

"Oh yeah?" Baron snorts, "If you hadn't called me, I wouldn't have come."

"If you hadn't gone back on your word of not making contact with her, this would not have happened."

Baron thrusts his chin forward, "If you hadn't—"

The sound of a whistle blows through the space and we freeze, turning toward Sinner, who glares between us. "Woulda, coulda, shoulda. You assholes know better than to spend time talking about what already happened. Question is," his gaze narrows, "what are you gonna do about it now?"

I glance at the faces of each of my friends. They regard me with expressions varying from curiosity to empathy to hope.... Fucking hope. It's the one thing I don't have. If she doesn't choose me, I have nothing. I left the one thing that mattered to me, for her, and if she turns away from me... I pivot and face the window. "F-u-c-k." I bunch the fingers of my free hand into a fist. *Don't go there. Don't even contemplate that. What you left behind... What you gave up... That's not on her. It's what you wanted to do.* It's not that I had been unhappy with my choice to join the seminary. It's not that I had not been fulfilled. It's not that I hadn't found joy in helping others... Something which I hope I can still do.

It was more... The gnawing, aching, emptiness deep inside of me, the one that hadn't gone away, even after weeks of retreat. When I had turned to Him for help, had spent days in meditation and prayer, searching for an elusive answer. And all I had found was temporary peace. One that went away as soon as I returned to my duties. When worshipping him and dedicating my life to others...still did not fill the nothingness that infused me when I went to bed.... Greeted me when I woke up the next morning, knowing that something was missing. And that restlessness had grown, until I'd met Ava and had been able to put a name to it.

Apparently, I am more human than I thought. More fallible, more vulnerable. I am not invincible. Hell, I'm not even cut out to be a man of the cloth. I know I need her to feel alive. Need her to help me get in touch with that part of me that I have hidden so carefully over the years. Need her to help me embrace the ugliness inside of me... For when I am with her, everything seems so possible. Yeah, she gives me hope...and it's why I can't lose her. I square my shoulders, then turn back to the silent room.

"We," I clear my throat, "we're gonna come up with a plan."

"Thought that's what you already did?" Sinclair arches an eyebrow.

"A real plan." I glance at Baron, who scowls back at me. "One that is fair for Ava. One in which neither of us is going to outdo the other. One which gives us both an equal...probability of being with her."

He opens his mouth as if to say something, then shuts it. He cracks his neck, regards me thoughtfully, "You have something in mind."

I nod.

"You going to share what you're thinking?"

I glance around the faces of my friends, "I think your job here is done." I tip up my chin. "You feel me, guys?"

Sinner holds my gaze a second longer, then jerks his chin. "Better get this sorted, you two." He turns to leave, then pauses. "There is one more thing."

He glances between Baron and Weston, "The guy who Edward put out of commission? I assume he's still unconscious?"

Baron nods, then turns to Weston, "And the fucker Edward shot? I want to know why they came after Ava."

"He's not yet in a position to speak," Weston replies.

"Hmm." Sinner rubs his jaw. "That's too bad. I was hoping they'd have some information on what we need to know to get to the bottom of these attacks on us."

"Attacks?" Baron frowns, "What attacks?"

I exchange a glance with Sinner, who jerks his chin. "It's a series of incidents, which have affected most of us, in some form."

I take in the faces of the rest of the Seven. "If the rest of you are okay with it, I can recap for Baron?"

Damian, Weston, Saint and Arpad nod in my direction.

"It begins with Damian's girlfriend and child being in a fatal car accident." I rub the back of my neck. "One we now speculate that the Mafia was behind."

"The same Mafia who were behind our kidnapping?" Baron frowns.

I nod.

"Shit," Baron mutters. "That's…" He sets his jaw, "that's just…" He turns to Damian, "I'm sorry man, truly."

"Yeah." Damian swallows. "Life, huh? What can I say?"

Baron walks toward Damian, grabs him by the shoulder and draws him close, "I'm sorry I wasn't there for you when it happened."

Damian half smiles. Baron pulls him in for an embrace. They hug, clap each other on the back, before he pulls away.

"What else?" Baron scowls. "What else did those bastards do?"

"They kidnapped Victoria," Saint snarls, "Assholes took her from under my nose. Good thing we tracked down the bastard behind it."

"You did?" Baron frowns. "What did you do with him?"

"He's working for us, behind enemy lines," Sinner says with some satisfaction.

"Then Weston's mother was poisoned," I murmur, "They got her to the hospital in time, but we now speculate that the Mafia was behind that too."

"Assholes," Weston growls. "When we finally get the perpetrators who were behind it, I am going to wring their necks."

"They also attacked Weston's wife in her apartment," I point out.

"Good thing I reached her in time." Weston grunts. "If I hadn't..."

"But you did," I remind him, "and Amelie's safe."

"And there were, uh, certain benefits, shall we say, in the aftermath of that particular incident, all of which, I was the beneficiary of, so there's that..." He smirks.

The rest of the men chuckle.

"Now, the homeless man," I glance between the men, "Guess Baron told you that he was a student at St. Lucian's?"

Damian nods, "We also know that he used to be a junkie, hard up on his next fix, who was used by the Mafia to supply the whereabouts of our locations to them."

"And yet," I tilt my head, "he helped all of you at various points."

"He did?" Baron scowls.

"He's played a role in smoothing the way for the five of them to get their women."

"Not me," Sinner points out, "though I admit, it was intriguing to read his Byron quotes... Shit," He straightens. "Byron. He quoted Byron."

"So?" I turn to him. "You remember something, Sinner?"

"Summer's father, before he died, he mentioned something about Byron. Fucking hell." He drags his fingers through his hair. "I never could understand the significance of it...but it's too much of a coincidence, don't you think, that the homeless man was quoting Byron?" He glances at me. "Surely, he must know more than he revealed to you."

"Only way to find out is when he wakes up." I turn to Weston,

"Which could be when, Doc?"

"Anyone's guess." He narrows his gaze on me, "You sure lost your shit there, Ed. It's not like you to cause bodily harm to anyone."

"Yeah, well," I chuckle dryly, "apparently, there's a lot about me that I am discovering for the first time."

The guys stare at me with something like understanding...empathy... Even pity, on their faces. Jesus...and now I am using the Lord's name as a swearword. Which, I shouldn't, but I can, now that, technically, I've walked away from the priesthood, but bloody hell... I am, clearly, losing my head right now.

"I think it's time you guys left," I mutter. "Baron and I have shit to sort out."

No one moves. They stare at me, then at Baron.

"What?" I bark. "I may have almost strangled one man. Doesn't mean I'm going to do anything to Baron, who, by the way, can defend himself really well, considering he is the ex-soldier here."

"You're not too bad at holding your own in a fight, Fath—I mean Ed," Saint finally says. "Shit, it's going to take some getting used to, to not call you Father anymore."

"Tell me about it," I say bitterly.

Sinner stares between Baron and me, then nods. He turns to Weston, "So, you'll tell us when either of the men awakens?"

"You guys will be the first to know," he affirms.

"Well, then," Damian straightens, "time to get the hell out of here and let these two jokers sort their shit out."

The guys, one by one, hug Baron, then me. They say their goodbyes and walk out of the door. I rub the back of my neck, then turn back to the booze. I pour whiskey into my glass, top up another and push it toward Baron.

We raise our glasses, toss back the drinks. I place my tumbler back on the counter with a thump, then turn to him.

"About Ava," he begins at the same time as I say, "We need to talk—"

We both chuckle, then he gestures to me, "You first."

I top up my glass, then his, pick up mine and stare into the depths of the amber liquid. I take a sip, turn to him, "I have a plan."

15

"You know what I really hate? Boys. Okay, maybe I don't hate them but I hate
how my mind reacts to them. I get so freaked and panicky about them. If I
message them and they don't reply straight away, my mind's like, 'he's moved
on to talk to another girl,' or 'you've pissed him off now; well done.' I also feel
like I reply too fast to their messages… But maybe that's just irrational
thinking. The thing is… I'm kind of scared of them. As in, I'm scared of what
a relationship is (not friendship—I can be friends, easily). It's like foreign
ground. I've never done the whole relationship thing. I've always thought you
should start out friends to stop the awkwardness, but if someone doesn't want
that, what are you supposed to do? Anyway, I'm going to go sleep or do
something else that is totally unproductive whilst I try not care about boys…"
-From Ava's Diary

Ava

"I still can't believe you threw him out," Isla stares up at me from the corner of the dressing room in my studio. I glance at the door of the studio for, like, the hundredth time in the last hour. Will I ever feel safe in here? I mean, it's silly. Since those guys had broken in, Baron had insisted that Karina, Arpad's wife who runs a security agency, beef up the security on the place, and I had agreed. The door is reinforced, and all of my students have to be buzzed in, which does make me feel safer.

Still, this is where Edward was shot, and that...is something I don't think I am going to forget anytime soon. At least, I still have the space. If it were up to Baron, he'd have moved me to a completely new studio...at his expense. Not that I'd have allowed him to do that. I don't want to feel beholden to him... Or to Edward. In any form, right now.

Shit, stop thinking about him and Baron. This is supposed to be a complete break, remember?

When Isla had dropped by, carrying two cups of coffee, it had been a welcome break between classes. She'd tried reaching me by phone, then when I hadn't answered the phone, she'd decided to drop by. For the past half an hour, I have been trying to explain the situation to her, or rather, trying to justify the reason behind what I had done, both to her, and I suppose, to myself. And it had been the right thing. It has to be, right? If I can't stop getting intimate with either of them when I see them, then clearly, this arrangement isn't working.

"I kissed Baron," I repeat, "then I walked into the house and made out with Edward."

"So?"

"So?" I scowl at her. "Seriously, Isla, that doesn't sound right to me."

"You are too influenced by what society thinks."

"What is that supposed to mean?"

"I mean, just because conventional wisdom dictates that you can be only with one man at a time —"

"For a reason," I look her up and down, "I mean, how would you feel if Liam carried on with you and another woman —"

She scowls, holds up a finger, "Firstly, don't talk about that bastard. And secondly," she holds up another finger, "he *is* with another woman. He's getting married, remember?"

"How are the arrangements going?"

"He showed up for the first rehearsal, but I haven't seen him since. I feel sorry for his fiancée."

"Thought you didn't like his fiancée."

"I don't."

"Then why are you defending her?"

"Dunno, maybe I just think that she deserves better."

"Really?" I peer into her features.

She nods. "I mean, it can't be easy being engaged to the jerkass. He's, apparently, told her that she can do what she wants. He doesn't care." She flips her hair over her shoulder, "I mean, he's paying for all of it. The least he can do is make sure he's getting his money's worth."

"Maybe he trusts you?"

"Not likely, considering I barely know the man." She snorts, "In fact, I am beginning to empathize with his fiancée."

"You are?"

She nods, "She's a lovely girl, actually. A bit naïve; he'll probably chew her up and spit her out."

"But not you?"

"Huh?" She frowns.

"He'd have met his match in you?"

"Stop." She glowers at me. "Don't go turning the spotlight on me, bitch."

"Yeah, okay." I raise my shoulders. "I tried. I mean, your love life is far more interesting right now."

"Ha, ha," Isla deadpans. "That's a joke, right?"

I give her a dirty look.

"I'm not the one getting boned by two hot alphaholes."

"I am not getting boned by them," I protest.

"Surely you've thought about it?" She waggles her eyebrows, "Imagine two dicks at the same time. Not to mention, you'll have two pair of hands, two sets of lips, two tongues and —"

"I can count," I say dryly.

"Can you, though?"

"What?" I groan, "Come out and say it, Isla." I place my now empty coffee cup down on the floor and lean forward in the tiny dressing room, "What's on your mind?"

"That pushing both of them away is not the way to go about this."

"Why not?"

"It's the proverbial *hiding your head in the sand and hoping that it will all go away.*"

"If only it were that simple," I mumble. "Not that I am not trying, believe me. I've tried to regulate the time spent with each of them and, clearly, that's not going to work."

"You barely gave it a chance to work," she points out.

I snort, "I only have to spend a few moments alone with either of them and things just get out of hand, so yeah, not going down that path."

"So, you decide you're not going to see either of them?"

"Well, yeah." I raise my shoulders. "What would you have done?"

"The opposite?"

"Huh?"

"Spend time with both of them?" She stares at me as if I am a complete idiot.

"Wait, what?"

"I mean, spend time with both of them."

"At the same time?"

"YES."

"So, what? Like, double date, except it would be a threesome of sorts?" I frown

"Yes."

"No." I shake my head.

"Yes." She nods.

I jump up, brush past her into the studio and begin to pace. "This doesn't make sense at all."

She stands up from her chair and leans against the doorway of the dressing room. "Why not?"

I turn on her, "Hello, can you hear yourself?" I throw my hands in the air. "You're basically saying I should be with both of them, and risk them hurting each other?"

"Why would they do that?"

"You haven't seen how pissed off each of them gets, when they know I am with the other. They have come to blows at least twice now, already."

"So let them fight it out." She raises a hand, "They need to get it out of their systems; let them."

"They'll hurt each other."

"They'll heal." She shrugs.

I stare at her, and she scowls back, "What? Don't tell me you don't find the thought of two men fighting over you, hot?"

"Honestly?" I bite down my lower lip, "It is a little hot, I suppose." She grins and I hold up a hand, "But mostly, it gives me a headache." I rub at my temples, "How the hell am I going to figure this out?"

"Don't sweat it, babe." She walks toward me and grips my shoulder, "Let things happen organically."

"I tried that, remember?" I sigh. "I think I took the meaning of 'organically' to be too literal."

"Maybe you just need to sleep with both of them, so you can compare how you feel, you know?"

"I've done that already."

"But do it more consciously?" She raises her eyebrows, "So you can weigh how you feel, and not just physically."

"It doesn't seem right... You know?" I slide my hands into the pockets of the leather jacket that I had thrown over my dress before leaving earlier. "It feels too cold, too calculated... And it goes against everything I thought a relationship should be about."

"Well, these are extenuating circumstances, so..."

"But does it justify that I am actually, in effect, with two men at the same time?" I glance at her, stricken, "Shit, it does come down to that, right? I am a two-timing little slut." Tears form in my eyes.

She frowns at me, "Stop being so judgmental of yourself."

"Why shouldn't I be?" I sniff.

She glances around, spots the box of tissues I keep in the far corner of the studio and goes over to grab them for me. She returns, hands it to me, and I mumble my thanks. "I mean, it's not natural, having such a deep connection with two men and not being able to decide." I dab at my eyes.

"It happens." She eyes me closely, "And it's not completely your fault. After all, those two set you up."

"Yeah," I bite the inside of my cheek. "Still doesn't help me, though. After all, I am the one caught in between them."

"That," she smirks, "is the key point here."

"What?"

"In between them." She titters.

"You have a one-track mind." I roll my eyes. "Nothing like that is ever going to happen."

"You don't even know what I am thinking of."

"Don't I?"

She arches an eyebrow, "Again, don't tell me that you haven't thought about it."

"No." My cheeks heat. "Okay, maybe."

"Ha!" she crows. "What better way of comparing them, then having them side by side?"

"Stop." I slap my hands over my ears. "Seriously, Iz, I think you're sexually deprived; you need to get laid."

"Tell me about it." She blows out a breath, then glances at her watch. "OMG, look at the time. I need to get going."

"Another, rehearsal?"

"With Liam's fiancée and the dildo I now keep in his seat, since he doesn't turn up."

I gape. "No, you don't."

"Sure, I do."

"Seriously?" I giggle.

"It started out as a joke," she admits. "Now, Lila and I do it whenever he doesn't turn up. It makes it all kind of fun."

"It is funny." I chortle.

"Yeah, I know." She rises to her feet, grabs her things then glances at me, "So, what are you going to do, then?"

"Good question." I move toward my music console, flip a switch.

The strain of my favorite dance number *Girl like Me* by the Black-Eyed Peas and Shakira, fills the space. I raise my arms above my head, do a little shimmy, "I suppose I could always dance. It's one way of solving my problems." I move my hips, bump and grind. "I could pretend I am between the two of them, seducing them—"

"Umm, Ava?" I hear her call above the strains of the music.

"What?" I mumble, focusing on my steps—shake my hips, move my feet, bend, raise my arms. "Or I could rub myself up against one, then the other." I widen my legs, thrust my pelvis forward.

"Ava!" Isla says more urgently. "They are—"

"What?" I grumble. "Can I, at least, dance in my own studio, or what?" I shake my chest, undulate my body, "Maybe I could dirty dance with one, then the other, then with both, like—" I swirl around, come face to face with two heated gazes.

16

Ava

"Ah." I lose my footing, and would have fallen, but Baron and Edward both step up. Baron grips my left arm, Edward my right, and I find my balance. I glance between the two of them. From Baron's blue gaze that burns with that inner fire I am coming to recognize as uniquely his to Edward's golden one that sweeps down my curves and eats me up before coming to rest on my face.

The tension between us builds. Heat flushes my cheeks, my chest. My nipples pebble.

"Um," Isla clears her throat, "I guess I'd better be going. Call me if you need anything, Ava."

Her footsteps recede, the door slams behind her and then I am alone, with not one, but two hot, sexy, dominant-as-hell alphaholes.

I tug on my arms, but neither of them releases me.

"Hey, guys," I half laugh, "I think you'd best unhand me."

Neither moves. Both of them glare at me, like they want to hurt me, right before they kiss it all and make it better. OMG, stop thinking about them in the plural! What the hell is wrong with me?

"Baron, Edward, please, can you release my hands? You are hurting me."

Baron instantly releases me, Edward more slowly. I step back, wrap my arms about myself. "I didn't hear the two of you come in."

"I have the password," Baron concedes.

"Of course, you do," I complain. "Karina must have shared it with you, huh?"

"I didn't give her a choice." He smirks. "And if she hadn't, I'd have simply hacked into her computer."

"Another of your many skills, no doubt."

"Just something I like to play with in my spare time." His grin widens. "Of course, there are other things I'd rather be doing instead, if you must know."

My flush deepens. "Don't think I asked, or that I care, either way."

"Sure, you do." He chuckles, "Admit it, Eve, you are dying to know more about me."

"And I want to know more about you," Edward interjects smoothly. "It strikes me that you haven't had the chance to tell me more about yourself since we met."

"That's true, I guess." I glance between them again. "I mean, I've, uh, been busy, I suppose."

"What do you say we pick you up after class and take you to dinner?" Baron asks.

"Both of you?" I look from Baron to Edward, then at Baron again. "At the same time?"

"It's only dinner," Edward drawls. "What do you say?"

"I... I don't understand." I frown.

"You have to eat sometime," Baron urges. "So do we."

"But at the same time?"

"Why not?" Edward interjects. "We can have a civil meal, the three of us, can't we?"

"Can we?" I step back from them. "The last time I saw the two of you, you were getting ready to smash in the other one's face. Then, both of you were pissed that I was maybe getting...uh, intimate with the other. Now you're saying we should go to dinner together..." I purse my lips. "Do either of you care to explain what the hell is happening?"

They look at each other, then Baron nods at Edward, which is weird. Not that he nodded, but because it's like a sign has passed between them, which means they are communicating, and that is strange. These two couldn't stand the sight of each other. Now, suddenly, they are here asking me to dinner? Together? I shake my head, "What?" I frown. "What is it?"

Edward raises his hand, "We, uh, met up earlier, after you, ah, threw me out."

"I am not sorry about it," I mutter and he smirks.

"Opinionated too, huh?"

I flush. "You were saying? That you two met?"

His eyes gleam. "Yep, we did, and we figured we should come at this at a different angle."

"Which is?"

"That the two of us try to date you together, for a little while."

"So, the three of us," I circle the space between us with my finger, "do stuff together?"

Baron nods.

"So, we hang out together."

"Yep," Edward leans forward, "you okay with that?"

"More to the point, are you okay with that?"

His brow furrows, then he schools all emotions form his features. "For now." He nods, "Yeah, for the moment, I am."

"And you?" I turn to Baron, "You're fine with this arrangement?"

He squares his shoulders. "Temporarily."

"Hmm." I purse my lips. "I wonder how long that will last?"

Edward grunts. "Don't write us off yet," he admonishes me. "Neither of us wants to risk losing you. And while each of us hates the thought of you being with the other, it would be a lot worse if we upset you so much that you turned away from us completely, hence —"

"This arrangement," Baron picks up the commentary. "It's not ideal, but it means each of us knows where the other is in relation to you."

"So, there is some level of transparency?" I venture.

"Exactly," Edward nods. "Earlier, each of us kept speculating about what the other was up to. This way, at least, whatever is happening is out in the open."

"Right." I glance between them again. "You do know that I am not compromising on the no-sex clause."

Edward scowls. Baron glowers back at me.

"Well?"

Edward seems like he is about to say something, then firms his lips.

"I am not deviating from that." I draw myself up to my full height. "I am not sleeping with either of you guys."

Both stay quiet. The silence stretches.

"Guess neither of you is happy with that," I say softly. "But that's one thing I am not budging on." I glance between them again, "So what do you say?"

Baron's jaw tics and a nerve throbs at his temple. Edward glares at me, his amber eyes glowing with a golden light that seems to flare even brighter.

"Well?" I say. "Guess you are both not on board with it, then?" I hunch my shoulders. "If you're not, then I guess you should both leave now."

I am about to turn away, when Baron snaps, "Fine." He grumbles, "Fine, no-sex, for the time-being."

My muscles unwind. I nod, turn to Edward, "And you?" I murmur. "What do you say, Ed?"

"You're killing me, Eve," he says softly.

"Is that a 'no'?"

"It's a 'yes.'" He pinches the bridge of his nose. "I can't believe I am agreeing to it, but yeah, fine, no sex. Temporarily."

"No sex." I hold out my palm. "Promise me, neither of you will push it."

"What?" Baron scowls.

"What the fuck?" Edward glares at me.

"Promise me." I jerk my chin toward my upturned hand.

Baron growls, then places his large palm on my much smaller one.

"What-fucking-ever," he gripes.

My lips quirk as I turn to Ed.

He holds my gaze, then cushions my palm with his, sandwiching my hand between his and Baron's. Heat suffuses my spine. My thighs clench. Warmth from the point of contact with both of them sinks into my blood.

"Fine," Edward grumbles, "we'll do it your way."

17

Ava

I glance over the rim of my menu at the two men who sit opposite me. Luckily, we are seated at a round table at the restaurant, so we didn't need to argue over who was going to sit next to me. Not that they would have fought over that.... I blow out a breath. They totally would have fought over that. Who wants to bet that before the evening is over, the two of them will have come to blows with each other? Right now, though, they are both seated with their drinks in front of them, studying their own menus.

Baron's blond hair is combed back. He's wearing a button-down white shirt that sets off his tan. He's clearly made an effort to dress up for dinner. The strong chords of his throat flex as he takes a sip from his drink before placing his tumbler down on the table. Both men are, of course, drinking whiskey... And yes, it's the same brand. Their tastes clearly run similarly...including in women.

I wince, glance at Edward. His dark hair has shots of brown woven through it. His skin color is darker than Baron's, his jaw more pronounced. He's wearing a white T-shirt that stretches across his broad shoulders. It shows off his biceps, while the tattoo I'd seen on him earlier peeks from under his collar. His hair is disheveled, thick tufts falling across his forehead. Somehow, he seems untamed, unleashed...the mask he'd worn earlier having been ripped away from him at some point. He'd set aside his priest's collar and with it, apparently, the veneer of civility he had donned at one point.

How could I have ever thought of him as being gentle or disciplined? He is wild, this man. All those emotions that he had smothered have only just begun to be revealed. All that passion that he'd locked inside has only now begun to be divulged. The dam has begun to crumble, and when he reveals what he really is to the world... Will I be there to see it? To which woman will he share that deepest part of himself, the secrets that he hides inside? He raises his gaze and meets mine, and a flush heats my cheeks. I glance away, then back at him.

Edward smirks. "You look good."

I chuckle, "I am wearing exactly the same outfit that I had on when the two of you barged in earlier. You've had time to go back and change while I? I had to make do with spritzing my face with water and refreshing my make up."

"You don't need any embellishments." Baron places his menu card on the table. "Your inner beauty shines through, no matter what you wear."

"Oh." My cheeks heat. "That," I swallow, "that's some compliment."

"It's true." He holds my gaze and the heat spreads to my chest. My nipples tighten and my belly flutters. He reaches forward and holds out his hand, I place my palm in it. He winds his fingers with mine, "I knew it from the moment I saw you, Ava, that there was never going to be anyone else but you."

The hair on the back of my neck rises. I glance the other way and find Edward glaring at our joined-up fingers. Shit, knew it. Who were these guys kidding? Two minutes into the meal, and already, I can sense the beginnings of a disagreement.

I place the menu on the table, then hold out my other palm, face up. Edward takes it and I squeeze his fingers.

"You, okay?" I whisper.

He blinks as if coming out of a daze, then nods. "You?"

"I'll be fine once I get some food in me." I tilt my lips up, and his features light up with an answering smile. His face brightens. The gold in his eyes seem to catch fire. My breath catches in my chest. I turn away to find Baron scowling at Edward.

I try to withdraw my hands and both men hold on.

"Guys," I warn, "please."

The tension builds between us; first Baron, then Edward releases me.

I fold my hands in my lap stare and the menu blindly. Oh, jeez, this is going to be a disaster of an evening.

The waiter comes up to us. "Are you ready to order?" he asks us.

"She'll have the butternut squash ravioli with mushrooms and sage pesto," Baron replies.

"Get her the roast duck," Edward counters.

"I'm vegetarian." I mutter, and Edward blinks, then turns to the waiter.

"Get her the spinach and feta pie," he amends.

The waiter glances at both of them, then at me. I blow out a breath. Of course, neither of them had asked me what I wanted. Typical. The tension at the table grows. The waiter shuffles his feet. "Ma'am?" he urges me, and I roll my shoulders, feeling the beginnings of a stress headache. And this was supposed to be, a relaxing evening?

"I'll have..." both men stiffen, "neither," I murmur. I really wanted the ravioli, but dammit, I cannot show favoritism with these dumbasses without starting World War III.

I sense the surprise from both of them, but don't look at them. Instead, I turn to the waiter, "Can you get me the classic ratatouille, please?"

The waiter nods, turns to the men, who proceed to order. Baron orders the wine; Edward doesn't protest. Well, hallelujah. Apparently, they agree on something. Once the waiter leaves, they both turn to me.

"Thanks," Baron says. "We didn't handle that well, did we?"

I resist the urge to roll my eyes. "That's putting it mildly." I glance between them. "Why does everything turn into a competition between the two of you?"

"Old habits," Baron mutters, "we weren't always this —"

"Combative?" Edward offers.

"I was going to say contentious." Baron smirks.

"I'd settle for cut-throat," Edward muses.

"That too." Baron nods. "It's just, after the incident…"

He glances up at Edward, who toys with his fork. "Fucking incident," he growls, "the aftermath of which seems as if it will haunt us for the rest of our lives."

"What…" I swallow. "What happened to the two of you then?"

Baron's shoulders freeze. His features close and when I look at Edward his jaw is set. Neither man breaks the silence.

"Fine," I mumble, "I get the hint. Sorry if I asked about something I shouldn't have. I mean, this is supposed to be a getting to know each other date…or something."

Edward leans forward. "Hey." He tries to catch my eye. "Look at me, Eve."

I glance away. Why the hell do I feel hurt? I mean, it's not like they had promised me anything, except that they'd try to get along. And they had agreed to my no sex condition. Speaking of, that had been a surprise. I honestly hadn't expected them to agree to that. Totally hadn't. Why the hell hasn't either of them pushed their weight around on that?

Maybe, they don't really want to sleep with me… Oh, come on. Of course, they do. So, the very fact that they had agreed to it…is… something. Maybe they really do want to try to make this work.

"Ava," Edward warns, "don't ignore me."

I huff, then raise my gaze to his. "What?" I scowl. "What do you want?"

"It's not that I don't want you to know what happened then, but it's…" he frowns, "not easy to talk about."

"It's the single worst time of my life," Baron says, his voice hard.

I glance from his closed features to Edward's angry ones.

"Whatever happened then, it defined both of you. It changed your lives. It pulled you apart even as it connected the two of you together for life."

Edward glances at Baron, who shakes his head.

"Nice." I shake my head. "When it suits you, the two of you agree with each other and have silent conversations that I am, clearly, not privy to."

"It's not like that." Baron frowns at me.

"Then what *is* it like?" I wrap my arms around my waist. "Clearly, there's a part of your lives, a hell of a big chunk of your life experiences, that the two of you share. One which you'll never let me into."

"We will," Edward murmurs. "I promise you, Eve, we'll tell you everything, just not now."

"Then when?" I scowl. "When the two of you are done bashing each other up? Or maybe when both of you have decided that this temporary 'peace' is no longer valid and decide to fall out again and go your separate ways."

"When...*if* that happens," Baron growls, "you'll be on the same path as one of us."

"Not."

"What?" Ed frowns. "We've had this discussion. You are going to pick one of us."

"Maybe," I mutter.

"No, maybes," Baron snaps. "You will decide on one of us."

"And if I don't?" I firm my lips. Not that I mean to do so. I mean, come on. I have enough drama on my hands just by having the two of them in my life. I am hardly going to risk making both of them angry by going after someone else. Not that I can even think of anyone else. These two... Between them, my heart has been twisted into knots, something I am not going to recover from very soon. So...yeah, not going there at all. Doesn't mean I can't have a little fun with them, right?

"You will not look at anyone else." Edward's voice lowers to a hush, "In fact, you will not even think of anyone else. You will choose from one of us."

"Is that an order?"

18

Edward

"Yes," I growl, "it's a fucking order."

What the hell? *What's wrong with you? Why the hell are you commanding her, knowing it's going to piss her off?* Maybe I want to make her angry? Maybe I want to see her lip's part, the flush bloom on her cheeks, her green eyes glittering as her chest heaves and she leans forward, to thump her little knuckles on the table...

"What the fuck?" she snarls. "Did you really say what I think you said?"

I allow my lips to curl. "You heard me, babe." I buff my fingernails on my sleeve. "It's either me or Baron here for you."

"Is that right?" She rises to her feet, "You can't control me."

Baron raises his head, a slight quirk to his lips. He stares up at her, peruses her face. Oh, yeah, I get the appeal. It's that sass of hers, the steel in her spine, her feisty sprit that makes me feel alive. It's the same reason Baron's so fascinated with her.

I turn to Ava, "Sit down, Eve."

Her cheeks redden and her chest heaves as she draws in a breath, then another. Oh, yeah, she's certainly found her backbone, the woman who'd been a virgin not so long ago. She's changed, all right. She's found the will to resist and I love it, even as a part of me regrets that I tainted her. I spoiled her. If I had left her alone, she'd probably still be the pure, untouched Ava, who would have ultimately given her virginity to someone else—my pulse pounds at my temples and my belly knots—something which I would never tolerate. The thought of her being with anyone else...? I bunch my fists, press them into the table, much like Ava had done earlier. "Sit down, Ava. Now."

She blinks, stares at me, then at Baron, who jerks his chin.

She sinks into her chair. "There." She huffs, "Happy?"

"Not yet." I don't take my gaze off of her face as the waiter brings the wine. He pours out some for Baron to taste. He nods and the waiter fills our glasses halfway. I raise my glass and shift my gaze to Baron.

He lifts his glass. "To Ava."

I echo his toast, "To Ava."

She glances between us as a blush steals over her cheeks. She raises her glass, then takes a sip, swirls it around her palate. "It's good," she takes another sip, "really good."

"Only the best for my woman." Baron smirks at her and she laughs.

"Not your woman yet," she says.

"Oh, you will be." Baron's grin widens.

"You're awfully sure of yourself, Mr. Masters." She raises one eyebrow.

"No reason not to be." He shoots me a sideways glance. "No offense."

"None taken," I arch an eyebrow, "though if I were you, I wouldn't get too confident."

"Hey," she protests, "I am still here, you guys."

Baron opens his mouth to retort, when our food arrives. The server places the food on the table and leaves.

She frowns down at the food, "I think I lost my appetite."

"Eat," I order.

When she firms her lips, Baron, leans forward. "Eat, Ava, before the food gets cold," he coaxes her, and her gaze grows mutinous.

"Ava," I warn, "don't defy me."

She glances at Baron again, who stares down at her plate then back at her. "Go on, Eve," he cajoles.

She draws in a breath, then reaches for her fork and digs in.

Is she more responsive toward him? Does she place more importance on his words?

I scowl down, push the food around on my plate. Surely, it must be my imagination. Yeah, that's all it is. I reach for my glass of wine, take a sip, then place it down.

"So, Ava, why belly dancing?"

"Why the priesthood?"

"You first." I set my jaw, and she scowls.

"Why do I always have to give in?"

"Because you're submissive?"

Her jaw drops, "Of all the asinine —"

"I joined the army because it was the only way to deal with the ghosts of my past," Baron interjects.

Both of us turn to him.

He looks up from his plate, "In hindsight, it was the most cowardly and the most courageous thing that I had ever done."

"Cowardly?" She frowns.

He raises a shoulder "I simply placed all of my problems on the back burner. Only, they were still there when I returned."

"So, what are you going to do about it?" I murmur. "You going to face them head on now?"

He laughs, "What do you think?"

"I think," I reach for the wine and refill his glass, then Ava's, "you need to get drunk."

"What about you?" Ava asks

"I am the designated driver this evening."

"With your arm in a sling?" She scowls.

I smirk, take off the sling, and stretch my arm, "Surprise."

"Wow," she stares at me, "you're better?"

"The sling was just a precaution, to curtail movement, which would help the wound to heal faster," I explain, "but I'm definitely feeling better."

"Hmm," she purses her lips, "so you weren't as badly hurt as I thought."

"I just heal fast," I offer.

"Guess I didn't really need to ask you to stay with me, huh?"

My neck heats, but I refuse to look away. "You can't blame a guy for trying." I shrug.

"Edward," she gapes, "really... You actually pretended to be worse off just so you could get into my..."

"Pants?"

"I was going to say bed," she snaps.

"I suppose I should say I am sorry," I quirk my lips, "but I am not."

"Of course, not." She scowls. "Why should you? Doesn't matter that I was really worried about you, you...ass." She tightens her fingers around the stem of her wine glass, "Seriously, Ed, sometimes I don't think I recognize you anymore."

"Me neither." I glance away. I should apologize, really, I should, but I only did what was necessary to get a head start over Baron. What's so wrong with that? I glance at her tense face, then at Baron's smirking one. Bastard. I glower at him and he shakes his head.

"What should we toast this round?" He raises his glass and turns to her.

"To not lying?" She shoots me a dirty look.

I wince, then smirk back at her. She glances away and at Baron.

"To following your instinct," Baron quirks his lips, before raising his own glass.

"To..." I stare at Ava, "to you."

She tips up her chin, finally meets my gaze, her green eyes bright with defiance, and something else... Excitement? She is enjoying this thrust and parry, the chemistry between the three of us, something which, I admit, has caught me by surprise as well. I take in her flushed features, the pulse that beats at the base of her throat. She bites down on her lower lip and my dick twitches. She flicks out her tongue, licks her lower lip and the blood drains to my groin. This woman... She simply has to look at me and I want to throw her down on the table and take her right here.

Baron clears his throat and the two of us jerk our heads in his direction.

His features are hard as he stares between us. "Please pass the salt," he says in a toneless voice. I hand over the salt shaker and he seasons his food, before placing it aside. "What about you Edward? Do you regret joining the Church?"

"Never," I scoop up some of the fish, close my mouth around the tines of the fork. "It was a phase of my life...which was essential in so many ways. It gave me structure and discipline, helped me ground myself at a time when I needed a direction."

"Do you ever wonder what you would have been if you hadn't joined the Church?" Ava asks.

"I certainly wouldn't have been sitting across from you and enjoying a meal with you." I glance back at her. "So no, I don't regret a single thing I did with my life because all of it has led up to this moment, when I can look in your eyes and tell you just how much you mean to me."

A glass crashes to the floor beside the table. Ava visibly shakes, turns to glance at Baron.

"Oops, sorry," he murmurs, "I am being exceptionally clumsy today."

"Seems you prefer to have the focus of the table on you, ol' chap," I mutter without looking away from Ava's gorgeous face.

"You accusing me of being an attention seeker or something?" he replies.

"Or something." I reach for the bottle of wine, empty the rest of its contents into my unused glass. I slide it over to Baron, then hold up the bottle for the waiter, who materializes next to me. "Another bottle, please,"

He vanishes with the empty one just as one of the staff scurries toward the table and sweeps up the glass shards.

"Excuse me," Ava pushes back her chair, "I need to use the

restroom." She stands, then stares between us, "Can I hope that the two of you have not killed each other by the time I return?"

I frown. "Oh, come now, Ava. This is just friendly fire."

"Friendly fire?" Her voice rises in exasperation, "Seriously, why do I even bother?" She grabs her purse, then leaves the table.

I can't stop myself from taking in the sway of her hips, her thick auburn strands flowing behind her as she walks in the direction of the restroom. I glance up to find Baron's attention as riveted. A growl rips from my chest.

"What?" He frowns. "You're not the only one enamored with her, you know."

"Doesn't make this any easier to stomach." I scowl back.

"If we can't get through a meal together, how the hell are we going to make it through the next few weeks...maybe months?"

"Months?" I pale.

"You don't think this is going to get sorted out that quickly, do you?"

"It's only the question of all our lives." I grimace. "But months... I won't last. Seriously, when I am in the same space as her... All I can think of is...." I squeeze my eyes shut, take a breath, another, "It kills me to have you look at her." I finally manage, "I want to tear your eyes out, then beat you up, tie you up, and throw you into the Thames. That's after I've handed your balls to you, of course."

Baron winces. "Ouch, man. Spare the balls, at least. Not that I haven't had the same thoughts about you."

"How the hell are we going to manage this?" I grumble. The waiter arrives with a bottle of wine. "Thanks," I mutter, then indicate he can leave when he hovers at my elbow. Wish I was getting drunk as well.

"This is going to end badly." Baron takes a sip of his wine.

"It's not going to end well," I agree.

"This no sex thing is going to kill me." He slides a finger under the collar of his starched collar.

"It bloody sucks." I scowl. "I can't decide what's worse: that she's not sleeping with me, or that she's not sleeping with you either."

"I'd have said it's a relief that she's definitely not having sex with you... But hell, if it isn't a bummer that I can't get some either." He rubs his chin.

We glance at each other, and a chuckle breaks out from me. He smirks back. We both burst out laughing.

"Fuck," he rubs the back of his neck, "how did we get here again?"

"Afraid this one is my mess." I roll my shoulders. "If I hadn't picked up the phone and called you—"

"Which I am glad you did."

I stare. "You are?"

"Bet the rest of the Seven are pissed that you didn't reach out to them." His lips quirk

"Bet they are—" I chuckle.

"But seriously," he glances at the wine, "and maybe this is the wine talking... In fact, I am sure it is the wine talking..." He takes another sip. "You called at the right time."

"I did?"

"I guess I was waiting for an excuse to come back." He raises his shoulders. "I was tired of running."

"I was tired of..." Not feeling? Not letting myself think too deeply? Just having an existence which barely scratched the surface? Not facing my fears? My need to live life using all my senses? Not wanting to hide anymore? I take another sip of the water, "I was just tired..."

"You took the brunt of what happened during the incident." Baron's features harden. "If there was any way I could thank you for what you did..."

"You can leave her."

He starts, then laughs out loud. "You don't mean it."

"Don't I?"

"All these years and you choose now to call in that favor?"

"You asked."

"Doesn't mean I am going to give you what you want." His throat moves as he swallows. "Besides, she is not a thing...that we can pass around between each other. She deserves a chance to make up her own mind."

"With some help from us."

"I knew you had changed Edward," his jaw tics, "I just hadn't realized how much."

"And you, Baron." I tilt my head, "You haven't changed at all. You're still every bit as self-righteous, as focused on the straight and narrow as you were when you joined the army."

"Unlike you." He glares back. "You joined the priesthood to cover up just how twisted you really are inside."

"That's right." I bare my teeth. "And don't you forget it, you—"

Baron's phone buzzes. He pulls it out of my pocket, glances at the screen, then holds it to his ear, "Ava? Are you—"

The blood drains from his face.

"Who is it?" I snap.

He springs to his feet and so do I, "Baron, who the fuck was that?"

He shoves back his chair, runs toward the door, and I follow him, "It's Ava, isn't it?" I pant, "Is she—"

"They got to her."

I race after him toward the doors leading to the restrooms.

19

Ava

"Bitch, give me that." The man lunges for me and I scream. The phone slips from my fingers. I turn toward the door that leads to the restaurant but he's already there.

The breath catches in my throat and my heart begins to race. I pivot, heading up the alleyway, with the man in hot pursuit.

I'd finished at the restroom, come out into the corridor, but hadn't wanted to return. It would have been more of the same. The two of them going at each other like dogs fighting over a bone. Damn them, they have reduced me to this—a dog bone.

How could they? Are they both so blind that they can't see what it is doing to me to be stuck in the middle like this? I don't want to come between them, really. At the same time, I can't choose between them. My mind is too confused. And my heart? It's simply not going to be able to take another snarled comment from either of them.

They don't mean to hurt me, though. I am sure of that. They are just so busy trying to get one up on the other, even as they try to figure out a way to give me some space to figure out what I want. Ha, as if… I am giving them too much credit. They are thinking with their dicks, getting all possessive, when the other so much as looks at me. Yeah, this arrangement of the three of us spending time together is all going tits up.

I'd turned away from the dining room and walked toward the back door, instead. I'd pushed it open, stepped out into the cool night air. The sounds of the restaurant had faded away as the door had shut behind me. I'd stood there, simply enjoying the silence, when a man had pushed away from the wall where he'd been leaning. He'd asked me if I had a light, and I had said no. He'd come toward me and I'd stiffened as I'd recognized him. I'd reached into the bag, gotten my phone, and called Baron before he'd realized what was happening. That's when he'd reached for me. I'd evaded him, managed to speak to Baron, and he'd lunged for me.

Now, I pump my legs…trying to go faster… Well, as fast as my heels will allow. Damnit, today of all days, I had forgone my flats in favor of these kitten heels. That's what happens when you have two men in your life. You lose perspective. And when your brain is addled with trying to figure out who you want more, you screw up all other parts of your life. I can't believe I wasn't more careful. After being attacked twice now, you'd have thought I'd have a better sense of self preservation, but apparently, not.

His footsteps sound closer. I turn to glance over my shoulder and cry out. He's right behind me. Ohmigod, oh, my god! I straighten, put on a burst of speed, then scream when he grabs my arm. He yanks me back and I stumble against him. The stench of sweat and cigarette smoke engulfs me. My guts churn; the blood thuds at my temples. I try to pull away, but his grasp tightens.

"I am going to teach you a lesson, bitch. Thanks to you, my friends are in trouble. You deserve to pay for what you did to them."

"*I* did to *them*?" I growl, "Asshole, the three of you attacked me. They deserve what happened to them.

"Oh, yeah?"

He releases me, only to raise his hand. I duck…too late. He catches me at the side of my face and my vision blurs. Pain slices through my head; sparks of white flare behind my eyes. I lurch back, my knees give way, and I collapse. He straddles me, shackles his fingers around my neck. He presses down and my lungs burn. I try to take in a breath, cough. Spots of black flicker at the corners of my eyes. Terror bubbles up and my stomach churns. I paw at his wrists, his hands, but he doesn't release me. My vision wavers, darkness closing in. The next second, his weight is pulled off of me. I drag in a lungful of air, then scream when someone bends over me.

"Ava, it's me, Edward."

"Ed?" My chin wobbles and hot tears spill over as Edward touches my cheek. I wince and his beautiful features harden. I hear the sounds of a struggle, the unmistakable echoes of someone getting beaten. The ground seems to shake. I wince and Edward's scowl deepens. He rises, scoops me up in his arms.

"Your wound," I protest.

"Fuck that," he growls, and I begin to laugh.

"What?" He frowns. "What's wrong?

"I'll always remember how you said 'Fuck my vows' when you came to see me, right before you—"

"Left," he says in a sorrowful voice.

"Oh, Ed." I press my aching forehead against his chest. Behind me, I hear the pounding of footsteps as my attacker races away. Then Baron walks over to us.

"Bastard got away," he swears as he shakes out his fist. His shirt is torn, his jacket blood-stained, his hair is mussed up and he looks...glorious.

Fuck, what's wrong with me? These men saved my life again, and all I can do is think about how I want them to touch me.

"You okay, Eve?" He places his hand against my unhurt cheek and I burst into tears.

"What the—?" He glances at me, then at Ed, "What did I say?"

"N... nothing," I blubber, It's just...he...he..."

"He's gone," Baron says softly. "He won't hurt you again. Not as long as I—"

"—we," Edward corrects him.

"Not as long as we have anything to do with it," he agrees, and that only makes me cry harder.

"Shit, don't cry, Ava." Baron cups my cheek and I turn my face into the palm of his hand.

I coil into Edward's chest and allow the tears to fall.

Edward rocks me, Baron moves in closer and his crisp mountain air scent weaves with Edward's cut grass scent. Heat from both of their bodies envelops me, sinks into my blood.

"Shh," Edward croons, "you're safe with us."

I know.

Baron runs his fingers through my hair and I shiver. I hunch my shoulders, try to swallow down the sobs, and finally...finally... manage to turn down the waterworks.

"Better?" Baron whispers.

I nod.

"Sure?" Edward asks. "If you want, we could punch each other?"

"Wha—?" I stare up at him from under my spiky eyelashes. "Why would you do that?"

"To distract you, so you'd stop crying?"

"Like that would work?" I sniffle.

He stares at me and I hiccough. "Fine, fine," I mumble. "Be like that."

"You feeling better, Ava?" Baron peers into my face, "I think we need to get your face looked at."

"I'm fine," I mutter. "Just get me some aspirin for my headache and I'll be as good as new. Speaking of," I glance around us, "where's my bag, and my phone? I think I may have dropped them earlier."

Baron pivots, walks around the space. He pulls out his phone, shines the light close to the ground. "There." He picks up my bag, then spots my phone not far from it. He returns and hands both items over.

"Thanks," I mutter.

"There's water in the car," Edward tells him.

At Baron's nod, he turns, and they make their way to Baron's SUV.

He unlocks the car, opens the back and Edward lowers me onto the seat. He straightens and I grab his hand, "Thanks, Ed."

His features soften. "Anytime." He rubs his knuckles across my unhurt cheek, then straightens.

Baron comes around the other side, and slides into the back seat, next to me. Edward gets into the driver's seat, holds out his hand for the keys.

"You promise you'll treat her with respect?" Baron scowls at Ed.

Her? I glance between them. *Who are they talking about?*

Edward glares back at Baron in the rearview mirror, "Stop fussing."

"Not until you promise."

"Jeez." Edward cracks his neck, and Baron's scowl deepens. "Fine, fine." Edward blows out a breath, "I solemnly swear that I will drive Scarlet O'Cara with the due respect that she deserves."

I blink, "Did you just say Scarlet O'Cara?"

"That's what Baron calls his car." Edward smirks.

I lean my aching head against the side of the car. "You named your car after a fictional character?"

"Not just any celebrity." Baron frowns "It's Scarlet."

"A character."

"So?" He shifts uncomfortably.

"So...nothing." I stab my tongue into the inside of my cheek.

Baron holds up the key fob and Edward snatches it. He slams the door shut, then pauses.

"The bill for the dinner?" he asks.

Baron nods at his phone, "Just emailing the manager to take care of it."

"You also need to text Archer so he doesn't wait for me," I remind him.

"Already done." He flashes me a smile and my heart lurches. Shit, I am definitely a goner. And more confused than ever. My body doesn't seem to be able to differentiate between these two men. Neither does my mind. And my heart? What about my heart?

Edward glances about the space, then snatches the bottle of

water from its receptacle and hands it over to me. I accept it, dig out the aspirin from my bag and swallow it.

"You okay?" Ed asks as I cap the bottle and stow it below the window.

"Yeah." I lean my forehead against the car window. "Thanks for taking care of me."

"You don't have to thank me, Ava. You know that, right?" Our gazes catch, hold.

Despite my befuddled state, heat flushes my skin. I swallow. "I know," I whisper.

Baron pockets his phone. Then reaches over and tucks me into his side. "How's your face?"

"It hurts," I whine.

"Let's stop at a supermarket and get some ice for her, " Baron tells Edward, who nods. He sets the car in motion. I slide down, place my head in Baron's lap.

He runs his fingers through my hair and my eyes close. The next thing I know, something cold touches my swollen cheek. I sigh in relief as the throbbing instantly recedes. I hear the guys speaking in a low tones, as the movement of the vehicle rocks me to sleep again.

When I wake up next, it's to find that I am being carried into a house. "Where are we?" I yawn.

"At Edward's place," Baron answers.

"Edward has his own place?" I yawn so widely that my jaw cracks.

"I do now," Edward replies.

I am aware of being carried by Baron into a bedroom. Edward pulls back the sheets. Baron places me on the bed, removes my shoes, and then pulls the duvet to under my chin.

"Sleep." He bends to kiss my forehead. I am aware of another soft touch to the top of my head, and sleep, once more, overcomes me.

When I wake up next, I am alone. Light floods in through the crack between the curtains of the window. I sit up and every part of me feels sore, but I feel rested. I touch my face and it doesn't hurt as much. I push off the covers, swing my legs over the side. That's when I notice the glass of water and a bottle of ibuprofen next to it. Guess the guys must have left it for me. I swallow down a couple of tablets with the water, then walk into the bathroom. I shower, and brush my teeth with the toothbrush and paste I find; spot a bathrobe, and not wanting to wear the clothes from last night, slip it on, then gather my clothes. I'll have to look for a washing machine, I guess.

I bundle my clothes under my arm, walk out of the bedroom. The landing is square-shaped with two other rooms leading off from it. I peek into one, find it empty; so is the other. I walk down the steps to the ground floor and the smell of coffee greets me. The low murmur of voices draws me and I head toward it. When I reach the kitchen, I pause. The scent of coffee and food reaches me. How long have these guys been up? I peek inside to find Baron and Edward seated at the dining table. The plates in front of them indicate the remnants of their breakfast.

"Why would they do this?" Baron growls, "Why are they targeting her?"

"Fuck, if I know." Edward rubs the back of his neck. "The only reason I can think of is—"

He exchanges a glance with Baron, who blows out a breath. "Us," Baron declares. "Fucking hell. I should have been more careful. I returned to town, led them straight to her."

"I am as much to blame," Edward rumbles. "I should have realized that being seen with her would draw their attention straight to her."

"Whose attention?" Both men turn to glance at me.

20

Ava

I walk into the room and their gazes track me. Baron pushes back his chair, then walks over to meet me half way. "How are you doing?" He pinches my chin, turns my face this way, then the other. "The swelling is almost gone."

"It doesn't hurt anymore," I confirm.

He glances down at the clothes I am carrying, "Do you want those washed?"

I nod. He reaches down to take them from me.

"They're dirty," I protest.

He shoots me a glance and I shut up. He tugs the clothes from me, shoves the bundle under his arm, then turns and pulls out a chair for me. I slide in and he pushes the chair forward, "I'll get you coffee." He kisses the top of my head, then heads off for a side door that I assume leads to a laundry room. I turn to find Edward staring at me.

"What?" I murmur.

"You two look good together."

My cheeks heat "Yeah, well...guess we did spend some time together."

"More than what you and I spent together." He nods, then pushes his cup of coffee toward me, "Take a sip."

"Baron's getting me a fresh cup."

"Go on," he urges me, "you look like you need your dose of caffeine."

I smile my thanks and take a sip of the coffee, then make a face. "It's black."

"It's coffee."

"It's bitter." I grimace

"It's coffee, woman." He laughs, then takes a sip, "Hot as sin and as black as my heart."

"You don't have a black heart, Ed."

He peers into the depths of the mug, "Somehow I don't think the One Above will agree to that."

"Are you upset that you left the Church?"

"No," he says at once, "I don't regret it one bit. You know, I'd do it all over again if it meant I could have you."

"Oh, Ed." I lean forward, place my hand on his, "I never wanted you to give up what was clearly such a big part of your life."

"You didn't force me to do anything, Ava." He glances up, meeting my gaze, "It was a long time coming. You were merely the spark that triggered what I should have done a long time ago."

"Were you that unhappy in the priesthood?"

"Not unhappy." He rubs the back of his neck. "Incomplete. Then I saw you and knew my life had changed forever. That I'd never be whole, not until I had you in my life."

I glance away. "Ed, please."

"No pressure, Eve." He chuckles but his voice is serious, "You take your time deciding, honestly."

I peer at him from under my eyelashes, "Are you sure about that, Ed?"

"Of course." He turns his hand face up, so our palms kiss. Goose-bumps pop on my skin. Heat radiates out from the point of contact, and arrows straight to the space between my legs. I swallow and my throat feels too dry. He leans froward in his chair and his bare feet brush mine. Heat from his body flows over me, surrounds me, engulfs me. My thighs clench. His amber eyes flare and he closes the distance between us, places his lips right in front of mine. His nose bumps mine and we share breath. I part my lips and he tilts his head. When Baron opens the door that leads in from the laundry room into the kitchen, I spring back, my cheeks heating. I glance at Baron who watches us carefully.

"I didn't." I swallow. "We didn't... I mean." I stumble over the words. Oh hell, I didn't do anything wrong, so why the hell do I feel this guilty? "Baron, it's not what it seems like," I insist.

"It's okay, Ava," Baron says, his voice casual, "I understand."

"You do?"

He nods, "We had a talk, Ed and I, when you were asleep."

"You did?" I frown, glance between them. "What did you guys speak about?"

"You," Ed grins back, his tone lazy, "of course."

"Of course." I fold my arms in my lap, "And what was it that you guys discussed?"

"The terms of how we're going to stay here."

"Stay here?" I glance around the space, "Not that I have any complaints with it or anything... It's a nice house, but I need to get back."

"You're not." Baron pours out a cup of coffee, adds in three spoonfuls of sugar, plops in a drop of milk. He stirs it, then brings it over to me, along with a plate of food which he places in front of me.

I glance at the baked beans, hash browns, fried tomatoes and mushrooms, along with the thick slices of toast. Of course, he remembers that I am vegetarian. He's always one step ahead of me.

I dig into the food, am half way through the contents of my plate before I look up. Both of them are watching me with varying degrees of amusement.

"What?" I mumble as I chew on the hash browns, which have been cooked perfectly, by the way, something which I've never managed to get right. "Why are you two staring?" I scowl.

"You've got...something..." Edward leans forward and scoops up some food from the side of my mouth. He brings his finger to his mouth and licks it off.

Heat sears my skin. My toes curl. Shit, one gesture from him and I am putty. I place my fork down, reach for my coffee and take a sip. I can't stop the smile that curves my lips, "Just how I like it."

"You're welcome." Baron smirks.

"Doesn't change the fact that I need to return to my place. My classes are going to start in..." I glance around, can't spot a clock that indicates the time, "What time is it?"

Edward glances at his watch, "It's 10 am."

"In three hours." I take another sip of the coffee, place the cup down. "In fact, I need to be getting back right away."

I stand up, glance between them, "Which of you two gentleman is going to drive me back?"

They glare at each other. A look passes between them, then Baron turns to me, "You're not going anywhere Ava."

"What do you mean?" I laugh, "Of course, I am."

"Even if one of us were to drive you, which we are not," Edward tips his chin up, "we wouldn't reach your place in three hours."

"How far can we be from my place?"

"Have you taken a look outside?" Edward nods toward the window.

I walk around the table, to the kitchen window, and peer outside. Greenery stretches out as far as I can see, which is not unusual in London. There are parts of the city in the outer zones which stretch into the country side, unless... "Where are we?" I turn to glance between them, "We're not in London, are we?"

"Half way to Scotland." Baron replies.

"What?" I blink, "What the hell are you guys talking about?"

"We drove through the night, got here around two in the morning."

"Which is where, exactly?"

"Somewhere in the Lake District," Edward murmurs.

"And you're not going to tell me exactly where?"

Both men shake their heads.

The beginnings of anger twist my guts. "And why is that?"

They exchange another of those looks that makes me feel like they are in on something…and I am not, which honestly, is damn annoying.

"Well?" I tap my toes on the floor? "Why is it that you won't tell me where we are?" I prompt.

"So, you don't call anyone to come get you," Baron finally says.

"Ha!" I blow out a breath, "If you think, that's going to stop me from getting out of here, you have another think coming."

I march back up to my room, glance around the space, but there's no sign of my purse with my phone. Heat flushes my skin. What the hell are these two guys playing at? I stomp downstairs, back into the kitchen, to find both of them sitting where I had left them.

"Where are my bag and my phone?"

"Why don't you sit down first?" Baron gestures to the seat, "And we can talk about our plan."

"I want my phone first, and my things."

"We'll get you another phone." Edward glances at me.

I firm my lips, "I want *my* phone."

"It may be bugged." Baron explains.

"Bugged?" I stare. "I don't understand."

"We figured it's not a coincidence that you were attacked three times. Each time, you were alone," Edward replies. "The only way they'd have tracked you was if they knew where you were and when you were at the most vulnerable."

"Who do you think is tracking me?" I blink. "Who are you talking about?"

"We think," Baron leans forward in his seat, "the Mafia is tracking you."

"The Mafia?" I open and shut my mouth, "What are you guys talking about?"

"Why don't you sit down, Eve?" Baron gestures to a chair. "Please, give us a chance to explain things."

I walk over to the chair, sink into it. "The Mafia?" I repeat. "What do I have to do with the Mafia?"

"Nothing," Edward raises his shoulders, "and everything."

"Cut the crap, Ed." I scowl at him. "Seriously, what's going on here?"

"The Mafia are the ones behind the incident," Baron offers. "They kidnapped us, held us for ransom—"

"Except for Sinclair, that is, whose parents didn't have much money to begin with," Edward adds.

"They took him by mistake," Baron clarifies, "but that's beside the point. They abducted us. Our parents paid the ransom, and the cops found us—"

"Though by then, the damage had been done." Edward's lips twist. "Since then, the Seven of us have tried to track down the perpetrators."

"And apparently, we are getting close, because they are trying to get to you." Baron adds.

"Why would they do that?" I place my elbows on the table. "Why do they want to hurt me?"

"As a means of using you to get to us," Baron points between himself and Edward. "We think they are trying to send us a signal to back off."

"Which only reinforces our suspicion that we are getting close to finding out the real identity of who the kidnapper was," Edward adds.

"How do you know it's the Mafia who attempted to hurt me?" I frown.

"The man Edward shot; he had tattoos that identified him as one of them," Baron replies, "and the man he tried to kill earlier—"

"Hold on, he tried to kill someone?" I stare at Edward, "You tried to kill someone?"

Edward's jaw hardens. "He was responsible for getting us kidnapped. When I found that out," he tightens his fingers round the handle of his mug, "I couldn't hold back. He is responsible for everything that happened to the Seven of us. Do you understand?"

"Still," I swallow, "you tried to kill him, Ed."

"He didn't die," Baron reasons.

"That's not the point." I take in Edward's features, his amber eyes currently filled with an emotion that I can't quite place, those high cheekbones, the pouty lower lip... So familiar, and yet, not. He's changed so much since I met him. He's the same, and yet... He's not. I am not sure what to make of him. A dull pounding starts at my temples. My face feels numb. Maybe I'm not over last night's attack either. I mean, a girl can only take so much.

"So basically, you guys brought me here to ensure that you could watch over me, keep me safe until you know the danger has been averted?"

Baron and Edward stare at each other, then at me.

"Yes," Edward says, "We thought it best to get you here right away. We didn't want to risk going to your place, in case it tipped off anyone."

"My classes — ?"

"I've arranged to email the students that you are taking a temporary leave of absence." Baron explains.

And when I get back, I'll have to likely start from square one, because, well, students of dance are not necessarily the most loyal. My shoulders slump. "And my clothes — ?"

"I've asked Archer to arrange for a few changes of clothing to be delivered here." Edward replies.

"A few changes?" I tip up my chin, "Exactly how long do you expect us to stay here?"

"Until the danger blows over." Edward tilts his head.

"And both of you will stay here with me?"

They both nod.

"Also," Edward folds his arms across his chest, "you can fuck either one of us, at any time."

I choke on my sip of coffee. "Wha—" I gape at him. "Excuse me?" I sputter, "Wha...what do you mean by that?"

"Exactly that," Baron murmurs. "We realized it's not right to put you under any more constraints, especially after everything that you have been through."

"We thought it best to keep things simple, so if you want shag either one of us, you can do so," Edward adds.

"So, let me get this right." I narrow my gaze on Ed. "If I sleep with Baron, you'll be fine?'

Edward's jaw hardens, but he nods.

I turn to Baron, "And if I slept with Ed, you'd be okay?"

A vein pops at Baron's temple, "I have to be." He squares his shoulders, "It's the best way for us to see this thing through."

"And neither of you thought of asking me how I felt about it?"

Edward shuffles his feet, "Look, Ava, all we're saying is, we'll just act normal and if, at any point, you feel the desire to...shag one of us, the other one won't get in the way."

"How generous of you." I roll my eyes. "So, what you're saying is, if I get an itch, I should not hold back?"

Baron's jaw tics. "Let's just keep things natural, and allow them to progress organically." He rubs the back of his neck. "I realize how strange all of this sounds, but we've discussed it and believe that this is the best way forward."

We've discussed it. I stare between them and bite back the multiple sarcastic responses that stampede through my head.

Edward continues, "This way, there is no pressure on you, and there are no artificial conditions imposed on the situation. At the same time, if the situation arises where you want to sleep with one of us, then you can do so with a clear conscience."

I am literally speechless. This situation is completely insane. Seriously, the two of them talking about how we are going to stay in this place as fuck buddies, then negotiating the terms of how I am supposed to sleep with either of them if...when I feel like it...? Shit, this is going to be one cozy party... *Not.* Tiredness drags at my limbs. The headache at my temples intensifies. "I am not feeling well," I murmur. "I rise to my feet and both men get up as well."

"I am fine." I wave them off, "Really, I think I just need some rest."

"You need to finish your breakfast." Edward frowns.

My stomach churns. "No more food," I whisper.

I turn and my knees threaten to give way, but Baron is already there. He scoops me up in his arms.

"I can walk," I protest.

"I am taking you to bed." I sense him exchange a glance with Edward, who doesn't say anything. Turning, Baron walks out of the kitchen and up to my bedroom. He places me on the floor next to the bed. I shrug off the bathrobe, and Baron averts his eyes. I blink. *Whoa, what the—? Did he just glance away to give me some privacy since I am not wearing anything under the bathrobe?* That is some un-Baron-like behavior.

I slide under the covers. He tucks me in, then bends to kiss my forehead. I tip up my chin so our lips almost brush. At the last second, he turns his head and kisses my cheek.

"Wha—?" I frown, "Why did you do that?"

"You need to sleep, babe." His lips quirk, but his eyes are serious, "Get some rest; we'll talk when you feel better."

He turns to leave and my eyelids flutter down. Sleep pulls me under.

The sound of footsteps grows closer. I glance over my shoulder, but there's no one there. I increase my pace, reach the entrance to the subway, and hesitate. Do I want to walk in there? It's so dark. Just then, thunder flashes overhead, followed closely behind by rain-drops. Within moments, they plaster my clothes to my shoulders. Shit. I step inside the subway and the rain cuts out. Cold grips me and I shiver. Goosebumps pop on my skin. I walk into the narrow passageway. The darkness deepens. I half turn, hesitate, then push forward, increasing my pace. I continue walking. Footsteps sound again behind me. I turn and cry out. There's a man silhouetted at the entrance. His shoulders fill the space. No, no, no. I turn, race for the exit. Another man steps up to block the way. He's so tall, so big. He widens his stance, slaps his palms on his hips. My heart begins to race, my pulse pounding at my temples. Sweat beads my palms and I wipe them on my dress. Behind me, the footsteps grow closer. I turn to find the first man is closer. Fear bubbles up; my arms and legs tremble. I turn away, only to find the second man is moving toward me. "No, please, no." My voice echoes in the space. I stumble back, trying to put space between me and the two men who walk toward me. My back hits the wall. The first man moves closer.

"What's wrong, Ava?" Baron frowns. "We won't hurt you."

"Baron?" I swallow, "Is it really you?"

"Of course, Sweetheart, who else would it be?"

"Don't call her, Sweetheart," The second man draws abreast. His golden eyes glow, almost cat-like in the darkness. "She's not yours; she's mine."

Baron's jaw hardens. He pivots, grabs Edward by the shoulder, "She was never yours to begin with. She belongs to me, you hear me?" Baron throws a punch.

"She's mine," Edward blocks him.

"Mine," Baron growls. He raises his fist, sinks it in Edward's side.

"Mine." Edward lurches back, shaking his head to clear it. "I am going to rearrange your face." He leans forward on the balls of his feet, when I step between them.

"Stop it, you two!" I yell. "Stop."

I turn on Ed just as he throws a punch. My head snaps back as pain explodes in my head. I snap my eyes open, breath heaving, pulse pounding at my temples. A dream; it was only a dream.

Sweat drips down my back.

I sit up, shove the covers off and swing my legs over the side of the bed. Reach for the half-full glass of water and down the rest of it. At least, I don't have a headache anymore. Jeez, what was that dream? It seemed so real. Guess the incident from last night traumatized me in more ways than I realized. I need to put an end to this. But how? I glance toward the window, but it's already dark outside. How long did I sleep?

I take another quick shower, then slip into the bathrobe. My clothes must be dry by now. Guess I'd better go get them from the dryer.

I walk into the kitchen and spot a covered plate on the dining table. I walk toward it, find a note:

Eat!

. . .

That's all the note says. One word, written in a bossy-ass handwriting, which could belong to either of them. Of course, it's meant for me... They wouldn't dare talk to each other in such an over-the-top, demanding manner. Gah! I uncover the plate, take in the rice and curry on the plate. Whoa, how did they guess I like Indian food? More to the point, how did they manage to procure it here? Does one of them know how to cook? Or did they order it in? The spicy scent teases my nostrils and my stomach rumbles. I walk over to the microwave, heat up the food, then sit down at the dining table and inhale it. Yum. Washing the plate and cutlery, I stow them away, then head through the adjoining door into the laundry room. I pull my clothes from the dryer, glance at the dress, then grimace. It's clean, but torn. Guess I am not going to be able to wear it again. I fold it and place it aside, then walk back through the kitchen.

It's so quiet. I peer up the darkened corridor and see the outline of a closed door at the end, light peeking around the edges, giving it a foreboding air. I guess one of the guys is using it? I turn the other way, head toward a closed door that seems to promise solitude. I push it open, flip on the light beside the door, and gasp.

OMG, it's a studio. An honest-to-god, beautiful studio, with wooden floors, and a mirror that runs the entire length of one wall. The lights in the ceiling emit golden rays that bathe the space. I walk toward my reflection, trail my fingers across the barre in front of the mirror. I glance around, find a table at the far end with a tablet on it. I swipe the surface, and it reveals a playlist... The tracks are all dance songs—dance songs by my favorite artists. Yep, they are all here. The tunes I love dancing to. Who programmed this? And why does Edward have a studio in this place?

I take in the wood on the floor, which is marked from use. Clearly, someone used this studio before...but the playlist... That was programmed for me. The door on the far side rattles. I walk toward it, and find it unlocked. I push it open, step out onto the landing. In the gathering darkness, the countryside stretches out. Lush green and quiet.

"Feeling better?"

I half-scream, turning in the direction of the voice.

21

Ava

The glow of a cigarette lights up the darkness, then a puff of smoke haloes his features.

"Edward?" I frown. "How many cigarettes do you smoke in a day?"

"A pack, maybe more?" He raises a shoulder and I gasp.

"A pack? Seriously, Ed?" I admonish, "These things will kill you."

"But what a sweet death it will be, hmm?" He takes another drag and the fragrant scent of burning tobacco fills the space. "Apparently, when I decided to fall from grace, I took the express." He smirks.

I toss my hair over my shoulder. "Honestly, I never know what to expect from you anymore."

"You and me both." His smile vanishes as he surveys the tip of his cigarette, "I am getting very good at surprising myself as well."

I walk over to him, take the cigarette from him and put it

between my lips. I inhale, and instantly, my lungs burn. I cough, tears stream down my cheeks, and he laughs.

Smirking, he snatches the cigarette back and takes a healthy puff... Yeah, okay, so not that healthy. He takes another drag, this time blowing out a smoke circle.

"Why Father—I mean, Mr. Chase, I do believe you are showing off."

His eyebrows knit. "Maybe." His voice grows remote. Shit, what did I do now to piss him off?

"Sorry about the slip of the tongue... I guess, on some level, I still think of you as Father."

"Is it so difficult for you to perceive me as a normal man?" He scowls.

"Yes." I shake my head, "No. I don't know. Perhaps there was always an element of the forbidden about you earlier that attracted me, you know."

"You mean you are no longer attracted to me now?" His frown deepens.

"I didn't say that."

"Are you worried that I am going to lose my temper with you?" he asks softly, "Because I almost killed a man?"

I shake my head truthfully. "It's not that, either. I know I sounded surprised earlier, but that's only because it came out of the blue, to find out what you'd done."

"Then, what is it?" He reaches for the ashtray on the chair next to him and stubs out his cigarette. "Why is it that since I returned, you've held yourself at a distance from me?"

"Distance?" I fold my arms across my chest. "I don't think my behavior with you kept much distance between us."

"You mean my making you come?"

A blush sears my cheeks. Thank God, it's already dark. Hopefully, he didn't spot how fiery my cheeks are right now.

He prowls toward me, his massive shoulders outlined against the inkiness of the night. Heat spools off of his body, slams into my chest. I gulp; my throat dries. He pauses in front of me, the boots on his feet brushing against my bare feet.

"You're not wearing any shoes?" he murmurs.

"I, ah, I was on my way to get my clothes from the dryer."

His amber eyes glow, "So no underclothes either?"

Heat flushes my skin and my stomach flip-flops.

"Answer me, Eve, do you have any underclothes on?" His voice lowers to a hush and I shiver.

"No," I whisper, "I am naked under this bathrobe."

His nostrils flare, "Did you say that purposely to turn me on?"

"Wh-what?" I stutter. "Of course, not. You're the one who started out on this entire train of thought."

"But you're the one who brought it to the surface."

"What, because I said I was naked under—?"

"Shh." He places one thick finger on my lips, "Don't say anything else. Not unless you want me to take this conversation to its logical destination."

His voice is thick with lust. Desire pulses between us. The strength of his dominance pins me down, pushes down on my shoulders. My throat closes. I can't breathe, can't think, can't do anything except stare up into his hard features. His jaw tics and a vein throbs at his temple. "Yes or no, Eve?"

His tone is hard, yet wary. As if he can't predict my response to him anymore. And it's true, in a way, I am not sure myself how to react to him. To what this man gave up for me. How he changed his life completely, to such an extent that I don't know him anymore... And that's a side benefit of this trip, right?

A chance to understand both of them. To find out what makes them tick. To share of myself with them, in the hopes of finding whom I am more compatible with.

"What is it to be, Eve?" he demands. "Yes or no?" The tendons of his throat move as he swallows. Perhaps it's that slight giveaway, the clue that he's not as sure of himself as he portrays himself to be, which propels me to jerk my chin.

His gaze narrows, "Say it aloud, Eve."

"Yes." I clear my throat, "Ye—"

He places his hands on my hips, lifts me up, and I wrap my legs around his waist, the bathrobe parting to reveal what I've tried to keep hidden. He fits his lips over mine and licks the seam. I part my lips and he sweeps his tongue inside. He swipes his tongue across my teeth, closes his mouth over mine and drinks from me. I sense us move, then feel the wall against my back. He thrusts forward, fitting his swollen length that tents his jeans against my melting core. It's so good, so hot, a groan tumbles from my lips. He swallows it, slides his hand down the open neck of my robe. He pinches my nipple and the spot between my legs instantly grows wet... Okay, wetter. He presses kisses down my jawline, to the base of my throat. He nibbles on the pulse there and I can't stop the moan that wells up.

"These little noises you make, Eve..." he growls, "I've missed them. Fuck, I've missed you, baby. So much."

I wrap my arms about his neck, pressing his head down further. He kisses his way down to the valley between my tits, then nips at the curve of my breast. I feel it all the way down to my core. He cups my breast, squeezes, turns his head, and bites on my swollen nipple. Goosebumps flare on my skin. I squeeze my thighs around him, pushing myself into the bulge at his groin.

A growl rumbles from him, "I need to be inside you, Eve."

Yes.

"Say it aloud."

"Yes," I murmur, "Yes, yes—"

He slips his hand between us, thrusts two thick fingers inside my melting channel. *Oh, my god!* I pant, rolling my head back against the wall. He adds a third finger and I moan. He works his digits in and out of me, in and out, and my entire body shudders. "Edward, oh, my god, Ed."

He kisses his way up my throat, nips on my chin, then closes his mouth over mine again. All the time he's working my pussy, sawing in and out of me, wet, squelching noises filling the space. Heat flushes my skin as I realize that's me... It's my sopping pussy that's causing that filthy sound. And that only turns me on even more. I pant into his mouth, share his breath, as he thrusts his fingers inside of me. He pulls out, only to cram his fingers back in me with such force that my body bucks. The climax crashes over me. I curve my spine, throw my head back and scream... At least, I think I must have, but he absorbs every last sound.

He pulls his fingers out of me. I hear the clink of his belt buckle, the rasp of the zipper being lowered, then he lines himself up with my entrance. He thrusts forward, burying himself inside of me, and I gasp. Too much, too full; there's so much of him. "Edward," I moan, "Ed, pleas—"

"Shh." He stays there, stretching me, throbbing inside of me, allowing me to adjust to his girth. As if that were possible.

"Why do you feel bigger than before?" I whisper. "What have you been doing with yourself?"

"If you mean, did I masturbate while I was away, the answer is no."

"Wait..." I blink. "What? You didn't?"

He shakes his head. "How could I? When all I wanted was to feel your cunt—" he tilts his hips and pushes into me, "gripping my dick." He pulls out, then propels forward, burying himself to the hilt again. I moan. "When all I wanted to hear was the sound of your voice crying out for release." He slides his fingers behind to cup my butt, then drags the tip of his finger against my backhole, "When all I wanted to feel was you writhing against me."

Heat flushes my skin; my belly flip flops. He eases his digit inside my puckered hole. A moan slips from my lips. His dick thickens inside of me and I gasp. I clamp down on his cock and a groan rumbles up his throat.

"You're killing me, Eve."

He begins to fuck me in earnest. In-out-in, he nails me against the wall, and I am helpless, and turned on, and melting inside. I dig my fingers into his broad shoulders, feel the flex of his muscles as he rams into me again and again. His big body shudders, the planes of his back ripple, and hell, if that doesn't turn me on even more. I clench my thighs about his waist. He places his palm behind my head to cushion it, then tilts his hips and lunges forward. He hits a spot deep inside of me, one I didn't even know existed. The climax sweeps out from my core, shudders up my spine. "Ed, I'm—"

"Come with me," he rasps. "Come with me, Eve."

His entire body seems to tremble, then a groan rips from him. His dick pulses inside me and he buries his head in my neck as he shoots warm jets of cum inside me. My climax crashes over me and sparks flutter behind my eyes. I stay there, surrounded by him, engulfed in his masculinity, as the aftershocks grip me. He raises his head, kisses my mouth, my closed eyes, "You, okay?" he murmurs as he holds me close.

I nod, try to open my eyes, but it's like they are weighted down.

"Ed," I force my eyes open, "the studio. Why is there a studio in this space?"

"It's the reason I bought the place."

"I... I don't understand."

"When I was away from you, I knew when I came back, I'd do my best to make things up to you. Sinner helped me reach out to a few real estate agents about the kind of place I wanted to buy. This one just happened to be on the market, and when I read the details, I knew it was perfect.

"Because of the studio?"

"Because I knew you'd love to have a space of your own to work out and dance in." He swallows. "Because I want you to have a space where you can let go...in your own home."

"Oh." I swallow. "You remembered?"

"I remember everything, Eve. How you wrinkle your nose when you're unsure about something. How you move your hips when you dance. How you screw up your eyes when you smile."

"I don't screw up my eyes," I yawn and my eyes water.

He chuckles, "I think I wore you out."

"I'm just recovering from what happened yesterday."

His jaw hardens. "I'll never let anything happen to you, Eve. You have to believe that."

I glance into his amber eyes, and somehow, I believe him. This man... He'd take a bullet for me... Correction, he already took a bullet for me.

"I know." I rub my cheek against his chest. "I believe you, Ed."

He winds his arms around me and the familiar scent of cut grass envelops me. My muscles relax and my eyelids flutter down.

I feel a soft brush against the top of my head, "Sleep, darling, I've got you."

22

Baron

I push away from the desk where I've spent the last few hours working on my investments. I'd taken this room, which had been set up with a desk and a chair, and claimed it as my study. I'd needed a space where I could devote myself to the task of growing my assets.

All these years, I've been happy to coast along. The money that I've made through being a co-owner of 7A investments, along with the rest of the Seven, has been more than sufficient to take care of my needs. I haven't worked a day since I left the army—other than starting a security company with Archer, but I hardly consider that work—and yet, I am a billionaire...

Only, it's not enough now. I want more. I want to make enough to ensure that Ava never lacks for anything. I want to make so much money that my children and their children will have more than enough to have their every wish fulfilled. Some may say that's too much, that ultimately kids need to work for their living so they know the worth of their money, and a part of me agrees. Which is why I've already put a trust in place so the money I make will be held there until they come of age. It will be released to them on their eighteenth, then their twenty-first, twenty-fifth and thirtieth birthdays. Ava and my kids will not only be responsible, but they will also go on to become successful in their own rights. Whatever field they choose, whether it's a creative one like hers or a more finance-driven one like mine, they will shine. They'll be at the top of their game. The envy of everyone else, the —

The floorboards above me creak, and I pause. I glance outside to find that it's completely dark now. Where has the time gone? I glance at the watch on my wrist. It's nearly nine p.m. The last I'd checked in on Ava, she'd been sleeping. I had wanted to wake her up, to feed her, but she'd been sleeping so peacefully, I had held back. Instead, we'd prepared a plate and left it in the kitchen with a note for her. I push away from the desk, rolling my shoulders as I walk out the door. The lights in the kitchen are dim, the food gone; there's no one in the living room either.

Everything is silent, but I swear I heard the sounds of someone moving around upstairs. I take the steps two at a time, reach the landing. I peek into Ava's room, find it's empty. Turning, I head for Edward's room. I glance inside and pause. He's on the far side of the bed, under the covers, his body curled around Ava's. Their shoulders, which is all I can see above the covers, are bare. Clearly, they are naked. His arm is curled about her waist, her head is pillowed on his arm. Their eyes are shut, their breathing even. Guess I heard them come up to bed. Had they fucked before that? While I had been working...they had been working too... Only, on each other.

I curl my fingers at my side. F-u-c-k. The blood pounds at my temples. I grind my teeth so hard that pain tears up my jaw.

It's fine, right? This is what we agreed to. Things could unfold organically... If Ava wanted to shag him...she was entitled to. They'd had each other before I came on the picture. If Edward hadn't called me out of the blue, I might never have met her. In a way, they belonged to each other before I came onto the scene. And in some twisted way, I owe Edward... If it weren't for him, if he hadn't called me, I wouldn't be here today.

I haven't forgotten what he's asked of me… Except, I can't leave. Not yet. Not without giving her a chance to make up her mind. Not without allowing her to get to know me better. This isn't just about what I want or what Edward wants… It's also about her… And maybe it's my greed speaking… Maybe I am being selfish for giving this a little more time, but I can't give up on us, on her… Not yet, not when everything inside me insists that there's still a chance.

And yet, here she is… She chose to go to bed with him.

Fucking hell. I pivot, walk down the stairs to the bar in the corner of the living room. I grab the half-full bottle of whiskey, head for the study. Lift the bottle and take a healthy swig, then another. The liquor burns its way down, hitting my stomach. Warmth tingles out to my extremities. I can still feel though…

Can still sense the softness of her curves as they fill my palms, can scent the sweetness of her arousal as she falls apart under my ministrations, hear her moans as she gives in to her arousal… Fuck! My cock thickens; my groin hardens. I tilt the bottle to my mouth, chug down more of the alcohol. My throat burns as it slides down my gullet. I lower the bottle, walk over to my desk, glance at my laptop, the papers I had worked on. I had mapped out my future, planned how I was going to diversify, where I was going to focus, how I would build a life for us… I had strategized my future with her… Only, I hadn't thought she may not want the same things as me. And clearly, she doesn't. She'd gone to him, hadn't she?

She'd allowed him to fuck her. She'd participated in it, and while I had agreed to this, that she could sleep with both of us while we were here, fuck, if it doesn't bloody hurt. The band around my chest tightens, the blood pounds at my temples, and I swipe out my hand, shove the papers off the desk. My fingers touch the laptop that skids across to the edge, tilts, then falls to the ground with a thud.

A gasp reaches me from the direction of the door. The scent of jasmine infiltrates the space. I stiffen, don't turn around as muted footsteps approach me.

She touches my arm and I stiffen.

"Baron?" she whispers, and the sound of my name on her lips…

F-u-c-k. A hot sensation stabs at my chest. My guts twist. I raise the bottle to my lips, take another swig.

"Baron, are you okay?" She grips my arm and I shake off her hold.

"Go away," I say through gritted teeth. "Leave, Ava, or I swear, I won't be responsible for what happens next."

There's silence for a beat, another. Then, "And what if I don't want to?" she whispers. "What if I want to be here?"

"You don't mean it."

"I do," she insists. "I don't want to be anywhere else."

"I saw you with him," I growl. "You didn't seem like you wanted to be any place else."

"And now I am here."

"What do you want, Ava?"

"What do you think?"

"I am past thinking." I grit my teeth. "If I see you now, if I touch you again, I won't be able to back off."

"Maybe I don't want you to back off."

"You don't know what you're saying."

"Don't I?" she murmurs. "Or maybe you are too scared to acknowledge what you'll feel if you see me. It's why you still refuse to look at me. Funny," she chuckles, "I didn't think you were a coward Baron, you—"

I turn and freeze. "Fuck, Ava." I drag my gaze down her features, her plump breasts, her tiny waist, the sweet flesh between her legs with that narrow strip of hair that drives me insane.

"Why the fuck are you naked?" I growl.

"Why do you think?" Her lips tilt up. The minx chuckles. She actually chuckles.

"This is not funny," I growl.

"No," she wipes the smile off of her face, "it isn't."

I chug down more whiskey, wipe the back of my hand across my face. "If you think just because you are naked, I am going to bend you over the desk and rip into your pussy—" I bare my teeth, "you are abso-fucking-lutely, right."

23

Ava

"Oh." I swallow, "OH." Those filthy possessive words send heat racing down my spine.

I'd heard a noise and woken up from my dazed half-slumber to see Baron moving away from the door. I had a vague recollection of Edward carrying me up to his bedroom, and then to the ensuite. There he'd propped me up under the stream of water, then proceeded to wash every inch of my body. I'd barely managed to keep my eyes open as he'd cleaned himself. Then he'd dried me and himself, before carrying me to his bed.

I'd wanted to resist, but I had been so pleasantly tired, and besides, I didn't want to sleep alone. So, when he'd spooned me, I had snuggled into his embrace. I'd enjoyed the heat of his body, the feeling of ownership that his heavy arm around my waist had evoked. That is, until I'd spotted Baron. I'd seen him leaving and I knew he must be upset. Despite the guys insisting that it was fine for me to sleep with either of them, they were both too possessive, too alpha to not get jealous when I was with the other. It's why I had crept out from under Edward's embrace, and followed Baron down to the study. It's also why I hadn't worn any clothes.

Not that I want to seduce him... Ha! Of course, I do. But maybe it's also this sense of mischief rearing its head inside of me.

Could he actually refuse me if I turned up naked in front of him? Would he turn away from me as he had done the last time? Guess I am about to find out.

"Come 'ere." Baron crooks a finger at me.

I hesitate and he glares at me. "Don't defy me, Eve," he rumbles. "Come here, now."

His voice propels me forward. I pause in front of him.

"Good girl." He smirks and that edge of danger in his smile... OMG, he's the original bad boy, all right. He takes another swig from his whiskey bottle, then holds the bottle over my chest and tips it. The scent of woodsy alcohol deepens and the liquid trickles down my breasts.

He leans in, drags his tongue down the trail. He circles my breast, bites down on my nipple, and I shudder. He follows the stream down to my belly button, swirls his tongue in the hollow. Goosebumps pop on my skin. "Oh," I gasp. "Oh, my."

He laps his way down the slight swell of my belly, across the soft flesh of my pussy.

My thighs clench.

He nips on my engorged clit and my knees seem to give way. I stumble, and he grips my hip, holding me in place. He drops to his knees, buries his nose in my core and inhales. The gesture is so damn erotic. OMG. My nipples pebble and my thighs clench.

Heat explodes up my spine and my belly trembles.

He places the bottle of alcohol on the floor, grips the outside of my thighs. The calluses on his fingers chafe the sensitive skin, and my core clenches. A fat drop of cum slides out from between my pussy lip and he's instantly there. He laps it up, licks his lips, then stares up at me from under hooded eyelashes. "You drive me insane, Ava," he growls. "You taste so fucking sweet that I swear, no dessert will ever compare to the taste of you."

"Baron," I whisper, and he shakes his head.

"Don't talk," he warns. "Not one fucking word out of you, understand?"

I nod.

He lowers his gaze back to my pussy, stares at it. He urges me to part my legs, and heat flushes my cheeks, spreads over my chest. I force myself to watch as he continues to gaze at my flesh like it is the single most important thing in the world. The absolute attention he bestows on me is so hot, so damn sexy. Something hot stabs at my chest. I wriggle my hips, shuffle my feet, and he makes a warning noise at the back of his throat.

The rough sound chafes at my nerve-endings. My breath catches in my throat.

He blows on my heated flesh, and I shiver.

"All the time I was imprisoned behind enemy lines, every single moment that I was tortured, I swore to myself that if I ever got out, I'd live life to the fullest, never regret a single moment. I told myself that I'd fuck every single pussy I could get my dick into. Then I met you." He chuckles, "Turns out, I only wanted one wet hole. One tight, moist space to call my own. Why is it that you feel so much like home, Ava? Why?"

The pressure builds behind my eyes. A teardrop rolls down my cheek as he flicks out his tongue and swipes up from my opening to the swollen nub of my clit.

The rough texture of his tongue, the burn of the alcohol, the heat of his mouth... All of it goes to my head. The world spins. I grab at him, digging my fingers into his hair to steady myself.

He lowers his head, licking me again and again. He swipes his tongue between my pussy lips, swirling that wicked tongue around my clit. He bites down on my swollen core and I swear, I almost come right then. A whine escapes me as he thrusts his tongue inside my melting channel and proceeds to eat me. He weaves his tongue in and out of me, in and out; brings his hand down to grind the heel of his palm into my clit, and the climax sweeps up from my toes.

He pulls away and my orgasm recedes. I'm almost there... Almost. He rises to his feet and I blink. I open my mouth and he shakes his head. He walks around to stand behind me, and I force myself to focus. The heat from his big body pours over me, sinks into my blood. He leans in and his hot breath sears my ear. "Bend over."

"Wh...what?"

"You heard me." He bites the shell of my ear and I shiver. "Bend over the desk, or I'll make you do it."

He steps back.

I gape at him.

He jerks his chin toward the desk, "Go on."

I frown and he clicks his tongue, "Do it. Or do you want me to make you — ?" He takes a step forward.

I skitter back, toss my hair over my shoulder. Fine, if he thinks he can coerce me into bending to his will... He is absolutely right. I walk to the desk, lower my head onto my folded arms. Then I have to part my legs to accommodate the angle. Bet the alphahole knew that already.

I turn my head, press my cheek onto my arms. Heat envelops me and I know he's come up to stand behind me. I glance at him over my shoulder.

He shakes his head. "Don't move."

I frown, and he flattens his palm at the small of my back. He applies just enough pressure that I am forced to stay still.

He plants his thigh between mine, kicking my legs apart. Cool air hits the exposed skin between my legs, and I shiver. He palms my butt and a shudder runs up my spine. He drags his fingers up the seam of my pussy and my toes curl. My heartbeat ratchets up. He continues up the valley between my buttcheeks, playing with my puckered hole.

"Who took you here last Ava?"

I bite down on my lower lip.

"Tell me." His voice lowers to a hush, and damn him, when he uses that tone, I can't refuse him.

"Y-you," I stutter, "you did."

"Good."

I gaze at him from the corner of my eyes, in time to see him spit on his fingers. He slides his digit inside my backhole and I wince.

"Shh," he murmurs, "let me prep you."

"That's what I am afraid of."

"What did you say...?"

"I said—"*Oh shit, shit, shit.*

He nods.

"What did I say about speaking?"

You told me to shut up, you prick.

"Exactly." He smirks. "And did I tell you how I would punish you for your disobedience?"

I swallow, then shake my head.

"Guess I saved the best for the last, then, didn't I?"

He steps away and to the side, so I can't see him anymore. What the hell? I gulp. What the hell is he up to? I sense him move a second before his palm connects with my backside.

I jump. To be honest, it didn't hurt. It's more my ego that's taking a beating. What the hell is wrong with this man? I crane my neck, and he places his palm again on the small of my back. He holds me down with his hand even as his other palm connects with my backside. The shock of the impact courses through my veins. I yelp, bracing myself as he spanks me on one arse cheek, then the next, and again, alternating between the left and right cheeks until my entire backside seems to be aflame.

A trembling courses up my legs and my core clenches. My belly flip-flops and moisture drools from between my legs. I will not allow myself to be turned on, will not. I curl my fingers into fists, dig my heels into the ground as he pauses. He massages my burning butt cheeks with one large palm. The calluses on his fingers chafe against the sensitized flesh. Goosebumps pop on my skin. My thighs clench.

Fuck, fuck, fuck. This is not good. How can I be so aroused by what is, clearly, meant to be a punishment? He's trying to humiliate me, and I like it. Shit, what craziness is this? *Where's your ego? Your pride in yourself?* All gone... Kaput... Shredded to pieces by the asshole who dips his finger into my pussy. "You're soaking wet, Eve," he rumbles.

No shit, Einstein.

He drags the moisture up to my backhole, smears it around the rim. Scoops up more of my cum and slides his soaked digit inside my puckered hole. He slides his finger in and out of me and pinpricks of heat swirl out from the contact. He adds a second finger and I huff, grip the edge of the desk as he stretches me, preps me.

"Who'd have thought you had a taste for spanking, hmm? Makes me wonder what other secrets you're hiding from me."

As if I am going to tell you. I snicker and he pauses, then drives his fingers in and out of me at an increased pace. My toes curl, my belly clenches, and more moisture pools between my legs. He lowers his face into my line of sight. "I am going to wipe that smile off your face." He smirks. "By the time I am done, you'll remember nothing except my touch, my scent, the feel of my dick owning you, my cock buried deep inside your most forbidden place, you riding me, you coming all over me, you and me, baby, just us, you get me?"

I swallow, hold his gaze. The blue in his eyes deepens to a brilliant azure. Then he straightens. I hear the rasp of his zipper being lowered. The next moment, the crown of his shaft teases my back entrance.

Oh, hell. I draw in a breath and he pauses.

He drags his hand up my back, wraps his finger around the nape of my neck. He bends, placing his cheek next to mine. "Relax," he whispers, "I've got you."

I swallow. It's the same words Edward had told me. Shit, this is getting so very complicated. So bloody complicated, with no solution in sight.

I must have tensed against him, for he drags his hand down the side of my breast, down my hip, and around to strum my pussy lips. He teases my clit and a moan drips from my lips. "Beautiful," he murmurs, "you're fucking beautiful, Ava. If I die, this is the last sound I want to hear. Your voice calling out for me as you give in to the orgasm that I am going to fuck out of you."

He slips his fingers inside my soaking pussy, moving them in and out of me. Heat sizzles out from the contact. I give in to his touch, my muscles relax, and he slips past my sphincter. Too much, too full. I can feel him all the way inside of me. I gasp and sweat beads my brow as he straightens. I sense his gaze sweep down my back, to where we are connected. "If you could only see yourself Eve," he growls, "you're the fucking hottest thing I have ever laid eyes on." He pulls back, then slips inside again and a groan tumbles from my lips. "F-u-c-k," he growls, bending over me. The heat from his big body surrounds me, cocoons me, cajoles me into parting my legs wider, allowing him to slip even further inside as he increases the pace at which he finger-fucks me. My entire body bucks, and his grip on my neck tightens. His fingers are long enough to wrap around my throat, impeding the flow of air. He pulls out again, then propels forward, burying himself inside me with such force, the entire desk shudders. He speeds up, thrusting his fingers in and out of me, even as he fucks my arse.

I try to draw in a breath, but my lungs burn and spots of black dot the edges of my vision. He thrusts into me, hits a spot deep inside, at the same time as he curves his fingers inside my channel. The climax whispers out from my womb, swoops up my spine. He releases the hold on my neck and orders, "Come."

Instantly, the orgasm roars forward, crashes behind my eyes. Floating. Darkness. Peace. When I open my eyes, I find him staring into my face.

I hold his gaze, bring a finger up to touch his mouth. "Kiss me?" I rasp. My throat hurts. Did I scream? I must have. It's the only reason I can imagine my throat feels so raw, right?

He brushes his lips across mine once, twice. So sweet. My eyelids flutter down as he straightens, pulling out of me. He hauls me up and into his arms as I yawn widely.

"You need to eat," he mutters, and I shake my head.

"Sleep... I need to sleep." I yawn again and my jaw cracks.

He chuckles, then pulls me close. I curl into his chest, closing my eyes.

I fall into a deep sleep, and when I open my eyes, I am in bed. I stare at the broad back, the dark hair, the tattoo of the snake crawling up his back and know the man I am staring at is Edward. I try to turn and find I can't move. Glance down to find a thick arm around my waist. Follow the corded muscles up to find Baron is behind me... He's spooning me. I swallow. I am in bed with both of them? Is that good? Not like I am trying to hide from one what I'm doing with the other, right? Shouldn't it be easier like this...? So why do I feel uncomfortable, like I've been caught doing something wrong?

How did I get here anyway? I frown. I fell asleep in Baron's arms. And he carried me up here to Edward's bed? Why the hell would he do that? Does he want to cause a massive disagreement, or what? I try to push his hand off of me, but of course, it's too heavy. Bloody hell. There's movement next to me. The hair on the nape of my neck prickles. I glance up to meet Edward's amber gaze.

24

Edward

I take in her flushed features, her sleepy gaze, her thick hair flowing about her shoulders. Gorgeous, beautiful, a vision to wake up to every day. She bites her lower lip and I feel the tug all the way to the tip of my dick. She shifts her shoulders; I drag my gaze down to where the covers are pulled up to the tops of her creamy breasts. I reach out, tug on the sheet, which slips down to catch on her nipple. I trace the outline of the swollen bud, and her breath catches in her chest.

I raise my gaze to hers. "Good morning," I whisper, "how did you sleep?"

"Good." She swallows. Her hand jerks, as she traces a path down the forearm of the man sleeping on her other side. "I... I can explain Ed." She gulps, "It's just... I um, woke up and, well—"

"Shh," I touch my finger to her lips, "are you hungry?"

"Hungry?" She blinks.

"Breakfast?" I tilt my head, "I could make you my special?"

"Your special?" She opens and shuts her mouth.

Guess I've surprised her with my calm acceptance of the three of us being in the same bed. Hell, if I hadn't surprised myself with my lack of outburst at having woken up last night to find the two of them in my bed. Maybe I'd been too tired, maybe I was just tired of fighting, or maybe they had looked so peaceful sleeping curled around each other in my bed, that I hadn't had the heart to wake either of them. For a moment, my mind had drifted back to when Baron and I were kids, fighting over our favorite toys, learning to take turns, and having sleepovers. Ah, the innocence of youth. I'll never admit it, but I swear, I think I almost felt like it was supposed to be this way. Like we could have had this easy peace between us, if not for the incident.

So, I had contented myself with wrapping my arm around her and falling asleep. I had woken up to the most gorgeous sight ever. Of her in my bed, her face turned toward me, the sheet poised low on her breasts, barely covering her nipples. I'd give anything to wake up to that sight every day. My heart stutters in my chest, as I hold her gaze, "You do eat eggs don't you?"

She nods.

"Good." I throw back my end of the covers, swing my legs over and stand; reach for my sweat pants and shrug into them. When I turn, I find her gaze fixed on me. I drag my fingers down my chest and her breath hitches. I slide my hand toward the waistband and she jerks her gaze up to mine.

I smirk.

She scowls. "Jerk," she mouths the word without heat.

"Your jerk," I whisper back.

She opens her mouth, and I raise a finger to my lips. I glance at the slumbering Baron next to her, then jerk my head toward the door. "Come on," I say in a low voice, "let's not awaken Sleeping Beauty here."

Inch by inch, she slides out from under his arm. Baron stirs in his sleep and we both freeze.

He was a soldier and I'd have expected him to wake up with all this movement around him, but instead, he slumbers on. Maybe he's more tired than usual?

Maybe it's the fact that he slept with her that exhausted him, and sated him? I set my jaw, watch as she scoots all the way over to the end of my bed. Then she swings her legs over the side, glancing around for something to wear. I grab my T-shirt and hand it to her. As she shrugs into it, I walk over to the closet, pull out a pair of my boxer briefs, and return with them. She slips into them and they hang around her hips. The t-shirt dwarfs her. It reaches almost down to her knees and covers the boxers completely, but it'll have to do for now. I walk out of the bedroom and she follows me. I wait for her to precede me, carefully shut the door behind us, then follow her down to the kitchen. She switches on the coffee maker while I pull out the ingredients needed for making pancakes.

"I do eat milk, butter and cheese, as well; and fish," she ventures. "I guess I am a fake vegetarian."

"When did you give up meat?"

"When I was thirteen, I saw a documentary on how livestock are butchered to provide meat, and that was that." She shudders. "I gave up not only meat, but also fish and all animal products, but it was exhausting." She sighs. "Our society is so geared toward animal products… Sometimes I think there is a larger conspiracy at play. Big corporations want to rule our dining tables and dictate our eating choices. I resisted for as long as I could."

"You did well," I mutter as I crack the eggs and whip up the pancake mixture, "Looking at you, though, I'd have never guessed how ecologically and politically conscious you are."

"Why, because I am a belly dancer?" She frowns. "So, of course, I shouldn't have a single original thought in my head?"

"Hold on, spitfire," I say lightly, "you know that's not what I meant."

"Hmm," she purses her lips, "then what did you mean?"

I toss some butter onto the hot skillet, then turn to her, "Just that there's more to you than meets the eye and I, for one, can't wait to unpeel all the layers and get to know your deepest, darkest desires."

She draws in a sharp breath. "Edward," she shakes her head, "sometimes you…you…"

"Impress you?"

"Shock me."

"But you still find me irresistible."

"Whatever," she mutters.

"The sassy Eve, at a loss for words?" I smirk. "That's a first."

"The alphahole, whipping up a meal, in the hopes that he'll get into my pants?" She sticks out her tongue at me and I fix my gaze on her luscious mouth.

"Keep that up and I promise I'll bend you over the table right now and…"

The sound of someone clearing their throat reaches me. I glance up to find Baron in the doorway. He takes in the scene, winks at me —bastard, then saunters over to the table. He bends his head, kisses Eve on the lips. "Good morning, beautiful," he rumbles.

Her cheeks tinge pink. Fucking adorable. She glances at me, then at Baron, who wanders over to get three cups from the shelf; then he proceeds to pour coffee into them. He slides a cup over to me, then doctors one of the remaining two with sugar and cream, before walking over to the dining table. He hands a cup to Ava, places one at the setting next to her, before turning back to pull out plates and other utensils.

I turn back to the pancakes, pour the batter over the sizzling butter in the skillet. Behind me, I hear Baron bustling around as he sets the table.

By the time I walk to the table with a stack of pancakes, he's set three places, and also placed other condiments on the table. I plate out the pancakes, seat myself.

"Can you please pass me the maple syrup?" Ava murmurs.

Baron slides the bottle over to her, as I pour honey over the stack on my plate.

"This place is certainly well-stocked," she muses. "How did you manage to get a hold of all this?" She gestures to the table.

"When I realized that the Mafia was targeting you, I mentioned to Baron the possibility of using this place as a hideaway."

"You did?"

I nod, "We both agreed that the only way to keep you safe would be to bring you here until the danger had passed."

"That's when I reached out to Archer and had the place stocked up," Baron adds.

"Hang on," she scowls, "so you guys have been planning this for a while?"

"Just over the last week." I raise a shoulder.

"And I thought you two didn't get along?"

"Oh, we don't." I glare at Baron, who scowls back. "But when it comes to your safety, we agreed that we won't compromise."

"It's annoying how the two of you gang up on me when it suits you." She rakes her hair back from her face.

"Only because the one thing we both agree on is that we'd do anything to keep you safe," I offer

She snorts, then glances between us, "And that includes cooking up an elaborate dinner?"

Baron frowns. "You mean yesterday's Indian food?" He jerks his chin at Edward, "That was all him."

She narrows her gaze on me, "Really? You cooked yesterday's dinner?"

"Are you doubting my talents?"

She purses her lips.

"You don't think I could whip up a lavish Indian meal for you?"

"Well," she blinks, " I mean —"

"Relax." I smirk. "I had a chef cook meals and freeze them for us."

"You did?"

"Of course, not." I grin. "I didn't have enough time for that, but I did ask Archer to stock up on a bunch of frozen lunches and dinners. All of the best quality, of course."

"Of course," she echoes. "So, all that time, when the three of us were discussing the best way forward, while I was trying to be fair to both of you, you two were secretly plotting a way to get me here?"

She scowls at me and I raise my hands, "And we were right in having a plan."

"After that third attack, it was clear that you need to be protected until we track down the remaining two guys who came after you in the subway," Baron reminds her.

She shivers, folds her arms around herself.

"I don't mean to bring this up to scare you, Eve." I lean forward and take her hand between mine. "It's just, we want to make sure you understand how serious this threat is. Which is why," I gesture to the space around us, "we brought you here."

She blows out a breath. "I understand. I really do." She glances between us. "I just wish I, at least, had a phone. My father's getting married tomorrow, and uh, he wanted me to be there. If I can't make it, I should, at least, let him know."

"Do you want to go to his wedding?" I hold her gaze. "Do you, Eve?"

She swallows, then glances away.

"If you did..." Baron tilts his head, "If you did, we'd make it happen."

She bites down on her lower lip. "To be fair, I'm not sure." She shakes her head. "It's only been six months since my mother died and while she, apparently, approved of the woman he's chosen to marry, I don't know." She shakes her head, "It's too soon. I mean, my parents were married for twenty-five years. They had me and my sister. It's not like it was some fly-by-night relationship, you know. They had a wonderful marriage, a close family... And then, just like that..." she snaps her finger, "she fell sick one day and was gone in a few months." A tear rolls down her cheek, "It was terrible."

I push back my seat, walk around and put my arms around her. "I am so sorry, Eve."

"And now he's getting remarried." She wipes the tears from her cheek. "I can't believe he's replacing her so quickly."

"Maybe she wanted him to marry?" Baron offers. "She'd have wanted him to be happy, right?"

"That's what he claims." Ava sniffles and my heart seems to break.

"Don't cry, babe. If you want to go and see him..."

"I do want to see him," she says in a fierce voice. "It's what my Mum would have wanted."

"If you want to go, we'll take you." I meet Baron's gaze over her head.

"It's dangerous," he cautions. "We'd be revealing our whereabouts."

"Not if we are careful."

"However, as many precautions as we may take, there's nothing stopping anyone from spotting us, then tracking us back here."

"We'll be very cautious."

He blows out a breath. "Is this important to you, Ava?" he murmurs. "Do you definitely want to go?"

"My father and my sister will never forgive me if I don't turn up." She smiles, then adds, "Also, Isla is organizing the wedding and she won't be very happy if I didn't turn up for it."

"Right." Baron scowls at me.

"Right." I jerk my chin at him.

"Where are they getting married?" Baron finally asks.

"In Windermere," she replies.

"That's the next town over," I offer.

"It is?" Ava's face brightens. "That means we can get there and back really quickly, right?"

"It's a forty-five-minute drive, at the most," Baron interjects.

Both of us turn to him.

"We can't stay too late." He raises a shoulder, and Ava's face breaks into a smile. She holds out her hand. Baron glances at it, then back at her. "You also can't leave my and Edward's side."

"I promise." Her grin widens. "Now, will you take my hand, you stubborn man?"

He grabs her palm, kisses the back of her hand. "You sure there's space for two more people?"

25

"I LOVE my dad so much. I mean, I never really talk about him. I normally just talk about my mum, and leave my dad out. But that isn't fair because I love him... Obviously, because he's my dad. I'm lucky to have him as a dad, anyway. Plus, he bought me clothes yesterday! What a lovely, generous man! And omg, I desperately want these shoes that I saw... If I tell him, do you think he'll buy them for me? No, I am not a brat, really I am not..."
— From Ava's Diary

Ava

I glance at the suited man driving the SUV. Baron's broad shoulders are encased in a black jacket. He'd refused to wear a tie and his shirt buttons are open to reveal the demarcation between his pecs. That stubborn lock of hair falls over his forehead and his jaw is hard as he focuses on the road ahead. He looks delicious, and sexy, and so damn hot. My stomach flip-flops and my thighs clench. Being with him would have already made me the envy of every single person at the wedding...

Then, add in the man riding shotgun with him. In his dark jacket and yellow tie that picks out the golden flares in his eyes, Edward is the epitome of suave masculinity. His shoulders are as broad as Baron's, while the rest of him is leaner, which still means that he's a big guy, with his muscled physique, broad chest, tapered waist and those powerful thighs currently clad in what are, surely, tailor-made pants.

After we'd spoken yesterday, the guys had had Archer drop by with their clothes and a suitcase full of garments. Baron had compromised and allowed me to use his phone—which was, apparently, secure—to call Isla to tell her that Archer was on his way. Of course, she had been curious about where I was, and I told her I couldn't reveal my location, which had prompted a flurry of questions. To which I'd said that I would tell her more when I met her at the wedding.

At least, I was able to give her instructions on the clothes she had to pack for me, which included this dress. Made of layered silk, with a modest neckline and a back that dips almost to the cleft of my butt, the pale pink dress coordinates beautifully with my burgundy shawl. Paired with matching lipstick, the combination is both sexy, as well as modest enough, to not steal attention from the bride. Not that it matters. I wouldn't care, either way. I'm not there for Lina. I am there purely to support my dad. I don't want to disappoint my family; that's all.

"You, okay?" Edward meets my gaze in the mirror. "You've been awfully quiet."

"I'm nervous."

Which is true... I am walking in with two men, and don't exactly want to be questioned about why I am there with both of them.

"You worried about raising eyebrows?" Baron asks me. Typical Baron. Never one to mince words, he always puts out there the stuff that others hesitate to say aloud.

"I suppose," I finally concede. "It's not every day that a woman walks into a social occasion with not one, but two gorgeous men, who are, obviously, not gay."

Baron snorts.

Edward arches an eyebrow. "Are you really that worried about being seen with both of us?"

"Yes?" I raise a shoulder. "No. I don't know. This entire situation is confusing enough without my having to try to put a name to this," I wave a hand in the air, "for everyone else."

"I'd say fuck 'em all," Baron drawls, "but I know that wouldn't work for you."

"Not." I chuckle. "No, I am not sure what I am going to say if anyone asks why I am with both of you."

"Tell them the truth," Edward suggests.

"Which is...what? That I am fucking both of you?" I glance out of the window. "Do you realize how that makes me look?"

"Like you are irresistible?" Baron meets my gaze in the mirror, "Which you are. You should know that, Ava."

"You are a gorgeous, confident, young woman who can have anyone you want." Edward turns to me, "And that's what you should tell anyone who asks you."

Baron nods.

"It really is annoying when the two of you gang up on me," I gripe.

Edward chuckles. Baron's lips twist in that smirk which is hot and mean, and so damn filthy. My ovaries spasm. No, seriously, they do. Heat fills my cheeks and I glance out the window as we turn off the highway. Well, here we are then; time to face the music.

I knock on the door of my parent's bedroom. Old habits... I've always call it my parents' bedroom. Just because my mother is no longer there doesn't mean I am going to call it by some other name, alright?

"Come in," my father calls out and I walk inside.

He places the photograph of my mum and him on their wedding day back on the dresser.

I walk up to him, glance down at the photograph. "She was so beautiful," I whisper.

"I saw her across a crowded house party in London and knew she was the one for me."

I've heard the story of how they met a thousand times, and yet, I can't resist asking, "What was she wearing?"

"A sleeveless dress that reached her knees. I saw the back of her neck, the curve of her bare shoulder, and I was a goner."

"And you?" I murmur, "What were you doing?"

"I was in a pair of shorts, wearing a Santa hat while I jumped up and down on the couch." He chuckles.

"Was it Christmas?"

"Not quite. It was the middle of summer, but I was high enough on life… And yeah, enough alcohol to not give a damn. Then I saw her and knew that my life would never be the same again." His voice breaks and I turn to him in time to see a tear run down his cheek.

"Oh, Dad." I grip his arm. "I'm so sorry, Dad."

"Me, too." He swallows. "You meet your life partner and you think you'll be together for the rest of your lives. You think you'll always have them next to you, that you'll be old and wrinkled before you have to say good-bye. Yet one day, they are gone, and you are left to pick up the pieces of your life and move on… Even as the grief consumes you from the inside, and you try to put on a brave face and smile because that's what they would have wanted. I don't want your Mum to be upset. I want her to feel like I am still living my best life for her."

"Oh, Daddy." I stand up on tip-toe and hug him, and he puts his arms around me and holds me close. The woodsy scent of his after-shave is so familiar, so comforting, that I almost break down. I bite back my tears, pat his shoulder, "I am so sorry I said those horrible things to you earlier."

"I think we all say things we don't mean when we're upset." He rubs his cheek across my hair. "You were hurting. So was I. We were all trying to figure out how we were going to go on without her."

"You're doing the right thing by marrying Aunty Lina." I lean back and he releases me. "I hope the two of you are happy, Daddy."

"Thank you, sweetheart." He smiles down at me, "It means a lot to me to hear that."

There's a knock on the door, then Raisa peeks in. "Everything okay?" She glances between us.

"Yeah," I sniffle, "I was just catching up with Dad, that's all."

"I am so happy you came, Ava." She smiles at me.

"Me, too." I look up at the ceiling to keep the tears from falling and messing up my make-up. "Thanks for being so patient with me, big sis."

She screws up her face, "Don't call me that. Not that I am not your older sister, but it makes me feel old when you do."

"Some things never change." I chuckle.

Her smile widens. "And some things do." She peers into my face, "You ready for this?"

"Yeah," I square my shoulders, "I am."

"Good." She turns to my father, "And you, Dad, you ready to do this?"

He blows out a breath. "Yes." He straightens his spine. "Yes, I am."

He tucks me under his arm, then holds his other arm out to Raisa. She walks over to us, and the three of us hug.

"Thank you," Dad says hoarsely. "Thank you for understanding."

Two hours later, I watch from the sidelines of the small dance floor that had been erected in the backyard of my childhood home. The large white marquee that had hosted the ceremony is aglow with twinkling lights strung from the ceiling. The sides of the tent are open and a gust of air sweeps through, rustling the table cloths behind me. The DJ on the far end plays a tune that has me tapping my foot in rhythm.

"Hey, you," Isla comes up to stand next to me, "long time no see."

I glance at her sideways, "Speak for yourself. You've been missing all through the ceremony."

"Don't ask." She mimics wiping sweat from her brow "Last minute issue with the DJ, but I finally pulled in a favor." She waves at the tall man behind the console, who grins at her before turning his attention back to the set up.

"Thanks again for packing my clothes for me," I gesture to the dress I am wearing. "Thanks to you, I am, at least, properly dressed."

"You can thank me by telling me more about what's up with you." She arches an eyebrow, "What's up with all the secrecy?" She frowns. "And where are you staying anyway?"

"Uh, I told you, it's just a security thing," I mutter. Shit, I hate not being able to share the details with her, but the guys made it clear, I am not to tell anyone about where I am staying.

Even now, the two of them stand on opposite sides of the tent, keeping a wary look out over the crowd. During the wedding, they'd both parked themselves on either end of the small group of invitees and kept a vigil, as well. It's like I am traveling with my own security team, in a way.

"Ava." Isla hisses at me, "Ava, you listening to me?"

"Eh?" I give her my full attention, "Sorry, what did you say?"

"You are so not acting yourself." She frowns. "Is everything okay?"

"Of course, it is." I take a sip of my champagne. "Your wedding arrangements, as usual, have been top-notch. I am glad you were able to take on the wedding preparations so last-minute."

"Not as last minute as the weddings I've had to put together for the Seven." She snorts, "I mean, your dad gave me an entire month to plan. Imagine that."

I dig my elbow into her side. "Stop being so snarky."

"You stop being so secretive."

"I am not being secretive." I glance about the room and feign innocence.

"Oh?" She peers into my face, "So why is it that you didn't mention to me that you were going to be here with both of them?"

"Who?" I frown. "Who are you talking about?"

"Seriously, Ava?" She scowls. "Don't give me that. This is not like you, at all, to hide things from me."

"Yeah," I hunch my shoulders. "Look, it's complicated, okay?"

"When isn't it?"

A waiter passes by and Isla grabs my empty champagne glass, sets it on his tray, and grabs two more. "Thanks, Mark." She nods at the young guy, who blushes before scurrying off.

"Do all of your team have a crush on you?"

"Only the young impressionable ones." She hands me a glass, before sipping from her own. "And don't change the topic, Slick."

"Would I do that?" I widen my gaze.

"And stop giving me the innocent act." She glowers at me. "Tell me what's happening with you, Ava, seriously."

I take a sip of the champagne, and the cool, crisp liquid slides down smoothly. "Well, basically, I am sleeping...with both of them."

She chokes on her champagne, and I pat her back as she splutters.

"Easy, easy," I mutter, "don't go drawing all the attention to us now."

"You're doing fine in that regard all on your own, considering those two have ensured you are always in their line of sight since you guys walked in."

"That's only because they are protecting me."

"Protecting you?" She frowns. "What do you mean?"

"I was attacked..." I mumble, "again."

"Wait, hold on." She stares at me. "You were ambushed in the subway, then in your studio.... Are you saying, it happened again?"

I wince, and her features soften. "Oh, honey, I am so sorry. I didn't mean to bring back any flashbacks by talking about it."

"I'm stronger than that," I lie.

"No one is that strong, Ava. We can pretend to ourselves that things don't affect us, but everything does. Even tripping and hurting ourselves when we are children leaves scars on our physical body. Our cells remember everything. The memories in our body stay with us, whether we like it or not. They change us; they have ramifications for how we act and react. The only thing we can do is manage the stories we tell ourselves about it."

"Wow," I stare at her, "that was profound."

"Right?" She shakes her head, "Sometimes, even I don't know where I come up with this shit."

"You never do talk about your past, you know." I take in her features. "I go on and on about my family and you... You never tell me about yours."

"But we are not talking about me, are we?" She waggles her eyebrows. "You were talking about bedding both of them. How is it?"

"How is what?"

"You know, DP."

"DP?"

"Double penetration?"

"Oh." I stare at her. "OH." I redden. "No, no, no. I don't know about that."

"No?"

"I mean, I don't sleep with them at the same time." I wave my hand in the air, "How could you even think about that?"

"Aw," her lips turn down, "and here I was, hoping things were finally getting exciting."

"Trust me, I've had enough excitement just trying to keep up with two of them in my life at the same time." I shake my head, "Seriously, I am at my wits end."

"Whose dick is bigger?"

"What?" I redden, and she chuckles. Gah! She's always trying to catch me out, this one. I purse my lips, push my finger into my cheek and pretend to consider the question. "You do know, it's not just about the size; it's also the technique." I sniff.

"And?" She taps her feet on the ground, "Give, girlfriend, which one wins?"

I lower my chin. "Sadly, it seems they are neck and neck on both accounts."

She clicks her tongue, "Poor Ava, you have such a hard life." She shakes her head, "All that double dosage of cocks and lips and hands and legs and balls... Girl, you lead a tough life."

"Stop it." I choke. "Seriously, it's not at all how you make it out to be."

"Oh, well," she takes another sip of the champagne, "things could be worse; you could have neither of them."

"Yeah, tried that, and it didn't work, either." I grimace.

"Well, if you can't beat 'em, join 'em."

"Okay, I am getting tired of trying to keep up with you here." I scowl, "What are you trying to say, Isla?"

"Just that you should have a good time, while you can, babe." She snatches my glass from me, then hands both flutes over to the hovering Mark.

She jerks her chin at the DJ, who nods, then speaks into the mic, "Can we have the newly wedded couple on the floor?"

Applause breaks out as my father leads Lina onto the floor. Throughout the dance, she stares up at him with adoration in her eyes. My father seems a little tired, and maybe sad. She places her palm against his cheek, leans up to say something. He chuckles and some of the weight around his shoulder dissipates. Maybe this really is a good thing. Maybe she'll make him happy, and maybe she does deserve him, after all.

I watch as they glide around the dance floor. The song comes to an end, and everyone claps as my father leads Lina off the floor. He smiles at me and I blow him a kiss, then nod at Lina. They move over to talk with their friends and the DJ switches to a throbbing beat. "Okay everyone, time to get on the dance floor." The DJ speaks into the mic, "Let's all celebrate the wedding of Lina and Christopher!"

"Okay, this should be good." Isla grabs my arm and yanks me onto the floor.

"What are you doing?" I laugh.

"Come on, Ava, you've been dying to dance, and I've made sure the music is good for the kind of dancing you like."

"Is that right?" I chuckle. The music changes again, the familiar beats of a fast dance remix come on. I can't stop myself from tapping my feet against the floor, swaying my hips, shimmying my waist, my shoulders.

"Woohoo!" Isla hoots. "Go for it, babe." She launches into her own bump and grind version of a dance that's both seductive and funny at the same time.

I laugh, shake my booty, fling my hands up in the air, drag them down my body as I move to the rhythm. Isla mirrors my moves and soon the two of us are shaking it up, dancing with each other, and to the music. Around us, the dance floor fills up.

More people join and soon we are pressed in from all sides in the tiny space. The music moves to an even faster beat, the lights dim, and strobe lights are flicked, transforming the atmosphere closer to that of a night club.

The crowd seems to thicken even more. Sweat beads my fore-head, slides down the valley between my breasts. A man jostles Isla. She turns at the same time as him. He apologizes to her, she laughs. The two begin to dance together. My dress sticks to my back. Shit, I'm too hot. I push my way through the swaying bodies, to the edge of the dance floor. Then walk across the lawn to the side of the house. I can still hear the music, but there's no one here. Besides, it's cooler.

A breeze blows over my fevered skin and I lift my face to it.

The thump of the beats reaches me across the space. The cadence seeps through my veins, sinks into my blood. I close my eyes, letting the rhythm wash over me as I move my feet. I widen my stance as I grind my arse, sinking down in a semi squat, before I thrust my hips out, then my breasts, then weave up to straighten.

I sense a change in the space in front of me, then a pair of warm hands land on my hips.

I snap my eyes open, take in the strong chords of his throat, the sculpted pecs and the black marks of the tattoo exposed by the open neck of his shirt. His broad shoulders block out the sight of every-body else, and I gulp. I lift my eyes to meet his amber gaze.

Edward moves in sync with me, his gaze intense as he takes in my undulating body.

The hair on the nape of my neck prickles. Heat sears my back. I glance sideways, already knowing that I'll find Baron behind me.

His big body towers over me and his biceps stretch the tight fit of his light blue shirt that set off the flint in his eyes. He must have abandoned his jacket at some point—not that I am complaining. He's rolled his sleeves up to expose his thick veiny arms, the powerful forearms dotted with dark brown hair. His wide palms rest on my shoulders, the heat of them burning through the thin material of my dress.

Baron's movements are stiff...as stiff as the unmistakable bulge that tents his crotch. He moves in closer and his pelvis cradles my hips. The thick column of his shaft nestles against the curve of my butt. Lust thickens my veins; moisture laces the hollow between my legs.

I turn forward as Edward bends his knees slightly. His movements are smooth, coordinated, a self-assurance to his steps that hints at some kind of formal lessons. I tip up my chin, rise on tip toe.

"Where did you learn to dance?" I murmur.

"Ballroom dancing classes." He smirks.

"What?" I gape. "No."

"Oh, yes." His smile widens. "One of the few things that my mother cared about. After all, I had to dance so she could take me to parties and show me off. At least, in this, she was determined that I appear civilized." He bares his teeth and my knees threaten to give way from under me. This man... He's deadly. OMG—my thighs clench and my heart begins to thunder in my chest.

I turn my head sideways, "And you Baron?" I tilt my head, "Clearly, dancing isn't one of your hobbies?"

"Is that a challenge?" He growls.

"It's an...invitation?" I bat my eyelashes at him and his grip tightens on my hips.

His forehead furrows and he picks up his pace, matching his moves to mine... To the left, to the right, circle...and to the right again. I face forward to find Edward matching us step for step. To the left, right, circle, again. Just like that, the three of us are in sync. Flying. Floating. When you have the right beat, the right partner— or partners—dancing is like flying.

I raise my arm, wind it around Baron's neck. Bring my other hand up and place my palm against Edward's cheek. His amber eyes gleam. Edward moves in closer, until we are joined from chest, to hip, to thigh. Baron tilts his hips behind me. His throbbing length seems bigger, hotter, more insistent. My throat closes and sweat slides down the valley between my breast. I tip my chin up as

Edward lowers his mouth to mine. He kisses me deeply, smoothly, thrusts his tongue between my lips. A grasp on my chin urges me to turn my head. Edward releases my mouth, for Baron to replace it with his. He brushes my lips once, twice, then swipes his tongue across my mouth. I groan, parting my lips, and instantly, he swoops in, closes his mouth around my tongue, sucking, nibbling, biting on my lower lip, and my pussy instantly clenches. Ed kisses his way across my cheek, down my throat, to the valley between my tits. He cups my breast, tweaks my nipple so hard that I cry out. The sound is swallowed by Baron's mouth. He kisses me harder. I pant against his lips, press my fingers into the side of his neck. A moan ripples up my throat, and he shudders. He tears his mouth from mine, then growls, "To the car, right fucking now."

26

Ava

I walk inside the house, then pause in the middle of the living room. The door shuts behind me and I shiver. A ripple of apprehension runs down my spine. Shit, shit, shit, what am I doing? On the way home, none of us had spoken in the car. Baron had driven, barely keeping under the speed limit, and the SUV had seemed to eat up the miles. He'd barely parked when Edward had jumped out of the car and come around to open my door, then led me to the house. After unlocking the door, he'd gestured for me to go ahead. I'd moved in, conscious of his gaze eating me up. I'd headed for the stairs, then stopped.

Shit, what should I do? Go straight up to my room? To Edward's room where we had spent the night? To Baron's room? What is the right protocol to follow when you are about to bed two guys? Two guys... Gah! For someone who'd been a virgin not too long ago, I've, clearly, come a long way. OMG. Two guys. Two alphaholes... Two massive dicks... How the hell is this going to work? Can I handle both of them at the same time?

Why the hell had I thought this was a good idea?

At least I had had the presence of mind to move away from the dancefloor and the crowd of people. With some luck, no one should have seen the three of us engaged in that little dance-fuck-fest.

Why did I care what they thought of me anyway?

Most of the people there were my parent's friends...and I had always been the rebel. The girl who'd dropped out of medical school to become a belly dancer. I mean, who does that, right? So, I shouldn't worry about the fact that I was dancing with two men. Still, I am fairly certain that no one saw us.

Besides, most people had been drinking since the afternoon. Everybody had been happy and ready to dance, and no doubt, the champagne had helped lower my inhibitions too. And the dance... It had been the music which had seduced me. It had gone to my head and I had gotten carried away. I had allowed myself to be seduced by the heat of their bodies, the feel of their hands on my hips, their lips on mine.

Edward stops not far from me. He looks me up and down as he unknots his tie and allows the length to hang down from either side of his collar. Heat zings in my belly. My throat goes dry. Footstep's approach. I glance past him as Baron stalks over to stand next to him. His blue gaze holds mine. He reaches for his rolled-up sleeve and smooths it down his arm. I gulp.

Baron's lips twitch. "You want a drink, Eve?" he rumbles.

"Yes," I breathe, "yes, please."

His smile widens. He knows I am nervous, and he's enjoying it. Jerk. At the same time, he's offering me a drink to help distract me. Typical Baron. Confusing, a little mean, and a whole lot gentle. He stalks over to the bar, grabs a bottle of whiskey and swigs from it. He ambles over, hands it to Edward, who drinks from it without taking his eyes off of me.

He offers me the bottle and I glance from him to Baron, then back at Ed. I twist my fingers together in front of me.

"What's the matter, Ava?" Edward murmurs. "You scared of us?"

I shake my head.

"You changed your mind, Eve?" Baron quirks an eyebrow. "If you have—"

"No," I rush out, "it's not that."

"Then?" Baron takes the bottle from Edward, tilts it to his lips. The strong chords of his throat move as he swallows and a pulse flares to life between my legs.

"What is it?" Edward studies me. "What's wrong?"

"N...nothing."

Baron tilts his head, "It's something." His lips kick up, "Go on, you can tell us anything; you know that."

"It's just," I shake the hair away from my face, "it was different on the dance floor, you know? It was more organic, more natural, and here... It just feels forced."

"Hmm." Baron's eyebrows draw down. "You know we won't force you into doing anything, Eve."

"I know."

"Nothing you don't want us to do to you, that is." He smirks and goosebumps pop on my skin. OMG, that's what I am afraid of, and I don't know how to categorize the feelings that bubble up from somewhere deep inside.

It seems natural to be with both of them...and yet... It's unusual. This is not what normal people do. This is not how one is supposed to choose between two men... I mean, I feel something for both of them. I've tried scheduling time with each of them. I've tried not sleeping with them, only to sleep with each of them separately... And now, here I am, faced with both of them... Actually, on the verge of doing it with both of them at the same time. It should feel odd...but it doesn't. Which should count for something, right? If only I could, somehow, get past the strange reluctance that grips me.

I lower my hands to my sides, walk up to Baron. I take the bottle from him, tilt it to my lips and take a healthy swig. The liquor burns its way down, leaving a trail of heat in its wake. I take another sip and warmth flushes my skin. A pleasant numbness radiates out from my stomach. I raise the bottle and Edward takes it from me.

"Enough," he scolds, "don't want you getting drunk."

"As if." I toss my head, pivot and head for the stairs. I stop with my leg poised on the lowest step. Turn to find them walking toward me. Oh, hell, this is it. I turn, take the steps up to my room. Yeah, if I am going to do this, then it is going to be on my turf. Not that I am going to be able to control much of what is to come, but hell, if I am going to give in to everything. At least, I am going to initiate the proceedings. Take the lead in something. Famous last words. I stop at the foot of the bed, glance toward where the men stand just inside the doorway of the room. I reach for the sleeve of my dress and shrug it down, then the other side. It slides down, pools around my ankles, I kick it off along with my heels.

Baron's chest rises and falls.

Edward's nostrils flare.

I reach behind me, unhook my bra and drop it to the ground. Then, without taking my gaze off of them, I slide my panties down to the floor and kick them aside.

Baron's jaw tics. He walks toward me, grabs his shirt at the back with one hand and—in that way that men do—yanks it off and flings it aside. He pauses in front of me, and I gesture to his pants.

"Take them off," I rasp.

He toes off his shoes, unbuckles his pants and shoves them down along with his boxers and socks. He folds his clothes, places them on a nearby chair then straightens to reveal his long, thick cock that points straight up. The head is fat and swollen, almost purple with arousal. I can't take my gaze off of its heavy perfection. Precum oozes from the crown and my mouth waters.

He bends, grabs me by my waist and throws me on the bed. I squeak, bounce on the mattress once, then lay there with my hair across my face. I reach up to push the hair from my face and he points a finger at me.

"Stop."

"Wh…what?"

"You don't get to direct the proceedings, little Eve."

"And…you do?"

"Damn-fucking right." He grabs his already erect dick and

pumps himself once. His shaft seems to lengthen even more and my breath catches. Oh God, have I actually had that inside of me?

I glance past him to where Edward watches the two of us, an indecipherable look in his eyes.

"Ed," I swallow, "you okay?"

He doesn't reply. He fists his hands at his side, rakes his gaze down my naked body.

"On your knees," he snaps.

"Wh...what?"

"Do as he says," Baron orders.

Well, hell...again, the two of you gang up on me... And this time, it's going to lead to a gang bang. OMG. I snort and Baron glares at me.

"Do it," he growls, "or else." He takes a step forward and I flip over, then push up to my knees.

"Good girl," Edward praises me and I flush.

His footsteps approach and he comes around to stand in front of me. I glance up to find him undoing his shirt, leisurely, one button at a time. He pulls off his shirt, along with his tie, drops them to the floor.

He toes off his shoes and does the same with his pants and briefs. He turns to me and I take in his erect cock. It juts up, thick and heavy, a vein running up the underside. His dick is not as long as Baron's, but what he lacks in length, he makes up in width. Fuck. As I watch, his cock seems to swell further—fat, turgid, and so damn huge. How the hell am I going to take not one, but two, monster cocks inside me at the same time?

He lowers his head, drags his lips over mine. I part my lips, and instantly, he slides his tongue inside. He kisses me, long and deep, and with such intensity that my head spins.

The bed dips, heat sears my back, then big palms grip my hips.

Baron slides his fingers around to strum my pussy lips and I moan. He slides two fingers inside of me and I arch back and into him. Edward cups my breast; he tweaks my nipple and I shudder.

He releases my mouth and Baron instantly replaces it with his. He swipes his tongue across the seam of my lips, licks into my mouth, and drags his tongue across my teeth. My pussy clenches around his fingers and he groans. He presses kisses across my cheek, to the shell of my ear. He sucks on my earlobe and my entire body jolts.

"Fuck." he breathes, "you're so fucking sexy, little Eve."

He shoves my hair aside, kisses his way down to the curve of my shoulder. He bites down and I tremble. Edward cups both of my breasts, bringing them together. He bends down, bites on one nipple, and I shudder. He kisses his way to the other, then sucks deeply on the nipple and I feel the pull all the way down to my core.

"Bloody hell, you're soaking," Baron growls. "You're dripping all over my hand, Eve."

Yeah, well, you have two men, two pair of hands, two pairs of sinful mouths kissing you, sucking on you, licking their way across your most sensitive parts, and then we'll see how you do.

As if he heard me and wants to punish me for my impertinent thoughts, Baron shoves two more fingers inside of me and I moan. He begins to work his fingers in and out of me. The wet squelching noises fill the space, and it's so dirty and so raw that I can't stop myself from panting, from throwing my arm up and around him, pushing my breasts deeper into Edward's roaming mouth. He squeezes my tits with so much pressure that a sound of protest leaves my lips. Baron closes his mouth over mine again, as if he can't bear to let the sound escape. He bites down on my lower lip, then licks into my mouth again. I wind my fingers around his neck, pulling on the hair at the nape of his neck. He shudders, releasing my mouth, just as Edward rises up to kiss my chin. He brushes his mouth across mine again, nipping on my lips, slurping on them, before thrusting his tongue inside my mouth and sucking on my tongue.

Baron increases the pace with which he's moving his fingers in and out of me. At the same time Edward lowers his head to my other breast. He bites down on my nipple and heat sears my spine, my pussy clenches, my thighs spasm and I almost collapse, but Baron's hold on my waist keeps me upright.

He kisses his way down the slope of my shoulder, down my spine, just as he curves his fingers inside me.

Edward releases my breast only to massage my thigh. He slides his fingers around and into the valley between my butt cheeks. That's when the orgasm rips through me.

It washes over me and I pant, close my eyes, and allow the waves to carry me up...higher up...before they fade away. I slump against Baron, who pulls his fingers out of me. He brings it to his mouth sucks on it.

"Fuck," he groans, "you taste fucking sweet, Ava."

I open my eyes in time to see them exchange a glance.

"What...?" I clear my throat. "What was that about?"

Edward glances down at me. "I'm hungry."

"Umm." I swallow. "We had dinner already," I remind him and Edward's smile widens.

"We missed dessert."

"Oh."

"Time to make up for that."

He glances at Baron, who runs his hands up to cup my breasts. He begins to massage them, running his rough callused digits across my sensitive nipples. A moan bleeds from my lips.

"Oh, my god," I groan, "Oh my g—OD."

I cry out as Edward drops to his knees on the floor. Baron positions me to face Edward, so he is at eye level with my pussy. Immediately, Ed fits his mouth to my cunt and begins to eat me out.

"Jesus," I moan as he crams his tongue inside my channel. My thigh muscles turn to jelly. My legs slide apart further, giving him better access. He grips my hips, holds me in place as he tilts his head and sticks his tongue in and out of me, again and again. Meanwhile, Baron continues to knead my breasts. He sucks on my earlobe, then inserts his tongue inside my ear, and my eyes roll back in my head.

"Oh," I gasp, "oh, my fucking god."

I hear Baron chuckle, right before he catches my nipples between the forefinger and thumb of each his hands. He pinches with such precision that I yell. Heat sluices down my spine, and I throw my head back and groan as moisture gushes out from between my legs.

Edward licks it up, slurps his tongue up my melting slit with long, deep swipes that seem to penetrate to the core of me.

Baron releases his hold on one breast, only to pinch my chin, turning it toward him, before he places his mouth over mine. "Come," he growls. "Come right now, Eve," he says, as Edward closes his mouth over my pussy. That's when I explode.

This second orgasm whips out from my womb, up my spine, to crash behind my eyes. Seconds later, I open my eyes to find myself slumped against Baron. I glance up at his blue eyes, which bore into me.

"Wow," I mumble. "What was that?"

"That," Edward rises to his feet, "was just the first course."

I turn to gaze up at him from under heavy eyelashes, "I thought you said that was dessert."

His grin widens, "I lied."

He glances at Baron, who places both of his hands on my hips. He lifts me up, then turns me around before placing me back on my knees, so I am facing him.

"Oh." I blink. "Now what?"

"Now we fuck."

27

Ava

My muscles have turned to jelly. There is not a single, solid bone left in my body. My brain cells have all melted into a gooey mess. It's the only reason I don't protest as the two men maneuver me as if I don't have a single thought in my head. Which, to be fair, I don't.

Baron lies back, and Edward positions me over Baron, with my knees on either side of his thighs. He grips my hips, and Edward releases me. The bed dips, heat sears my back, and I glance over my shoulder as Edward kneels behind me. He places his hands on my waist, above Baron's hands. There's a least an inch of space between them, as if there's a tacit understanding between them not to touch each other.

Baron increases his pressure on my waist. I turn back to him just he lifts me up slightly so I am positioned a little above him.

Edward leans in so his hard chest is pressed into my back. He reaches under to play with my pussy and I huff. He slides his fingers in and out of me, scoops up my cum, and brings it up to smear it around my backhole. I shiver.

"Ed," I breathe, "please..."

"Please what?"

Please be gentle, is what I want to say. But just then he inserts a finger inside my backhole. I freeze.

"Shh" He brings his other hand up to my chin, turns me to face him, bends down and licks into my mouth. He nibbles on my lips until I part them, then sweeps his tongue inside. He kisses me, tilts his head and swipes his tongue across my teeth. He deepens the kiss, floods my mouth with his taste until I relax.

Baron walks his hands up my waist, cups the undersides of my breasts. He drags his fingertips across the sensitive skin and I shiver. I raise my arm wind it around Edward's neck, just as he thrusts his fingers in and out of me. He scoops up more of my cum, slides it inside my backhole. He inserts a second finger and I part my legs further apart, allowing him deeper access. Baron cups the heavy weight of my breast in one hand, brings the other hand down to strum my clit. He weaves his finger about my clit and a shudder runs up my spine.

Edward pulls his fingers out from my backside, only to slide them in again. He scissors his fingers and my back channel stretches to accommodate him. A groan ripples up my throat and my thigh muscles threaten to give way.

"Fuck," he breathes against my lips, "you're so tight, baby."

Heat sears my skin, and my pussy clenches and comes up empty.

"Please." I clear my throat, "I want..."

I glance down at Baron and he slides a finger inside my soaking pussy.

He adds another finger, a third, and I arch my spine, reach out with my free hand... Searching, wanting. His strong fingers twine with mine. My belly clenches... Needing...wanting... More. I angle my head to meet Baron's gaze. The blue of his irises deepens; green flares in their depths.

I need this. I want this. I am so, empty. So...so...empty.

Baron's nods. He pulls out his fingers. At the same time, with his other hand on my hip, he guides me down until the crown of his dick breaches me. A trembling grips me. I lower my thighs, sink down another centimeter onto his fat shaft. Sweat beads his brow and the skin around his eyes creases. He tightens his grip on my waist, applies more pressure, and I slide down the rest of the way.

"Oh." I throw my head back, impaling myself on his cock. His dick stretches me, chafes against my sensitive inner walls. Ripples of pleasure radiate out from the contact. My nipples harden. My chest heaves.

Edward runs his hand down my spine, flattens his large palm at the small of my back. He applies pressure and I lower my arm from around his neck. I flatten my palm against Baron's hard chest, then lean forward and over him. He brings up his hand, fastens it around my nape. He eases my head down, until my face is poised close to his. He rises up to meet me half-way, rubs his nose against mine. My lips curve and he brushes his mouth over mine, and again. He releases my hand only to slide his down and pinch my nipple. My core clenches and my muscles tremble. Behind me, I sense Edward move. He positions his dick against the rim of my backhole, and I freeze.

"Shh," Baron tightens his grip on the nape of my neck, and some-how, it's reassuring and arousing. I feel claimed, and turned on, and incredibly horny. He licks into my mouth and I part my lips, allowing him further access. He kisses me, even as he massages my breast. He deepens the kiss, sucks on my tongue and my eyes roll back in my head. I am melting inside. My thigh muscles quiver. My shoulders tremble. I give in to the kiss completely, and that's when Edward pushes into my backhole.

A moan trembles from my lips and Baron swallows it down. "It's going to be so good for you, baby," he croons, "so good." He feathers kisses against my jawline, down to my mouth. Licks the edge of my lips. "Oh, Eve." He groans into my mouth, "You're fucking glorious."

I relax further and Edward thrusts forward, past the tightness. He hits a spot deep inside and my insides quiver. It's too much. Too full. Like nothing I've ever felt before. The burning in my backchannel is balanced by the fullness in my pussy. I gaze into

Baron's eyes as Edward pulls out. He plunges forward and my entire body bucks.

"F-u-c-k," Edward breathes, "you're so fucking tight, Ava. So hot." The heat from his body sears my back, flows over my shoulders.

Inside me, Baron's cock thickens, pulses. "Touch your tits," he orders.

I slide my hand up to squeeze my breast. I play with my nipple and a whine spills from my lips. My pussy clenches, and a groan rips out of Baron. He thrusts up and into me just as Edward pulls out. Edward grips my hips, squeezes, then plunges back into my back channel. Heat sears up my spine as Baron pulls out. He thrusts into me, as Edward retreats. In and out, in and out. They move in rhythm, fucking me, pounding both my front and back holes. The vibrations from the impact radiate out, my toes curl, and my fingers tremble.

There's so much of them in me, it feels like I am no longer in my skin. It's like they've literally fucked me out of myself. A chuckle spills from my lips and Baron frowns. His lips curl, his eyes gleam, then he picks up the pace. He pistons his hips forward and impales me, again and again, just as Edward pounds into me from behind. Edward's hands on my hips... Baron's hold on my neck, his fingers meeting around the front of my throat... His grip tightens and spots of black flicker at the edges of my eyes.

Edward brings his hand to my breast. He shoves my palm aside, and tweaks my nipple so hard that pinpricks of pleasure pool in my belly...

Oh, God. Oh, God. I throw out my hand and Baron catches it. He twines his fingers through mine. I try to draw a breath, my lungs burn, my pussy clenches, and my back channel quivers. Every part of me is stretched and tensed and aching for release. I open my mouth, but no sound comes out. *Please, please, please.* My eyelids flutter down.

"Open your eyes, Ava," Baron commands. "Look at me."

I snap my eyelids open, hold his blue gaze, just as he releases his hold on my throat. The climax rips through me. Edward grips my chin, turns me toward him. "I fucking love you, Ava," he growls as he thrusts into me one last time. The orgasm crashes into me. The breath rushes out of me. My eyelids roll back and sparks flare in front of my eyes. I swear, I do see stars... No, really, I do. When I open my eyes, it's to find I am slumped over Baron's chest, with Edward hunched over me. Someone—Baron?— rubs my back. Someone else—Edward?—drags his fingers through my hair.

"You okay?" Baron asks, at the same time as Edward.

They stare at each other, then Baron turns to me. "How do you feel?"

"Awful."

"What?" Baron frowns.

"What?" Edward growls. He drops his head down to peer into my face, "Are you okay? Did we hurt you? If we did—"

"Relax." I smirk. "I am good. In fact, I don't think I've ever been better."

"Ah," Edward's brow clears, "you little tease."

He wraps his fingers around my thick strands of hair and pulls. My scalp prickles. Goosebumps pop on my skin and I shiver.

"The only thing that can improve things is..." I turn and lock gazes with Baron, "If the two of you come inside me, right now."

"We don't have to," Baron murmurs, even as his cock throbs inside my pussy.

"We could just jerk off..." Edward grimaces, "if you're too sore."

I squeeze down with my inner muscles, and both men groan.

"Fuck," Baron swears.

"Bloody hell," Edward groans.

"Please," I bite the inside of my cheek, "I insist."

They look at each other, then another of those stupid, mysterious male glances passes between them.

Edward leans in. He kisses me as he starts to thrust into me, again and again. Sweat beads his brow, his jaw hardens, and his dick thickens inside of me as he grunts.

Under me, Baron pistons his hips up, thrusting inside me. Vibrations shiver up my spine and heat flushes my skin. I groan as they fall into an easy rhythm. Baron thrusts, Edward retreats. Edward lunges forward, Baron pulls back. In-out-in, their movements grow more frantic. I glance at Edward's face. His amber eyes gleam and a nerve throbs at his temples.

"I am going to come, Ava." He plunges inside me, ramming into me with such force that a whine tumbles from my lips. I turn back, lock gazes with Baron. His blue irises glow, his jaw tics, and sweat glistens on his forehead. He pulls me down, kisses me as he thrusts up and into me. His dick thickens, and he hits a spot—or was that, Edward? It's difficult to say when both of them are pounding into me, filling me, touching me so deeply inside that I know I'll never feel this possessed again, this changed by another experience.

Baron groans, while behind me, Edward grunts. Then they come, simultaneously shooting their loads inside me.

Edward kisses my cheek, my neck, then straightens. He pulls out of me at the same time that Baron does. I glance down to find cum sliding down my inner thighs.

"Fuck, that's hot," Edward murmurs. He throws himself down on the bed, and I ease down to lie between them. My arms and legs tingle. Then, as the adrenaline fades away, they feel weighted down. The sweat dries on my skin and I shiver. Baron pulls the cover over us. I turn over on my side and he spoons me. I snuggle into Edward and he slides his hand under my neck. My eyes close and I fall asleep. It's the deepest, most dreamless sleep I've had in years. When I wake up, light creeps in from between the curtains. I glance around to find that I am alone in bed.

28

Ava

I slide out of bed and my core hurts. I head toward the bathroom and other parts of me protest. I step under the shower and the heat soothes away the ache in my tired muscles. I get out of the shower, brush my teeth, then head for the closet. The clothes that Archer brought me earlier are still in the suitcase he delivered to me. I pull out fresh underwear. Thank God, Isla had been able to get it for me. It would have been mortifying if it had been Archer who had to pack the bag; not that either of the men would have let him do that. Both of them are too possessive to tolerate that. No wonder Baron had agreed to my calling Isla. They must have realized it was the only way they could get fresh clothes over to me. I finish dressing in a skirt and a blouse, then pull a thick pullover on top, finishing off with a pair of thick socks, before walking down the steps.

I enter the kitchen to find Baron tapping away on his phone at the dining table. Edward's at the stove, making breakfast. The scent of whatever he is cooking wafts over to me. My stomach grumbles. The toaster pops and he pulls out the bread and places it on a plate.

Baron glances up when I enter. His features brighten. He rises to his feet, walks over and kisses me on my cheek. Huh? No demanding kiss on the lips? When was the last time he did something this innocent?

"Eve," he rumbles, "did you sleep well?"

I can't stop the blush that rises to my cheeks.

He peers into my face and his lips quirk, "So you did sleep well."

I nod.

"Good." He leads me to the table, pulls out a chair for me, then eases it back in after I am seated.

"Ava." Edward walks over to place a fully-loaded plate in front of me. "Did you get some rest?" He bends, kisses me on the forehead, then pours some orange juice for me.

Baron heads over to the coffee maker and returns with a steaming mug of coffee. He places in front of me. I glance down at my breakfast, then between the two of them.

"Wow," I mutter, "that's some service, you guys."

"Only the best for my girl." Baron squeezes my shoulder before sitting down.

Edward points at my plate, "Eat, you must be starved."

"The way the two of you constantly go on about my eating, you are going to have to roll me out of here."

"I don't see an issue with that." Edward looks me up and down and heat sears my cheeks. I glance away, devoting myself to my breakfast.

Baron puts his phone aside, accepts the plate that Edward sets down in front of him. Then, Edward takes his place and the three of us eat in silence. When I've managed to put away most of the omelette and the toast and fruit salad, I pick up my coffee, wait until the guys have finished eating.

"So," I ask when Baron sets down his fork, "are we going to address the elephant in the room?"

"If you're talking about Ed, here, I see him more as a rhino."

"A rhino?" I blink.

"He constantly butts in where he's not needed and tramples over everything." Baron smirks.

"I rather see myself more as a cheetah." Edward yawns.

"And I'm what, a lion?" Baron's grin widens.

"And I'm confused." I glance between them. "Aren't you two supposed to hate each other?"

"Temporary truce." Baron raises his shoulder, "You have to admit, that entire going at each other's throats dynamic was getting a little passé."

"And that was a good diversion," I scowl, "but as I was saying earlier, aren't we going to talk about — ?"

"No." Baron shakes his head.

"Nope." Edward scowls.

I gape, "You don't even know what I am going to — "

Baron holds up his hand. "We're never talking about it." He exchanges a glance with Edward, who nods.

"Never," he agrees.

"So..." I set down my mug of coffee, "let me get this right." I glance between them. "We are not going to talk about what happened last night?"

"What happened last night?" Baron fixes me with that impenetrable gaze.

"Yeah, do enlighten us." Edward tilts his head.

I can't believe this. They are going to make me recap the details. Jerks. Fine, if they think I am going to back down from it, they have another think coming. "I slept," I glance at Baron, "with you," I turn to Edward, "and with you." I glance between them and wave my arms, "at the same time."

"And it's not happening again," Baron says in a hard voice.

"Never again," Edward emphasizes, "and that's the last we are ever going to refer to it."

I throw up my hands. "There you two go again, doing the thing...you do..."

"What?" Baron scowls.

"Excuse me?" Edward arches an eyebrow, all cold and mean-like.

Well, whatever. This time, their over-the-top sexiness is not going to distract me.

"When it suits you, the two of you unite against me, and when it doesn't, you decide to fight over me."

"Which is stopping right now," Edward drawls.

"It is?"

Baron nods, "We're done behaving in such an immature fashion."

I snort, "Famous last words."

"We mean it this time." Edward leans forward, "We had a talk this morning."

I push back my chair and jump up, "Another talk? And once more, I am not part of it?"

"You were tired." Edward scowls. "We let you sleep in."

"Oh, you let me sleep in." I scoff. "If you expect me to thank you, prepare to be disappointed," I snap. "Besides, who's fault is it that I was tired?" At their blank looks, I continue. "I handled the both of you, at once, Jesus, do you know how difficult that was for me?"

"I don't know, babe," Baron mutters, "from what I saw, you enjoyed yourself tremendously."

"Asshole." I pale. "The both of you... Fuckers. Wankers. Tossers of the first order." My chest heaves, "I hate both of you. I wish I'd never met either of you."

"Done having your tantrum?" Baron says in a cold voice that, honestly, pushes me over the edge.

"Done?" I glance between them. "No, I am not done." I grab my plate with the remnants of my breakfast and smash it to the floor. Neither of them reacts. *Oh, yeah? That's how it's going to be, is it?* I seize Baron's plate with his leftovers and throw it down, reach for Edward's plate when he grabs my arm. "Let me go," I snarl, "let me the fuck go."

"Sit down, Eve," Baron snaps.

"No."

"Do it, or I'll make you." I shoot him a sideways glance, take in his hard features, the tic of his jaw, the nerve that throbs at his temple. I hold his gaze and his blue eyes turn even colder. Chips of ice that can burn me, cut through me, slice me to the bone and I'd never be able to stop him. Never. I release my hold on Edward's plate, sink down into the chair.

Baron pushes a glass of water toward me. "Drink," he orders.

I lift the glass and my fingers tighten around it. I so want to throw it in his face.

"Don't," Edward says in a mild tone.

I glare at him, take a few sips, then keep it down.

His lips twist, "Now we talk."

29

Ava

"Talk?" I purse my lips, "I thought the two of you said that you would never again discuss what happened last night."

"We're not doing it again Eve," Baron rumbles. "That was a one-off."

"Oh, why is that?" I stare at him. "Because you two decided so?"

"Among other things." He nods, and I blow out a breath, "See, this is the problem, the two of you deciding things that concern me, without keeping me in the picture."

"We let you decide how to manage the situation first, and see what happened then?"

I pale. "That...that's not fair," I say in a low voice. "I tried my best to be fair. I tried to figure out how best to allocate my time between the two of you."

"And it made you miserable." Edward leans forward, "You were torn apart and unhappy. You put so much stress on yourself that you stopped finding enjoyment in life.""

"Not true." Actually, it is. That entire phase of trying to be with each of them separately, only to feel guilty when each became jealous of the time I spent with the other was nerve-wracking.

"Exactly," Baron nods, "which is why we are taking the onus off of you."

"I thought that's what bringing me here was about."

"That was for your safety," Edward clarifies.

"And both of you sleeping with me at the same time?" I frown. "What was that?"

The two exchange glances, then Baron turns to me, "That was a one-off."

"A one-off?"

"It was..." he blows out a breath, "inevitable."

"Inevitable?" I scowl. "You could be a little more complimentary about the experience."

"Fucking you is as close as it gets to a spiritual experience," Edward growls. "Is that what you wanted to hear?"

"It's like coming home," Baron snaps, "but you know that already."

"Oh," I mumble, and my cheeks burn again. Shit, I am not used to this... I mean, sleeping with the both of them was...like...mind-blowing. But talking about it? Hell... My pussy clenches, my back-hole hurts, and every part of me seems to come alive. My heart begins to thud in my chest. Shit, just thinking about it...is sending my libido into overdrive. "And it is...an experience I am never going to forget."

"But it won't happen again," Baron growls. "You understand?"

"Either we sleep with you individually, or not at all," Edward grumbles.

"And for now, we choose not at all," Baron interjects.

"Wait," I blink, "what do you mean?"

"It means, for the moment, sex is off the table," Edward murmurs.

"Neither of us is gonna shag you," Baron clarifies.

"B...but, why?" I grip the edge of the table. "I mean...are you two sure you can go without shagging?"

They glare at each other, then both nod.

"Yes," Edward rolls his shoulders, "I can."

"I'll make it work," Baron mutters.

"But...why?" I drag my fingers through my hair, "I don't understand the rationale behind this decision."

"Sex only confuses the issue," Edward offers. "I should know, right?" he says in a self-deprecating voice. "Apparently, the Church was onto something, in this respect, at least."

"This way, that particular source of tension is dispelled. So, you can focus on the individuals." Baron drums his fingers on the table. "We can all focus on the relationship aspect instead. Gives us the opportunity to think with a clear head."

"Do I get a say in this?" I glance between them.

Baron sets his jaw.

Edward folds his arms across his chest.

"No, don't answer that." I raise my hand, "You've already made up your minds, and of course, why does what I think about it matter?"

"You know, it's the right thing to do," Baron says softly. "You do, Eve."

"It will help you in coming to a decision faster." Edward reaches for my hand and I pull away. He frowns and I firm lips. Just because they are right, doesn't mean I am going to let them know that I agree, right?

"Fine." I rise to my feet. "Whatever."

"So, you're okay with this?" Baron asks cautiously.

"Do I have a choice?"

"No," Edward replies. "No, you don't."

"Well then," I raise a shoulder, "there's nothing left to say anymore."

Turning, I storm out of the kitchen. I suppose I should help them clean up the mess I created, but too bad. Since they are making all of the decisions, they can handle this on their own.

I head back to my room, unpack the rest of my clothes, put them away, have a long bath, wash my hair and dry it, take a nap. When Baron peeks his head inside and asks me to have lunch with them, I refuse. For once, he doesn't insist and I'm both relieved and pissed off. I mean, he'd never have allowed me to go hungry nor would Edward... And now, they are letting me stew here on my own? Gah!

As the day wears on, I can't bear being locked up in here further.

I grab my hip-scarf from the closet—thank God, Isla had packed it for me—then I head down to the studio. I shut the door, pull up the playlist to a medium beat song, one that I can stretch to, and ease into a rhythm. By the time I am on my third song, my heart is pumping and sweat beads my brow. I throw myself into a choreographed routine that I've been working on, in the hope that I can professionally compete someday.

I shimmy my shoulders, grind my hips, raise my arms, allow the music to sink into my blood as I move my body to the beats. I close my eyes, twirl again and again, and once more. I throw back my hair, tip up my chin and see Edward at the doorway. I continue to dance, undulate my shoulders, lift my hips, drop them heavily, then lean into a lighter half-drop.

His gaze narrows. The beat on the track kicks in.

I lift my hips upward and slightly forward in a strong, accented move. Activate the outside of my thigh and my hip to give the movement oomph, drop slightly, then lift again.

His chest rises and falls. He takes a step forward, then another.

Sweat trickles down between my breasts. I shift my weight from leg to leg, straighten my supporting knee, and release the other, then slide my hip out to the side, then back.

He swallows, closing the distance between us. He places his big palms on my hips, then sinks to his knees. I continue to lift one hip and drop, then the next, and the first.

A groan rips from him. He stares at my curves, slides his palm down to cup my butt cheeks. A moan slips from my lips. I keep moving, lift and drop, thrust to the side and drop. He doesn't release me. He leans in and presses his cheek against my stomach. The warmth of him sears me through the clothes I am wearing. I dig my fingers into his hair and tug. Urge him to look up.

He glances at me from under his long sooty eye lashes. "You slay me, Eve," he whispers. "You are my downfall and my saving grace."

"Oh, Ed." I sink down to my knees, cup his face, "I love you, Ed."

He leans in close enough for our eyelashes to tangle. The music winds down, then switches off completely. Our noses bump and we share breath. My heart begins to pound in my chest.

"Edward." I whisper, and he stares down at my lips.

"I want to kiss you, Eve."

"Do it." I swallow and my throat hurts. "Do it, Ed."

His lips part, then he raises his gaze to meet mine. "I can't."

He rises to his feet. "I'm sorry, Eve, but you understand, right?"

"No" I jump to my feet. "I fucking don't."

"You heard us earlier; no sex."

"Fuck that." I curl my fingers into fists. "Fuck the stupid, idiotic condition you guys have laid down."

"I can't," he mutters. "We all agreed."

"No, the two of you agreed." I throw up my hands. "Oh, for fuck's sake."

I brush past him, out the door, and run into Baron. He stares at me, then at Ed, a strange look in his eyes.

"What?" I snap. "What do you want?"

"Eve, please." I hear Edward approach, and fuck, I really don't want to talk to either of them now. I brush past Baron, take the steps two at a time. I reach my room, slam the door and bolt it, then throw myself on the bed.

"Bloody hell." I bury my face in my pillow. This entire situation is untenable. I really have to get away from them. Just be on my own, get a respite from this crazy sexual tension that's always there when I am with either of them. It's just not possible that I am so attracted to both... That I can't make up my mind if I prefer one over the other.

Someone knocks on the door.

"Go the fuck away," I growl.

"You missed lunch," Baron calls out.

"I am not hungry."

"I am leaving your plate by the door."

"Go away," I yell, then bury my face in my pillow again. Exhausted, I fall asleep, and when I awake next, the light is fading outside. My stomach grumbles. I slide off the bed, walk to the entrance and open my bedroom door. I glance outside, then on the floor. On a tray near the door is a covered plate. I snatch it up, shut the door, then sit on a table near the window and polish off the sandwich. It's a little soggy, but still delicious.

Wonder who made it? Baron or Edward? Probably, Edward made it, and Baron brought it to me. Gah! The two of them have a certain understanding between them that comes from having known each other for years. There's animosity between them, no doubt, but they seem to be getting along better than ever. And hell, if I am not beginning to think fondly of both of them. This, despite the fact that both of them feel that they have the right to order me around.

Shit. I really need to find a way out of here. If I can get to the main road, I can hitchhike back, right? Why couldn't the alphaholes have trusted me enough to give me a phone? Well, this is why... Because I'd have found a way out of here much faster. Damn it, why can't they treat me like I can make up my own mind? Because I can't? After all, I am still dithering over which one of them is my 'one'? Bloody hell, all this thinking is definitely not helping me any. I jump up, begin to pace. I only have to stay awake until they go to bed. And then I can leave.

I can try to find the keys to Baron's SUV...and then drive away. They might hear me leave, but that's okay. They don't have another mode of transportation. By the time they figure out a backup plan, I'll be long gone.

They haven't mentioned any security around the place. I haven't seen anything either. Bet they thought keeping an eye on me was enough, right? Would it be safe, though? Is it safer to stay here? Not for my sanity, at any rate. I am done bending to their will. It's time for me to strike out, assert my independence. I've come this far, haven't I? I've forged my own way in the world, despite everyone telling me I couldn't make it. I'm only twenty-one, and an entrepreneur already. I founded my studio, cultivated a successful clientele... I can do this.

· · ·

An hour later, I am dressed in jeans and a shirt, with a jacket. I still have my handbag, so I pull out my wallet, check the money I have, and my credit cards. Yeah, I'll be okay. I pace a little, glance out of the window, wait. A few hours later, I hear the sound of footsteps ascending the stairs. The footsteps approach, stop outside my door. Then there's a knock.

"Ava," Edward calls, "are you coming to dinner?"

"I'm not hungry," I call back.

"Did you eat your lunch?"

"Yes," I snap, "now go away."

"You still sulking?"

"What do you think?"

"If you come down, we could provide you with free entertainment."

"If you mean the two of you bashing each other up," I snort, "you forget, I've seen that already."

There's silence, then he says, "We only want what's best for you, Eve."

"You're not my parents," I yell, realizing as the words leave my mouth that I sound like a spoiled child. "Now, go away."

I sense rather than hear him sigh. "I'll leave dinner outside the door for you." A few minutes later, I hear his return and the sound of a tray being placed on the floor. Then, his footsteps recede.

I wait another half-hour before I peek out the door, grab the food and demolish it. The pasta is yummy. Shit, Edward can cook. Or was that Baron? I know he can cook, but there's so much more I don't know about him. I can stay, of course, and get to know him better. And then what? I'll still be as confused as I am now. And honestly, I can't bear that anymore. I can't.

I pace a little more before finally laying down on the bed. When I awaken again, it's completely dark outside. I slip on my shoes, slide my wallet into my back pocket, then crack the door open. It's dark outside and the doors of the other two rooms are closed. I walk across the landing, down the stairs. One of the steps creaks. I freeze, wait... Nothing moves. I blow out a breath I hadn't been aware I was holding, then walk down, past the living room, to the table near the front door, where I'd seen Baron toss the keys. The bowl is empty. Shit.

I glance around the living room, head for the coffee table. Nothing. I walk down to the room that doubles as Baron's study, crack the door open, peer inside. It's dark. Good. I walk across to the desk, and spot them. There, next to his laptop. I snatch the key fob, retrace my steps to the front door. I swing it open, slowly, expecting something. Maybe alarm bells to go off?

Nothing moves. An owl hoots somewhere and the wind rustles the leaves of the trees. The house is silent. I step out, close the door behind me, then reach the car. I press the key fob, and the door beeps open. Shit, the beep is too loud. I'm sure they definitely heard that, right? I glance at the still silent house, but there's no movement. I open the door to the driver's side, haul myself inside. Adjust the seat, then start the car. Sweat beads my palms and my hands slip on the steering wheel. Shit, shit, shit.

Keeping the headlights off, I grasp the wheel tighter, then ease the car down the short driveway, and onto the country road. I drive carefully, then when I I feel confident enough, I switch on the headlights. I steer the car down the narrow road, until I reach the highway. A car whizzes by. I glance both ways, accelerate onto the main road, and head in the direction of London.

I speed up, keep a look-out in the rearview mirror. The road is empty. I blow out a breath, peer through the windshield at the road ahead. Cars pass by, and I continue on. A few more minutes pass and my muscles relax. Maybe...maybe I'll make it. Even if they do catch up with me... Well, big deal... Maybe they'll punish me... I smirk... More likely, they'll lock me up in the room like an errant child. Seriously, those guys need to get a life. If only they had included me in their decision-making, maybe I'd have stayed. Maybe not. I glance up at the rearview mirror and freeze. Headlights light up the space behind me. Shit. I step down on the accelerator and the car behind me speeds up too. I accelerate further; the car keeps pace. Shit, could it be them? I can make out two passengers in the front of the car, but they are too far for me to see their features. Shit, how the hell could they have gotten hold of a car that quickly?

I glance at the road, then back at the mirror, to find the car gaining on me. Shit, shit, shit. I accelerate further, and the car behind me increases its speed. Hell, ugh! I can't lose this round... Not that it's a competition, but I have my pride. I am going to outrun them if it's the last thing I do. I step on the accelerator, grip the steering wheel more tightly. The SUV leaps forward. The headlights light up the road and there, straight-ahead, eyes stare back at me. I scream, swerve to miss the deer. The brakes screech and the car hits the bank of the road, hurtles down the short slope. A tree looms ahead, there's a loud bang, then everything goes dark.

30

Edward

"She's gone."

"What the fuck?" Baron swears aloud.

I'd thought I'd heard a beep, followed by the sound of a car driving away, had glanced outside and seen the SUV gone. I'd rushed into her room...knowing already that it would be empty. Then stepped out to find Baron at the doorway to his room.

"The SUV's gone."

"Fuck. The car keys." He races down the steps to the study. I follow him, knowing already what he is going to find. He reaches his desk and swears. "Fuck, fuck, fuck." He turns to me, "The car, we can track it."

He stalks out of the study, up the stairs to his room. I follow him. He snatches his phone, pulls up the app. I reach him, glance over his shoulder at the green dot on the screen.

"Well?"

"It's not moving."

"What does that mean?"

"How the fuck do I know?" He turns on me, "This was a bad idea. We should have spoken to her, reasoned with her, not acted like overbearing brutes..."

"Which we are." I grimace. "Let's get to her first, then point fingers at each other."

He nods. "Fuck, fuck, fuck." He squeezes his fingers around the phone, the skin across his knuckles stretching white. "If something happens to her, I'll never forgive myself."

"Hold on, man." I grip his shoulder. "We'll find her."

"I should have walked away when you asked me to." He squeezes his eyes shut, I stayed on. I couldn't bring myself to leave, and now she's gone."

"We'll find her, Baron," I insist. "She's not far. You said so yourself; we just need to hurry before anything happens to her."

He snaps his eyelids open. "Shit," he shudders, "if they get to her first."

"They won't."

He drags in a breath, "We'll find her first."

"We will."

"And when we do, I—"

"Not now," I snap. "Pull yourself together. Focus, solider. Let's get going."

"Right."

"Right." I clap his shoulder, "See you downstairs." I head for the doorway, when he calls out.

"Edward, how do we get to her? She took the car."

I glance at him over my shoulder, "You didn't think I'd allow you to have the only ride in town, did you?"

His eyes gleam, "Bastard."

"Wanker." I smirk. "See you in a minute."

By the time I pull on my clothes and reach the door, he's already there. I walk around the back of the house, to the garage in the far corner. A few minutes later, we pull out of the driveway in my Aston Martin.

"You had this in the garage, all this time?"

I raise my shoulders. "I had Sinner equip the place with the essentials."

"Remind me to thank him..." He shakes my head, "No, actually, don't. That would only feed into the bastard's ego, and he has more than enough of that to go around."

"As do you."

"And you," he reminds me.

"It's what got us into this situation in the first place."

Baron stares straight ahead.

"Fuck," I slam my palm down on the steering wheel. "Bloody fuck." I turn onto the highway, press down on the accelerator. "How much further?"

"Another few miles." Baron repeatedly glances down at the phone, then up at the road, finally cautioning me, "Slow down. We should be coming up to it."

I lose speed, search the area as I drive.

"There," Baron exclaims.

I slam on the brakes, park on the side of the road. By the time I am out of the car, he's already at the SUV. He races over to the passenger side and freezes. "She's not here."

I take in the car's front end, which is crumpled against the tree. "The airbags deployed," I state unnecessarily.

"Where the fuck is she?" he swears.

I walk around to the driver's side, spot the trampled grass around the space. "Look at this"

Baron stalks around the car, follows my gaze, and his features pale. "Fuck," he growls. "Fuck, fuck, fuck."

"They got to her."

"We need to find her before they hurt her."

Baron's phone rings just then. We glance at each other, then he answers the phone. "Archer?" He listens for a few seconds, then disconnects and stares at me, "The man you injured at the church? He's awake."

. . .

Two hours later, we pull up at the safehouse outside of London, where both the homeless guy and the guy who'd broken into Ava's studio, have been taken.

I park the car behind two other SUVs and follow Baron into the house. We walk past the empty living room to the bedroom where the homeless guy is. Archer straightens from his position by the window.

"Has he spoken?" Baron takes in the figure on the bed.

"Not yet." Weston glances up from his chair next to the bed. When Archer had moved the injured men here for their own safety, Weston had opted to come with them, staying available to monitor their progress.

I walk around to stand over the man. He's a big man, and his bulk takes up most of the narrow bed. His eyes are shut, his hair in disarray. His features are ashen, the marks around his neck standing out in contrast against his skin. I curl my fingers into fists. I should have killed the bastard; too bad he didn't die. I take a step forward and Baron grabs my shoulder.

I turn to him and he shakes his head. "Let me question him."

I scowl. "Asshole was responsible for what happened to us."

"And he may have information that can help us find her," he reminds me. "Information that I can pry from him."

I open my mouth to protest and he raises his hand, "This is my specialty, Ed." He rolls his shoulders, then continues, "The guy who broke into Ava's studio—the one you shot? He would have more information on why Ava was kidnapped."

"But he's still unconscious," I point out. "Whereas the homeless guy is awake."

Baron purses his lips.

"Also, he did mention that he's involved with the Mafia." I add, "Surely, he must know something about Ava's abduction?"

The sound of a car pulling up outside reaches us. This is followed by the sound of a door slamming, then footsteps approaching from the front of the house. We exchange glances, then look at Archer.

"Did you alert the rest of the Seven?" Baron asks him.

"I did," Weston confirms.

"What the fuck?" I scowl at Weston.

"Why did you do that?" Baron growls, before turning to Archer, "Did you know about this?"

"Uh." He rubs the back of his neck, "It's—'

"Not his fault," Weston interjects. "I threatened to go to the cops unless he agreed to let me call the others."

"The fuck?" I turn on Wes, "Why would you do that?"

"Because you guys need back up." Weston leans forward in his chair. "Something which you two are too proud to ask for. So, I took the decision out of your hands."

"Seriously?" Baron balls his fists at his sides. "It's bad enough we agreed to let you monitor this bastard in the safehouse."

"Not that you had a choice. I am his doctor and he's my patient." He leans forward to check the vitals of the guy, who stirs.

"He doesn't deserve an ounce of care," I growl. "Bastard's behind our kidnapping... And chances are, the same people are behind Ava's kidnapping."

"Ava?" Weston straightens. "The hell you talking about?"

"She ran out on us," Baron rubs the back of his neck, "and they took her."

"And both of you couldn't do anything about it?" Weston scowls.

Baron's face flushes. He leans forward and I slap a hand in his chest, "Easy, ol' chap, we need to keep our cool here."

"This bastard," Baron glares at the man on the bed, "he'd better have some answers."

The sound of wheels on gravel reaches us, car doors slam, then Damian walks in, followed by Arpad, Saint, and finally, Sinner.

They take up positions around the room.

"Well?" Sinner levels his gaze at Baron," You going to question him or what?"

Baron draws in a breath. Degree by degree, he seems to force himself to relax. He unfurls his fists, rolls his shoulders. He pulls another chair up to the bed. He stares at the features of the man on the bed, then stiffens.

"Shit," he swears aloud, "now I know where I've seen him before."

"You've seen him before?" I growl, and he nods.

"I thought I recognized him when I first saw him, but couldn't place him."

"But you can now?" Arpad straightens.

"Yeah." Baron blows out a breath and looks at Saint. "Remember the time you and I fought at the underground parking lot and I defeated you?"

"You didn't defeat me."

"Sure, I did," Baron smirks, "though that's not the point." His features harden. "I saw him in the crowd that day."

"You did?" Arpad frowns.

"You sure?" Sinner asks.

"Yeah." Baron squares his shoulders. "Best to get on with the questioning." He glances toward me, "Do you know his name?"

"Anton," Weston interjects, "Anton Ruzlovksy."

I whip my head around, "He's Russian?"

Arpad stiffens; he stares hard at the figure on the bed. "I am going to call Nikolai in on this."

Arpad's wife is Nikolai's sister; their father is *Pakhan* of the Bratva. Arpad, himself, is part of the Bratva...as a special consultant, of sorts...or so he claims. Asshole is probably more in with the Bratva than he is letting on.

He straightens, exchanges a glance with Baron, who nods. Arpad pulls out his phone and walks out, while Baron leans over the man, "Anton, can you hear me?"

Anton's eyes flutter.

"Anton Ruzlovsky?" Baron's voice is firm, "Nod if you can hear me, Anton."

Anton swallows. His eyes flutter again, then he nods almost imperceptibly.

"Good," Baron says in an encouraging tone. "I'm Baron. Baron Masters. Can you tell me who you work for, Anton?"

He opens and shuts his mouth, but nothing emerges.

"His vocal chords suffered some trauma," Weston mutters, "but he should be able to speak."

"Can you hear me, Anton?" Baron asks.

Anton nods.

"What do you have to do with Ava's kidnapping?"

The guys stiffen.

"Ava was taken?" Sinner snaps.

Neither Baron nor I reply.

"Fuck," Saint growls, "this asshole had better start talking, and fast."

I scowl down at the prone figure, who takes in the faces around the room. His chest planes move.

"Anton, hey!" Baron snaps his fingers and Anton jerks his attention back to him. "Ava," Baron growls, "what do you know about Ava's abduction?"

His lips move. Baron presses his ear close to Anton's mouth.

He clenches his jaw. "You are lying," Baron growls. "You do realize, we are not going to go easy on you. The only way you can alleviate what's coming to you, is if you tell us the truth."

Anton swallows, then shakes his head again. His lips move and Baron straightens. "Asshole insists he had nothing to do with the kidnapping."

Anger coils in my gut. "We don't have time for this," I growl. "We're here holding our dicks in our hands, while Ava is, at this moment, being held by kidnappers."

"I know," Baron growls, "I fucking know."

"Ed," Damian cautions me, "take it easy, man."

I glare at Baron, who glowers back at me.

"You too, Baron," Damian says in a low voice. "The two of you fighting is not going to help anyone, especially not Ava."

Sinner straightens. "Ask the asshole who's behind the incident? Who did he give the information to?"

"Who did you work for, Anton?" Baron growls. "Who asked you for information on the seven boys which led to their kidnapping?"

His lips move and Baron leans forward. "What was that? Can you repeat yourself?" Anton's lips move again. Baron stiffens; he stares at me. "Byron?" He scowls. "Did you say Byron?"

A ripple of tension runs round the room. I scowl at the prone man. "Do you have a full name, you asshole?"

Baron holds up a hand and I purse my lips. "Ask him Baron," I insist and Baron glares at me, before turning to the guy.

"Do you have a full name for us? Does Byron have a surname?"

The man's lips move again. Baron leans in, presses his ear close to the man's mouth. His scowl deepens. "Michael Byron? Is that right, Anton?"

Anton nods.

"Did he send you to talk to us?"

Anton shakes his head.

"So why have you been interacting with each of the Seven? Why have you been appearing at crucial junctures at each of their lives? Why have you been tracking them?"

Anton's lips twist, he whispers again, and Baron pulls back to stare at him, "You expect me to believe that?"

Anton's lips curve. His shoulders shake. Is the asshole laughing? What the fuck? I move forward, but Baron reacts before me. He shoots out his hand and his palm connects with Anton's cheek. Anton coughs, or at least I think that's what he does because no sound emerges. His face reddens and spittle flies out of his mouth. He shakes his head, then beckons Baron closer.

Baron leans in and Anton tips up his chin. The tendons of his throat strain. "It's true," he whispers, and I catch the words this time. "All of it." He swallows. "I wanted to make up for what my actions did to all of you. I wanted to make sure you found some measure of happiness."

"We didn't need your help," Saint growls. "We were doing fine on our own."

Anton snickers. Saint's face reddens. He thrusts his chest out, takes a step forward, and Sinner grabs his shoulder.

"Steady, ol' chap," Sinner mutters, "he's trying to get you worked up."

"Well, he's succeeding." Saint shakes off Sinner's arm. "Asshole has two seconds to come through with some information of use, else I swear, I am going to finish what Father—I mean, Edward here, started."

I scowl at him. "I am no longer a priest, you prick. Best remember that."

"Priest? Somehow, now that you are no longer one, this new nickname suits you." Saint looks me up and down, "Hey, Priest." He snickers, "How are you, Priest?"

I ball my fists at my sides, glare at him. "The fuck is your problem, you piss-head?"

"Welcome to the real world, ol' chap," Saint grins, "where you are allowed to speak your mind without fear of a larger power striking you down for your sins... Unless you are like our man on the bed here, in which case, it's only a matter of time before they catch up with you. And no one can save you from what's about to come next." He glares at Anton, "You catch my drift, motherfucker?"

"You heard the guy." Baron straightens his spine. "You have one last chance to tell us something that's going to help find Ava, else I am going to let Saint, here, take a shot at you, and I can tell you, there's nothing holding him back. Not the law, not the fear of any repercussions. Sadly, the man has enough money to buy out not just the cops, but also governments, if needed, not to mention the Mafia. He can kill you right now and vanish your body and no one would ever know."

Anton's lips twist... Did the asshole just smirk? I glare at his face. "So, you expect us to believe that you followed us around to make sure our lives didn't go to shit?"

He nods.

"And you came to me to confess, because you knew I was one of the Seven?" I scoff.

He stills, then nods again.

This doesn't make sense. I stare at him, hard. "I still don't understand why you came to see me. Clearly, you wanted me to lose control. You knew there was a good probability I'd react exactly the way I did with you... Unless..." I roll my shoulders. "Unless you guessed that I was at the end of my tether. You knew I was falling for Ava and conflicted about how to balance my feelings for her with my calling."

He tilts his head.

"You were hoping that your revelations would push me over the edge, that it would make me do something that I would regret enough to leave the priesthood? That it would nudge me toward her?"

His lips twitch and anger curls in my chest. My blood hums and my pulse rate ratchets up. I step toward him. "Or were you hoping to get exactly the kind of reaction you got from me, where I almost killed you? Did you hope to die in church at the hands of a man of God as a way of repenting for your sins?"

Asshole stays quiet. He doesn't even blink.

"Answer me, you motherfucker," I bark. "What kind of game were you playing when you came to see me?"

His jaw hardens but he doesn't say a word. Bloody-fucking-hell. I clench my fists at my sides.

He'd better start speaking, or else, Saint will have to get in line behind me. Strange how, once you go down the path of sin... Each progressive one becomes simpler, easier, faster until you forget the true nature of your actions, until everything is tainted by the same brush, until... To err becomes a part of you...and then you walk the line between light and dark, knowing you'll always be a shade of grey. It's only the intensity of that in-between color which changes... And well, that doesn't count for much. It's still grey.

"You have one minute," Baron growls, "sixty seconds before I step away and let these guys beat it out of you..." he shrugs, "so what's it going to be?"

Anton glances around the room, then back at Baron. He tips up his chin and Baron places his ear next to Anton's mouth again. Anton's lips move. Baron's features grow stonier. He shoves back his chair and heads for the door. I follow him.

"We're coming with you." Sinner pushes away from the wall.

"No." We both say in unison. I nod, then Baron turns to glance at the guys.

"This one's ours."

31

"My happiest moments are in a car. Looking out the window, the music on full blast, without a care in the world. I just like watching the world go by. I get this overwhelming feeling as I pass fields upon fields or people upon people. It's like I'm in a film. And then, that perfect song comes on and the sun shines and it's pure happiness."
-From Ava's Diary

Ava

My head pounds and my mouth is so dry. I swallow and my throat hurts. I try to move and my shoulder screams. I try to open my eyes, only to find my eyelids are glued together. I pry them apart, and stars burst behind my eyes. I groan, and the sound echoes around the space. Where am I? What the hell happened? I remember being in the car... The deer... I'd veered off the road. I remember the headlights of the car lighting up the tree and then... Nothing. Shit, I must have crashed. So how did I get here? I try to move, find my arms are bound behind me. I glance down to find my legs are tied to the legs of the chair that I am seated on. What the hell?

My heart begins to race. Had they found me? The men who had assaulted me, then broken into the studio... Had they finally gotten to me? It must have been them who chased me on the highway. And I'd thought it was my guys. Shit, if only it had been Baron and Edward who had been after me. I never should have left the house...but they hadn't included me in their decisions and I had been so mad. Shit, had they realized that I was gone? Would they come in search of me? Of course, they would, but how quickly could they find me?

A bead of sweat slides down my back.

I glance around the space, taking in the rest of the room. High ceilings, walls which must have been white at one point but which are now a faded gray. Near the doorway there's a pile of cloth— looks like faded carpet. Had someone bought the material with the hope of doing up this room, then abandoned it? A ray of sunlight filters in through the only window, and motes of dust dance in its path. I stare at them, watch as they are highlighted by the sunshine, only to disappear.

Shit, life really is fleeting. Time doesn't wait for anyone. It hadn't for my mother. She's gone, and we are left grappling in the after-math. A family broken and grieving for her, yet unable to come together to comfort each other. My father had done the right thing. He'd moved on, not from my mother, but from wallowing in self-pity. He'll never forget her and he's chosen to honor her memory by living.

And me? I am still stuck there—in my head, a girl without a mother, someone who misses her so much, and yet, has refused to spend time with her family. I've rebuffed my sister at every turn, not wanting to comfort her or let myself be comforted. I've allowed my selfishness to override everything else. I've clung to my grief, nurtured it, not allowed anyone or anything to touch it. I've held it close, reveled in it, thinking as long as I had it, I had a connection with my mother. I am still holding onto the memory of how it was to be with her. As long as I house that grief in me... At least, I have some last vestige of connection to her physically... I haven't wanted to move on and I have blamed my family for dealing with it, for coming to terms with it, for wanting to honor her memory by staying in the present. Me... I am still stuck there...with her...the memory of the last breath that she took.

And then, when I had been so attracted to both of them, it had only pushed me to withdraw into myself. No wonder I hadn't been able to make sense of my feelings for both of them. No wonder I hadn't been able to choose. How could I, when so much of me was still trapped in coming to terms with the grief in my life? The grief I am ready to relinquish.

No, I won't forget my mother...but... I am ready to live for her... Ready to make her proud of me. To fulfill my potential completely, to let my true nature shine in everything I do. Whether it is dancing... or love. I am going to give it my all... I am finally ready to make my choice. I know what I want. I know who I want to spend the rest of my life with, and no asshole kidnappers are going to come between me and the kind of life I have always wanted.

Heat presses down on my shoulders and sweat beads my forehead. Why is it so hot? Did they crank up the heating in here? I glance outside at the sun shining through the window, the warmth amplified by the glass panes. Where are Baron and Edward? Do they know where to look? If they don't find me... No, they will. They are smart. More than smart, they are tenacious. They'll track me down. They wouldn't let anything happen to me.

My palms sweat. I tug on the ropes that restrain my hands, but it only seems to tighten them further. Shit, whoever tied me up knew what they were doing. I force myself to relax my muscles, blinking away the sweat that drips into my eyes. Why the hell is it like a sauna in here?

A low vibration hums through the space and the hair on the back of my neck stands on end. Shit, what was that? What the hell is happening? I strain my ears, close my eyes, and try to focus in on the sounds. The scent of smoke reaches me. I cough, snap open my eyes. Is someone smoking out there? The scent of burning intensifies. Bloody hell, is the house on fire? My heart begins to race. "Help," I yell, "Help me!"

I tug on my ropes, yank at them, but they don't give. I push down with my feet, managing to move the chair slightly. My muscles protest. Sweat pours down my face. Shit, this is not good, not good. "Help," I cry out again. There's silence, except for the crackling sound, which I swear, has grown louder. The heat in the room pushes down on my chest, my shoulders. My throat closes; the band around my chest tightens. Shit, if there's a fire, am I going to stay here like a sitting duck? I stare at the door, then back at the window. If only I could creep a little closer. Surely, the air nearer to the pane would be fresher?

I push against the floor, leaning toward the window. This time the chair moves a little more. I force myself to push again, and again. My breath catches, panting. I focus on the window pane. I've managed to move, maybe a few inches. It's just the angle at which I have been tied to the chair—it's all wrong. OMG! I am going to burn in here. Shit, shit, shit.

Why are the guys not here? Surely, they should have figured out where I am by now? And if they haven't? What if there are no clues to lead them here? What if they have no idea where to look?

Tendrils of smoke slitherin from under the door frame and I cry out. "Please, no," I gasp, "no, no, no." I push against the floor, leaning in the direction of the window. *Pretend it's a belly dance, but one where you are burdened with weights. Where your arms and legs are bound and it's up to you how well you can put the muscles you've gained thus far to use.*

I undulate my hips, wriggle my torso, even as I push my heels into the ground and careen to the right. With a screech the chair moves toward the window. I repeat the action, and again. My head pounds, my heart hammers so hard against my chest that I am sure it's going to break through my ribcage. I pant, draw in a breath and cough. I panic as I realize the room is filling with smoke. Shit. My eyes water and my pulse thuds at my temples. Damn, if I am going to go down without a fight. I lean my torso to the right, push off with my feet. This time, the chair careens to the right, then tips over. "No..." I scream as the chair hits the floor, my cheek smashes into the wooden planks, the reverberations sweep through me, and the hammering in my head intensifies. "No...please." I sob, "No, I don't want to die like this. Please."

32

Baron

"What the fuck is that?"

I stare through the windshield at the smoke that rises into the air. Edward leans forward, peering through the windshield. "Fuck." He presses down on the accelerator and the car leaps forward. He negotiates the winding country road, screeching around the next corner, as I fix my gaze on the plumes of black smoke.

"If anything happens to her, I'll never forgive myself," I reach for the phone, dial 999. As soon as the operator comes on the line I give them the location of the fire, then hang up.

Edward clutches the steering wheel, the skin stretching white across his knuckles. "F-u-c-k!" he yells. "This is fucked up; why the hell would they want to harm her?"

"To get to us?"

"We were wrong in not discussing everything openly with her." He slams his fist on the steering wheel and the car wobbles.

I brace myself against the door, staying focused on the scene ahead, "If we get her out unhurt... I'll..." I can't bring myself to say it. I can't walk away from her, can I? But I'd heard her tell Edward that she loved him. That must mean something, right? I should have walked away when Edward had asked me to. I hadn't, and now, here she is, likely trapped in the burning house.

"Fuck." I grab my hair and tug on it. "She's going to be fine; she has to be fine."

Edward careens around the next corner, pulls into the driveway of the house. I've unbuckled my belt and jumped out before the vehicle has come to a stop. I race toward the doorway, Edward in on my heels.

I try to push open the door and it doesn't budge. I put my shoulder to it and it barely moves. "Motherfucker."

Edward notches his shoulder against the door "On my count: one, two three..." We put our strength behind it and the door shudders.

"Once more," he grunts. "One, two three..."

We smash our shoulders against the door and it creaks, groans, then comes away at the hinges. We stamp across the fallen door, into the hallway. Smoke fills the hallway, and I cough. Heat sears my skin, sweat beads my forehead.

"Fuck." My heart pumps in my chest like it wants to escape. "This is not good."

"Where the fuck could she be?" Edward cries.

We stare around the space. "I'll take the stairs, you check the rooms on this floor."

"Hurry," he urges me.

We split up, I race for the steps, hit the landing on the first floor. Glance down the corridor and swear. Smoke swirls across the space. I tear off my jacket, hold it to my nose. Four rooms; there are four on this floor.

Ahead, flames zip up the doorframe. The door catches fire then crashes to the floor. The sound sweeps through my mind—the zing of bullets, the cries of soldiers. All of it overwhelms me. My stomach churns, bile boils up my throat. Images flood my mind and I am powerless to stop the flashback.

Smoke, so much smoke, so thick that I can't see in front of me. My foot brushes something. I glance down, take in the charred body. My guts twist. Bile splashes up my throat. I swallow down the acidic taste, grip my gun, keep going. I can't see my hand in front of my face. Cries fill the space, more bullets, the thump of bodies hitting the ground. I keep my gaze trained forward. Keep moving. I just need to get to the other side. A bullet whizzes past me. My pulse rate ratchets up. Adrenaline laces my blood. I train my gun, take aim and fire. And again. And again.

There's a touch on my shoulder and I snap out of the memory. I turn to find Edward next to me.

"She's not on the ground floor." He coughs. "I am going to search the rooms on the top floor." He peers into my face, "You got this?"

"Yeah." I swallow.

I pull away, head for the first room, kick down the door, and see it's empty. Head for the second one, step through the doorway. Smoke fills the space. I cough, try to draw a breath and my lungs burn. The smoke parts, I glance around the space, realize she's not here. I race down the corridor, and up the stairs. As I reach the landing, I hear Edward cry out, "I found her."

I spring forward, toward the only room with an open door. I dash through the smoke, to find him bent over a prone figure tied to an upturned chair.

"Fuck." I rush to him, drop to my knees.

"Found her unconscious," he murmurs, as he unties the ropes on her feet.

I reach for the knots that tether her wrists together. My fingers slip. I swear, draw in a breath, then pick at the knot again. It loosens. I pull the rope apart, attack the second knot, which falls away. I tug at the rope again and it slackens enough for me to pull it down and off of her.

She slips from the chair and I grab her just as Ed completes untying the ropes on her feet. I haul her up in my arms, move toward the door just as a stack of fabric near the doorway catch fire.

I've barely made it through before a lick of fire flares up behind me. I turn, to find Edward on my heels. Behind him the doorframe is on fire. I head for the stairs and am halfway down the last flight when I realize Edward is not with me. I turn to find him frozen at the top of the stairs. What the hell? I retrace my way up the stairs, and pause a couple of steps below him, "Edward," I yell, "What's wrong?"

Sweat beads his forehead, his gaze is focused on a point in the distance. His muscles are locked, and he seems frozen, in shock? Shit, "Edward!" I growl, "Get a grip, man." I step up next to him, nudge him with my shoulder, "Ed! Jesus Christ, man, snap the fuck out of it."

He blinks, then turns his gaze on me, "Baron?" He murmurs, before his gaze moves to the woman in my arms.

"Go," he gestures, "get her to safety."

"Oh, I will, I promise, but you are coming."

He tilts his head, "I can't."

"The fuck you mean?"

"I must atone for my sins."

"Sins? What sins are you talking about?"

"I gave him up and now I must pay my due." His voice is without inflection as if he is in a dream, or in shock? "This is not the fucking time to have a crisis of faith." I snap, "You need to come with me, now."

He shakes his head, "Take her out of here, Baron."

Behind us, something crashes to the floor and the entire building seems to shudder.

"Fuck." I glare at him, "I am not leaving without you."

"Ava." His voice grows haunted. He glances down at her again, then back at my face. "She's the priority here."

I hesitate.

"Go." He points down the stairs, "Go, before it's too late. I'll be right behind you."

Fuck, fuck, fuck. No way, am I leaving him, but if I hesitate, I'll endanger Ava as well. *Bloody hell.* I pull away from my friend and race down the last flight of steps, only to slip. I lose my footing, tumble down the rest of the stairs and turn my body at the last second to cushion the impact.

Her limp body collapses on top of mine. My back hits the floor and pain flashes behind my eyes. My guts churn, nausea bubbles up, and I swallow it down. I draw in a breath, scoop her up in my arms as I straighten, then race out of the doorway. I draw in gusts of fresh air as I place her down on the grass, then lean away, coughing, gasping. Next to me, she stirs, coughing, and I turn to her. I cup her face, "Eve?" I plead. "Ava, open your eyes. Please."

Her eyelids flicker open. Her gaze widens as she takes in my features. "Baron." She swallows, "Oh, my god, Baron." She coughs as she rises up and throws her arms around my neck, "The fire... I was so afraid."

"You're safe." I close my arms around her, bury my face in her hair. Smoke, burning wood, and below that, the faint scent of jasmine. My heart stutters. "Fuck, Ava, if anything had happened to you..."

"I'm fine." She coughs again. "I knew you'd come." She begins to cry, "Knew you and Edward would find me in time."

I stiffen and she must sense the tension in me, for she pulls back, and peers into my face, "Edward." She swallows, "Where's Ed?"

"The important thing is that you're safe."

"Edward." She grabs at my collar, "Where's Edward, Baron?"

I stare toward the burning house, then back at her.

"No," she shakes her head, "no, no, no." She scrambles away from me.

"Ava, stop."

"Oh, no," she snaps, "don't you dare ask me to stop. If Edward's in there, I am going in." She staggers to her feet, hobbles toward the flames. I spring up, dash after her and grab her arm, "He'll be fine. He said he'd be right behind us."

Just then a creaking sound reaches us. We glance up to find flames shooting up from the roof of the house.

"No!" she screams. "No, Edward!"

She tries to break free and I throw my arms around her, "Shh, Ava, please..."

"No!" she screams and turns in my arms. "I can't let anything happen to him, Baron." She grabs my collar and rises up to tiptoe, "I love him, don't you understand?"

Something cold stabs at my chest. I glance down at her sobbing face.

"You love him?"

"Yes." She sobs, "Please, help him, Baron, please... He went in there to save me. If anything happens to him, I'll never be able to forgive myself. Please, Baron... Please."

I circle her wrists, pull them away from my collar, before I release her. Then I brush past her and walk into the burning house.

33

Edward

I glance over my shoulder at the flames that lick the far end of the corridor. If I am going to die, at least, I know that she is safe. That I'll be sacrificing myself for her.

The crown molding catches fire. The flames edge toward me as I watch, trapped in my own personal hell.

If there was going to be a way for me to go, then it makes sense it would be like this—bathed in fire, purified of my sins. The cross that I have borne since the incident. The event that had scarred my life, had ruined me for any relationship… Until her. She had given me a reason to haul myself out of the unfeeling, unseeing existence I had settled for.

I believed I had found my calling… And in those years, I had found a certain kind of peace, dedicating myself to the higher good… Focusing on everything else… *Anything else,* but the festering mass of pain deep inside that had only grown, bigger, wider, more solid with time... Until it had lodged in my gut, had weighed me down, anchored me to a state of being from which I couldn't escape.

If becoming a priest was the single most courageous act I had undertaken, then walking away from everything familiar was the riskiest one. One I hadn't hesitated to take, because the path led to her. She saved my life, and I willingly sacrifice myself for her...and in that...there is a certain poetic justice.

I will die, consumed by the fire that will finally purify me. That will wipe away the hate I carry deep inside, the scars, which are all that remain of the boy I had once been.

And she won't be alone. She has Baron to protect her, to take care of her. She'll be safe and happy. *My woman and my best friend.* I clutch my fingers at my sides. My woman. *Mine.* Fuck... I close my eyes. Why is it I find it so difficult to let go of her, even now?

Baron is right for her. He isn't tainted, like me. He is right for her. He has to be. Fucking Baron. Seems, he was always destined to come out ahead of me... *It's not a fucking competition, Ed.*

Of course, it is. The race to capture the heart of a woman who means so much to me... It's right I don't win this one. I don't deserve her.

"Priest, motherfucker."

I snap my eyes open, turn to find Baron, racing up the stairs.

"The fuck you doing, asshole?" He pants as he comes to a stop next me.

"What the fuck is it to you?" I scowl.

"I don't give a rat's ass what you do to yourself, but the woman out there... She's losing her shit, and if you don't get out of the fire, she's walking right into it with you."

I lower my chin to my chest, "I don't fucking deserve her, man."

"You can say that again." Baron growls, "But it's not for you or for me to decide. She gets the final choice in this matter." His jaw tics. "And she chooses you."

"What?" *She wants me? She chose me? She needs me? She wants to be with me?* I frown and Baron's features soften; there's an indecipherable look in his eyes.

"Yeah," he closes the distance between us, "she wants you, man.

You're her first love. Hell, it was always you and her. Me? I was the interloper."

"You watched over her, took care of her while I sorted my shit out."

"And that's all it was ever meant to be." Baron's features harden. "I was wrong to think otherwise. I should have stayed true to my word to you. I should have bowed out a while ago... It's just... I couldn't."

"Baron, I—"

Fire licks up the wall, the chandelier hanging from the ceiling in the hallway shudders before the crystals explode. "Fuck." I throw up my arm to protect my face. Pain slices up my side. "Shit, we need to get out of here."

"Now, you're talking." He bares his teeth.

There's a high-pitched whine, and the ceiling above us groans.

"Motherfucker." Baron charges down the steps, and I follow him.

The stairway seems to tremble. Intense heat overwhelms me.

Behind us the crackling, popping sound intensifies. Flames hiss and a lick of fire lashes out from the side. I duck, then jump down the last step.

34

Ava

Come on, come on, where are the two of you?

I gaze at the burning house, at the flames that leap up into the sky. The fire's gotten even more fierce in the last few minutes. Shit, shit, shit.

It's bad enough that they risked their lives to save me. I shouldn't have sent Baron in there...but Edward. Oh, my god, Ed. How could I have allowed him to be consumed by the fire? They are going to be okay; they have to be. The sirens wail in the distance and I close my eyes and sob. *Help is on its way. It's going to be fine, you guys. Just make it out of there. Please, just make it out.*

Only when my knees touch the ground do I realize that I am praying. I clasp my palms together, stare at the entrance of the house. *Come on, come on, please.*

God, I am so sorry that I tempted him away from you. Please don't take your anger out on him. Please. Let them both live. Please I beg you.

The sirens draw closer, then the fire-engine pulls up next to me.

The firefighters jump out. One of them squats next to me. He's saying something, but I can't focus. Can't take my gaze off the doorway. *Come on, you guys. What's taking you so long?*

The firefighters swing into action. They unravel their hoses, train them on the house. A torrent of water zooms forth. Someone places a blanket around my shoulders. My thighs tremble and my heart flip flops in my chest. I stare at the doorway. *Please, please, please.*

"Miss, you have to move away; you are too close to the fire."

I shake off the arms that grip me. *Not close enough. I am not nearly close enough. Please, you have both got to make it through. I'll never forgive myself if anything happens to either of you.*

I close my eyes, tilt my chin-up. *Please, if you are up there and watching over us, I am sorry if I took him away from you. You know I didn't do it to hurt you. I wasn't being vindictive. It just felt right. Please don't punish him for that.*

More sirens sound, then an ambulance drives up and a medic jumps out. Someone's talking to me. I ignore them. *Please, please, please.* I repeat the word like a mantra. *If anything happens to either of them...please no, you can't be that cruel. Please help them. Please.*

A cry goes up around me. I snap my eyes open, lower my gaze to the door, to the two figures outlined against the burning inferno. I am on my feet and running. They stagger toward me and I throw myself at them. Edward catches me, then sinks to the ground, with me on top of him. "Ohmigod, ohmigod," I blubber, "ohmigod, Ed. I thought I'd lost you."

He rubs his palm down my hair and his fingers catch in a knot. My scalp tingles and it's so familiar, so comforting, that my tears intensify.

"Shh," he holds me close, "it's okay, I am here."

"Thank god, Baron got to you in time."

Edward kisses my forehead, "He saved my life." He glances past me, "Baron, where is he?"

"He was right here." I turn around to find he's gone. "Wait, where did he go? Baron?" I call.

A few firemen surround us. One of them wraps the blanket

around me again. "Miss," he says firmly, "we need to check him out and treat his wounds."

"Of course." I move away from Ed, who holds out his arm.

"Don't go too far." He smirks.

"I won't," I promise, half-smiling, half-crying. I glance around for Baron and can't see him anywhere.

One of the medics tends to my wounds. Another attends to Edward. They place a mask over his face, then strap him onto the stretcher. I follow him toward the ambulance, glancing around again. *Where the hell is Baron?*

One of the medics walks past me and I hail him, "Excuse me, do you know what happened to the second man who walked out of the building?"

"If you mean the guy who saved your friend, he left."

"What do you mean, he left?"

The medic raises a shoulder, "He refused to be treated."

"But…he was hurt. How could you just allow him to leave?"

"Can't force him to accept help, ma'am." The medic urges me into the ambulance. *Shit, shit, shit. This isn't good. It can't be good. Why did Baron leave and without saying a word to me or Edward?*

The medic slams the door of the ambulance, which sets off. I bite down on my lower lip. My fingers tremble, and I squeeze them together in front of me.

Edward pulls the oxygen mask off of his face. The medic protests and he dismisses her concern. "Just need a second," he insists.

She frowns, then nods at him.

He turns to me, "What's wrong, Eve?"

"It's Baron," I murmur, "he left."

"What do you mean, left?"

"He walked away. One of the medics saw him leave. He literally just took off, without saying a word to me. Why would he do that, Ed?"

Edward draws in a breath. "Maybe," he says carefully, "maybe he's telling you by his actions what he can't say in words."

"You mean," I swallow, "you mean, this is him saying goodbye?"

He reaches over and takes my hand in his, "You knew this was inevitable, Eve." He weaves his fingers with mine. "One of us was always going to come away empty-handed."

"It's not fair." A tear runs down my cheek. "I love him, Ed. I love both of you."

"I know." He tugs and I sink down on the floor of the ambulance. I place my head on his chest. He flinches.

"Shit," I mutter, "you're hurt."

"Nothing I can't bear," he assures me. "I love you, Eve." He runs his fingers down my hair.

I turn my nose into his chest, breathe in the scent of smoke, of cut grass and testosterone. My belly trembles, my thighs clench, yet the emptiness in my chest gapes. More tears well up and I swallow them down. "I love you too, Ed."

A day later, I park the Aston Martin in front of my house. Edward had wanted to drive, but when I'd pointed out that he was on painkillers to combat the burns he'd suffered, he hadn't protested.

His wounds hadn't been extensive though, thank God. All in all, we had escaped with minor injuries, considering how serious the fire had been.

Within hours of arriving at the hospital, the rest of the Seven had turned up, wives in tow. The men had huddled in conversation with Edward over the next few hours, while the women, including Isla, had kept me company.

I'd sensed their curiosity about the situation, though none of them had asked me where Baron was, and for that, I was grateful.

It seems he made my choice for me... Which is fine. I had told him that I loved Edward, after all; and I do. I am happy to be coming home with him, right?

But why couldn't he have told me that face-to-face? Why did he have to leave without a word? I had tried calling him, but had only gotten his voice mail. I'd tried texting him, but he hadn't replied.

None of the Seven had heard from him either.

He had disappeared on his friends once before... And apparently, he is doing it again now. Does he just want to lay low for the moment? Away from me...and his friends. He had returned to his life and now, thanks to me, he had decided to go quiet on them again. Shit, I curl my fingers around the wheel.

"You, okay?" Edward turns to me. He's wearing a black T-shirt, a jacket on top, and jeans with his usual shit-kicker boots. I am still getting used to seeing him in such normal clothes, I guess. With his hair long enough to brush his collar and the makings of a beard clinging to his chin... He looks so different... So rough. So not like the sleek, powerful man I saw slicing through the pool that day. He's the same...yet not. And I know I caused the change in him... And it's thrilling, but also...a little bit overwhelming. Does anyone want to take on the onus of changing someone else's life that completely? Had meeting me caused him more harm than good?

"Don't," he mutters. He reaches out, places his palm against my cheek, "Don't overthink it."

"Yeah." I glance away and he pulls his hand back.

"It's safe for you to go back home, if that's what you are worried about."

Ed had told me that the man he'd almost killed—Anton was his name—had given them more information on the men who were behind the attacks and my abduction. With Archer's help, they had tracked down the men as they had been about to board a flight to Sicily. The men had confessed to all the attacks on me, including kidnapping me then setting the building on fire before leaving. They said that they were only following instructions. Their goal had been to send a message to the Seven, to stop enquiring after the Mafia.

They should have known that everything they did would only strengthen the resolve of the Seven to go after whoever was behind the attacks.

In this case, the Seven had made the decision to hand the two men over to the police, along with the third man, who is still unconscious. While the Seven prefer to stay away from the cops on most occasion, this time, they felt it was the best way to put the men behind bars long enough for them to not be a threat to us anymore. Of course, Ed mentioned, they have a contact in the police force who helped them to put the men away with the least fuss possible.

Of course, they do. The Seven are nothing, if not powerful and resourceful. They take care of their own. Which is why I don't understand why they've decided to allow Baron this time away? I mean, aren't they concerned that he might be upset enough to do something that he shouldn't?

I turn to Edward. "I am not worried about my safety," I murmur, "I know you guys have dealt with my..." I swallow, "my attackers."

Yeah, it is still difficult to say that aloud. Given a choice, I'd prefer to forget about how they'd ambushed me, then broken into my studio, and ultimately, kidnapped me and left me, restrained, in a burning building. Thankfully, there are no other lasting injuries, though the last two nights I still haven't slept properly. Which is to be expected. It had been an emotionally traumatic experience. And this, despite the fact that I had been so sure that the guys would get to me.

I can only imagine how difficult it must have been for them after the incident. I had been kidnapped and held for a few hours. They had been kidnapped and held for closer to a month. The kind of scars they both carry... Are, clearly, so much more intense.

"Then what is it...?" he murmurs. "You can tell me, babe."

"It's..." I close my eyes, "It's nothing."

"It's something."

How can I tell him, that while I am happy to be with him, a part of me misses Baron? Somehow, I had not thought that he would leave. While I'd chosen Edward...technically... I hadn't realized that's what I was doing, and I hadn't completely comprehended that it meant losing Baron. Shit, why do I feel so...forlorn? Like I lost something vital, something I didn't know had ended, until it was gone.

"It's Baron, isn't it?" Edward blows out a breath, "You're thinking of him."

"No," I lie, "it's just...everything over the last few days has been so much to take in."

I sense him peruse my features and I turn my face away. If I meet his gaze now, he'll see exactly how little truth there is in what I am telling him.

I push open the car door and walk around to the curb. Edward steps out. His ankle is bandaged, and he has a cane to help him walk. It's just a sprain. The burns on his back are more serious and will require daily visits to the burn unit for debridement.

I tuck my handbag under my arm—a new handbag that Isla had gotten for me. She'd also helped with packing my clothes at Edward's house. Archer had packed up some of Edward's things and helped transfer everything to my place.

I'd asked him about Baron, but Archer had confessed that he didn't know where Baron was. He'd told me that he was moving Baron's things into storage. That's when I'd asked him for Baron's home address—and he'd revealed that Baron had left the city. Temporarily, at any rate.

Which is good. It's good that he's away, that there is no temptation to go check on him.

No, I have Edward. The man I had fallen in love with first. This…is everything I had hoped for. So, why am I not happier?

I reach for Edward's backpack and he scowls at me. "No woman's carrying my load."

"Of course, not," I mutter. "God forbid, you admit to actually needing someone's help."

"Eve," he scowls, "that's not what I mean."

"Hmm." I turn away, as he heaves his pack on his shoulder, then takes a step toward me.

"I know how you can help me," he says.

"Oh?"

"Yeah." He holds up his arm, points at the space next to him. "Come 'ere."

I notch myself under his arm, and he leans on me. I wrap my arm around his waist, take some of his weight. Gah, he's too heavy, but I am not going to say anything.

"Happy?"

I scowl up at him and he chuckles.

"Shall we go inside?"

35

Ava

It's been a week since Edward and I returned from the hospital, and things are going… Fine. Every morning, he cooks me breakfast, then I do my admin stuff for my studio, while Ed gets on calls with the rest of the Seven. He's been taking an active interest in 7A, the company that he owns with the rest of the Seven. The money he's made, up until leaving the Church, has all been in a trust that carries out charitable work, and he doesn't want to touch that. So, he's working on a separate 'starter portfolio' with the Seven that he can grow and invest. The gains will provide an income from which he is going to live. And when I say live, I mean he can live a very good lifestyle off the money he's set to make.

His sprain healed up quickly, and while I took the tube to work the first two days, from the third day onward, Edward has insisted on taking me. I can tell that leaning back against the car seat—any seat, really—causes discomfort, but he denies it.

Now that the men who attacked me are behind bars, at least, I've been able to regain some level of independence. I have told Ed he doesn't need to drive me, but he insists.

While I am in the studio, he heads off to the offices of 7A or makes calls, or sometimes, simply heads back home to work on his assets some more. He's always back in time to pick me up... And yeah, he has cameras stationed within my studio, so he can keep an eye on me. And yeah, also tracking devices in my phone—a new one that he bought for me.

We normally have dinner together, which he insists on cooking, and then, we sleep in my bed. He spoons me as I fall asleep and I am glad for his warmth. Still, most mornings I wake up on the opposite side of the bed from him. It's like he's giving me time and space to come to terms with the decision. And somehow, it's not helping.

I wish he were more demanding, more dominating, more the kind of Edward he was when he'd sauntered into my home and fucked me before taking off. Somehow, that Edward had been raw and hurting. He hadn't cared that he was going to upset me when he left... Or if he did...he hadn't shown it. And it had been honest and real and... Everything that I had been looking for. Now, he's the same man... So, why do I feel so unsettled about being with him?

Today, after the last student departs at the studio, I decide to stay a little longer. I text Edward to let him know that I need a little more time. Then I flip the music to one of my favorite pick-me-up dance songs. The beats of *Gasolina* by Daddy Yankee fill the space. It's reggaeton, not strictly belly dancing music. But told ya, I love to interpret belly dancing in my own style.

I shimmy my shoulders, lift one side of my hips, drop, swirl into a figure eight, then lift my arms, allow the beats to thrum over my skin, sink into my blood. I plunge headlong into the rhythm, the music already pounding at my temples. Lift and drop my hips...lift and drop, let the beats ripple down my spine, curve my torso, my hips, twirl on my toes, and again. Drag my fingers down my arms, turn, and crash into something hard. My heart hammers in my chest and my eyelids snap open. I meet Edward's amber gaze.

"Oh," I press my hand to my heart, "you scared me."

He grips my shoulder to right me. "Did I?" He peers into my face. "You didn't expect me to come in, did you?"

"N...no." I step back and he lowers his arm. "I won't be long, I just wanted to take some time to perfect a new routine."

"That's okay," his lips twitch, "I love watching you dance."

And there was a time when I'd loved having him watch me. I walk over to the panel in the wall and shut off the music. Silence descends. My breath still comes in pants from my earlier exertion. I reach for my towel, mop my forehead. "I really won't be much longer," I murmur.

I sense him move, hear his footsteps approach, and stiffen.

He bends, pressing a kiss to the curve of where my neck meets my shoulder. I freeze.

He takes my shoulders, urges me to turn around. I drag my feet, allow him to position me so I am facing him.

I stare at the tendons of his throat, the familiar square jaw, now set in uncompromising lines. He notches a knuckle under my chin, tilts it up. I raise my gaze, meeting his eyes, then glance away.

His chest rises and falls; he blows out a breath.

"It's not working, is it?" he asks, almost tenderly.

"What...what do you mean?" I swallow. My heart begins to race. Shit, shit, shit. And I thought I had disguised my emotions so well.

"Don't hide from me, Ava." His voice softens even further. And somehow, that makes it all so much worse. I wish he'd rage at me. That he'd throw a tantrum; that he'd demand that I give him my full attention, that I dance for him, strip for him, that I drop to my knees in front of him... But he does none of that. He wipes the tear that trails down my cheek, before urging me to glance up at him.

I raise my gaze reluctantly, gazing into those glowing golden eyes. Eyes that have seen so much. That see me now, for what I am. A woman in love with his best friend. The man I've missed since he walked away from me.

"It's okay," he says, "I understand."

"No, you don't..." I burst out. "How can you, when even I don't get what's wrong with me?" I pull away from him and begin to pace. "You are my first love, Edward. You swept into my life, you turned it upside down. It was so full-on, so everything, so much that I wanted and then—"

"I left."

I pivot to face him, take in the set lines of his features.

"I hurt you, Ava. I broke your heart. I was selfish... I'd like to think I wasn't but... Maybe it was all too much for me. Maybe I had been waiting for a sign, for something or someone to push me to take that step, to force me to face my demons... Maybe all of that came to the fore when I met you. I wanted you, Eve... I still do... But I lost you then. I came back and expected to take up from where I had left off."

"And that's what I wanted too," I blurt out. "You're everything I want, Ed."

"But I am not everything you need."

I frown, "What...what do you mean?"

"Look at you, Ava. You're not fully here. You haven't been since the fire. Since Baron left. You go through the motions of the day, but you barely pay attention to the food that you are eating. At night, you flinch when I wrap my arms around you. You wake up on the opposite side of the bed from me—" So, he had noticed?

"You've been going to the studio earlier and earlier, preferring to stay later."

Argh, have I been doing that? Have I become that much of a cliche?

"And even now, when you were dancing, you weren't really there, were you?"

I jerk my chin around and meet his gaze.

"You were miles away; you hadn't realized when I walked into the studio... You didn't even sense when I was in your personal space, Ava."

"Oh, Ed," my lip trembles and my eyes well, "this is such bullshit."

"It's love." His lips curve in a sad smile. "We don't choose who we fall in love with, when we fall, or how we fall... Indeed, sometimes we don't realize it until it's all but lost to us."

"Ed, no," I shake my head, "please don't do this."

"It's done." His throat moves as he swallows. "You are too good a person. You'd stay with me, just out of a sense of duty...of purpose, even, but you and I both know, your heart is elsewhere."

"Oh, Ed." A ball of emotion clogs my throat. "This...this isn't how I wanted it to be."

"It is, what it is, Ava." He raises his hand as if to touch my cheek, then lowers it to his side. "Know this. I want you to be happy, Ava. I wanted to make you happy. When you chose me, I had been thrilled and excited and flattered and... I'd wanted you. I'd wanted to make a life with you. I'd looked forward to spending the rest of my days with you. I'd wanted it all and returned here with you... Only, something had shifted."

I stare at him through tear-drenched eyes.

"Whenever I've tried to kiss you over the last few days, you've flinched."

"I... I have?"

He nods, "Even now, when I try to touch you—" He reaches for me and I lean away from him.

"See?"

I swallow, "It's...it's not intentional."

"Exactly." His lips twist. "Your body recognizes what your heart has been trying to communicate to you for days."

"Which is..."

"That you don't belong to me, Ava. Not anymore."

"Oh, Ed." I take a step forward and he holds up a hand.

"Don't feel badly, Ava. I am not going away completely empty-handed."

"You...aren't?"

He shakes his head. "It's thanks to you that I found a new lease on life. The Church was everything I needed at that stage in my life to stay sane, calm, and feel loved. You showed me I am still human, that I could feel that pull toward another person, someone who could calm me and help me feel normal. In a way, I transferred the dependence I had on the Church to you. But really, what you did was give me a starting point. You opened me up to other possibilities in life, to forgiving myself without the crutch of blind faith—not that faith isn't helpful, but blindly following isn't healthy—and that's where I was."

His gaze softens, "You taught me that it's possible to find that one person I could truly trust, help, and be helped by. You also made me realize that I can't replace one obsession with another. You've shown me that I need to find myself first."

"I have?"

He nods.

"If I don't discover who I truly am, how can I give myself up to another?"

"I think, you're giving me too much credit," I murmur.

"Or not enough." He tilts his head, "You were at the right place at the right time...for me. Call it serendipity or call it an act of God," he smiles, "but you showed me I could keep my faith in the Power Above, without having to bind myself to an institution to nurture it. You set me free to explore, to discover who I truly am, and for that, I will always be grateful."

"Oh, Edward," I fold my fingers together, "whenever you decide you are ready for a relationship, whoever it is you decide to be with, she is going to be a very lucky person."

"And you and Baron are lucky to have found each other. You have what so many of us will spend a lifetime looking for."

"Hopefully, you'll find her well before that."

He tilts his head, "If you or Baron, ever need anything...at any time..." He shakes his head as if to clear it, then turns and heads for the door.

When he reaches the exit, I call out, "Edward, stop."

He pauses, his big body almost filling the doorway.

"I... I did love you, Ed."

"I know," he says softly, "but you love him more."

36

"So... everybody says that nobody's normal and that everyone is different right? The definition of normal is conforming to the standard or the common type; usual; not abnormal; regular; natural. So, if everyone is different, then doesn't that make being different normal? And if being different is normal then everybody IS normal, but at the same time, they're different. So, in actual fact, everyone is normal BECAUSE they're different. Ugh...sooo confusing!"
From Ava's Diary

A month later

Ava

I ring the doorbell to Summer and Sinclair's townhouse on Primrose Hill. I'd barely managed to complete the practice session after my classes at the studio before I'd changed and raced over, for a get together with the rest of the girls.

I haven't seen Edward since he left my place a few weeks ago. And while I initially was upset about it, I realize now, he was right. It would have been wrong for both him and me, if we had stayed together—not when my heart is clearly dwelling on another. Since then, I had thrown myself into work and my studio is flourishing. Which, in turn, has given me the confidence to compete.

Yep, I had finally put aside my fears and am now practicing for the next World Belly Dancing Championships. Apparently, I am done hiding my talent from the world. This is my passion, this is what sets my heart on fire, so I am going to embrace it and share my talent with the world. I am going to do it for myself this time, and not because I am trying to prove anything...but because... I enjoy it, thrive on it, and I know I am good at it. Baron was right. I needed to have more faith in myself. Now, I do. I am gonna aim for the first prize. No half measures anymore for me.

The door opens and Summer stands there wearing a pink jumpsuit that declares: *Mommy To-Be.*

I glance at it, then at her face.

"Too obvious?" She quirks an eyebrow.

"No," I laugh, "it's you." I step forward and hug her. "You are glowing," I compliment her.

"So are you." She moves back, looks me up and down, "Yep, definitely glowing."

"Must be the sweat from practice." I chuckle. "I didn't have time to take a shower."

"We women glow, period." She grins back at me, "You can take a shower in the guest room, if you want."

"Oh, can I?" I cry gratefully. "That would be perfect."

"Come on," she pulls me inside, then glances over her shoulder at the hovering butler. "It's okay Jeeves," she waves at him, "I've got this."

He lurks there for a few more seconds, then half bows. "As you wish, Madam." He pivots and leaves.

"Is his name really Jeeves?" I whisper as she shuts the door behind me.

"No, but he answers to it." She giggles, "And he definitely looks like a Jeeves. I've yet to get Sinner to respond to any of my Bertie Wooster jokes though."

"Good luck with that." I frown. "I can't see the grouchy Sinclair Sterling laughing at anything."

"Oh, he laughs alright; he has a weird sense of humor."

"Only because you bring that out in him." I tilt my head at her.

"Yeah, guess that's the sign of a healthy relationship, right? I mean, I am sure Baron would laugh at—" her voice trails off. "Jeez, sorry," she blinks rapidly, "didn't mean to bring the B word into our conversation."

Yeah, well, I'd had a few very drunken nights with the girls over the past week where I had poured out my heart to them.

"It's okay," I murmur, "I can't hang around you and the Seven without mention of Baron, or Edward, for that matter."

"Hmm," she peers into my face, "so he hasn't contacted you at all?"

"Who?"

"You know who I am talking about." She leads me toward the flight of stairs.

"If you mean Baron, no, and I don't expect him too either."

"Hmm." She huffs again.

"What?" I scowl. "What is it?"

"Nothing."

"Tell me," I pause with my foot on the first step, "please, Summer."

"It's probably nothing, but Baron has been in touch with the Seven."

"He has?"

"He's taking an active interest in all of their investments, so he attends all of their calls."

"Oh." I swallow. "And how is he? I mean, has Sinclair mentioned anything—?

She reaches down and grips my shoulder, "He's apparently, okay, and back in London. He's staying at a service apartment that he's renting from Saint."

"A service apartment." I swallow, "You...uh, you don't happen to have the address, do you?

Her eyes twinkle. She whips out her phone from her pocket and fingers flies across the screen.

My phone dings and I pull it out, glance at the message she sent me. "Thanks, Summer."

"You're welcome." She nods toward the front door, "Go girl, what are you waiting for?'

37

Baron

I glance at the view outside the window of my penthouse apartment. The lights of London twinkle back at me, their cold, silvery haloes a reflection of my surroundings. Chrome and steel, blacks and browns. The colors and lack of textures is perfect for how I feel.

I raise the glass of whiskey, drain it. Then head back to the bar to top up my glass. At this rate, I am going to become an alcoholic, which is probably not a bad idea. Though, even the alcohol is not helping me of late. The thoughts in my head, the visions of Ava laughing, dancing, teasing me... The images overwhelm me. Truthfully, I haven't tried too hard to stop thinking of her. Why should I, when it is all I have left of our time together?

Sometimes I wonder if I imagined it all. Spending time with my best friend and my woman... It had been a special kind of heaven... and hell. Both, rolled into one. I had done the right thing...leaving her... So, maybe it had been cowardly. I hadn't been able to face her, to tell her that I was giving her up. Hell, I'd been worried that if I saw her face, I'd lose all reasoning, that I'd plead with her to walk away with me. And she didn't deserve that. She didn't need me putting her on the spot again.

I slide my hand inside the pocket of my pants. My fingers brush something. I pull it out, glare at the purple hairband. *Her* purple hairband that I've carried around with me, since the day I first met her outside her house. I bring it to my nose and sniff it. Instantly, the lingering scent of jasmine laced with raspberries fills my senses. My groin hardens, heat flushes my chest. Fuck. I'll never be rid of her. I'll never get of her... and she...? She loves Edward. I had seen the distress in her eyes, when she'd thought he was trapped inside the burning building. I'd seen the relief in her eyes when we had both staggered out. How she had run to him, and embraced him. And seeing them together had clarified everything for me. I'd done what was needed. I had taken care of her while Edward was away. And now... I need to get out of their way. They need to get on with their lives together... While me? I have to figure out how the hell I am going to live mine.

I stuff the hairtie back into my pocket.

One step in front of the other, soldier. Keep going. Don't stop. Tunnel vision. Focus on...what? Making money? Yeah, that's the one thing I'm good at. I may not have worked directly with the Seven the last few years, but I haven't lost my touch for keeping on top of my investments. Truthfully, work is the only thing that has managed to distract me. When I am applying my mind to mathematical equations...and tinkering with the algorithm that Saint and Sinner invented to forecast the movements of the stock market... For those few hours, at least, I have been able to push her to the back of my mind... Kind of...

Frankly, she is always on my mind. The scent of her is entrapped in my skin, the taste of her, a remembrance on my palate. The memories of her coil in my heart. And I guard them jealously. If this is all I have to hold onto... Then I'd be a fool to forget a single moment of the time I had with her.

I drain my glass, reach for the bottle again, when the intercom buzzes.

I walk over, depress the button and the porter's face appears. "I have a Ms. Ava Erikson here for you."

"Excuse me?"

"Ms. Ava—"

"Send her up."

I step back from the screen. What the—? What is Ava doing here? How had she found out where I'm staying? Probably, through one of the Seven... Or their wives. I shake my head. Why had Edward allowed her to come? Likely, he doesn't know. He hasn't been on the last few calls with the Seven either. I figured it's because he needs time to concentrate on his new relationship. I have tried hard not to be angry or jealous about it... And have failed. In a way, it's good that Ed hasn't been on the calls. Likely, I wouldn't have been able to disguise my bitterness. So, I had given her up. Doesn't mean I have to be gracious about my loss, does it?

So, what the hell is she doing here? I head back to the bar, topping up my glass.

Behind me, I hear the elevator doors part. I hear the click of her heels against the marbled floors. Is she wearing the same purple tipped boots that I had seen her in so often? The scent of jasmine invades the air, and the blood rushes to my groin. Fuck. I haven't even seen her, and already, my body is betraying me. I cannot think of her in this fashion, cannot allow her to play havoc with what little bit of restraint I have managed to hold onto.

"What are you doing here?" I growl.

She doesn't answer, but the scent of jasmine intensifies. Her footsteps approach. I raise my glass to my lips, and damn it, my hand trembles. It actually trembles.

"Answer, the question," I snap.

"No, you answer mine first." Her voice cuts through the space.

I turn, look her up and down. "Making demands, are we?"

"Not in a good mood, are we?"

"I was, until you came through the door."

Her lips tighten. "Still the same old alphahole, I see."

"Leopard. Spots, and all that," I drawl. "Why did you come here, Ava?"

She glances around the space, then back at me, "Uh, nice place."

"It's cold and boring." *Everything you are not.* "Next?"

She locks her fingers together in front of her body. "Ah, can I get a glass of water?"

I hesitate and she frowns, "Come on. Surely, even you can extend that much hospitality to me?"

"Not." I growl, "But what-fucking-ever." I head behind the bar, pour a glass of water and hand it to her. Keeping the barrier of the bar between us is cowardly, I know...but it's best this way. If I stand next to her, I won't be able to keep my hands to myself.

She drains the water, places the glass back on the counter.

"Well?" I glance at my watch, "Better make it quick. I have a date."

"No, you don't."

I arch an eyebrow, "And you know that, how?"

"Because you love me."

Shit. I feign a yawn. "There you go, deluding yourself. If I loved you, I wouldn't have left you."

"It's because you love me that you left me."

I smirk. "This isn't one of your sweet romances."

"I only read erotic romances. The ones in which the villain is also the hero."

"Neither of which I am." I place my elbow on the counter. "I don't play any part in your story, babe."

She pales. "I don't believe you."

"Better believe it."

"You still love me."

"And you love Edward."

"I love you more."

"And you arrived at that brilliant piece of deduction, how?"

"Sometimes it takes absence and time to put things in perspective. After you left... I missed you. Nothing was the same. I was with Edward but..." she swallows, "all I could think about was you. I realized that you are the one I want. You are the one I need. You are the person I want to be with, Baron."

Something hot stabs at my chest. I fold my fingers into fists, glare at her as she shuffles her feet.

"Edward and I are no longer together." She lowers her chin and folds her fingers together in front of her. "It's been a month since we decided to break up."

"A month?"

She nods. "I wanted to give myself enough time to make sure that I knew exactly what I had to do next."

"I know what you need to do next." I jerk my chin toward the door and her gaze widens. "You should leave."

"No."

"You need to get out of here, Ava."

She shakes her head, "I know you're upset Baron—"

"Upset?" I laugh, "That's putting it mildly. You made up your mind; I've made peace with it. I am ready to move on—"

"No, you're not."

"Oh?"

"If you were, you wouldn't be glaring at me like you'd like to spank me and kiss me simultaneously."

My cock twitches; my groin hardens. The thought of marking that sweet curved backside of hers, right before I turn her over and bury my face in her melting core—I stiffen, and no, I don't mean only my dick. I square my shoulders, crack my neck. "Nice dialogue—" I drawl, "but it's too late."

"It's not."

"It's time you took that sweet tush of yours out of here."

"Not yet." She places her bag on the counter, pulls out her phone and places it face-up. Then swipes across the screen. She pulls up a playlist.

"What are you doing?"

"Something I should have done a long time ago."

She digs in her bag, pulls out her hip scarf and ties it around her hips. The material clings to her luscious curves, emphasizes the tiny span of her waist. She takes a few steps back into the center of her room, and juts out a hip. She places a hand on it, then tips her chin up, "Can you press play, please?"

38

Ava

His blue eyes glower as he eats me up with his gaze. The skin around his eyes tightens and his lips thin.

"Please," I urge him. "Please hit play."

"No," he snaps, and I draw in a breath. *Fine, I can do without the music.*

I bend my knee to drop the hip. The tiny coins at the edge of the hip scarf jingle. I straighten the knee to lift the hip, keep my knees soft and centered. Drop hip downward, then flow into a heavy deep-seated drop. Every tiny move is amplified by the sound of the coins rubbing against each other.

His chest rises and falls. He leans forward, his gaze captured. He watches my every step as I rise up and into a lighter half-drop. I trace a circle with my hip, out to the side, then back, then pull into my center.

I keep circling, keep an open connection between my hip and

heart, drawing energy in my movement. Keep everything supple and flowing, allow the energy to flow around my body.

I sense him walk around to stand in front of the bar. Good. He's caught in the energy, the rush of the performance. As am I.

I lift my hip upward and slightly forward, activate the outside of my thigh and hip to give the movement oomph. Drop slightly, then lift.

He takes a step closer, leans forward on the balls of his feet.

I bring my shoulders up together, then let both go. Another fast shoulder drop, while swaying my body from side-to-side. I ground my feet and shift my weight to the side, push my hips back, then round to the other side.

I peek up at him from under my eyelashes, and flinch. The coldness in his arctic eyes—it's freezing. His gaze intensifies. I hold the connection, refuse to look away as I move into a figure eight. I twist my hip forward, shift the weight onto the front of the foot, then turn the foot and the hip inward.

He swallows, clenching his hands into fists.

I twist my hips inward, then out again. I lift and drop, lift and drop again. Shimmy shoulders, undulate my waist, as I flow into a figure eight, this time in the vertical direction. Keeping my movements fluid, I channel the energy from my belly. Again. And again.

Sweat beads his forehead. The skin around his lips whitens. I twirl my fingers, beckon to him, and he takes a step forward, and another. I reel him in and he closes the distance between us. He glares down at me as I hold up both of my arms, lean my torso forward. My breasts brush his chest and he hisses.

"I need you, Baron." I tip my chin up, and his lips firm.

"You're stretching my patience." His jaw tics and a nerve throbs at his temple. His blue eyes deepen into that almost cerulean color that takes my breath away.

"Fuck," he growls. "F-u-c-k."

"Yes, please." I widen my legs, shimmy down his length in a wide plié squat. I lower my butt until I almost touch the floor. Then gaze up at him from under my eyelashes. His glare intensifies and his chest heaves. The blue in his eyes is stormy, tortured, tormented.

Tension rolls off of him; the force of his dominance pins me in place, and I stay there, poised. A beat, then another. My throat dries, my thigh muscles protest, but still, I don't move.

The band around my chest tightens, my leg muscles scream at me to move. I begin to straighten and he clicks his tongue. "Don't even think about it," he growls.

I freeze, tip up my chin, and hold his gaze.

"Did you mean what you said?" he finally asks.

"A...bout?"

"About making up your mind?"

I nod.

"Are you sure this is what you want?"

I jerk my chin.

"Are you convinced that you belong to me?"

Yes. Yes. Yes. I tip up my chin, meet his gaze. Allow him to read the expression on my face. "

His throat moves as he swallows. Then his jaw firms. "If we do this, if I fuck you now, there is no going back."

I don't take my gaze off of his face.

"If I take you now, I am never letting you get away."

My scalp tingles, my fingers tremble, and a pressure builds at the back of my eyes.

"If we are together, Ava, I'll ask everything of you. I'll strip you bare, I'll infiltrate your deepest desires, your most secret dreams, the most intimate of your places. Nothing about you will be off limits. Not your thoughts or your words, not your body or your mind... Certainly not, your soul. I'll imprint myself in every cell of your body... Your every breath will belong to me."

My toes curl, my belly trembles, and moisture pools between my legs.

"The flutter of your eyelashes as you fall asleep, your dreams, the first thing you see when you wake up in the morning... All of it will be mine. I'll be in everything you see, in every taste you draw into your body. Every sensation that filters to you will originate from me... Do you...understand what I mean?"

I draw in a harsh breath. The band around my chest tightens. My skin feels too tight for my body. This man, these words... They are etched in every particle of my being.

"Do. You. Understand?" he snaps.

I jerk my chin. My legs threaten to give way from under me, and I push my heels into the ground to hold steady.

"Say it, then," he growls. "Say you are mine."

"Yours." I swallow. "I am yours."

"That you get that there's no going back.

"No going back."

"That you belong to me."

"You." I nod.

"That—"

"I love you," I burst out. "You, Baron, only you."

His breath catches. His gaze bores into me. The emotions rolling off of him vibrate between us, thicken and swirl. Heat spools off of his body, slams into my chest. I gasp, trying to draw in a breath, and my lungs burn. The strength of his intention lassoes around my shoulders, ties me to him. Then he moves. He dips his knees, swoops down and grabs me between my legs. He straightens, hauls me up with him, by my pussy, and my entire body jerks.

"Last chance, Ava," he cautions. "Leave while you can."

"I... I can't." I lick my lips and his gaze darts to my mouth.

"If you stay, I am not letting you go, not until I have fucked the thought of any other man out of you."

Heat flares low in my belly. My core clenches, and he must feel the instinctive reaction, for his lips curl.

"So, you in or out? Eve?"

Oh, my god. My nipples pebble, my breasts ache, and all of my brain cells seem to combust. "In," I rasp, "I'm in."

"Good." He releases me so suddenly that I lose my balance and wobble. He steps back and the warmth of his body recedes. A shiver runs up my spine.

"Take off your clothes," he growls.

I hesitate and he arches an eyebrow.

"Now." He lowers his voice to a hush and my nerve endings spark.

"Do it." He leans forward.

I spring into action. I untie the hip scarf. It pools around my feet, and the coins jingle. I toe off my boots, kick them away with the scarf. The clinking rises then fades away. I lift the skirt of my dress, grab my stockings and begin to roll them down. I pull them off, hold them up, and let them slide through my fingers. They flutter to the ground, and neither of us glances that way.

"All of it," he grates out. "Take. It. All. Off."

My mouth dries. Not that I haven't been naked in front of him before, but this...feels different. Like it's the first time that he'll be seeing all of me. Nude and vulnerable and completely bared for his inspection.

I undo the top button on the front of my dress, then the one after it, and the next. Push one sleeve down, then the other side. I tuck my elbows close to my sides and the dress flutters to the ground. I step out of it, then shrug off the camisole I am wearing as well.

I stand in front of him, clad only in my purple bra and panties.

He looks me up and down, "You know what they say about purple, right?"

"N...no," I stutter.

"It's a sign that you haven't been fucked enough, something I need to rectify...soon."

He smirks, and goosebumps pop on my skin.

Shit, all this build up. It's doing me in. The cool air in the room brushes over me and my nipples pebble. Or maybe it has to do with how he's staring at me, like he's going to eat me up. Oh, how I do hope he does.

He raises his gaze from my chest to my face. "Off with it," he growls.

A giggle bubbles up and he frowns.

"What?"

"That was a very imperious command."

His glare intensifies. His shoulders flex. "If you need help taking the rest of your clothes off—" he leans forward, and I hastily reach back and around for the clasp of my bra. I undo it, shrug it off. Reach for my panties, roll them down and step out of them. I stand before him without a shred of clothing. Without a shred of armor. He takes his time perusing my form—from my eyes, to my lips, my breasts, my stomach, the flesh between my thighs, to my feet. By the time he raises his gaze to my face, every part of me feels like it's on fire. My nipples are so hard, they are twin points of pain. My belly trembles and my core feels too moist. I squeeze my thighs together and he shakes his head. "Not yet. You don't have any right to relief. Not until I give you permission."

Oh, hell. I gulp, "This is going to be a long...long night."

"You have no idea." His lips twist. He makes a circle in the air with his fingers. I frown and he lowers his chin. "I can help you...if you want." He closes the distance between us and I instantly pivot, turn my back on him. Heat from his big body flows over me, cocooning me. The contrast between that and the cooler air on my front makes me shiver.

His breath sears the shell of my ear as he whispers, "Bend down; grab your ankles."

"Wh...what?"

"Don't make me repeat myself."

He places his palm at the small of my back, urging me to do his bidding. I widen my stance, lean over and grab my ankles. I glance between my parted legs as he sinks to his knees.

"What the—?"

He slides his tongue up my exposed slit from the entrance of my pussy to my backhole.

"Oh, hell." I gasp, "Oh, my, bloody hell."

"Indeed." I sense his lips curve against my tender flesh. He thrusts his tongue inside my cunt and my thighs tremble. I would fall, except he grabs my hips, holding me in place. He thrusts his broad shoulders in between my legs, forcing me to slide them apart further.

He thrusts his tongue in and out of me, in and out. Bringing his hands up to grip my inner thighs, he pries them apart, pulls his tongue out of my pussy, only to bite down on my swollen clit. I scream. The climax screeches up my legs and that's when he releases his hold on my cunt. He straightens, and my orgasm retreats. I blink. What the hell? What's that all about?

He bends forward, winds his fingers around the nape of my neck, urges me to unbend, stand straight. He pinches my chin so I turn to glance at him, and he licks my lips. He brushes his mouth across mine and the taste of him, laced with my essence, sinks into my palate.

"You fucking taste of honey, you know that?" He groans into my mouth and my heart hammers in my chest. "You're so damn irresistible. Once I let you in, I'll never be able to get you out of my head." He stills, "Who am I kidding?" He murmurs as if he's talking to himself, "You're already imprinted on my heart, Eve, and I don't know what to do about it."

I swallow.

"When I thought that I'd lost you, I swore that I'd never let anyone this close to me again. Why should I trust you again, Eve? Why?" He stares into my eyes, "Tell me what stops you from leaving me again?"

"I... I won't," I promise.

He holds my gaze and somehow, something in his eyes tells me he doesn't believe me completely yet.

"How can I prove it to you?" I murmur. "Tell me what I should do, to show you how much you mean to me."

"You won't be able to do it."

"Try me."

"You're sure?" His eyes gleam.

I nod.

"Move in with me."

"O...kay."

"Marry me."

"What?" I blink. "What did you say?"

"Marry me, Ava."

39

Ava

"Is that a proposal?"

"If that's what you want it to be."

I stare at him. "You sure are romantic." I strive for a light tone, but my voice comes out all breathless.

The expression on his face doesn't change. He holds my gaze, "Well?" He tilts his head, "What do you say?"

"Okay." I blow out a breath,

"Is that a yes?"

"It's..." I swallow, "It's a yes."

"Good." He releases the nape of my neck, steps up and around me. "Come." He jerks his head.

"Wh...where?"

"I'll show you to your room."

Right. I bend to pick up the clothes I had kicked aside earlier, then grab my bag from the counter and trail behind him. He leads me down the short corridor and pauses at the first room on the right. He pushes the door open, gestures for me to enter. I walk in, take in the double bed, the nightstand, the walk-in closet in the corner, the dresser pushed up against one wall, a writing table and chair on the other side. My feet sink into the thick carpet, and I wriggle my toes. "It's nice," I say.

"It'll do."

He retreats to the exit and I stop him, "Wait."

He turns to glance at me.

"Where...where are you sleeping?"

"My room is across the hallway."

"So...uh, we're not sleeping together?"

"When you're in my bed, you won't be doing much of that."

Oh, my god. He sure has a way with words. And that's not the only thing he knows his way around. My breasts feel too heavy, my scalp tingles, and moisture beads between my legs. His nostril's flare and his eyes gleam. Damn it, he knows exactly what his words do to me.

"So...we are going to have separate bedrooms?"

"Only until the wedding." He turns to leave and I take a step forward.

"But why?" I blurt out. "Why this distance?"

He pauses, then continues toward the door.

"Is it because you want to punish me for not coming to you sooner?"

He doesn't say anything, but the set of his shoulders, the way he holds himself so erect that his spine is totally upright gives him away.

"Just so you know," I lower my hands to my sides, and my stuff falls to the floor, "I am not going anywhere."

He stares straight ahead.

"Also, it's really not fair that you judge me this harshly. You were there, Baron. You saw how conflicted I was between the two of you. It was difficult for me to untangle what I felt for each of you."

He holds up a hand, and I firm my lips. Damn him. Only Baron can have this effect on me. His one gesture, and I want to follow his lead. His one look, and I want to throw myself at his feet and ask him to take me. His one touch, and I am ready to debase myself to please him. This...this is what I missed. The surety of his demeanor. The way he can be hard toward me and yet gentle, at the same time.

There is a poetry to his actions... A certain push-pull at play that always keeps me on the edge. It makes me want to hit him, then kiss him again. The way he constantly challenges me, forces me to become a better version of myself. And the fact that he loved me enough to walk away from me...? It's what clarified everything for me.

Not that Edward wouldn't have made me happy. He'd have loved me and protected me. Hell, he took a bullet for me, for hell's sake... But Baron wanted my happiness enough to turn his back on me. He thought that I deserved to be with the man I had confessed to love. He still thinks that I don't love him enough.

But he's wrong. He'd been there for me when I'd needed someone the most. Second to losing my mother, the time I had been away from him were the worst days of my life... Especially because I hadn't been able to put a name to the emptiness, the desperate sensations that had eaten away at me from the inside. It had taken me a while to figure out what it was. Luckily, Edward had loved me enough to point me in the right direction. As soon as I had sorted out everything in my head, I had come to him.

And I am not leaving. Not now. Not ever. This is it for me. But how do I convince him?

He takes another step toward the door and I call out again, "Wait, if I am moving in here, then what about my stuff?"

"We can go get it tomorrow."

"And my classes, my studio?"

He turns so I can see his face in profile, "None of that needs to change. I want you for my wife, not my captive."

He faces forward, and I call out. "Wait..."

He glances over his shoulder.

"I... I need a T-shirt or something to change into for bed."

He looks me up and down, "You can survive for one night. I'll arrange to have your things delivered tomorrow."

This time when he leaves the room, I don't try to stop him.

I glance around the room, then back at the door. Shit, shit, shit. So that's it? We live under the same roof, have our own rooms, then we get married and what? He fucks me?

I chose to come to him…and he what? Holds me at arm's length? This is not the kind of welcome I foresaw. When he'd asked me to bend over, I'd been sure he'd fuck me… Instead…he'd aroused me, brought me to the edge of an orgasm, and then he'd pulled away. Bastard. What the hell is he trying to do here?

I pick up my bag, place it on the nightstand, and drape my clothes over the chair. I grab a quick shower then slip into my panties and camisole, before sliding under the covers with my phone. I dial Isla. Her phone rings, then she picks up the call. Her face appears on the screen.

"Hellooo," she sing-songs. I hear voices in the background, see lights, a blur of people…

"Sorry, are you busy?"

"Not for you, babe." She steps out of the room; a door closes behind her and the sounds fade.

"Where are you?"

"Out with a bride who needed a shoulder to cry on."

"You mean…" I lower my chin

"Yeah," she blows out a breath, "the bride of the man who shall not be named." Her lips firm. "Except for the one wedding rehearsal, asshole didn't turn up for any of the tastings or for any of the other meetings. It's like he really doesn't care. I really feel sorry for the bride…so…"

"So…you're hanging out with her?"

"So?"

"So, you broke your rule about not socializing with the clients."

"She was just sooo sad." Isla grimaces, "When she asked me out for a drink, I couldn't refuse."

"Or maybe, you wanted to get more info on Li—"

She frowns.

"I mean, the man who shall not be named."

"Of course, not." She purses her lips. "Not really. I mean, I did lend a sympathetic ear to her as she poured out the details of their relationship, which is beyond dysfunctional, but really, I was just doing my job."

"Hmm," I scowl, "if you say so."

"And we are not here to talk about me." She raises an eyebrow. "What's up? Everything okay with you and Baron?"

"Wait, what?" I blink, "How did you know about...?"

"Why else would you be calling me?

"You mean, I only call you when I need a sounding board?"

She smirks.

"Iz..." I scowl.

"Not that I mind. I mean, your life is far more interesting than mine right now."

"Trust me, I'd trade mine for something tame and boring..." I mutter.

Her gaze narrows, and I rush to add, "Not that I could ever accuse you of that. Not now that what's-his-face is occupying so much of your time."

She glowers and I motion zipping my mouth, "Okay, won't go there."

"So... Baron?"

I deflate a little. "I am at his place."

"Finally." She blows out a breath, "I mean, honestly woman, what took you so long?"

"I just needed some time to cleanse my palate."

She stares at me and I point a finger at the screen. "I didn't mean it that way."

"Then how did you mean it?"

"Just that I needed a little bit of space from both of them... Enough to sort out my thoughts." I raise a shoulder, "I mean, I admit I surprised myself when I realized it wasn't Edward but...Baron that I want... But uh, I may have needed a little bit of time to get my courage up to face him, you know?"

"And?"

"And what?"

"You're in his house, but you're not with him...so?"

I narrow my gaze, "Jesus, woman, give me a chance to tell my story."

"Go on..." she says impatiently, "why the hell isn't he ravishing you as we speak?"

My cheeks pink. "Uh, I thought that's what he was going to do."

"And then?"

"Then he pulled away."

"Like, literally pulled away?"

My cheeks heat, "He, uh, asked me to marry him."

"He what...?" She opens and shuts her mouth.

"Yeah." I bite the inside of my cheek. "It surprised me too. As much as him putting me in another room and telling me that he isn't going to sleep with me until after the wedding."

"And you agreed?"

I raise my shoulders, "Umm...yeah?"

"So, you are going to, once more, toe the line."

"Uh, not sure he gave me a choice."

"So, first he...comes onto you physically, only to retreat and ask you to marry him. Then he puts you up in his guest room."

I nod.

She taps her cheek, "Seems to me, your alphahole is insecure."

"Well, that's an oxymoron. Alphaholes don't get insecure... But," I hunch my shoulders, "I have to concede, you may be right, in this case. He did ask me if I was going to change my mind again."

"How dare he?" She grimaces, "I mean, it's a valid question. But seriously, how could he question your intent?"

"Yeah," I nod, "I mean, I am here; I am not going anywhere. This is where I want to be. With him. And I told him so, and I thought he believed it, but—"

"He's having trouble accepting it."

I nod.

"His mind gets it, but it hasn't quite sunk in."

"Exactly."

"So, you know what you have to do, right?"

"What?"

"Come on, Ava, do I have to tell you everything?"

"Gah." I sit up in bed, clutching the sheets under my arms "Can you please tell me what you're thinking?"

Her eyes twinkle. "If he doesn't come to you, you'll have to go to him, Ava."

40

Baron

I lower my whiskey glass, as I stare at the screen of my computer. What the hell had come over me? When she'd walked in... When I had seen her, it was like I could finally breathe. All that time away from her, I'd thought I was alive. I was so wrong. How could I be, when my heart no longer belongs to me? She'd walked into my apartment and I couldn't believe that she was really here.

At the same time, I knew... I know it's right. That she belongs with me. Has been mine from the moment I laid eyes on her. I'd known it, and yet, I'd walked away. I'd thought, he deserves her. After everything he's done for me, I'd thought I owed him this much... I owed him a chance at happiness. So, I'd left... And she'd come to me.

And I'd wanted to throw her down and tear into her pussy. I'd wanted to bury myself in her tight little cunt; I'd wanted to cram myself in her arse, and fill her mouth with my cum. I'd wanted to paint every inch of her body with the evidence of my arousal, my ownership. I'd wanted to lick her up and bite down on the sensitive skin between her legs. I'd wanted to mark her creamy thighs, redden her bottom with my handprints. I'd wanted to... Fill every hole in her body and show her who she belongs to. Hell, I wanted to put my ring on her finger and mark her as mine for the world to see.

So yeah... I'd run with it. I'd asked her to marry me... Until that very moment, I hadn't realized how much I wanted her to be mine, in every sense of the word.

Which is all good; but the distance? Putting her in another room while I stay in mine... Shit, what was I thinking?

I'd checked in on her earlier, to find that she was sleeping. She seemed to be naked. Her clothes were dumped on the chair by the desk, the soldier in me had cringed. I'd walked over and folded her clothes, then sat there next to the bed. I'd watched her sleep. Like that's not creepy or anything. I was simply making sure that she was okay. She'd slept deeply, her cheeks pink, her lips slightly parted. Her auburn hair was in a cloud around her face. She'd looked innocent and at peace, and I'd wanted to cover her body with mine and bury myself inside of her...

That's when I'd gotten up and left. I'd ended up in the third room, which is my temporary office. I'd gone over my investments, put in calls to Asia and the US. That's the benefit of running a portfolio with global interests. There's always someone, somewhere in the world who is working.

As I wrap up my last call, my phone rings again. Damian's picture—or to be more specific, that of him and his pregnant wife Julia—shows up. I stare at it, take in their laughing faces. Will I ever have that? Do I want that? Can I have that with Ava, given everything we've been through?

I answer the call and Damian's face fills the screen. "Hey, motherfucker." He smirks.

I groan, "Now I know why I stayed away from you guys for so long."

"And we're going to make up for it with a vengeance."

"We?" I frown, "What do you—?"

Another face appears on the screen. Sinner; it's bloody Sinner.

Then Saint, and Arpad, and Weston. I grip my phone, am about to chuck it aside, when Sinner warns, "You want to hear what we have to say, asshole."

"Do I?" I growl.

"Stop being a bastard," Saint barks, "and listen to what we have to say."

"Look who's talking." I roll my shoulders. "The biggest bastard of them all."

"At least, I know who I am," he mutters.

"What's that supposed to mean?"

"Exactly what I said." He smirks. "I've never shied away from what I am. I wear my proclivities on my sleeve."

"That wife of yours needs to have her head examined for staying with you," I snipe.

Saint's features freeze, and for a second, I am sure he's going to explode. Probably drive over and bash my face in, which I deserve, considering I had broken the only rule... One I had repeatedly violated during my interactions with them since I'd returned... Wives and significant others, including kids, are off the table when we speak to each other. Specifically, when we insult each other. I had just broken the rule again... So, what's new?

The rest of the Seven threaten...and posture, but with the exception of Edward, they all conform, one way or the other. It's only me and Ed who'd tried to forge a different path to cope with the aftermath of the incident. We were hurt the most and we'd lashed out at life... At ourselves. Then at each other. And look where that has gotten us. In a mess I am still trying to make sense of.

"Apologize." Saint's features are hard. "You're not yourself, so I understand why you said something you didn't mean. Say you're sorry, you piece of shit."

I stare at Saint. *Whoa? What? No raging and tearing things up? No threats of punishments...? He isn't coming over to physically beat the shit out of me? Something which I had actually been looking forward to, if I am being honest.* Nothing like being able to use my fists, to be able to let off steam. Of course, I could walk in next door and fuck my woman... I shake my head. Not yet. She isn't mine yet. *She came to you, remember?*

She wants you. This time, she chose you... But hell, if a part of me inside, still can't believe it.

Just like I can't believe Saint—motherfucking—Caldwell is ready to forgive me for my error of judgment.

"I'm sorry," I say through gritted teeth. "You're right; I didn't mean it."

"You're angry." He nods, "It's understandable."

"I apologized, didn't I?" I growl. "You don't have to pretend to get what I am going through."

"Oh, but we do," Weston says, his voice soft. "If we, the alpha-holes who've been brought to our knees by the right women, don't get what you're going through, then who can?"

"That why you called me up at—" I glance at my watch, "four in the morning?" I smirk. "Thought you guys had your families and stuff to take care of."

"That's what we are doing." Damian's smile widens.

"What?" I frown.

"Taking care of family, you turd," Saint growls.

"I...ah..." My throat closes and a pressure builds behind my eyes. "The hell are you guys trying to say?"

"Want us to spell it out?" Sinner sighs, "Fine, you are our family, you tosser. We are each other's family. We have been since the incident and you know it, and you have been fighting it."

"No, I have not." I scowl.

"Yes, you have." Saint nods. "Edward was the stubborn one, but you were the sensitive one."

"Sensitive?" I laugh, "You guys been drinking...? Oh, wait," I pretend to think, "you guys don't do that anymore, now that you are the responsible ones."

"Nice try," Arpad smirks, "but you can't distract us."

"None of us realized how much you had been hurt," Weston picks up the narrative. "If we had any indication just how much you and Edward had been impacted..."

"It's done; it's behind us," I say through gritted teeth.

"Is it?" Weston, tilts his head. "Edward managed it by joining the priesthood, and it was there for him when he needed it most.

However, he eventually realized just how much of a crutch it was, and opted out. He's still trying to find his mooring, and that's okay. He's already started on the journey. But you?" He shakes his head, "You have your destination in front of you, but refuse to recognize it."

"If this is about Ava—"

"Of course, it is about Ava, you toff," Sinner growls. "We know that she left Edward."

"And that she came to you last night," Damian murmurs.

I glare at them. Not a surprise that they know she's here. Much as I'd like to deny it, the Seven of us are up in each other's business. Put the wives and girlfriends into the mix, and well... You have communication pinging back and forth faster than a ball at a Wimbledon tennis match. Ava must have, no doubt, spoken to one of the women, and that would have alerted the entire network to what's happening.

"Remember what you said earlier, Saint, about not talking about the women?" I remind them.

"This is different." Saint glares at me, "We're talking about *you*, and your completely asinine attitude in refusing to accept what's right for you."

"And you guys know that, how?"

"Experience." Sinner blows out a breath, "Like we've said, been here, done that. And we're not allowing you to fuck up your life... No more than it is right now."

"Not sure you guys get a say in that," I mutter

"Might be a little too late for that, ol' chap." Arpad chortles.

"What do you—?" The intercom app on my phone buzzes. I'd switched off the connections in the rooms so it wouldn't disturb Ava. "Hold on."

I switch out of the call and place the phone to my ear, "Yes?"

"A Mr. Chase to see you, sir."

"Chase." I frown.

"Should I—?"

"Send him up." I switch back into the call to find the rest of them waiting.

"Well," Damian asks, "is it him?"

"Who?"

"Cut the crap. You two finally going to bury your differences, or what?" Saint growls.

"You guys behind this?" I mutter.

The guys stay silent. I take in their faces and blow out a breath. "The fuck, you think you're doing?" I growl. "What the fuck is wrong with you? If you think this is going to help, you are so wrong."

"Hold on," Sinner's glare intensifies, "we were only trying to—"

I switch out of the call and raise my phone, intent on throwing it, then stop. Fuck. That would only wake up Ava, and that's the last thing I want." I place the phone on the table, then get up and head out of the study. Making sure Ava's door is firmly shut, I head for the living room, just as the elevator dings. It opens and Edward steps out.

41

Edward

When the guys had called me earlier, I had been pissed. But then they'd reminded me, again, how I'd intervened when each of them had been at a critical juncture in their lives. What I didn't tell them was that I had been a different person then. Someone who had literally divorced myself from what was going on inside of me. Someone who was focused on others, on the betterment of my flock. In their happiness lay mine. Which, honestly, wasn't a bad space to be in. Only, it had meant that I had locked away every damn feeling of my own. I had turned away from myself, had turned my back on my emotions, on the guilt and recriminations I had carried inside for so long. I hadn't been able to save him... Hadn't been able to save myself.

Until she had come along. A bright light at the end of a period of soul-searching darkness. Ava had been the catalyst, and I had been ready to break my vows. It was as simple as that. And I had loved her, truly… And it was that part of me which had known that she would be happier with Baron.

The guys had asked me to bury my differences with Baron. The truth is, there's nothing to forgive. So why hadn't I joined their conference calls? Why hadn't I been able to face Baron before this? Honestly, I don't have an answer to that. Now, as I step out of the elevator and take in the unsmiling countenance of the man who glares at me, I know he's hurting. As much as me.

I walk toward him, and he doesn't move. I pause in front of him, hold out my hand.

"Friends?" I murmur. "You ready to be friends?"

He glares at my proffered hand then back at my face, "What are you, ten?" He pivots around, heads to the bar, and pours out whiskey in two tumblers.

Well, at least, he hadn't asked me to leave. Though that's not Baron's style. I'm the one more liable to lose my temper nowadays. Breaking free of the discipline of priesthood has, apparently, unleashed an entire range of emotions in me, many of them unused for decades. Is that good or bad? The jury's out on that.

I stalk over to the bar, pick up the tumbler from the counter. "Ava?" I murmur.

"She's asleep."

I raise the glass to my mouth, and toss back the alcohol. Baron does the same. He fills up both of our glasses, then contemplates his own tumbler.

"What are you doing here, Ed?" he asks.

"I had to see you."

"What for?" he growls. "We've said everything there is to be said."

"Have we?" I peruse his brooding features, "We've never spoken about the incident."

"There's nothing to speak about." He begins to prowl about the space. Walks around, restless, before he comes to stop by the window. "There's nothing more to it."

"There's everything to it." I tilt my head, "We need to address what happened that day. We couldn't face it afterwards. Both of us agreed we'd never tell a soul what actually transpired that day..."

"And we haven't." He glances over his shoulder. "It's gone, buried, forgotten."

"But it isn't, is it?" I place my glass on the counter with a thump. "It's festering away within each of us. It's eating us inside. We didn't confide in our families, not our therapists, not even in the Seven. Hell, we haven't spoken about it to each other since."

"So?" He shrugs, "Neither of us turned out the worse for it."

"We could have put ourselves out of our misery a long time ago, if we had acknowledged how much it had scarred both of us. It's no joke when two young boys have to bugger—"

"Stop." He pivots so fast that some of the liquid sloshes over the side of his glass, "Shut the fuck up, Priest."

"Yeah," I glance at him thoughtfully, "I left the priesthood, and the rest of you seem to have adopted that nickname so naturally. Apparently, you can try to leave your past behind, but it always tags along somehow, know what I mean?"

"Go preach somewhere else," he growls, "I am not in the mood."

"Well, too bad." I stalk forward and he stiffens.

"The fuck you up to, Ed?"

"Just trying to put things right."

"There's nothing to righten," he snaps

"There's only everything to lose if I don't."

"Fuck off," he snarls, "don't come the fuck closer, man."

"Oh, yeah, what are you going to do if I do?"

He bares his teeth, "You wanna fight? Is that it, asshole?" He tosses back the rest of his drink, then flings his glass aside. It hits the floor and shatters. He throws up his fists, jumps forward as I rush him.

We meet somewhere in the middle. I bury my fist in his shoulder, but the asshole gets one in, right in my injured side. Fucking bullet injury—it hasn't healed completely. Pain slices through my head. I shake to clear it. Punch him in the stomach. He staggers back, only to straighten and lunge at me. He head butts me and the breath leaves my lungs. He gets in another punch to my solar plexus. I reel from it, then lob one at his side. His chest heaves, he lurches back, then throws himself at me. I take his full weight, and the bastard's fucking heavy. I sidestep the shards of glass on the floor but my feet slip on the drink he'd spilled earlier.

I crash to the ground, him on top of me. It's like a brick wall has collapsed on me. My lungs burn, my side screams, and my shoulder hurts like a bitch. I shove him to the side and away from the broken glass. We roll over and over, until we come to a stop, me leaning over him. I dig my elbow into his throat. "Give up," I growl.

"No fucking way," he snarls.

I increase the pressure until the color leaves his cheeks.

"Give the fuck up."

He glares at me. Anger, hatred...and something else. That fucking helplessness I'd witnessed in his eyes, that I'd felt when we'd locked gazes during that fateful time.

"Fuck," I growl, "F-u-c-k." I release him, only to lower my forehead to his. "Fucking hell, man." I swallow. "I am so fucking sorry for what I did to you."

"Yeah." His breath emerges on a rattle. "Me too. No one's more fucking sorry than me for what I did to you that day." He grabs the back of my neck, searches my eyes, "It wasn't your fucking fault though, you understand?"

"Yeah." A hot sensation stabs at my chest. "It wasn't your fault either." I hold his gaze.

"I forgive you, man," I finally say. The pressure builds behind my temples. My throat closes. I draw in a breath, then another. Force myself to feel every single fucking emotion that coils in my chest. "I forgive you; you hear me?"

"Me too." He swallows. "I forgive you."

That's when I hear footsteps approach us.

"What the hell is happening here?

42

Ava

The sound of voices had woken me up. I had pulled on my clothes then crept out of the room. I had peeked into the living room, to find the two of them engaged in conversation.

I had hesitated, not wanting to interrupt, when Baron had charged Ed. They'd sprawled to the floor, rolled over. I had stepped toward them, intent on breaking up the fight; that's when Ed had placed his forehead against Baron's in what was, clearly, an emotional moment between the two.

They had spoken in low voices. I crept close enough to hear them forgive each other... And the way they had looked at each other... There was so much pain, so much shared history, so much...anger, and underneath all of that, so much...connection. It was such a private moment... I had felt like an intruder. It didn't feel right, somehow. I had witnessed what was, clearly...something very emotional between them and they weren't even aware of it... That's when I had spoken up.

Now, both of them glance at me, until Edward springs up. He holds out his arm to Baron, who hesitates, then grabs it. Ed pulls him up. Both men turn to face me.

"Well?" I glance between them, "What was that all about?"

Both men hold my gaze; twin expressions of stubbornness greet me.

"Come on," I blow out a breath, "I heard you guys speak, and this wasn't a normal bro-to-bro conversion, the kind you guys normally indulge in."

"Bro-to-bro?" Edward mutters. "What does that even mean?"

"I mean, it wasn't the kind of posturing you Seven indulge in when you get together. This felt...raw...and real...and painful."

"That's because it was." Baron blows out a breath. He glares sideways at Ed, and the two exchange one of their looks.

"See?" I throw up my hands, "This is what I mean. You guys have a shared history and neither of you ever shared it with me."

"It wasn't the right time earlier." Baron stalks over to me, "But it is time now." He cups my cheek. "Believe me when I say, it's not an easy story to tell but," he swallows, "you deserve to know."

I glance past him at Edward, who nods at me.

"Okay." I swallow. "Tell me then."

Baron leads me over to the settee, then sinks down next to me. Edward sits in the chair opposite us. He glances at Baron, who takes my hand in his. He weaves his fingers through mine and the gesture is so...tender, so unlike how Baron has been with me before. And it's not like he hasn't been affectionate... But this, is almost more like a plea for my support... My heart stutters. My throat closes. *Oh, hell, do I really want to know about what they are going to tell me?*

"So," I square my shoulders, "what is it?"

He hesitates and I glance down at my palm that is swallowed up by his much larger one. I bring our joined hands up and kiss the back of his. "You can tell me anything, Baron."

His chest rises and falls. I glance up to find him staring at me with such vulnerability in his eyes, my breath grows shallow and my heart begins to pound. "What is it?" I murmur, "You're scaring me, Barry."

"Barry?" He blinks. "No one calls me Barry."

"Guess I do, now."

His lips quirk. He rolls his shoulders before composing himself. "You know about the incident, of course, and I guess you've heard something about how Ed and I..." he firms his lips, "how we were hurt the worst by it?"

"It's what I gathered from the girls, yes." I nod.

"When we were kidnapped, Ed and I were initially held with the rest of the Seven," Baron says in a hard voice. "We were all blind-folded and gagged then, so we could hear the rest of the boys, but not see them."

"Baron managed to free himself. He got to me and freed me. We'd been best friends since the first grade. Before we could remove the restrains of the other boys, they got to us. They separated us, took us into a different room," Edward murmurs. "And then," he swallows, "then one of the men raped me."

"Oh, Ed," I swallow, "I am so sorry." My heart feels like it's going to shatter; tears prick the backs of my eyes. I swallow them back and my throat burns.

"The worst thing was, as he buggered me, I was actually aroused. I was twelve-years-old. I didn't understand the difference between physiological reactions and desires, and they used my naiveté to shame me." Edward pauses to gather his thoughts, or maybe, his courage. "But it gets worse... They forced me to use the erection on Baron."

"What?" I cry in horror. "How could they? Oh, my god!" I glance from Ed to Baron, who stares into the distance.

"I refused, of course." Edward murmurs, "so they began beating him up. I could see them hit him, hear his groans." Ed swallows. "It was..." He shakes his head, "When I finally couldn't take it any longer, I agreed."

"You...a...agreed?" I blink.

"It was either that or stand by and watch him being beaten to death." Ed sets his jaw." When I agreed, one of the men raped me again. He forced an erection on me, and this time, I had to use it on Baron."

"Which, in turn, elicited an erection from me, and when they asked me to use it on Ed, I—" Baron's throat moves as he swallows, "I knew if I didn't, they'd only beat him up, or beat me again and... I couldn't bear the thought of it...so I did it."

Edward jumps in, "They made it seem like they were giving us a choice, which only added to the guilt each of us felt—and still do—but the truth is, we didn't have any other option. They used our shame to manipulate us. The thing is, if you want to cause serious psychological harm to a child, use shame. It's the most powerful emotion, and the hardest one to erase."

"We didn't know how to handle it, so we buried it," Baron adds. "As you may have noticed, that didn't work out so well." He grimaces and shares another look with Edward.

"There were so many times, when I was sure that I was going to break, that I couldn't bear it anymore. It was the courage in Edward's gaze that kept me going. Baron's voice cracks, and I grip his palm between both of mine.

"Oh, my god." Tears flow down my face and I wipe them away. "I am so sorry for what they did to you guys. You were so young, just coming to terms with your own sexuality. It would have hurt you, and scarred you for life."

"And it did." Edward lowers his chin. "So, there it is, our sordid little secret."

"Now you know." Baron tries to pull his hand away from me, but I hold on.

"And you haven't told anyone else about this?"

Both men shake their head.

"So why tell me?"

"Because," Baron turns me, "I want you to know. We," he jerks his chin toward Ed, "we want you to know about what happened between the two of us. You need to know everything about me, so we can make a fresh start."

"A fresh start." I tip up my chin, "Is that what it is?"

"It's," he peers into my face, "whatever you want it to be, Eve."

I swallow down the sobs that threaten, "Okay." I half smile, "It's going to be okay." I reach up, brush the hair off of his forehead, "Thank you for telling me."

He nods.

I turn to Edward, "Thank you for sharing this with me. Thank you for trusting me."

"I came today because," he links his fingers together and leans forward, "because I wanted you two to know that you have my blessing…" He chuckles. "Not that a blessing from an ex-priest means a whole lot." He lifts a shoulder, "And it's not that you two need it, but for what it's worth, I don't hold a grudge against either of you."

Baron wraps his arm around me and pulls me close. I recognize his gesture for what it is. Possessiveness, a mark of ownership, establishing his claim in front of his friend… And I can't blame him. After everything we've been through, this feels right. And organic and natural, and so real.

"Thanks, man," Baron murmurs, "it…means a lot to hear that from you."

"You better treat her right," he says quietly, "else you'll have to answer to me."

"Edward," I swallow, "I… I'm so sorry."

"Don't be." His lips twist. "You gave me a new lease on life and I'll always be grateful for that." He rises to his feet, "And now, I need to get going."

He has almost made it to the elevator when Baron calls out to him, "You're coming to the wedding, right?"

Ed stiffens, his shoulders go solid, then he seems to force himself to relax. He jerks his head in our direction, "I'll make sure to swing by."

43

Baron

The elevator doors close behind Edward. Silence descends in the room. I pull my hand from between Ava's grasp and stand. "I am going to bed."

I begin walking in the direction of my bedroom, when she calls out, "That's it?" Her voice is incredulous, "That's all you have to say about what just happened?"

I tilt my head, "Well, that was a surprise. I hadn't expected to reveal my background quite that way... But now you know."

"What happened wasn't either of you guys' fault." Her voice grows closer as she walks up to me. "You know that, right?"

I raise a shoulder, "Doesn't matter whose fault it was or wasn't; it happened."

"And you are not responsible for it."

"Maybe so," I rub the back of my neck, "but surely, I could have done something to prevent it."

"Like what?" She reaches me, presses her palm against my back, "You were kids, and you had been kidnapped and —"

"Spare me the details." I drag my fingers through my hair, "I was there, remember?"

I move away from her, pushing open the door to my bedroom, "Goodnight, Ava. Get some rest."

I turn to close the door, getting a glimpse of the hurt on her face. Her features are ashen, those big green eyes wide with hurt and... empathy. Shit, this is why I hadn't been able to tell her what had happened. This is exactly why I had refused to tell anyone else about the incident. I don't need anyone's sympathy. Certainly, don't need them telling me how sorry they are.

Shit happens. You deal with it... Or not, as the case may be. Either way, you move on. As I had.

I had left for the army, and while the rest of the Seven may think it was a way of escaping what had happened, and perhaps it was, it had been my way of dealing with the shit-show of cards that I had been dealt. Besides, I had come back, right? I have faced the music, so to speak. Hell, I've even buried my differences with Edward...

So why the hell can't I let this woman, who means so much to me, in? Why is it so difficult for me to take that final step and allow her into my life completely?

I close the door gently, shutting out the sight of those gorgeous green eyes. My heart squeezes in my chest and I ignore it. I strip as I head to the bathroom, stand under the shower. Not that it helps. I need more.

I. Need. Her. Need to bury myself in her sweet core and forget about the world for a while. I need to wrap myself around her curves, draw in her scent, lick her lips and taste her cries as she comes. I need to bite down on the tender skin where her neck meets her shoulder, and mark her as mine. My dick throbs as the blood rushes to my groin. But I refuse to jerk myself off. I hurt her. Again. I deserve to live with the discomfort. It is the least I can do.

I switch off the shower, dry myself on the way out of the bathroom. Dropping the towel, I climb under the sheets.

I close my eyes, and instantly, the sound of my screams fills my ears.

"Don't hurt me." I cough. "Please don't." I throw up hands to protect my face, even as the vicious kicks continue—in my side, in my stomach, on my other side. Pain rips up my spine and I gasp for air.

"Stop." Edward voice sounds behind me, "Stop beating him. I'll do it. I'll do as you say."

The blows stop and I slump against the floor. My back aches, my shoulder screams in pain. My entire body is one throbbing mass of hurt.

Hands grip my pants and someone pulls them off of me, along with my briefs. Someone else pulls off my shirt. The cool air hits me and goosebumps pop on my fevered skin. I want to cover myself, want to draw into myself and pretend I am not here. But I can't. I won't. I will survive this. I will do what is needed to come out of this alive. I will do what is needed to keep myself and Edward in one piece. Edward, I need to get to him. I push myself up to my hands and knees, beginning to crawl toward him.

Laughter follows me. "Look at him go," a voice yells. I jerk my head around and glare at the masked man with the gray eyes. I memorize the shape of his eyes, his height, the width of his shoulders. If I get out of here alive, I am going to hunt down these monsters and kill them. I am going to make them pay for this.

"What are you looking at, you piece of shit?" He takes a step toward me and I scramble away. I crawl as fast as I can until I reach Edward. "Ed," I grip his shoulder, "Ed, you okay?"

"Baron," he blinks rapidly, "Baron... I am so sorry."

"I am sorry too, Ed."

"Enough." Someone kicks my thigh from behind and I fall onto my side. He kicks me in the stomach and I groan, double over.

"Stop," I pant, "please, stop."

Behind me, I hear Edward growl, "Stop hurting him, you prick."

"Insult me, will you?" The man steps around me, and kicks Ed in his side. Edward groans, throws his hands up to protect himself.

Shit, shit, shit. "Stop," I yell, "we'll do as you say. Stop hitting him, you bastard."

Something—someone kicks me in the side. Pain explodes up my spine. "When will you two learn to stop speaking, and do as you are told?" Another kick to my already bruised ribs, and I cry out. Another to my legs, my arms. Someone plants his foot in my stomach and my entire body bucks.

"Stop," I howl, "don't hurt me."

"Baron?"

"Stop it," I cry. "Stop."

"Baron!"

Something closes around my neck. Someone's hands. My breath traps in my chest. I can't breathe; my lungs burn. I lunge toward my tormentor. I swoop out and my fingers brush something. I grab hold of an arm, tug. The breeze rushes over me as he stumbles and falls, his hold on me loosening. Instantly, I am on him. I reach for the direction of his face, wrap my fingers around his neck, begin to squeeze. *I am going to kill you. Kill you.*

"Baron, stop! You're hurting me."

I snap my eyes open, and meet her wide green ones. My fingers are around her neck, squeezing down, as I lean over her, straddling her on my bed. She coughs, digging her fingers into my palms, "Stop," she gurgles, "stop it."

I loosen my hold and she draws in a breath, coughing. Tears run down her cheeks. I bend and lick them up. She gasps. Her chest rises and falls. I peer into her features as I press my thumb into the pulse that flitters at the base of her throat.

"What are you doing here, Ava?" I lower my voice to a hush and she pants.

"I... I..."

"Couldn't keep away, could you?" I drag my palm down to her breast, squeeze.

A moan spills from her lips. "I... I heard you scream, came in to check, and saw that you were caught up in a nightmare."

"You shouldn't have come." I rub my thumb across the nipple

outlined against the cotton of her camisole. "You should have known that once I get you in my bed, I am not letting you go."

She stops struggling, glances up at me.

"Or maybe that's what you wanted, hmm? You wanted to catch me at my most vulnerable, so you could slip past my defenses?"

"Baron." She swallows, "Th...that's not true."

"Oh?" I drag my fingers up her throat to notch them under her chin. I push up and she lifts her head, holding my gaze.

"I... I came to help. I know you have flashbacks from the incident, and now I understand what happened to you."

"Do you?" I tilt my head. "Do you really understand how it is to have been through what I have?"

"I..." Her lips tremble, "I can't claim to know how that feels. Whatever happened to you was terrible and completely wrong. And I have not the tiniest inkling of how it is to live with it. But...if I can help ease the burden somewhat."

"And how would you do that?" I lower my lips until my mouth is positioned just above hers. "How would you, as you say, lessen the pain of what happened, little Eve?"

"With my body..." she gulps. "With my body, I thee worship. With my heart, I will ease your sorrow. With my soul... I... I'll share your grief. With my hands I will soothe the loss of the little boy you once were. With my cunt, I'll... I'll welcome you into me so you never feel alone again."

My breathing grows ragged. My chest tightens, my throat hurts, and a burning sensation crawls up my spine. "Is that right?" I choke out. "Is that how you mean to sacrifice yourself for me?"

"It's not a sacrifice, if it's what I want to do," she murmurs. She reaches up to cup my cheek, "I want to ease your agony, in any way I can, Baron. That is," she peers up at me from under her eyelashes, "if you'll let me."

Bloody fuck, this woman... She guts me. How can someone so young and so beautiful be this... Profound, this intense, this ardent in her intentions. Her green eyes gaze up at me like I am the center of the world. My heart stutters and my groin hardens. In all my life, I have never felt this...connected...this vulnerable...yet this powerful. I want her. I have needed her since the moment I saw her. And now she is in my bed, in my space. With nothing and no-one standing between us. It's time...she finds out what it means to be owned by a man who is never going to let go of her again.

I hook my finger in the center of her camisole and tug.

44

Ava

The cloth tears. I yelp, glancing down to find he's torn my camisole right down the middle. He lowers his mouth to my breast and bites down on my nipple.

"Oh, my god," I huff, "Baron."

"Shh." His hot breath sears my skin. He licks the swollen bud, then turns his attention to my other breast. He swirls his tongue around the nub of my nipple, and my pussy clenches. He glances up at me as he closes his hot mouth around my aching flesh. Goosebumps rise on my skin. He increases the pressure around my neck and my breath catches.

"Baron," I whisper, "please."

He bares his teeth as he reaches between us. He slides his fingers inside my panties. His fingertips brush my soaking center and I shudder. Closing his palm around my pussy, he squeezes. Heat shivers out from his touch. I squeeze my thighs together, trapping his hand there, and his eyes gleam.

"Who does your pussy belong to, Ava?" he growls.

"You," I groan, "it belongs to you."

He slides two fingers inside me and I gasp, "And your cunt?" he asks. "Who does your cunt belong to?"

"You," I gasp, "only you."

He brings his face close to mine, as he pulls out his fingers, only to shove them in between my lips.

"And your mouth?" His gaze intensifies, "Who does your mouth belong to?"

"You." The sound emerges garbled as I speak through his fingers, "You, Baron."

He nods. He pulls his fingers out, wipes them on my chest, and the gesture is so filthy, so hot that I have to squeeze my thighs together again. His nostrils flare and a pulse beats to life at his temples. He reaches down to slide his fingers between my arse cheeks. His fingers brush my backhole and I flinch. "And this hole?" He growls, "Who will you let inside here, sweet Eve?"

"You." I moan, "only you—"

He pulls back, only to shove his fingers between us. He snaps the delicate strap that holds up my panties and I shiver. He reaches down, positions his dick against my entrance. "I am going to fuck you now, Eve."

He hooks an arm under my knee, pulling up my leg so it is bent and next to my chest, then he plunges forward.

A scream rips from me as he buries himself to the hilt. Too much. Too full. I throw my arms about his shoulders, holding on, as he stays there, filling me, stretching me, possessing me. His dick throbs inside of me. Every hard ridge imprinted against my melting channel.

"Fuck," he groans, "you're so fucking tight, Eve."

He pulls out, then propels his hips and impales me again. His balls slap against my butt, his cock lengthens, thickens, as he begins to fuck me. He pounds up and into me, and my entire body bucks. The headboard of the bed hits the wall, something crashes to the ground. I can't stop the giggle that bubbles up, and his gaze intensifies. "You find this funny, Eve?"

His fingers around my throat tighten as he pulls out, stays poised at the rim of my entrance, only to propel forward as he buries himself inside me again and again. He hits that spot deep inside of me that makes me tremble.

"Oh, my god, Baron. Oh, Baron."

He thrusts into me again as his fingers tighten around my neck. Darkness mars the edge of my vision as he pounds into me. The climax rips up my legs, threatens to overwhelm me. That's when he loosens his grip on my neck. He lowers his mouth to mine and commands, "Come," and I shatter.

My orgasm shrieks over me, or maybe that's me screaming. He closes his mouth over mine, absorbs every last sound I make as he continues to nail me. In and out, in and out. My entire body shudders. The aftershocks grip me as he rips his mouth from mine, pushes his forehead against mine and groans. He pulls out of me, releasing his hold on my neck and leans back on his haunches as he comes.

He paints my stomach and chest with hot streams of white. He drags his fingers up his cock as he squeezes out every last drop. Then he rubs his cum into my breasts, down my stomach, into my pussy. Then he flips me over. He pulls me up so I am poised on my knees and forearms. He scoops up the cum, slathers it into my back entrance, then fits himself there. I stiffen and he winds his fingers around the nape of my neck. "Shh," he whispers, "I've got you, Eve."

I swallow as he leans down and kisses my shoulder. He nibbles his way up to my cheek, urging my face toward him. Then he kisses me. He presses his mouth to mine, licking my lips, sucking on my tongue. Warmth fills my chest. He slips inside my backhole and I groan. He swallows the sound. Brings his other hand around to play with my pussy lips. He slides one finger inside my cunt, and a whine slips from my lips. He works two fingers, then three, and it's so full, so much. Every hole of my body is filled with Baron. His touch, his lips, his fingers, his cock as he slips in through the tightness. He presses his heel into the nub of my clit, as he thrusts his tongue inside my mouth. Simultaneously he plunges forward, owns my arse as his dick throbs in my back channel. He begins to move, sawing in and out of me, as his cock seems to thicken inside of me. That feeling of fullness as he slides one more finger inside my pussy is too much. Too soon. Oh, my god. I am going to—

"Come," he growls against my mouth, "come all over my fingers."

The orgasm floors me. It seems to go on and on. My knees give way and it's his hold on my nape that keeps me upright. He thrust into me one more time, then buries his face in my neck. He bites down on my shoulder, as his dick throbs and he empties himself inside of me.

My eyelids flutter down, and I slump. I am vaguely aware of him leaving me, and I protest.

"Shh," he kisses me, "I'll be right back.

I vaguely hear the water run in the bathroom, then footsteps sound and the cool wetness of a washcloth presses into my pussy, then between my arse cheeks. I flush, open my eyes to find him wiping his dick, before he tosses the cloth aside.

"You forgot to clean the parts of me where I am wearing your cum."

"Good." He laughs, "Now you can't forget who you belong to." He climbs into bed, pulls me to him and I pass out again.

When I come to, I am resting on his chest. His arms are around me; the thud-thud-thud of his heartbeat is a comforting sound against my cheek. I peer up at him from under my eyelashes to find him gazing at me. His blue eyes burn in the dark, the look in them, contemplative.

"What," I clear my throat, "what are you thinking?"

"Why are you so good to me," he murmurs, "when all I have done is hurt you?"

"You saved me," I whisper. "You showed me, it's possible for me to be anything I want. The only limitations are those I set on myself."

"I did?" He frowns. "How's that?"

"By being you." I rest my chin on his chest, "When I think of everything you've been through, and yet, you never lost hope. You continued to believe."

He chuckles, "You sure you're talking about me?"

I nod, "You watched over me, protected me, loved me..."

He frowns, opening his mouth, and I place a finger across his lips, "Shh, I know you do. It's only a technicality that you haven't said it yet."

"A technicality?" He blinks.

"I mean, you do love me. Why else would you ask me to marry you, and then break your condition—which was stupid anyway and destined for failure—of not sleeping with me until the wedding?"

"Stupid?" His lips curve and his eyes gleam.

Before I can react, he flips me over so I am on my back, and he's bracketed me in between his arms. "I'll show you exactly how stupid it was."

He pushes forward and impales me. I am still so wet that he slides inside to the hilt. My pussy spasms around his dick. His thick, fat shaft pulses and a groan spills from my lips.

His chest rises and falls, his shoulder muscles tense, and his biceps bulge as sweat beads his forehead. "How is it that every time I am inside you, it's like the very first time?" He growls, "Why is it that I can't get enough of you? What is it about you that pulls me back to you again and again? That I want to stay buried inside you... If I were to die like this, I'd be the happiest man ever."

He hooks his arms under my knees, pushing them up, until my thighs are pushed in next to my chest. He lowers his mouth to mine, kissing me deeply as he begins to move. Slowly, so I can feel every ridge of his cock, he buries himself inside me and pulls out, again and again. I wrap my fingers around the headboard, as he tunnels into me.

"I am going to fuck you so hard, you won't know where you begin and where I end. I am going to come inside you again and again until your every pore leaks with my cum. You feel me, Eve?"

"Yes," I pant against his mouth, "yes, Baron."

He pulls out, then slams into me, hitting that spot deep inside, and I cry out. He propels his hips forward again and again, hitting that very same spot, and my entire body bucks. He doesn't stop until my orgasm screams up my spine, when he growls, "Look at me, Eve."

I stare into his blue eyes and the connection is so hot, so real, so everything that I shatter. He holds my gaze, as he empties himself inside me with a hoarse cry. Sweat clings to his beautiful shoulders as he slumps over me. His weight pushes me into the bed, holding me down, pinning me in place... And I know, there's nowhere else I'd rather be.

The next time I open my eyes, he's gone.

"Baron?" I call, and my voice echoes in the empty space. I slide out of bed, find a shirt he must have folded and put aside earlier. There are so many facets to this guy, I don't think I'll ever really get to know him completely. It's what draws me to him, knowing I can never really predict what he's going to do next.

I pad out into the hallway, peek into the living room, then the kitchen, finally, walking down to the partially-closed door at the end of the corridor. I push it open to find him standing at the window, wearing only his sweats. His broad shoulders block out the view of the early morning sky. I walk over to him. His shoulder blades bunch and I know he's aware of my presence. I slide my arms around his waist, rub my cheek against his back.

"I missed you," I whisper. "What are you doing here?

"Waiting for you."

"Were you?"

He nods, then turns around and lowers himself onto one knee.

"Baron..." I open and shut my mouth. *OMG, it can't be, can it? Is he going to —? No, is he, really?*

He slides his hand into his pocket, then pulls out a ring. He holds it up and the light glitters off a band made of jade.

"Oh." I swallow. "Oh wow, how...how did you get this? Where did you get this from? Did you know I was coming here?"

"I had hoped." He smiles. "As for the rest, I got this made the day after I met you."

"You...you did?" I gape, "No, seriously?"

His lips twist. "What can I say? I saw you and knew you were going to be my wife. I should have asked you right away, but I hesitated. Not anymore."

He holds out his palm and I place my hand in his.

"No gems are free of conflict and I know how important ethical sourcing is to you." He slides the ring onto the finger of my left hand. "The green reminds me of your eyes, and the jade is forever."

"Forever." I stare down at the band on my finger.

"Will you be mine?"

"Yes," I cry, "yes!" I take a step forward, go to throw my arms around him, but he moves aside. Huh? I frown, "What is it, Barry?"

"There's one more thing you need to know," he murmurs.

My heart begins to thud and my pulse rate ratchets up. "What?" I whisper, "what do you want to tell me?"

He walks over to the coffee table and I follow him. He picks up his wallet, pulls out a photograph and hands it over to me.

"It's the photograph that I carried in my purse. I thought I'd lost it."

"I found it when I walked into your studio, the day Edward turned up," he replies.

I notice he doesn't directly refer to the attack that day, for which I am grateful.

"Thank you for returning it to me." I peer up at him from under my eyelashes.

That's you in the picture, isn't it? The girl wearing the red dress."

I nod, and he blows out a breath. "I knew it was you, the moment I saw you."

"Knew it was me?" I blink. "I don't understand what you're saying."

He moves away and begins to pace. "That day, when Edward left you and I found you on the sidewalk, it's not the first day I saw you."

"It isn't?"

He shakes his head, "I saw you first when you were much younger. Maybe you were ten or so?" He raises a shoulder. "You and your family were having lunch at a pub on the outskirts of London. I was there with the Seven. You were wearing this same red dress on that day."

"I was?" I blink.

"I noticed you because you were so happy, so utterly carefree, and wished I could be like you."

"Oh." I swallow, "That was a long time ago."

"It was," he agrees, "but I never forgot your face."

"I have a vague recollection of a family outing that summer," I murmur, "and I remember wearing that red dress. It was a gift from my mother. It was my favorite dress. She told me I resembled a shining light when I wore it."

My eyes fill and I glance away. I'll never get over losing mum. Just when I think the pain is lessening, something like this happens, and the loss seems so very insurmountable.

I hear the sound of footsteps and the next second his strong arms surround me. He pulls me into his chest. "Shh," he croons, "I didn't mean to upset you."

"You didn't." I rub my cheek against his shoulder, "It's just... I still miss her, you know?"

"You were lucky to have her. My family threw money at me and hoped my problems would resolve themselves. They didn't realize that all I needed was their support to get through the hellish after-math of the incident."

"You have me now." I glance up at him. "And apparently, you knew I existed long before I met you."

"I saw you again, you know?" he murmurs. "Two years ago, on one of my infrequent visits to London. I was at Paddington Station, about to catch the Heathrow Express to the airport, and I heard your laugh."

"My laugh?"

"Your laughter is the most beautiful sound in the world. I heard it that day at the pub and never forgot it. Every time I remembered it, it made me feel hopeful and happy and wistful, all at the same time."

"Wistful?"

"You were so young, just a child, and yet I couldn't forget your face. And then I saw you all grown up on the railway platform, and knew you were the one for me, but the timing was all wrong."

"All these years," a ball of emotion fills my throat, "all this time, you knew?"

He nods. "I thought I'd never find you again." He cups my cheek, peers into my eyes, "And then when I did, I knew the most important thing was for you to be happy. It didn't matter who you were with, as long as you were happy."

"That's why you left?"

He nods, "And I thought my life was over. I thought..." His throat moves as he swallows, "I thought that I'd lost you, Eve."

"But you didn't," I glance up into those glistening blue eyes, "I am here and I am never leaving you again."

"I'll hold you to that." He smirks, "There's one more thing I need to confess."

I tilt my head, "What?" I frown, "What is it?"

He slides his hand into his pocket then holds up something purple.

I blink. "My hair tie?" I turn to him, "Where did you find it?"

"At your place, that first day I carried you home. I took it without telling you." He glances at the purple hair restraint then back at me, "I needed something of you to carry around, apparently."

He holds the hairband out to me and I shake my head, "You found it, you keep it. It's yours now."

"And you?" He searches my eyes, "What about you?"

"I'm yours, Baron. Only yours."

"Mine." He lowers his lips to mine.

45

Ava

I glance at myself in the mirror in Summer's town house. The simple white gown I've chosen has a sweetheart neckline and cinches in at the waist before flowing down to my feet. My hair's flowing around my shoulders, just how he likes it. On my feet, I am wearing green colored heels which match the green of my ring. My make-up is light, a touch of lip gloss, and purple eyeshadow to bring out the green of my eyes.

"What do you think?" I meet Isla's gaze in the mirror. "Too simple?"

"It's," she looks me up and down, "gorgeous; very you."

"Not that I had much time to find a dress," I mutter. "I mean, how did he manage to accelerate all the paperwork so we could be married in 24 hours?"

"Welcome to the brotherhood of the Seven." She grimaces, "Each of them seems to try to break the record of the previous one, when it comes to organizing their wedding. And of course, each of them has to ask me to organize it. And of course, I can't say no." She mock wipes her brow, "The number of grey hairs they have given me over the past few months is not funny."

"You like the challenge; admit it," I giggle.

"Yeah, right." She blows out a breath, "At least, I am not marrying one of them."

"No, you decided to set your sights on the older brother to one of them."

"Gah, stop it." She throws up her hands, "Liam's getting married in a week, and that will be that." She dusts off her palms.

Summer peeks in, "Isla, I think Amelie needs your help with the catering."

"Of course, she does," She turns and marches toward the door, then points a finger at Summer, "You make sure she gets down to the back garden in ten minutes, you hear me?"

"Yes Ma'am." Summer chuckles as Isla throws me a smile, then disappears down the corridor.

"Whew, she's in a mood." Summer saunters in, then sinks down into a chair. "How are you feeling?" She peers up at me. "No nerves or anything?"

"Nope," I smile, "I feel good."

"Good."

"Only thing."

She leans forward, giving me her full attention.

"He hasn't yet told me that he loves me."

"Hmm." She places her fingers together. "But he asked you to marry him and pulled out all the stops to get this ceremony underway as soon as possible."

I nod.

"And he found you a ring that's exactly the kind you'd have wanted."

"Mm-hmm." I jerk my chin.

"Seems to me like love."

"It is love," I declare. "It's just, I wish he'd say those three words aloud, you know?"

"When Sinclair asked me to marry him, it was part of a transaction." She tilts her head at me, "Did you know that?"

"No," I blink, "but you two are so much in love."

"Oh, the alphahole was in love with me, all right. It just took him a while to figure it out. Hell, it took me a while to figure out what my feelings for him were."

"But it all worked out."

"And how." She laughs as she places her palms across her belly. "I can't believe how thrilled I am to be carrying his baby."

"You're glowing." I smile back at her. "You look radiant."

"I feel radiant." She grins back, before glancing away. "If only my sister were here to share my happiness."

"Karma, right?" I turn to face her, "Hasn't she been away in Sicily, with her new beau?"

"That's the thing," Summer pushes her hair back from her face, "I've never met this man, and it's not like Karma to be away for so long."

"But she does call?"

"She texts me most weeks. Why she can't just pick up the phone and call me, I don't know. She doesn't answer when I call, just texts me back, which is really strange. I messaged her to tell her that I'll be coming over there if she didn't visit me soon, to which she didn't reply." Summer scowls, "I mean, meeting someone who sweeps you off your feet is all well and good, but what the hell is so pressing that she hasn't come back to visit even once in all this time?"

"Maybe he's possessive?" I chuckle. "He doesn't want to let her out of his sight."

"Don't we know all about that?" Summer rolls her eyes. "If you think Barons' bad now, wait until you get pregnant. He'll chain you to his side."

There's a knock on the door, then Julia walks in. In her hands is a bouquet of cascading greens. She offers me the bunch of eucalyptus, ferns and sage.

"Wow," I gaze at it, "it's beautiful. It's exactly what I would have chosen for myself." I had been so preoccupied with everything else, I had forgotten about the bouquet. "Thank you so much," I cry as I reach for the bouquet.

"Thank your husband to-be." Julia laughs, "He had this ordered especially for you. Clearly, he knows you well."

The blood rushes to my cheeks. I bring the bouquet up to my nose and sniff at it. "I think I am going to cry," I sniff.

"Don't you dare," Summer admonishes, "don't want to spoil your make up, now do you?"

Just then Amelie pops her head in, "There you are." She smiles at Summer, "Your man's been looking for you."

"I saw him, not ten minutes ago," Summer mutters.

"Yeah, but the Seven." Amelie chuckles.

"The bloody Seven." Summer laughs as she rises to her feet, "Speaking of, it's time for you to officially join our collective." Summer grins. She walks over, taking my hands in hers, "You ready?"

I weave my hand through my father's arm, and clutch my bouquet of cascading greens.

"You look beautiful," my father says as he places his palm over mine.

I blink away the tears that his softly spoken words elicit… Christ, what's it with me and the waterworks? "Thank you for being here with me, Daddy." I sniff, "And after how horrible I was to you."

"You know, you could say anything to me and I'd never take offense." My father pats my hand, "It's a child's prerogative to say what's on your mind, and it's a parent's prerogative to forgive."

"Oh, Dad," I glance up at him, "I was so wrong to judge you. I understand now that it's possible to love two people. Ma was your past and Lina is your future. I get it now."

"You've grown up, Ava." My father glances down at me, his eyes shining., "My little girl is a woman, ready to start her new life."

"You're going to make me cry," I sniffle.

"Oh, no." He beams down at me, "No tears today, only smiles."

Isla gestures to us that it's time to walk down the aisle. I draw in a breath, as my father leads me onto the garden path.

We'd decided to marry in the picturesque backyard of the Sterling's home, with the slopes of Primrose Hill, stretching out before us. We'd also decided to exchange vows in front of our friends and family and without having anyone officiate the wedding.

I glance up and my gaze collides with Baron's searing blue ones. The connection is instant. Electrifying and sexual, caring and full of those emotions he seems to carry under that hard exterior of his.

We reach him and my father places my hand in his. Baron brings it up to his lips and brushes his mouth across my knuckles. I shiver. His lips curve against my skin and his gaze intensifies as he stares deeply into my eyes. My thighs clench and my palms grow sweaty. I part my lips and his gaze drops to my mouth.

I blush. Baron smirks. He moves away, but doesn't release my hand. I lift my chin up, hold his gaze as we exchange our vows.

Then Baron grasps both of my hands in his. He leans down as I tip my head up. He gazes into my eyes, and in his blue ones, I see that unsaid emotion again. His irises deepen, until they seem almost azure in color. He lowers his lips to mine. "I love you," he whispers, then kisses me.

I pause my conversaton with Raisa to glance around at the faces of my friends and family. Saint stands with one arm around Victoria, the palm of his other hand on her five-month pregnant belly. Amelie leans into Weston as she converses with Victoria. The two men gaze down at their wives, looks of such adoration on their faces, that honestly, if I hadn't seen it for myself, I'd have never guessed that they could be such alphaholes.

The doors to the house are flung open to reveal a piano, with Damian seated at it. He plays the keys and the notes float across the distance. I watch as Julia leans a hip against the piano, then leans over to kiss him.

Meredith, assistant to the Seven, and in many ways a guardian to all of them when they were younger, looks on with a smile on her face. Next to her is Peter, Sinclair's chauffeur and Meredith's now fiancé. That's the thing with the Seven. Despite being gazillionaires, none of them allow class or economic status to define what they are or who their friends should be.

Arpad and Karina are seated at a table, engaged in an animated conversation. Summer and Sinclair stand nearby, their arms around each other.

Raisa nudges me and nods toward a particular group, making me smile. Baron converses with my Dad and Lina—yes, I invited her—periodically laughing and looking my way. I am trying my best to accept her. I realize now that she is not trying to replace my mother. She reached out to me and told me as much. I can see how much she and my Dad love each other, and somehow, in light of recent events, and knowing how it feels to be torn apart by my feelings for two men, I can empathize with their situation too.

Isla walks over to me, a glass of champagne in hand. "Congratulations, babe," she smiles widely, "that was a gorgeous ceremony."

"All thanks to you." I tip up my chin, "You have one hell of a talent in organizing the best weddings in such a short time." I grip her hand, "Seriously, Iz, thank you for putting this together so quickly."

"Oh, pfft." She tosses her hair over her shoulder, "Anything for you, babe. At least, I didn't have to herd guests, considering you guys wanted to keep this so intimate."

"Speaking of," Raisa nudges Isla with her elbow, "who are those three delicious men in that corner?"

I turn in the direction of her gaze to the far corner, where, as if they are keen to distance themselves from the rest of the married folks, three men—and the only bachelors among the group—level hard looks at each other as they engage in some, evidently, serious conversation.

"The growly one is Isla's Liam," I say, then chuckle and duck when Isla smacks my arm and protests, "Not my anything, that one."

"The one in the grey suit is Hunter Whittington, a friend of Baron and Liam's." I continue, "And the third guy is Karina's brother Nikolai Solonik. All three do business with the Seven."

Raisa opens her mouth to ask a question when the barking of a dog cuts through the space. Max—Summer and Sinclair's dog—tears across the garden toward me. I bend down, hold out my arms as he jumps up and licks my face. His paws brush my dress, leaving doggy prints all over it, but I don't care.

I giggle, pet him as Jeeves hurries over to me. "I am so sorry, Madam; he escaped me."

"It's okay." I laugh as I pat the excited dog. "He's so cute," I chuckle as he evades Jeeves outstretched arm and darts off with the butler in his wake.

"He's certainly ensuring that Jeeves' fitness levels have shot up." Summer smirks as she approaches me. Sinner follows, not far behind, with my husband next to him, holding two glasses of champagne.

My husband... Gah, he's my husband. Baron hands me a flute, then raises his glass to me as he raises his voice to our guests, "I'd like to propose a toast." His lips quirk.

Isla and Raisa move away as the group hushes.

Baron gazes into my eyes, "When I saw you the first time, I knew you were the one. When I am with you, I like myself more. When I look at you, I know I can weather any storm. When I hold your hand, I know you are what was missing all along. When I think of you, I become a better person. When you are with me, I know I can overcome any challenge. When we are together, anything is possible. Now that you are mine, I can't think of anything I want more than to take care of you, to love you, to cherish and protect you. As long as I am alive, you'll never want for anything, and after I die—"

I reach up and place my finger on his lips, "No talk of dying today."

He smirks, "As you wish, my love."

He raises his glass, "To my wife, the most beautiful woman on this earth, and to me, the lucky bastard who doesn't deserve her."

He kisses my fingers and I blush, raising my glass to my lips. Baron takes a sip from his flute, then glances past me at the sound of a loud engine. He hands me his glass, and at my puzzled look, he bends down, kisses me on the cheek, and says, "I'll be right back."

He walks past me, and I turn to find him stalking toward a familiar figure. Edward stands by his motorbike, on the other side of the house. He's wearing a leather jacket, his helmet under his arm. The wind ruffles his dark hair as Baron approaches him. He holds out his arm. Baron eschews it, instead throwing his arm around Ed. Ed hesitates, then hugs him back. The two talk, then as one, they turn to me. Edward waves at me, a smile splitting his face. I wave back. The two men converse some more, then Edward claps Baron on his shoulder. Baron returns the gesture, before stepping back. Edward slides on the helmet, mounts his bike, then raises the stand and starts the machine. The double barrels thunder, the noise clearly heard even at this distance. He takes off, and Baron turns and prowls over to me. I hand him his glass as he bends to brush his lips over mine.

"How is he?" I murmur.

Baron frowns, "He'll be fine… I think."

Jeeves walks in just then. He hovers at the side until Summer turns to him,

"What is it?" she asks.

"Umm, I'm sorry, madam, but your sister and her husband are here to attend the wedding, though they haven't been invited."

"My sister?" Summer scowls, "What do you mean, my sister? And she's not married, even if she is my sister. Which she can't be, because my sister is in Sicily, so..." She glances past Jeeves, then pales, "Oh, my." She swallows. "Oh, my god," she squeals, then takes off in the direction of a woman who's wearing a pant suit. She's standing next to a tall, broad man whose cold, dark eyes take in the gathering.

"Karma." Summer throws her arms around the woman, "Oh, my god, Karma, you're here! I missed you so much. Why didn't you tell me that you were coming? I would have sent the car for you."

"There's no need for that," the man next to her interjects, "my wife has my car and chauffeur at her service."

"Wife?" Summer steps back. She tips up her chin and plants her palms on her hips, "And who are you?"

The man casts a glance around the garden, making sure to meet the gaze of each of the Seven who is present. My husband tenses. He wraps his arm around me and pulls me close. Saint and Weston move forward as one. Their shoulders are a solid wall that blocks their women from the man's line of sight. Arpad rises up from the table and flanks Weston, effectively blocking Karina. Peter wraps an arm around Meredith, while Damian rises up from the piano. He covers Julia with his bulk as he steps up to the double doors that lead to the garden.

O-k-a-y, what the hell is this? Some kind of battle lines are being drawn here that I can't quite figure out. "What's happening?" I whisper to Baron. "Who's he?"

Sinner stalks toward the new arrivals, and plants himself in between Summer and the man. "My wife asked you a question," he rumbles. "Who are you?"

"I," the man's lips turn up in a semblance of a smile, one that resembles a shark who's sniffed his next prey, "I am Michael Byron."

EDWARD DOES GET HIS OWN HEA. SUBSCRIBE TO MY NEWSLETTER TO READ THE REST OF HIS STORY WHEN IT RELEASES, HERE

GET MAFIA KING - KARMA & MICHAEL BYRON'S STORY HERE

READ AN EXCERPT FROM MAFIA KING - KARMA & MICHAEL BYRON'S STORY...

Karma

"Morn came and went—and came, and brought no day..."

Tears prick the back of my eyes. Goddamn Byron. Crept up on me when I am at my weakest. Not that I am a poetry addict, by any measure, but words are my jam.

The one consolation I have, that when everything else in the world is wrong, I can turn to them, and they'll be there, friendly steady, waiting with open arms. And this particular poem had laced my blood, crawled into my gut when I'd first read it. Darkness had folded into me like an insidious snake that raises its head when I least expect it. Like now. I'd managed to give my bodyguard the slip and veered off my usual running route to reach *Waterlow Park*.

I look out on the still sleeping city of London, from the grassy slope of the expanse. Somewhere out there the Mafia was hunting me, apparently.

I purse my lips, close my eyes. Silence. The rustle of the wind between the leaves, the faint tinkle of the water from the nearby spring.

I could be the last person on this planet, alone, unsung, bound for the grave.

Ugh! Stop. Right there. I drag the back of my hand across my nose. Try it again, focus, get the words out, one after the other, like the steps of my sorry life.

"Morn came and went—and came, and brought no day..." My voice breaks. "Bloody, asinine, hell." I dig my fingers into the grass and grab a handful and fling it out. Again. From the top. I open my eyes, focus on a spot in the distance.

"Morn came and went—and came, and...."

"...brought no day."

I whip my head around. His profile fills my line of sight. Dark hair combed back by a ruthless hand that booked no measure.

My throat dries.

Hooked nose, thin upper lip, a fleshy lower lip, that hints at hidden desires. Heat. Lust. The sensuous scrape of that whiskered jaw over my innermost places. Across my inner thigh, reaching toward that core of me that throbs, clenches, melts to feel the stab of his tongue, the thrust of his hardness as he impales me, takes me, makes me his.

"Of this their desolation; and all hearts
Were chill'd into a selfish prayer for light.."

Sweat beads my palm; the hairs on my nape rise. "Who are you?"

He stares ahead, his lips moving,

"Forests were set on fire—but hour by hour
They fell and faded—and the crackling trunks
Extinguish'd with a crash—and all was black."

I swallow, squeeze my thighs together. Moisture gathers in my core. How can I be wet by the mere cadence of this stranger's voice?

I spring up to my feet.

"Sit down."

His voice is unhurried, lazy even, his spine erect. The cut of his black jacket stretches across the width of his massive shoulders. His hair... I was mistaken. There are strands of dark gold woven between the darkness that pours down to brush the nape of his neck. My fingers tingle. My scalp itches.

I take in a breath and my lungs burn.

This man, he's sucked all the oxygen in this open space, as if he owns it, the master of all he surveys. The master of me. My death. My life. A shiver ladders its way up my spine. *Get away, get away now, while you still can.*

I take a step back.

"I won't ask again."

Ask. Command. Force me to do as he wants. He'll have me on my back, bent over, on the side, over him, under him, he'll surround me, overwhelm me, pin me down with the force of his personality. His charisma, his larger-than-life essence that will crush everything else out of me and I... I'll love it.

"No."

"Yes."

A fact. A statement of intent, spoken aloud. So true. So real. Too real. Too much. Too fast. All of my nightmares... my dreams come to life. Everything I've wanted is here in front of me. I'll die a thousand deaths before he'll be done with me... and then, will I be reborn? For him. For me. For myself. I live first and foremost to be the woman I am... am meant to be.

"You want to run?"

No.

No.

I nod my head

He turns his head and all of the breath leaves my lungs. Blue eyes, cerulean, dark like the morning skies, deep like the nighttime, hidden corners, secrets that I don't dare uncover. He'll destroy me, have my heart, and break it so casually.

My throat burns. A boiling sensation squeezes my chest.

"Go then, my beauty, fly. You have until I count to five. If I catch you, you are mine."

"If you don't?"

"Then I'll come after you, stalk your every living moment, possess your nightmares, and steal you away in the dead of midnight, and then..."

I draw in a shuddering breath; liquid heat drips from between my legs. "Then?" I whisper.

"Then, I'll ensure you'll never belong to anyone else, you'll never see the light of day again, for your every breath, your every waking second, your thoughts, your actions... and all of your words, every single last one, will belong to me." He peels back his lips, and his teeth glint in the first rays of the morning light. "Only me." He straightens to his feet, and rises, and rises.

He is massive. A beast. A monster who always gets his way. My guts churn. My toes curl. Something primal inside me insists I hold my own. I cannot give in to him. Cannot let him win whatever this is. I need to stake my ground in some form. *Say something. Anything. Show him you're not afraid of him.*

"Why?" I tilt my head back, all the way back. "Why are you doing this?"

He tilts his head, his ears almost canine in the way they are silhouetted against his profile.

"Is it because you can? Is it a... a..." I blink, "a debt of some kind?"

He stills.

"My father. This is about how he betrayed the Mafia, right? You're one of them?"

All expression is wiped clean of his face, and I know then I am right. My past... Why does it always catch up with me? *You can run, but you can never hide.*

"Tick-tock, Beauty." He angles his body and his shoulders shut out the sight of the sun, the dawn skies, the horizon, the city in the distance, the whisper of the grass, the trees, the rustle of the leaves... All of it fades, and leaves me and him. Us. *Run.*

"Five." He jerks his chin. Straightens the cuffs of his sleeves.

My knees wobble.

"Four."

My heart hammers in my chest. I should go. Leave. But my feet are welded to this earth. This piece of land where we first met. What am I, but a speck in the larger scheme of things? To be hurt. To be forgotten. To be brought to the edge of climax and taken without an ounce of retribution. To be punished... by him.

"Three." He thrusts out his chest, widens his stance, every muscle in his body relaxed. "Two."

I swallow. The pulse beats at my temples. My blood thrums.

"One."

Michael

"Go."

She pivots and races down the slope. The fabric of her dress streams behind her, scarlet in the blue morning. Her scent, lushly feminine with silver moonflowers, clings to my nose, then recedes. I reach forward, thrust out my chin, sniff the air, but there's only the green scent of dawn. She stumbles and I jump forward. Pause when she straightens. *Wait. Wait. Give her a lead. Let her think she has almost escaped, that she's gotten the better of me... As if.* I clench my fists at my sides, force myself to relax. *Wait. Wait.* She reaches the bottom of the incline, turns. I surge forward. One foot in front of the other, my heels dig into the grassy surface as mud flies up, clinging to the edges of my £4000 Italian pants. Like I care? Plenty more where that came from. An entire walk-in closet full of tailor-made clothes, to suit every occasion, with every possible accessory needed by a man in my position to impress... everything, except the one thing that I have coveted from the first time I had laid eyes on her. Sitting there on the grassy slope, unshed tears in her eyes, and reciting... Byron? For hell's sake. Of all the poet's in the world, she had to choose the Lord of Darkness.

I huff. All a ploy. Clearly, she'd known I was sitting near her... No, not possible. I had walked toward her and she hadn't stirred, hadn't been aware. Yeah, I am that good. I've been known to slice a man from ear to ear while he was awake and fully aware. Alive one second, dead the next. That's how it is in my world. You want it, you take it. And I... I want her.

I increase my pace, eat up the distance between myself and the girl... that's all she is. A slip of a thing, a slim blur of motion. Beauty in hiding. A diamond in the rough, waiting for me to get my hands on her, polish her, show her what it means to be... dead. She is dead. That's why I am here.

Her skirts flash behind her, exposing a creamy length of thigh. My groin hardens; my legs wobble. I lurch over a bump in the ground. The hell? I right myself, leap forward, inching closer, closer. She reaches a curve in the path, disappears out of sight. My heart hammers in my chest. I will not lose her, will not. *Here, Beauty, come to Daddy.* The wind whistles past my ears. I pump my legs, lengthen my strides, turn the corner. There's no one there, huh?

My heart hammers, the blood pounds at my wrists and my temples, and adrenaline thrums through my veins. I slow down, come to a stop. Scan the clearing.

The hairs on my forearms prickle. She's here. Not far. Where? *Where is she?* I prowl across to the edge of the clearing, under the tree with its spreading branches. *When I get my hands on you, Beauty, I'll spread your legs like the pages of a poem. Dip into your honeyed sweetness, like a quill into an inkwell, drag my aching shaft across that melting weeping entrance.* My balls throb. My groin tightens. The crack of a branch above shivers across my stretched nerve endings. Instinctively, I swoop forward, hold out my arms. A blur of red, dark blonde hair, skirt swept up in a gust of breeze. She drops into my arms and I close my grasp around the trembling, squirming mass of precious humanity. I cradle her close to my chest, heart beating thud-thud-thud, overwhelming any other thought.

Mine. All mine. The hell is wrong with me? She wriggles her little body, and her curves slide across my forearms. My shoulders bunch, my fingers tingle. She kicks out with her legs and arches her back. Her breasts thrust up, the nipples outlined against the fabric of her jogging vest. *She'd dared come out dressed like that...? In that scrap of fabric that barely covered her luscious flesh?*

"Let me go." She whips her head toward me, her hair flowing

around her shoulders, across her face. She blows it out of the way. "You monster, get away from me."

Anger drums at the backs of my eyes; desire tugs at my groin. The scent of her is sheer torture, something that I had dreamed of in the wee hours of twilight when dusk turned into night. She's not real. Not the woman I think she is. She is my downfall. My sweet poison. The bitter medicine I must imbibe to cure the ills that plague my company.

"Fine." I lower my arms and she tumbles to the floor, hits the ground butt first.

"How dare you?" She huffs out a breath, her hair messily arranged across her face.

I shove my hands into the pockets of my fitted pants, knees slightly bent, legs apart. Tip my chin down and watch her as she sprawls at my feet.

"You... dropped me?" She makes a sound deep in her throat.

So damn adorable.

"Your wish is my command." I quirk my lips.

"You don't mean it."

"You're right." I lean my weight forward on the balls of my feet and she flinches.

"What... what do you want?"

"You."

She pales. "You want to... rob me? I have nothing of value. I'm not carrying anything... except." She reaches for her pocket.

"Don't." I growl.

"It's only my phone."

"So you say, hmm?"

"You can..." She swallows, "you can trust me."

I chuckle.

"I mean, it's not like I can deck you with a phone or anything, right?"

I glare at her and she swallows. "Fine... you... you take it."

Interesting.

"Hands behind your neck."

She hesitates.

"Now."

She instantly folds her arms at the elbows, cradles the back of her head with her palms.

I lean down and every muscle in her body tenses. Good. She's wary. She should be. She should have been alert enough to have run as soon as she sensed my presence. But she hadn't. And I'd delayed what was meant to happen long enough.

I pull the gun from my pocket, hold it to her temple. "Goodbye Beauty."

To find out what happens next read Karma and Michael Byron's story HERE

Binge read the Big Bad Billionaire Series

US

UK

All markets

Start the series with Sinclair & Summer's story here

Read Saint & Victoria's story here

Read Weston & Amelie's story here

Read Damian & Julia's story here

Claim your FREE contemporary romance book. Click HERE

Claim your FREE paranormal romance book HERE

More books by L. STEELE

Join my newsletter

Follow me on AMAZON

Follow me on BookBub

Follow on Goodreads

Follow me on TikTok

Follow my Pinterest boards

Follow me on FB

Follow me on Instagram

Join my secret Facebook Reader Group; I am dying to meet YOU!

Follow me on Twitter

Read my Books HERE

Made in United States
Orlando, FL
06 April 2024

45528115R00182